ELLA had sensed horror and evil.

Mrs. Snell had heard bumps; so had Alice; and Alice had felt fright.

I had experienced despair, and should never forget it. Ignore it? I could try. What I could not avoid was wondering why. What had happened here? Once upon a time . . .

Gad's Hall

——◄◆►——

NORAH
LOFTS

FAWCETT CREST • NEW YORK

GAD'S HALL

THIS BOOK CONTAINS THE COMPLETE TEXT OF
THE ORIGINAL HARDCOVER EDITION.

Published by Fawcett Crest Books, a unit of CBS Publications,
the Consumer Publishing Division of CBS Inc., by arrangement with Doubleday and Company, Inc.

ISBN: 0-449-24040-1

Printed in the United States of America

10   9   8   7   6   5   4   3   2   1

Part One

"**I**T is Tudor," Bob said as the house came into full view.

His speech was still hesitant, uninflected; the product of much patient effort by speech-therapists, much dogged perseverance on his part.

But better; but steadily improving.

Driving over weed-greened gravel, between shrubberies of laurel and rhododendron, the flowers now faded and falling, I responded with cultivated garrulity. If one person can keep up a kind of monologue, it makes it easier for the one whose speech is impaired.

But better; but steadily improving.

"Yes," I said. "For once at least partially conforming to description." I had no need to refer to the advertisement, clipped from the Baildon *Daily Press*.

"I said, "Quote. Tudor farmhouse. Needs modernisation. 1⅓ acre of garden, partly walled. Secluded position. Unquote."

One of the many wise men had told me never,

never to do anything for Bob which he could conceivably manage to do, however slowly or badly, for himself. So, having brought the car to a standstill, I waited while he tried with his flaccid left hand to manipulate the handle on the car door. He failed, but, undeterred, reached over with his right hand, swung the door open and went through the pitiable—but admirable— business of getting himself out. Both legs together from a sideways sitting position; then his stout stick, and finally, there he stood, triumphant. His smile said: There you are, you see. I did it.

The wise man had said that the most important thing of all was the restoration of self-confidence. I understood. Fall off a bicycle or a pony and the only thing to do is to get up and remount. That way you may eventually ride again. Fall out of life, as Bob had done—sixteen days of deep coma . . . But he had got up, fearfully injured, but ready to live again.

So here we were.

While he struggled with the car door, the stick, the slow shuffle to the house, the huge key of which he had taken possession, and the business of turning it, I stood back a little and looked at the house critically. It seemed solid enough, and compared with some of the places we had seen, it was in good condition; no broken windows, no obviously sagging roof. Why it should be for sale at such an absurdly low price, and put on the market in such a curious, almost furtive, manner, mystified me completely.

The brief advertisement had given only a box number at the paper. Four days later I received a brief communication; typewritten. It informed me that the house in question was called Gad's Hall and was in Stonham St. Paul's. The key could be obtained from Park Farm, Stonham St. Peter's. And the price was £4,000. And that, as my mother-in-law remarked, wouldn't buy a decent bungalow, these days. Ella—

that is her name—always gives the impression of belonging to another age, no specific period, just some pretty, flowery time of her own; and she professes not to understand decimal coinage; she still translates pence into shillings; but she is sound where pounds are concerned; and it was true. Four thousand pounds would not buy a bungalow, decent or indecent. Bob and I had spent some time viewing cottages that looked like tumbledown haystacks and one tragic old stately home, twenty bedrooms, not one of them waterproof.

Bob unlocked the door, and then, forgetful of his disability, pushed and almost overbalanced. Naturally, they had told me, I must not let him fall on to a fire, but to be too ready with the helping hand would be a mistake, psychologically. And he righted himself, grabbed the door post and gave me a triumphant look. His eyes, these days, were far more expressive than the careful, acquired speech.

We stood in the hall together. Preparing myself as well as him I said with false lightness, "I fear the worst. Dry rot, damp rot; even death-watch beetle."

"No smell," Bob said.

It was true; there were none of the warning smells. The hall was well lighted, a deep-set window on either side of the door. Other doors, one to the right, one to the left. A very solid staircase with shallow treads ran up to a half landing and then turned. At the bottom, and at the turn, the bannister rail broke into carved knobs, each bigger than a pineapple.

Bob said, "No sliding . . . down bannisters." He smiled; I smiled. In his mother's elegant little Georgian house, the bannister was one smooth tempting curve. John, who was ten, had negotiated it safely; then Alice, almost two years younger, must copy, fail to brake in time. No actual harm was done, except to Alice's nose, but Ella's big blue and white Chinese bowl, full of pot-pourri, and the frail-legged table on which it stood had

escaped catastrophe by a millimetre. Ella had been
very nice about it—she is an extremely nice woman—
but next day the table and the bowl had been moved,
though I had forbidden sliding down bannisters, with
fearsome threats, mayhem the mildest punishment.

That was why Bob and I smiled at each other. The
fact that we still could smile seemed to confound
people. What had happened to Bob shouldn't have
happened to any decent man; but it had happened, and
what were we supposed to do? Set ourselves on fire?
Go about weeping forever? Ella cried very easily. In
fact she once told me that she could hardly look at
Bob without wanting to cry. And for that, if for no
other reason, I was anxious to get away. Did Gad's
Hall offer an escape hatch?

It seemed to do. I detected no sign of damp and de-
cay on the ground floor. The room on the left of the
hall gave upon a long drawing room, papered, green
and gold arabesques, faded in places, the colours repeated in the tiles of the very Victorian fireplace. The
room on the other side was papered too, warm crimson
once, now darkened to a kind of liver-colour.

"Good workroom," Bob said, and I agreed. Dear
Bob, poor Bob, he hung on like a bulldog to the belief
that, handicapped as he was, he could begin again,
making designs for engines or machinery. It was possible, of course, he'd always had an inventive and inquiring mind.

There was a third room on the ground floor. That
had hardly been altered at all except that what had
plainly been a wide open fireplace had been closed in
and fitted with one of those free-standing—except for
the pipe which led into the chimney—all-night-burning
stoves. Here the panelling had neither been ripped out
nor covered with canvas and wallpaper; it was painted
white; and there was a big square-bowed window jut-
ting out and overlooking a strip of lawn and a rosebed
and a stretch of water. From the front I had not real-

ized that Gad's was partially moated. The bow window
had window seats along its three sides, and somebody
had not thought it worth while to take the cushions
away. They'd been blue once but had faded to grey.

Bob said, "Nice," and sat down gladly. I dived into
one pocket of my jeans and produced cigarettes and a
lighter.

I'd never been an addict; I could smoke a cigarette
in order to be sociable, nothing more. Bob had been
what is idiotically called a *heavy* smoker. I'm inclined
to be fussy about the use of words and before I would
accept that term I'd want proof that somebody, having
smoked a packet, weighed more than he had done
when he opened it. But, when Bob was still speechless,
reducing to scribbling on pads, he had understood the
dramatic change in our financial position and had written—I'll give up smoking.

That struck me as very sad; he'd lost so much. Some
losses were natural—he'd given up rugger, officially,
when he was thirty, saying it was game for the
young—but if by any chance one of the Scunwick team
dropped out, there he was in a flash. He'd stuck resolutely to cricket, good for another fifteen years; and to
tennis no limit, so long as your eyesight served. Now
all that kind of activity was lost forever and I couldn't
bear to think that he was voluntarily renouncing one
small pleasure. So I took to smoking, and Bob smoked
with me, not breaking his vow, just being companion-
able.

Now, on the window seat, the sun warm on our
backs, we smoked together. Bob said, "What . . . do
you . . . think?"

I said, "All right so far; but there must be *some*
snag."

"Tudor kitchen."

"That wouldn't deter me. I can handle a brick oven.
Or rig up a spit if I have to." All the same, I thought, I
mustn't sound *too* eager to get away; Ella was Bob's

mother and her behaviour couldn't be faulted. Our decision to look for a place of our own had been tacit. I had never said—though I had often felt—that I'd be happier camping out in a tent.

"It's been . . . wired," Bob said, pointing his stick at a light fitment in the ceiling, a power plug in the skirting. I certainly hadn't expected that; not in a house so cheap and advertised as in need of modernisation.

The kitchen gave me a shock, in a pleasant way. It had been completely modernised except for one wall which was almost entirely taken up by a huge dresser, built in, part of the house itself. There was a stainless steel sink and a small electric geyser over it; some of what are called kitchen units, and an electric cooker; not perhaps the very latest model, with an eye-level grill, but not all that old. Who, in his right senses, would leave such a thing behind?

One door in the kitchen opened into an airy larder, the other upon a flight of scrubbed wooden stairs.

"I'll take a look at the bedrooms," I said, leaving Bob an option; he could go back to the window seat if he felt tired.

"Other stairs better for me," he said. I knew he hated being watched on stairs, going up as a child just learning would do; sound leg first, a pull on the bannister, his limp leg pulled up on to the same stair.

By the time he reached the landing from his end I had had time to look into several bedrooms, looking for one thing only, those betraying damp patches on ceilings which betrayed a faulty roof. I found none. At his end Bob opened a door and made a noise which in a man with normal control of speech would have been an exclamation. Then he said, "Jill. Look. Bathroom."

So there was, and again quite modern, except for its size. It was large by present day standards. Basin, bath and loo were all pink, and the bath was served by another electric geyser, bigger than the one in the kitchen.

"Move in . . . tomorrow," Bob said, his voice still expressionless but his eyes eloquent.

"One more river to cross," I said. For snag there must be; and the stairs up from the kitchen, having debouched onto the landing, went up again. There was another floor and there, I imagined, I should find the evidence of roof damage that I dreaded. But actually the top, or attic, floor covered only a small part of the house. There was one room that still smelt of stored apples; one completely empty, and one with a padlocked door. Assuming the room behind it to be about the same size as the others, in total this floor could offer protection from damp to only about a third of the house. And both of the attics into which I could look seemed sound and dry.

It simply was too good to be true.

Had we come to the wrong house?

Anybody to whom the impossible has happened is forever vulnerable; the impossible may happen again.

We had followed instructions and gone to Park Farm, Stonham St Peter's, and been told, by a neat, elderly woman, that Mr and Mrs Thorley were both out, but if our name was Spender and we wanted the key to Gad's, here it was; and she had kindly told us how to find the place; turn left at the church, up the hill, left again and into the lane and there'd we be.

And here we were. But it was just possible that we were not at Gad's. It was possible that Mr Thorley had two houses to sell, and that the kind woman facing me had made a very common error, thinking of her left as my right. Somewhere in the opposite direction there might be a house which was worth so little and did need modernisation.

Of this horrid suspicion I said nothing to Bob; for although he was to be treated as far as possible as a normal person, he was not to be subjected to either physical or mental stress.

I ran down the stairs and said, "Sound as a bell. I'll just look at the garden."

Of what I hoped to do, of how I intended to make a living, I had said nothing to anyone. Not to Bob, it would have sounded as though I distrusted his ability to make a living for us all; and not to Ella, who thought that the solution to our problem was for us to buy a nice little house in Baildon and for me to go back to my job as librarian. And Tony could go to a play-school in the mornings. She or Elsie—her faithful retainer—would fetch him at the end of the morning session, give him lunch, see that he had his afternoon's nap and entertain him as best they could until I collected him. John and Alice posed no problem; they'd both settled down happily in their school, took what was called school dinner. John, as extrovert as his father, had joined a number of ex-classroom activities and sometimes was not home until eight o'clock.

I'm old-fashioned; I still believe that up to the age of five at least a child's best friend is his mother. And I could see other flaws in Ella's neat little plan; the difference between school and library hours, and holidays; I couldn't bear to think of Bob, himself liable to accident, being alone, or in charge of two lively children and a toddler, not perhaps often, but at any time. That was why I had cooked up my scheme and looked only at properties with gardens. My farming blood informed me that, given a bit of land and a modicum of luck, I could make a living.

Gad's had more than a bit of land. It had a treasure house. Against the wall which partially surrounded it fruit trees were espaliered; there was a rather broken-down greenhouse, and in it a vine which despite its exposure to the weather through some broken panes had flourished and fruited. There were free-standing trees of apples and pears; there was a bed of the best asparagus I have ever seen, thick spears thrusting up through last year's debris.

There was also a lawn, which had been cut not long ago, and on the pergola which divided the pleasure garden from the utilitarian part, the roses did not sprawl in a neglected way.

I thought of how easily typing errors are made. Perhaps that piece of paper should have said £40,000.

In my mind I bade it goodbye. Wrong house perhaps; wrong price perhaps—or, a third possibility struck me as I went back through the kitchen, somebody else in partial possession. Some lucky, lucky person who had forestalled us, done a bit of modernisation, tidied the garden. Advertisement departments in papers are not infallible. There could have been a ghastly mistake somewhere. Bob and I might be in the wrong place, or even in the wrong time. I noticed for the first time that the whole house was extremely clean; none of the litter that most people, moving out, leave behind them, and come to that it didn't *feel* unoccupied. I am not, I think, an unduly fanciful person, but some of the houses that Bob and I had seen in the last few weeks had seemed to appeal for salvation and I'd always felt a bit sad as I turned my back on them. Gad's—if indeed this were Gad's—had none of that pathos and as we slammed the heavy door behind us I felt no sorrow for the place, only self-pity for myself because something, somewhere had gone badly wrong and I knew perfectly well nobody, in these days, bought for £4,000 a perfectly sound, modernised house and one and a third acres of fruitful, reasonably well-conditioned ground.

We went back to Park Farm, a new boot-box of a house, covered with pink plaster and separated from the road by flowerbeds, each as rectangular as the house, and planted out in a style reminiscent of public gardens, pink geraniums and blue salvias. The windows were wide and without panes, the front door of ribbed glass. For the second time that afternoon I rang the

bell, and this time a man came to the door. Behind the
ribbed glass he looked enormous, and only slightly less
so when we stood face to face. Well over six foot,
broad, but lean. His face was so tanned that his grey
eyes looked very pale.

"Mrs Spender?"

"Yes."

"I'm George Thorley." He held out a hand, the
palm hard as wood. And he looked at me, so search-
ingly that I suddenly felt improperly dressed. Since
he was himself in his shirt sleeves and braces, a pair of
old corduroy trousers, and his slippers, this was no
mean achievement.

"It's about Gad's? Well, how did you like it?"

"Very much." I did not intend to say more until I
knew that we were talking about the same house; and
the same price.

"We must talk things over. My wife has just made
tea. I'll fetch your husband."

"No. I'd better. Just at the moment he's—rather
lame." Despite the searching stare, the man had a
kindly expression; he'd be just the type who'd try to
help Bob out of the car, hand him his stick, offer his
arm.

"We're invited to tea," I said.

"Good. I can . . . do with it," Bob said, beginning
his struggle.

Going, this time more slowly, between the flowerbeds I noticed the garage, integral as advertisements
say. The lift-at-a-finger-touch door was open and a
smart MG and a solid Jaguar stood side by side.

Mr Thorley had the good sense enough not to offer
his hand to a man whose right bore heavily on a stick.
He said, "Good afternoon, Mr Spender. Come in," and
led the way through a rectangular archway, into the
dining room.

"My dear," he said, "Mr and Mrs Spender. They're interested in Gad's. I'll get some more crockery."

Mrs Thorley was no longer young, but she was well-made-up. I know some women do have blond hair and brown eyes, but I guessed that her blondness was artificial, a shade too golden, and her eyes were black, not brown; also her throat and the bare arms, which her very fashionable, sleeveless shift frock left exposed, were sallow.

She seemed to find it necessary to apologize for the substantial and very delectable meal.

"Mr Thorley is busy hay-making, and I had an appointment, so we had a very light lunch."

"So did . . . we," Bob said.

One of his doctors had told me that a great point in his favour was that his condition did not embarrass him. He was a very rational person; what had happened to him had happened, there was nothing shameful about it and so far as he could manage, nothing pitiable either.

There was, in fact, I thought, some resemblance between the two men now at this table—the beautiful quality of imperturbability.

Mr Thorley carved ham of a kind seldom found nowadays, we passed green salad and potato salad to and fro.

The inquisition began.

I said, "What we must know, Mr Thorley, is whether the house we saw this afternoon was the house you advertised; and whether it really is for sale for four thousand pounds." A forkful of food got as far down as just behind my collarbone and there stopped, growing red-hot, as I waited for the answer.

"Well," he said, "I've only the one place to sell and old Hattie gave you the key. The price, four thousand, was what I thought reasonable."

Mrs Thorley said, "Mr Thorley is very sentimental about Gad's."

"Maybe I am. My family has been there for a long time. Before Domesday Book. Not in the house, that came later, but in the barn—the Danes called that the hall. To tell you the truth I wouldn't sell it now, for any amount of money, but for the way things are going."

Bob said, "Com . . . Compulsory purchase. Squatters."

"Just so," Mr Thorley said. "Our lords and masters can have two or three houses and no questions asked, but the ordinary man . . ." He paused for a second, mastering what I recognised as violence, and then went on with that deceptively calm manner. "I didn't intend to see Gad's turned into lodgings for lunatics or cosy retreats for bad boys. And I didn't want it to be just a week-end place. I went about it carefully. That box number was a protection. I chucked out most of the letters; townees, speculative builders. I wanted no truck with them."

It was plain that he felt strongly about Gad's—so why did he live in a pink plaster boot-box? Mrs Thorley, as though catching my thought, said:

"Mr Thorley and I lived there ourselves until about five years ago. It was inconvenient for him—his herd is here, on the main road. And it was lonely for me. Nobody will live in nowadays; even *au pair* girls won't take country jobs. And with Mr Thorley so often away on business, or attending some committee . . ."

"Let's face it," he said mildly, "Kitty never liked the place. That's why the modernisation is such a makeshift job. Just enough to get by with, till she was settled—which she never did. Have either of you lived in the country before?"

"Baildon . . . Cambridge . . . Kidder mi-minister," Bob stumbled on the word but pressed on. "Scunwick."

"There's a sugar factory there."

"I was manager."

"Ah," Mr Thorley said. His grammar was faultless,

his accent barely perceptible, yet in a way his speech was countrified. Only a countryman—and old-fashioned at that—could put so much into one syllable. His "Ah" said, "Yes, before you had your stroke. I understand. I'm sorry for you."

I said, "Scunwick was almost suburban by the time we left. But I spent a lot of time in the country when I was young. In my grandmother's house—rather like Gad's, but not modernised at all."

"I reckoned you were country-bred the moment I set eyes on you."

"George!" Mrs Thorley said sharply.

"What's wrong with that?"

"So personal!"

"I'm just making sure. Mrs Spender, did you happen to notice the dresser in the kitchen?"

"Who could miss it? It's part of the house, isn't it? In fact I imagined it with crockery." I deliberately used his own, slightly outdated word. "Or better still, pewter, but that is scarce now and expensive."

"It takes all sorts to make a world," Mrs Thorley said. "Frankly, I thought it was a monstrosity. It was impossible to make a proper, streamlined kitchen with that great thing looming. But Mr Thorley said that to remove it would bring the whole wall down."

I'm not—I hope—one of these U and non-U observers, but her constant reference to Mr Thorley did indicate something. I know that the Queen's use of four simple words—my husband and I—is good for a sick giggle any day, but it is correct usage. I thought to myself that Kitty Thorley had come up in the world, learning a lot, but not *quite* enough. Then I said to myself: Snob; you're as bad as Ella!

"So," Mr Thorley said, "you think you'd be happy at Gad's. That's all I ask. Somebody happy there and being fond of it."

Bob gathered his forces and said, "Love at first sight," without any hesitation at all.

"I feel the same," I said.

"All right, then. It's yours. Move in tomorrow, if you like. I know lawyers make a business of it. Something they call searches. Necessary where a property has changed hands. Gad's never did. Straight down from father to son. It's never been in hucksters' hands. Mine to sell; yours to buy. Let's call it a deal."

"It'll be a weight off your mind, George," Mrs Thorley said amiably. "No more running up to Gad's to see if a tile blew off, or sending a man to mow and prune."

Sometimes my mind slips and suddenly I had a ridiculous thought: If her hair weren't dyed and her face coloured, she'd have been exactly like Anne Boleyn, whose hold on Henry VIII had been, while it lasted, absolute. She was the example which sprang immediately to mind, but there were hundreds of others, women who without any specific effort had gained ascendancy. What did they have that the others of us had not? Better in bed? But I could think of several cases where complete infatuation had preceded the bed test, or had never been subjected to it. Just one of life's mysteries. Stop meandering; get back to business.

"We can't move in tomorrow, much as we would like to. At the moment we don't possess so much as an egg-cup."

And why should that confession make Mr Thorley look so pleased.

"In that case," he said. "If I might make a suggestion . . . I brought some stuff away. Just a few things I couldn't bring myself to part with. It's up in a loft here. If you liked the dresser, Mrs Spender, you might like some of that."

"I'm afraid we shall have to furnish on a shoestring."

"This wouldn't cost you a penny. I'd be very happy to see the old things back in their proper places."

"I said Mr Thorley was sentimental, didn't I?"

"Lofts not . . . for me . . . just yet," Bob said. "I'll wait in the car."

"Oh no. Come into the lounge. With tea so late, it's time for a glass of sherry."

I waited in the hall while Mr Thorley changed back into his boots. The house was built on the open plan, possible only with very efficient central heating; and the whole thing was singularly like a Show House in an exhibition; all the furniture very expensive, Swedish style, possibly more comfortable than it looked. The only individual touch that I could see in the section of the lounge within my view was a flower piece, delphiniums and peonies and poppies, very formally arranged. I heard Mrs Thorley say:

"You mentioned Baildon. I do know a Mrs Spender who lives there."

"My mother. We're . . . staying with her."

"Oh really!" The surprise was blatant.

"We'll cut through the garden and the orchard," Mr Thorley said. Flower garden, vegetable garden, all immaculate, orchard of young trees, all regimented, then into the past again; an old farmhouse, nothing like Gad's for size or style, but a place I should have been very glad to buy for £4,000 only an hour ago.

"That was the original Park farmhouse. It was derelict when I took over, but I made it into two good houses—for stockmen. Two minutes' walk from the job." He jerked a thumb towards some much more modern-looking buildings across the yard. "Rent free. Now everybody is up in arms about what they call tied cottages. Did you ever hear anything so daft? If Joe Snell went to work for a garage in the village and I asked him to leave, I'd be a villain. Well, here we are."

The place still smelt faintly of horses, though it now housed only a LandRover, a pick-up truck and a lorry. The way to the loft was up an absolutely perpendicular

ladder made of stout slats nailed to the wall. I climbed
them without thinking, emerged through the square
opening in the floor of the loft and stood in near
darkness until Mr Thorley, following me, went and
flung open the wide doors through which, in the time
of horses, fodder and bedding had been forked from
high-piled wagons. Long rays of light, full of dust
motes, streamed in.

The stored furniture lay under stack tilts, under
dust-sheets, under sacking.

A dismantled four-poster bed, definitely Tudor; a
long heavy table, probably older, its top one solid
plank of oak which under a little surface dust revealed
the patina that beeswax and elbow grease and sheer
use had given it. A high-backed settle. A round rosewood pedestal table; a long-case clock; an elegant little
chiffonier. Too much to take in at a glance. But I did
specially notice a framed sampler, only slightly faded.
Worked by Mary Thorley and completed in June 1815.
Under her name and the date she had stitched "God be
thanked." Because the tedious work was done, or because the war had ended? I thought of Mary Webb's
most touching poem about a little girl working a sampler through "those leafy Junes, those ancient dark De-
cembers . . ."

I said, "Mr Thorley, have you any idea what these
things are worth?"

"To a museum, you mean? To be gaped at. That I
did not intend to have. In fact I mentioned all this stuff
in my will. I said it was to be burnt. And it would have
been. What a man says while he's alive is easily over-
ridden, but wills are still respected. There's an oddity if
you like; people are still afraid of offending the dead.
Well, take anything you can use, and welcome."

"I can take it all. And I promise to take good care
of it." I even knew where the long-case clock had
stood—on the half landing; it had left its ghost there as
very solid pieces of furniture do, dusted round.

"There was a time," he said, "when I hoped. I thought any son of mine—or come to that a daughter—would have grown up and taken to Gad's and put these things back in place. But I've no children."

He said it as though he were making a comment on the weather. I wondered why, and how long it had taken him to reach such a resigned, dispassionate attitude towards a situation which to him, so devoted to Gad's and its long tradition, must have been more painful than to men who had no roots.

"What a pity."

"It is that, but it can't be helped. I'll send this and a couple of men to shift it, up to Gad's tomorrow. But you'll need more. I didn't store anything the moths could get at. If you take my advice you'll go to Bidwell's."

Bidwell's was a shop in Baildon High Street; very up-to-the-minute and extremely expensive.

"Beyond our means."

"He has another department. Go down Pump Lane at the side of his big shop, and there's a secondhand department; and he's a good, honest chap."

Abruptly I found myself face to face with what I liked to think was my one phobia.

I'd met it first when I was about ten; living with my grandmother, and provided with two little playmates. A wet morning, so we sought some sheltered place to play in and found a loft, twin to this one. We'd had a happy morning, then the elder of the two, who had a watch, said it was lunchtime. She and her sister had gone down the vertical ladder as easily as they had mounted it; I tried to follow and just could not. The slats of the ladder extended above the level of the square hole; all there was to do was to take the top rung in one's hand and step off the edge of the square opening, on to one of the rungs; and I just could not do it. My knees turned to jelly at the thought, and my hands were equally useless. My friends came up and down several times to show me how easy it was; and then—their mother was strict about time—they ran off.

My grandmother came. She was nearing seventy, but very spry; she came up, went down, to show me how easy it was. Standing well away from the abyss, I said, "I can't. I can't," and cried. My grandmother said, "You'll come down when you're hungry," and went away.

I was hungry already. I was also deserted—by man, not by God. My grandmother was a very religious woman, not ostentatiously pious but firm in her simple and beautiful faith. I shared it then; so I knelt and prayed for courage and it did not come though I edged towards the abyss again, trying to show God that I did believe . . . At the sight of the emptiness into which I must step, the sight of the top rungs which I must grasp, weakness assailed me again. I couldn't do it. I should have to stay here until I died of hunger.

Some very long hours passed before I realised that there was another way down. The floor of the loft stopped short of the wall on its inner side so that hay could be pushed over and into the manger immediately below. Not much of a drop, not much of a drop; no waiting void. I jumped, scrambled out of the manger and made for the house, where my grandmother was just starting her pudding. "I knew you could it," she said placidly. I never told her how I had done it.

Now here I was, thirty-five years old, a married woman with three children, faced with the identical situation: obliged to make a humiliating confession to a man I'd known less than two hours. This time I had no need to jump. He went and stood in the manger and reached me down, as he would have done a doll from a shelf.

"There's no accounting for such irrational fears," he said. "Believe it or not, when I was a boy I was sure there were wolves in Layer Wood. And my fear seemed to communicate itself to my pony. Winter afternoons he'd cut through Layer like a race horse."

Physical contact, there in the manger, as he lifted me from one level and set me down on the other, had meant nothing, but suddenly as we went back to the pink plaster boot-box I found myself telling him what I had told nobody—my plans for making some sort of living at Gad's. "Until," I said, "my husband can get some of his ideas going. He's really a brilliant engineer, you know. And although some of his motor nerves suffered, they're mending. His *mind* is all right."

"Anybody can see that. But it'll be a while before he can dig. And if you go ahead with your plan, there'll be some digging to be done."

"I shall do it." I know that physically I am not impressive; quite tall, but so small boned that even as a fat adolescent I never weighed more than nine stone. Now much less, but all tough. And at the moment I was enjoying such a bout of euphoria that I'd have tackled the Great Pyramid and brought it low with a trowel.

"There's a slack time between hay and harvest," Mr Thorley said. "I'll lend you a man."

"I can't afford hired labour, Mr Thorley."

"Who said anything about hiring? I said lend. And he can bring good load of muck with him; it's starved land up there."

*

"Thorley," Ella said, "the name rings a bell. No, I don't mean this Mrs Thorley whom you met. I have *seen* her, either at the Ladies' Luncheon Club, or the Flower Club. Very smart."

My mother-in-law still made a distinction between having seen somebody, meeting somebody, and knowing somebody. "Wait. My memory is not what it was.

So infuriating! Really, I do know that we must all grow old and die to make room for the younger generation, but why we couldn't keep our looks, and our senses and our mobility, I shall never understand. But that is by the way . . . Thorley, Gad's Hall. Oh yes, I remember now. I only heard by hearsay. There was a Thorley at Gad's—quite wild, he squandered his substance. He broke his neck, hunting when he was well into his seventies . . . All long before my time, of course, but your father, Bob, had elderly friends who seemed to admire the old reprobate; though what is admirable about ruining one's family, I fail to see."

"Far from ruined . . . now. House worth forty . . . thousand, at least."

"And two cars," I said. "An MG and a Jaguar."

"And he proposes to sell Gad's Hall for four thousand. It must be in a terrible state."

"It isn't. I went over it thoroughly. I thought it was too good to be true. But Mr Thorley is sentimental about the place."

"I'm very fond of this house," Ella said, "but were I forced to sell it I should expect a fair price. I really think I had better take a look at it. And I'll ask Mr Gordon to look through the deeds." Mr Gordon was not the only solicitor in Baildon, but he was the only one that people like my mother-in-law would ever dream of consulting. He was one of the bridge circle.

"There aren't any; it's been in the same hands since Domesday."

"Presumably there are wills. Some proof of ownership."

"Man struck me . . . dead honest."

"We shall see."

"I'd like you to see it, Ella. Come with us, tomorrow. Unless it rains, Mr Thorley expects to have his hay in by mid-day and he's bringing the furniture across at around four o'clock."

"What furniture?"

That took some explaining, too, and Ella said that the only conclusion she could draw was that the man was mad. And, by implication, that Bob and I were, too—or so anxious to get away from the prim little house that we were willing to risk anything.

Bob, admitting to feeling a bit tired, but proudly refusing all offers of help, went to bed early and then Ella tackled me.

"I am well aware, my dear, that you need a place of your own. But if I have ever done or said anything that hinted that you were unwelcome here and that you must rush out and do something silly in order to get a roof over your head, I withdraw it, and I apologise."

"You never did. You've been wonderful. Kinder than God." Not perhaps the most acceptable compliment; absolutely orthodox in all her works and ways, Ella was a good church woman, a regular attendant at morning service, a stout supporter of any fund-raising schemes, coffee mornings, garden fêtes, Christmas bazaars.

"Has Elsie upset you in any way?"

"Of course not."

"Then why must you take on such an impossible place? At least six miles from the school where John and Alice seem happy and settled. That means running a car. And an old house, however well patched up, is going to be costly in maintenance. There'll be rates . . . I've been very careful not to decry Bob's idea that he can, one day, make some sort of living, but my dear Jill, you know as well as I do that he never can. So what will you live on? His miserable little pension?"

Back to her fixed idea; buy one of those reconstructed houses in the slum that had once been Scurvy Lane; four thousand down and the other two thousand and five hundred on mortgage; get myself a regular job in the Public Library, or, failing that, in a school. "Be sensible; be practical."

Ella must have been very pretty when she was young, and she was pretty still; neat little kitten face, blue eyes which the years had not faded, and soft, almost beige-coloured hair; she was short, but not plump, just nicely curved in just the right places, always wearing clothes, not quite old-fashioned, but a bit Old World-romantic, in soft pastel shades. But nobody knew better than I did that inside this very feminine, almost fondant appearance, there was a core of steel. In the terrible crisis which had overtaken us all, she had cried floods and floods of tears, and her attitude towards Bob was all wrong. She thought I was heartless, because, obeying instructions, I had left him to do things for himself—things not easily managed, I admit, but once accomplished, a boost to his self-esteem.

"Be sensible; be practical," Ella said, and I said, "Come with us tomorrow, and I'll show you how practical and sensible I intend to be."

I spent the next morning at Bidwell's, in the back street department. Mr Bidwell had such treasures to sell, at such extraordinarily low prices because when he sold new things from his smart High Street shop he would accept used furniture in part exchange—but, as the man who served me pointed out, only clean stuff, in good condition. Looking round, one could only conclude that some people bought new furniture just for the sake of change. I bought sparingly: I had no intention of using the big drawing room until our circumstances underwent a dramatic change. The room with the bow window would be our living room and would be adequately furnished with a high-backed settle and three chairs, one rather high one—easy to get out of, for Bob, two lower ones, less well upholstered. I bought three single beds, a kitchen table, six kitchen chairs, four matching and two odd, a pretty little dressing table which I thought would please Alice, two chests of drawers; a few other bits and pieces and all for just under fifty pounds. I had a preference for new mattresses, though those in the used department looked clean enough.

In the new department I bought, not only the mattresses, but, to show my faith in Bob, a proper swivel chair and one of those lamps which can be adjusted to any angle. Then nylon sheets, and pillowcases; foam rubber pillows, blankets. Carpets I must do without; Mr Bidwell did not take carpets in part exchange and his new ones were shockingly expensive, except for some rugs, plainly marked "Cotton" and giving the country of their origin.

As this bill was totted up I felt sick, thinking of all the things I had sold, at give-away prices, less than a year ago and of the things I had literally given away as keepsakes.

But now I had a bonus to come. The salesman in this department asked whether I wanted to pay cash or have credit and, when I said I would pay, said that Bidwell's gave a discount for cash; not in money, but in goods. I romped through the china and hardware department; in one choosing the cheapest, in the other the best. Crockery, as Mr Thorley called it, was vulnerable, a good frying-pan, properly used, could last for years. I slightly overran my discount and ended by owing another four pounds, fifteen pence.

Bidwell's delivered free within ten miles. Where did I want my purchases delivered; and when?

"Gad's Hall; Stonham St Paul's. And as soon as possible."

He went to one of those intercom telephones and came back with the good news that a small van was free this afternoon.

Mr Thorley did not come—a pity, I thought, because I wanted Ella to see that he was not mad; simply a man with an obsession. He sent three men, all sturdy, and with the usual admonishments—Bit more to your left, Joe. You silly bugger, only just missed my toe, they manhandled the heavy things into place. Then Bidwell's van arrived, with two men.

It was another hot afternoon and I felt badly about not being able to offer even a cup of tea, but Bob said women set too much store by tea and the men would much sooner have money and he had it ready.

Ella, fully as critical as I had been on the previous afternoon, had admitted that on the ground floor, at least, she could find no fault. Some of my purchases from Bidwell's she criticised. "Jill, there was no need to buy a teapot. I am sure I have at least three, never used."

In the end I got her into the garden and there her innate hostility to the scheme surfaced.

"It is far too big. How can you hope to manage a place this size?"

"I'm going to make it earn its living."

"You mean *sell* things?"

"Ella, we have both sold things, and suffered no ostensible damage."

"That was quite different. And look at that!" She pointed to the one space, not very wide, where the moat which held Gad's in a half embrace was open to the garden. Mostly the garden was shut off from the moat, by the south-facing wall, the old hothouse, trees and shrubs, and the outjutting wing of the house where the attics were. But there was this space.

"What about Tony?" Ella asked.

"I'll rig up some sort of fence. A few hurdles would do."

"Very effective, but not in keeping. I will give you, as a house-warming present, a length of that chestnut fencing. Much more suitable." With that word she turned abruptly away and went into the house. It was as though she was repudiating Gad's absolutely. I stood there for a moment and then remembered the asparagus bed. I went into the kitchen, found a knife, and, having as yet no basket, a cardboard box in which some of the things had been packed, and then I cut and cut, more asparagus and of far better quality than most people ever see.

When I returned to the house I found Bob and Ella in the living room. Half a glance informed me that it looked very nice; the settle and the round rosewood table looked as though they had never been away, and even the foreign cotton rug, borrowing dignity from its surroundings, looked almost Persian. A second half glance showed me that something had upset Ella. She and I had been through a good deal together, and I could see that although she was not—and had not been—crying, she had suffered some kind of shock and was maintaining composure by a great effort. Whatever it was Bob did not share it. He looked very happy, sitting in the chair I had chosen especially for him and talking about the other chair, the adjustable lamp and the wonderful solidity of the great table at which he would work. So why were the pupils of Ella's eyes so dilated that only a mere rim of blue showed? And why did her discreet, carefully applied make-up seem to stand out, as though behind it her face had grown pallid and shrunken?

Nothing was said on the way home, or in the evening until Bob switched on the nine o'clock news, which Ella often avoided, saying it was too depressing. At the door she turned and gave me a beckoning glance. I followed her up to the bedroom which was hers for the moment. She closed the door with something of a conspiratorial air, indicated that I should take the only chair, and seated herself on the dressing-table stool, her back to the glass.

"Jill, you must on no account go to live in that house."

"Why on earth not?"

"There is such evil there."

"Evil? What do you mean?"

"What I say. Evil. I hesitate to use the word haunted—I know you modern young people make mock of such things; and certainly I saw nothing, heard nothing; but I felt it. I was almost . . . overcome."

"Where?"

"On the attic floor. Perhaps you didn't penetrate so far."

"I did. I was looking for signs of damp. Two attics and a locked door."

"And you felt nothing?"

"Satisfaction that the roof seemed sound."

She gave me a look, half-pity, half-despair, as though I confessed an inability to spell cat.

"Then you must; you really must, my dear, be guided by me. I simply cannot allow you to buy that house."

"But we have."

"Don't be stupid! A few words across a tea-table! People retract from far firmer agreements than that. Now listen; ever since this afternoon I have been thinking of an alternative. As you know I have only my annuity and a few shares which depreciate every day. But I have this house. It is in the best neighbourhood, convenient for shops, church, everything. And it is small, easily run. It could be worth thirty thousand pounds. I'll sell it. Then we can pool our resources and buy a house in the country, with the kind of garden you want. What do you say to that?"

For a second or two, nothing. I was stunned by her offer.

She loved her elegant little house; as she said it was most conveniently situated and most of her friends lived nearby. And she did not really care for the country, except as a place to take a drive through, on a pleasant afternoon; she didn't own, so far as I know, a pair of walking shoes. She could not drive a car; in any country place she would be stranded—except for me—as though on a desert island.

"Ella, it's the noblest offer I ever heard of. But I can't let you make such a sacrifice."

I'm a realist; I know that people who make terrific sacrifices in moments of self-immolation regret it and come to hate those for whom the sacrifice was made. Also I could see myself perpetually trying to make up to Ella and wasting a lot of much-needed time, acting as chauffeur.

"I am not proposing that we would live in one another's pockets. We could find a house big enough to allow separate kitchens. I have Elsie to consider."

Snatching at a straw, I said, "Elsie might not fancy country life."

"When Elsie was my housemaid—we had housemaids then—she fell into a coma. Everybody thought she was dead; I didn't. I could run in those days and I ran for Doctor Taylor. It was a diabetic coma and Elsie, since then, has been kept alive by insulin injections. Which *I* give her. They have a contrivance by which diabetics can inject themselves, but Elsie could never bring herself to do it. So . . . every morning and every evening . . . I think it would take more than a change of house to make Elsie desert me."

I looked at those pretty, milk-white hands, their only sign of age the prominence of the blue veins, no brown blotches, no knobbly knuckles. Day after day, year upon year, performing a slightly disagreeable task. One from which I must admit I should have shuddered.

"That," my astounding mother-in-law said, "is just by the way. We were talking about Gad's Hall. I cannot possibly allow you to take Bob and those dear children to that dreadful place."

I said, "Look, Ella. It's a chance in a million. We can move in tomorrow—without disrupting your whole life. I'd be the last person to deny that *you* felt some-

thing. You may be sensitive to such things. I felt nothing. Bob isn't likely to tackle those stairs and if it eases
your mind at all I'll put the attics out of bounds for the
children." I began to improvise. "In the old days servants slept on that floor; some of them may have been
horribly unhappy—homesick; ill-treated by an employer or a fellow servant. I can *just* believe that a very
strong emotion can leave an impression which somebody with a kind of extra sense can pick up. And even
if Gad's were *known* to be haunted, I don't think it
would deter me. I can't think of a case where a ghost
ever did anybody a physical harm."

"Oh, can't you? I can. It was in the papers. A
Council house. A man was pushed downstairs, and his
wife received a heavy blow on the shoulder. The
Council rehoused them."

I was silent for a minute, thinking of one story; Lyt-
ton's about a haunted house in which a man intended
to sit up all night with a manservant and a guard dog;
the manservant ran away and the dog's neck was broken. But this was fiction; so probably was the experience of the people in the Council house.

My mother-in-law gave a sigh.

"Very well, if you must be so stubborn . . . Will
you do one thing for me, before you move in? Ask
your Mr Thorley to open that locked door."

❋

I don't think I've ever felt more foolish. Here I was,
having been offered, and having accepted, the biggest
bargain within living memory and quibbling about one
locked door.

"So far as I know, there never was a key to it," Mr
Thorley said. "My grandfather, or somebody before
him, locked it and so it stayed. I never knew him—he
must have been fifty before he married, and my father
didn't marry till he was clear of debt, so between my

grandfather and me there was a gap. I remember once *I* asked about that door and my father said mind my own business, he'd never seen inside it and why should I bother? And after that I never gave it a thought. But of course, if you want it opened . . ."

He used a pair of pliers and wrenched one staple free; the bit of chain dangled. The door opened upon nothing but another empty attic. It differed from the others only in one way. Its window was barred, slant-wise.

"I'd guess that was done," Mr Thorley said, "to guard against storm damage. This gable is a bit exposed and I seem to remember some talk about a window blowing in. But that was before my time."

"I can't understand why nobody had sufficient curiosity to break in before this. It might have held treasure."

"Treasure!" He laughed. "By all accounts my grandfather had disposed of everything that was disposable long before he died. All he left was debts and just the nucleus of a herd. It took my poor father . . . But you don't want to hear about all that."

"On the contrary, I find it most interesting. My mother-in-law, as soon as I mentioned your name, had some memory—about a hunting accident when he was . . . rather old."

"Very old, nudging eighty, and still wild as the devil. Well, are you satisfied that there are no skeletons in the attic?"

"To be honest, I never thought . . ." I began to move away, and as I turned my angle of sight and the angle of light coming through the barred window met, I saw, as you can see in some old churches, something that the whitewash had been intended to obscure. Not the biblical pictures intended to enlighten people who could not read; not, in fact, anything really recognisable, just some bits of faces with unpleasant expressions, and all partly smudged out by something other than whitewash. And even as I stared they seemed to fade away again.

I was able to report to Ella that there was nothing but an empty attic. I made rather much of the blown-in window. Imagine, I said, a maid sleeping up there on a night of howling wind, and having the window blow in; wouldn't that be terror enough to leave a lasting impression?

"It was not physical fear that I felt. However," she shrugged her slight shoulders, "I have done what I could. I feel that perhaps I should speak to Bob, but he is incapable of believing anything that can't be measured on a slide rule."

That day I spent shopping for food and Elsie unearthed a lot of screw-top jars; she never could bring herself, she said, to throw a good jar away; she'd always known they'd come in useful one day. She made a remark which had significance in its omissions; she'd miss Alice, she said. And certainly Alice, when not in John's company, was a very docile, quiet little girl. Apart from mentioning Alice, Elsie made no secret of her relief; before I had finished packing, she was making Ella's room ready for her again; you'd really have thought that the room had been occupied by squatters of a most unsavoury kind. On the other hand she showed goodwill by serving a very substantial tea, sausages and chips and by adding to what I had bought some jars of home-made jams, marmalade, chutney.

I tried to keep my word to Ella about the children and the attics. "It's a very old house," I explained, "and that top flight of stairs and the floor it leads to won't stand any rollicking about. Quite apart from any damage to you—" I looked straight at my son, "and that might mean a leg in plaster for weeks—it would run us into a lot of unnecessary expense." Poor John, he'd come a bit early to the question of what could and what could not be afforded. He understood. And in any case there was plenty to explore; more space, more funny little holes and corners than anywhere they had ever lived in their lives.

John was indeed a very sensible, logical boy and he immediately spotted the danger of that open space where the garden and the moat met. "Tony could fall in there, Mum."

"I know. Gran noticed it, too. She said she would give us a length of fencing."

"I'll see if I can rig up something in the meantime. Come on, Alice, you can lend me a hand."

When I was called to look at what they had rigged up, I remembered that the words engineer and ingenious were closely related. Out of an old window frame which John said he had found near the greenhouse, some logs and a sawhorse taken from a shed, and two packing cases left by Mr Bidwell's men, John and Alice—directed by him—had made a barrier quite sufficient to keep a toddler away from the water.

So, here we were, survivors from the wreck; Bob and I at last together again in a bed which we could consider in a way to be our own; in the big four-poster with the new mattress called king-size. I did not feel in the least guilty about Mr Thorley's generosity, or his waiving of formalities. His delight in seeing some of his family things restored to their rightful place had been so whole-hearted. And, after all, there were many people who felt so strongly about a family place that they'd hand it over to the National Trust—sometimes with a handsome dowry for its upkeep. There were also people who bequeath lots of money to anybody who will take care of a favourite cat or dog. Ella's remark that Mr Thorley must be mad didn't hold water. What was remarkable was that his need for a kind of perpetuation and our need for a home should have coincided. Just on the verge of sleep, I could look back, with a degree of calmness, on the train of events which had brought us here.

*

Bob, with an engineering degree from Cambridge and some chemical qualification too, could have found a post anywhere, and, given a bit of initial training, in almost any industry. He chose to make sugar from beet. I always said, teasingly, and he always denied it, that his choice was decided by the work hours. Beet sugar factories have a season, roughly from September to January or February, and during that time work never stops. Men work in shifts but technical people are literally on call day and night. Their summers are relatively free; not holiday exactly, there is always some old piece of machinery to be overhauled, something new to be installed, but a man who plans his jobs carefully can play cricket, and golf, go sailing.

We married when he got the managership at Scunwick. There was a house waiting for us, a Sugar Corporation house, quite large and well appointed. A thick belt of trees stood between us and the factory, hiding all but the two tallest chimneys of what everybody admitted was an ugly building. In an emergency Bob could cut through the trees and be on the scene in three minutes.

Scunwick was a pleasant, unspoiled old market town and we had many friends in and around it; it had two good schools, an above-average golf course, a decent library. We had our own hard tennis court. I was completely—perhaps dangerously—contented. So was Bob, except for one thing. He never could hit it off with his area supervisor, the man in charge of six factories of which Scunwick was one. Mr Beckworth was oldish, set in his ways, Bob said, dead stupid and that he had reached his exalted position simply by being there when somebody even older and more stupid dropped dead. Mr Beckworth did not, in fact, trouble us much but he made routine visits and almost every one of them ended with a row. Mr Beckworth had manners so good as to be almost courtly; Bob was, on the whole, an amiable person, but they kept up a long-drawn-out running battle about machinery, about procedure. They were in fact perfect examples of the generation gap.

I always made a point of asking Mr Beckworth to dinner and providing dishes that he liked. And inside the house both men dropped their grievances; Bob became the amiable host, Mr Beckworth the honoured guest. And always, on the next morning, I received a sheaf of carnations. A Beckworth Bunch, Bob called it.

I could not pinpoint exactly when the winter of Bob's discontent set in. It came, as all winters do, step by step. He said he'd run into a cul-de-sac; that he'd managed, despite Mr Beckworth's sabotaging activities, to make Scunwick at least 40 per cent more productive than any other factory within the Corporation. And what thanks did he get? That sort of thing.

Then he went to one of the conferences which punctuated the summer, and met a man, a West Indian, who had shared a staircase with him at Cambridge. I had never been privileged enough to be part of Cambridge, or Oxford, but I had a vague idea that Humbert Wolfe, whose verse I much admired, had dedicated one volume to somebody who had shared his staircase at Oxford.

When I heard what Bob's staircase-sharer had proposed, I had an attack of schizophrenia—in the literal sense; a split mind.

Santa Barbara sounded, and looked—judging by the brochures and other photographs and literature which Bob had brought home with him—more like the Garden of Eden than anyplace on this earth. It was small, the Spanish and the French had never bothered to dominate it; it had fallen under English influence during the Napoleonic Wars. Nelson had for a time used it as a base and one brochure said that he had called it the pearl of all islands, free of that scourge, yellow fever. Its peaceful history had never been interrupted by slave revolts or political coups and it had moved, without incident towards independence within the British Empire.

It had a backward economy which Bob's Cambridge acquaintance had set himself to improve by increasing production, inviting investment, and attracting tourists. It had two very small, very antiquated sugar mills. Bob had been invited to go there and take complete control, at a salary three times as large as what he was earning at the moment. In fact, his friend who now bore the title of Minister for Economics had come to England to conduct a recruitment campaign aimed especially at men like Bob who were ambitious and discontented. He'd netted several doctors and schoolmasters already.

I could see that Bob wanted to go; and although my instinct was against it, I could produce no really valid arguments. I could say, "But you are a *beet*-sugar man." Bob said that meant nothing—the principles were the same—and that if somebody discovered how to make sugar out of old rope, he'd be perfectly capable of running a factory for that purpose. I could not plead the climate, for one of the tourist brochures mentioned a cool current which moderated the tropical heat; the immigrant doctors were to have carte blanche to establish a Health Service; the immigrant schoolmasters were going out to assure education for all.

To say the simple truth: I don't want to leave Scunwick, would have sounded too stick-in-the-mud for words. And if Bob heeded it, I should have a frustrated man on my hands.

There was just one frail hope of reprieve. Mr Beckworth had decided to retire from what he called active service and take his place on the Board of the Corporation. If Bob should be offered his job, as was indeed, his due . . . That would have satisfied his ambition, and it would, incidentally, have been extremely beneficial to the industry as a whole; Bob's factory was far and away the best in the group of six which made up the area, and with him in charge his area would have been the best in England. And although we might have to hand over the factory house to Bob's successor, we need not leave Scunwick; within a given radius, area supervisors could live where they liked and Scunwick was quite central.

Bob did not get the post; and when he heard to whom it had been given, he was infuriated. "Of course with Bloody Beckworth now on the Board, I didn't stand a chance in hell. Withersly got it because he's a yes man, a lickspittle. And if they think I'm going to work under *him*, they can think again. Damn it all, I told Chambers that if I did accept his offer, I'd stay and see this factory open in September. Now I shan't. I'll bloody well leave them in the lurch."

I saw his point. I thought of those tasty little dinners—all wasted.

In Santa Barbara, the brochure said, there were no hurricanes; it lay outside the belt; but in Scunwick there was a hurricane all right. Either Bob on the phone, or somebody on the phone wanting him. Ella rang several times, sometimes wasted calls because she began to cry. She was totally against it; she was inclined to blame me, of all unfair things.

At the centre of a hurricane there is an eye of quiet and so it was with us, once the decision had been taken. Bob was to fly out at the end of June. I was to stay and dispose of everything that didn't seem to be worth the freight charges, give him time to settle in, find a house, and then be there for Christmas.

Until then I should have a roof over my head. The new Works Manager, a nice man with a nice wife, were already established in a house which suited them perfectly, and had no desire to move. They had only one child and did not need more space. Nor, apparently, did anyone else. There was a scheme in the pipeline for turning the factory house Bob and I had occupied into two flats, but, pending such development, I was welcome to occupy it at the minuscule rent of three pounds a week. Such a decision must have been made at Board level, and perhaps after all, those tasty little dinners had not been totally wasted.

This is what is so very odd about fate, chance, luck, or—as my grandmother always called it—Providence.

Bob wrote me ecstatic letters; Santa Barbara was all and more than he had hoped for; he'd found a house, midway between the two sugar mills, and he was furnishing it with native-made, wonderful things; and even as he wrote, he said, all the plant, turbines, boilers and such things which he had ordered were being delivered. Everything was wonderful, and busy as he was, he was counting the days . . . So was I.

And but for Ella, we all, John, Alice and Tony, would have been there, in Santa Barbara, just before Christmas.

I had given a whole series of parties, all with a farewell tinge, and several things which I treasured I'd given away as pre-Christmas presents, keepsakes really, to my best friends. A few things, easily crated, and all from my grandmother's house, I had reserved.

And then Ella rang me and weeping copiously said what about Christmas? Hadn't we always spent Christmas together, and now, this which might well be the *last* Christmas . . .

Well it was true; Christmas had always been a time for some kind of reunion. Not always bang on the nose because Christmas came in the middle of Bob's working season; but he'd snatch a day and a night and we'd drive down to Baildon and he'd do a lot of little jobs which she had been saving up and have a sedate dinner party and then race home. With one child, all right, with two, just impossible, with three, a muddle. So after Tony's birth, she had come to us. I'd fetch her—from Scunwick to Baildon was only about sixty-five miles.

In those days we'd got on as well as two fairly civilised people with nothing but the family in common could do. When I was in her house I always felt I was walking on eggshells; when she was in mine, she felt, I knew, as though she were camping out amongst barbarians. When she entertained in her neat little, dainty little, precise little house dinner was served. In mine—except for Mr Beckworth's visits—hospitality was a bit haphazard. I'd offer cold meat and potato salad, green salad in season; or a washbowl of curry and another washbowl of rice—perfectly cooked, though I say it myself; every grain fluffy and separated. I added chutney, sour sauce, sweet sauce. And people helped themselves, wore what they liked, drank gin rather than sherry and plonk more often than vintage wines. I often saw a somewhat pained expression on Ella's face.

Still, here she was, weepy on the phone, begging me to spend Christmas with her; just this one last time; for who could tell where we should all be next Christmas?

I gave in, changed the times of our flight and sent a cable to Bob informing him of the postponement.

When on Christmas Eve I received a cable from him I thought it was just a seasonal message. But it said, Hold everything on my way home.

No alarm then. He plainly now had the kind of job which would enable him to come and escort us, or view some special piece of equipment.

On my way home could well mean that he could be with us for the latter half of Christmas Day. The excitement was enormous, the waiting endless. Finally we decided that if the children were to enjoy their turkey, and plum pudding, they'd better have them before they fell asleep and before both comestibles were totally ruined.

Red candles, holly, crackers containing funny hats and would-be funny jokes—can I ever face them again?

It was Alice, always the most reluctant to go to bed, who switched on the television.

Apologising for the interruption in the programme, somebody told us that violent revolution had broken out in Santa Barbara. As usual their men on the spot had been intrepid, indefatigable and there were some pictures, buildings burning, cars overturned, mobs on the move.

I rang Heathrow; clinging to hope by my fingernails. Bob was no fool; if he'd caught even the faintest whisper of this he'd be on his way home. And that explained the apparent abruptness of his cabled message.

Heathrow was sorry, but Flight 24X or some such, due at 14.50, had not come in. No, so far as Heathrow knew there had been no accident, no fog anywhere, no diversions.

Ella cried and cried and said that from the first she had thought about what had happened in the Congo. And so had I. At least we were together on that. Together, also, in our hope that Bob might have got away.

As a matter of fact he almost did.

What had happened in that peaceful, ideal little island was a late explosion; the ordinary people did not like the new ways or the new people brought in to make new things work. There had been a complete revolution. Bob and every other foreigner had been told to go home, taking nothing more than could be carried in an ordinary suitcase. There was, perhaps, a kind of rough logic in that, but none at all in what happened later. Some fanatic, not content that foreigners should go, threw a bomb into the place where they were gathered, waiting to go.

Thank God for America. It cares for its own, as En-

gland once did. There were about forty American cit-
izens on Santa Barbara when the boil burst; they and,
as a sideline, all foreigners were rescued by helicopters
which flew in and out unmolested, protected by the
presence of an American frigate in the harbour,
threatening instant reprisal if one shot were fired.

The bomb had killed seventeen people and injured a
great many others. Bob was one of those seriously
hurt.

We were informed, by cable, from a hospital in Miami.

I went, just as I was.

There was the coma; then the series of delicate, in-
tricate operations, and Bob emerged, unable then to
speak at all and partially paralysed. But he could write,
and what he wrote proved that his mind and his
memory had not been impaired. The doctors varied in
their prognostications; one told me that Bob's age was
in his favour and that a good deal of improvement
might be expected, in time. Another warned me to be
prepared to see him live on in this maimed state. What
mattered to me was that he was alive, and he seemed
to have found from somewhere a dogged optimism.
One of the first things he wrote was: Don't worry. I
shall get well.

Because of its suddenness and ferocity, and because
it happened at Christmas, season of peace and goodwill, the incident attracted more attention than one
might have expected in a world so ravaged with violence. Somebody got hold of the fact that I had rushed
to Bob's bedside, "without so much as a toothbrush,"
as one reporter put it, and because one of the operations performed upon his brain had been frankly ex-
perimental, Bob and I received more than our share of
publicity. We were overwhelmed with kindness. People
from all over America sent me gifts of clothing—one
woman actually sent me a mink coat. Offers of hospi-

tality poured in. One big store provided me with a complete outfit. The hospital waived its charges, the surgeons repudiated all idea of payment.

One day Bob wrote that he wanted to go home. I said:

"You shall, darling. I'll make arrangements straight away."

What arrangements?

The wolf of financial worry which was to gnaw at my vitals from then on took its first bite. Air tickets cost money and we had none. Ella would have sent it, even if she had been obliged to borrow it, but there were so many hampering restrictions. I could have borrowed it; Miami was full of rich, kindly people. I hated the thought.

My assets were the mink coat, my wedding ring and my engagement ring, pretty but not very valuable. It had been bought before Bob was made manager and I said, truly, that I preferred a sizable topaz to a small diamond; and anyway wasn't the topaz a talisman, guaranteeing marital happiness?

While I was thinking about how and where to dispose of such poor assets, I took counsel with the doctors. The paid-up member of the Optimists' Union said that he was sure Bob would benefit by being in his own country, amidst his own family. The Practising Pessimist appeared to think that an air trip could do no positive harm. Doomed anyway, his manner said.

Then, of all things, I was asked to appear on a television programme. Santa Barbara, now in the hands of a party suspected of Communistic sympathies, was still news.

The last thing I wanted to do, but Bob was all for it. He wrote: Chance to thank everybody. I'll come too. Let people see.

It was a composite programme. There was one American who had escaped unscathed; he was important enough to own his private aeroplane. There was a man who invested some vast sum in the beginnings of a canning factory, and lost the lot. He was angered as well as slightly dazed. There was—Oh, why bother? Yap about the too sudden transition from ancient ways to modern times. Yap about infiltration; about Cuba; about the Monroe Doctrine.

Then Bob and me. He was in his wheel chair. Before the operations his head had been shaved. No bandages—a well-stitched wound needing nothing but stitches, such stitches that they did not even need to be removed. They either sloughed off or were absorbed.

I made a few rather tremulous, but utterly sincere remarks about the kindness which we had met with; then Bob wrote with a pen as thick as a candle, on a great sheet of white cardboard, "Thank you all," and held it up with his good hand.

Within ten minutes of that broadcast we were offered free flights home.

Let me not decry the Health Service. It works, up to a point. But it cannot, cannot be expected to, cope with such an exceptional case as Bob was. But there were people and there was a place . . .

Everton Park had been established originally for servicemen who had suffered damage to their brains or their nervous systems. Few ordinary people had ever heard of it, for although ordinary wounds were regarded as honourable some slight taint still clung to any mental or nervous derangement. I only heard of it through a neurologist in Harley Street.

In the years since the war the number of injured servicemen had naturally decreased—though there were still a few; they, of course, were treated free. In order to lessen the Government's burden, Everton now took private patients; there was even a department known familiarly as the Jug and Bottle, where dipsomaniacs could be treated. The charges were extremely high.

Bob and I had been, perhaps, a little happy-go-lucky about money; nothing very extravagant, we'd lived within our means but we had lived well; there had seemed no reason to scrimp; he had a steady job at Scunwick, and always the hope of promotion. When he left for Santa Barbara, we had about six hundred pounds in a Building Society. Out of that I had paid the rent and our living expenses for six months. Bob, from his fine new salary, could send me nothing even had I been in dire need. The Santa Barbara Government was even stricter about letting money go out of the country than the Bank of England was. So the children and I had lived on our savings; I'd bought our flight tickets and my ticket to Miami; and when Everton, the best possible place for Bob, promising improvement if not cure, was first mentioned we had already consulted and paid various specialists.

We had about three hundred pounds in the bank and a week at Everton cost a hundred and twenty for residence and some treatments; others were extra.

I sold the mink coat, my grandmother's Rockingham tea set, her elegant old rat-tailed silverware, her carriage clock, a few other bits and pieces that I had intended to take with me.

Ella was marvellous. She had two lovely rings, the diamond that marked her engagement, the deep sapphire which had celebrated Bob's birth; she had a pair of diamond ear-rings. She sold them all and then started on her china, most of which was pretty but not worth much.

About parting with her treasures, and even the prospect of mortgaging her house, she was a stoic. Bob must have the best. The dreadful thing was that after one visit she had no faith in Everton. Bob had then been there a month and I could see some improvement—I went every day except Saturday and Sunday; driving like a maniac along roads which were fortunately not too full of lorries.

Ella hated driving fast, she let out little squeaks of apprehension, clutched at the door handle, looked anxiously at the speedometer. So she was in a nervous state when we arrived and seeing, as she thought, Bob no better, she broke down and upset him, so that he was *not* better. All the way home she lamented; about his state, about his circumstances; his room, she said was a bleak cell; had I felt his bed? Hard as a board. Had I seen an absolute gibbering idiot in the corridor? How could Bob hope to recover in such a place? We were being swindled.

Then we arrived home to find that John and Alice, left only to Elsie's supervision, had squabbled over the TV programmes and pushed or pulled so many competetive knobs that they had put the set out of action.

A fine day that was! Culminating in my writing yet another letter to the insurance company.

The Corporation naturally had its own insurance for all its personnel and plant, but Bob had taken out a policy on his own; one which made him, he joked, worth far more dead than alive.

Insurance companies are naturally on the defensive and take rather restricted views; they hadn't a slot into which to drop being struck dumb and partially paralysed. Another bother was that Bob, the insured person, was in his right mind and could write, so he had to do some form filling and from the first made light of his injuries. Even to me he still joked, writing on his pad, "Shall I ask them to cut my leg off? Then we'd qualify for loss of limb."

The insurance people knew about Everton and had suspicions. They pointed out that no policy covered alcoholism, which was neither an accident nor an Act of God. I had to keep writing covering, explanatory letters.

In the end, I'll give them their due, they admitted that Bob had met with an accident, suffered partial disablement and was entitled to six thousand pounds.

I was also writing to the Corporation. They operated a pension scheme which had always seemed a bit odd to me. From the wages of people below a certain level they deducted a few shillings a week, so that at the end of his working life a man who had stayed with them could count on something to add to his State Retirement Pension. From the salary of managers no such deduction was made; they were expected to provide for their own futures. I could not expect much, since Bob had left them, so suddenly and so early; but before he was made manager he had paid in his shillings and we were rapidly approaching a time when even a few shillings mattered.

One morning at Everton I parked my hard-driven car beside a great gleaming Rolls. Inside, in Bob's cell there was Mr Beckworth, two dozen dark red carnations and a bunch of black grapes.

The effect of the sight of his one-time enemy had not reduced Bob as Ella's had done; in fact I think it had helped.

Mr Beckworth, courtly as ever, greeted me and said:

"I would have come sooner, but news takes time to percolate. I heard only yesterday."

I said, "It was kind of you to come."

Trying his newly learned speech for the first time before a stranger, Bob said, "Very kind." There was no intonation in the words but from the look on his face I guessed that had there been, it would have been sardonic.

Mr Beckworth then tactfully confined himself to asking Bob such questions as needed only yes or no for answers, or inquiring about the children, and congratulating me on my fortunate escape. Then he said:

"I was told not to tire you, Spender. Would it tire you to talk business for a moment, or shall I leave it for a later occasion?"

"Go on," Bob said.

"Well, as I said, I heard only yesterday, just before a meeting of the Board. I was therefore able to raise the question under any other business. You were with the Corporation for three years before you became man-ager at Scunwick, and during that period you paid your contribution to the pension scheme—a total of a hundred and fifty pounds, I understand."

We were now in such low water that even that small sum sounded like a windfall. It would buy a week at Everton.

"As you know, the conditions for granting a pension in the normal way were not fulfilled, but I took leave to point out to the Board that you served for ten years at Scunwick, with results consistently above average. Taking that—and everything else—into consideration, it was decided to offer you two hundred pounds a year. The decision, I may say was unanimous."

"Mag-nanimous," he said, stumbling over the long word. There was, however, no flicker of gratitude in his expression.

"It is only a minuscule sum." Mr Beckworth sound-ed apologetic. "But it may provide a few cigarettes." I remembered then that he was a passionate nonsmoker.

I was as certain as though I had been there that we owed the little pension to Mr Beckworth, but I dared not thank him too heartily in Bob's presence. To do so would be to upset Bob, who was, I could see, remem-bering a few other things for which he had Mr Beck-worth to thank. However, I made an opportunity. I said:

"Mr Beckworth, is that shining chariot yours? Then I think I may have parked awkwardly. I'll come down."

I thanked him heartily and then went back to Bob, who had not yet sufficient command of his mended motor-nerves to indulge in the flaming angry speech he would have liked to make. So he wrote: Old vulture. Come to gloat. And sundry other derogatory things.

And I played along, saying, "Under any other business?" An expression which was to become a standing joke.

Everton was no swindle. When they thought they had done all they could, they said so, and laden with optimistic assurances and pessimistic warnings, I took Bob back to Baildon and began the hunt for a house within the six thousand range and with a garden by which I could supplement our certain four pounds a week and whatever Bob could earn.

And so we came to Gad's Hall.

*

I found a wonderful outlet for anything I could grow—the shop run by the Women's Institute in Baildon. It was patronised by the most discriminating shoppers, people who preferred local, fresh produce, not all shrouded in cellophane. The fruit from the south wall, ripening early, found a ready market. So did such things as thyme and parsley and chives which had survived neglect.

Mr Thorley's Joe Snell, in addition to digging, had mended the greenhouse and now there were several things sharing its shelter. Amongst them a bay tree. So many recipes said take a bay leaf, and the best most people could do was to take a dry one, desiccated and flavourless. I had newly plucked bay leaves to sell. Presently I should have big brown eggs, which could rightly be termed free-range. I had ten beautiful Rhode Island red pullets and one gorgeous cockerel in a run which extended across the whole end of the garden. There would be no eggs until late October or early November, but they'd sell like hotcakes.

Every morning I drove John and Alice to school, delivered whatever I had to offer at the WI shop, did a bit of necessary shopping, and most mornings looked in on Ella, for whom I reserved the choicest of what Gad's had to offer. I repeatedly invited her to visit us. It was such a glorious summer, but she always had some excuse which I accepted without question. We had interrupted the placid stream of her social life and she had a back-log to make up; and she did not like Gad's.

One morning, it was late July, almost the end of the term, as John and Alice scrambled out of the car, one of the teachers, plainly on the watch for me, came up and said, "Mrs Spender, if you could spare a minute . . ."

I knew her. I was a conscientious member of the Teacher-Parent Association; her name was Brewster and she was in charge of Art and Craft. Anything less Arty and Crafty in appearance God never devised; grey all over. Grey hair in an untidy bun at the nape of her neck, grey eyes, grey complexion, grey skirt, grey blouse. Grey voice.

"I felt I must have a word with you," she said. "About Alice. You will remember, she came to us in January. And when we first met I told you that I thought she was one of the most promising pupils I ever had. Definitely gifted."

"Yes, I remember, Miss Brewster. I was pleased. But if she has gone off . . . Children do, as you must know."

God forgive me, I thought the poor woman was apologising; perhaps for the fact that at this end of term exhibition of finished work Alice Spender would figure less prominently than she had done just before Easter.

"It isn't that. It is . . . a change. Quite sudden, and in my opinion disquieting. I wondered. You may think me impertinent, but to me a child's welfare outweighs mere good manners. Has she lately come under the influence of . . . well, let us say an extremist religious organisation?"

"No." I could give that positive answer. Ella went to St Mary's for morning service every Sunday morning and if Alice felt inclined she had gone too. Since we moved into Gad's, Alice had been subject to no religious influence at all. "What has that to do with it?"

Miss Brewster did not answer directly. She said:

"I know that TV is often grotesque; but not macabre in quite this way. Excuse me again, Mrs Spender. Do you supervise your children's reading?"

"Yes." I could give a positive answer to that. At least I didn't supervise, I took interest. I had, after all, worked as a librarian and my own children's reading patterns were absolutely conventional. "I think I could safely say that we have never had a macabre book in our house."

I had encountered Foxe's *Book of Martyrs* when I was too young. It was illustrated, too. I'd been careful about things like that.

"Then I find it difficult to account for," Miss Brewster said.

"What exactly?"

"Her work. Macabre. Done by an older person one might even say Satanic. Demons. Imps. Hobgoblins."

"It's probably a phase, Miss Brewster. Isn't there a theory that we all go through every phase that every one of our ancestors on the long climb out of the sludge, went through? Gills, crawling, rearing up on hind legs. Alice is going through a phase." She looked so worried that I felt she needed reassurance. I seized on the one word which made light of it all. "We all go through the hobgoblin stage, Miss Brewster; but we can't all express it in drawing, as Alice appears to have done. Please don't worry. I'll keep a sharp lookout."

Ella had her birthday in August and she wanted to have a party. There was a woman in the village who would baby-sit, if fetched and returned, provided with a snack meal. Bob wished to go to his mother's party, so

I engaged Mrs Snell—no relation, as she was careful to point out to the Joe Snell who, at Mr Thorley's bidding, had dug in the garden.

I put Tony to bed and left orders that John and Alice were to retire at eight o'clock, after sharing Mrs Snell's snack. I promised to be back at half-past ten at the very latest. I thought it might be sooner, for this was Bob's first full scale party, and he might tire easily.

In deference to Bob's lack of festive garments Ella had decreed that men should wear lounge suits but women could get themselves up regardless. That meant that Ella could wear an extremely becoming blue lace frock.

It was a small party, all people known to us, including Colonel Murray-Smith, known as The Boy Friend. He and Ella had had for years that happy, undemanding relationship, completely platonic, I am certain, which can exist between two people, growing old, both vain, both with some lingering attractiveness, and both well content with their own way of life. Even if at any time over the last ten years any thought of setting up house together had occurred to them, they would have come up against an insuperable obstacle. The Colonel's house was run with military precision by his ex-batman, a seasoned martinet; Ella's was run by Elsie. Neither of them would have tolerated the other for half a day. And it was impossible to imagine Ella making a home in that leathery, masculine establishment, or Fred Murray-Smith settling in Ella's ultra-feminine one. It suited Ella to have somebody to drive her about and to spare her the slight inconvenience of always being the extra woman which old-fashioned circles like hers seem to find so bothersome; and it suited him to have a still-pretty woman partially, not wholly, dependent upon him, to listen to him, ask his advice. They fitted perfectly.

Bob bore up bravely, but shortly after dinner I could see that he was tiring. I could also see that without us there would be eight people—just right for bridge; so pleading the children as an excuse, we left; but not before I had invited Ella and The Boy Friend to lunch on the following Sunday week. She had never visited us since we moved in, and I thought that perhaps in broad daylight, sustained by the company of a man whose courage had gained him more than one medal, she might overcome her fear of the place, and feel happier about it. And realise that I was right.

On the way home I told Bob what I had done; adding, maybe conceitedly, that the lapse of time would give me time to salt a piece of beef properly, for it is true that this once so-common dish had become a rare luxury. The art of properly salting a joint had been lost. Mr Beckworth had once said, I think sincerely, that even at Simpson's . . .

Now Bob said, "Good. Thorleys, too. Been very kind."

I agreed that that was a splendid idea. I knew enough of them by this time to realise that Kitty Thorley was a raging snob and that George Thorley was such a completely natural person, so inwardly sure of himself, that if, in his shirt sleeves, he had found the Queen of England on his doorstep, he'd have behaved to her exactly as he had done to us.

Mrs Snell was in the living room, knitting something in stripes of purple and bright orange, and finishing off a brew of tea.

I said, cheerfully, because it had been a good party and Bob had stood up to it well,

"Here we are, Mrs Snell, nice and early. Has everything been all right?"

"Once they settled down." I detected the ominous note. In the good old days at Scunwick I had employed baby-sitters from time to time and could recognise an incipient complaint a mile off. "It was all right till they started galloping about and woke the little boy. Then he knew I wasn't his Mummy and carried on like anything."

"I gave them strict orders to go to bed at eight."

"So they did. Then they got rowdy and woke the baby."

I said, "I'll sort them out in the morning." I thought, They always know! Left to Elsie they'd put Ella's TV out of action. Left to Mrs Snell, God knows what prank they might have got up to.

I said, "I am sorry, Mrs Snell. I'll drive you home now."

She speared the two balls of wool. I said to Bob:

"Darling, just look in on Tony and see he's covered."

Tony was usually a very sound sleeper. Anything that would wake him must have been rowdy indeed.

No mother should play favourites, but Nature is a bit of arbitrary, the first-born son, so like the man who had fathered him. . . .

"She started it, silly old cow," John said, giving me his straight blue stare. "I don't know what Alice was doing. I was reading. I was nearly asleep and she came bursting in, accusing us of galloping about. We hadn't moved. But she went into a flap and said we had, and that upset Alice. And she cried, and Tony woke up and yelled. I told you, didn't I, that we'd have managed without that silly old cow, clumping about and saying we'd been on the back stairs." I'd known that he resented my hiring Mrs Snell. He'd always been a responsible, self-reliant child, and during Bob's absences had come to look upon himself as the man of the family.

I didn't insult him by asking was that the truth; so far as I knew he'd always been dead honest.

Alice's story was slightly different.

"Mrs Snell heard the bumps, Mummy, and blamed us."

"What bumps?"

"On the back stairs. I've heard them before but John said I was making it up. But I wasn't. There were bumps. And last night Mrs Snell heard them, too. *She* woke Tony, shouting at us. And then I knew I hadn't made up the bumps; and I got scared."

"What exactly do you mean by bumps, darling?"

Alice considered carefully.

"Dull sort of noises. Like people moving something heavy. On the back stairs."

Fear *is* contagious. Just for a moment I felt the prickle of it between my shoulders. What Ella had said I'd dismissed very lightly; she was an overemotional creature and strictly conventional in all her reactions; a rather bleak landing, a locked door in a house that had not been inhabited for five years had had upon her exactly the expected effect; despair; sheer evil; haunted . . .

A child, not yet nine, was rather a different matter. But while thinking of Ella as conventional, I became conventional myself. Applying the old placebos, I said:

"Old houses do make odd noises, Alice. Boards creak and groan. When I was your age," I said, recalling something I hardly knew I remembered, "I lived in an old house. I'd go upstairs, and then every step would settle back into place; just as though somebody were coming up behind me."

(About that my grandmother had been as Draconian as about the loft. Psychologically sound, however. She stood in the hall and told me to go upstairs and listen, count the noises; then come down. Go up again, two steps at a time, and count the noises. Three at a time and count. She had convinced me.)

I said to Alice, "And there are water pipes in this old house too. But I would like to know why things should go bump. Next time you hear the tiniest bump, call me and we'll see why."

My modest luncheon party seemed to be successful. The salted beef, coddled and turned about, had the right, the now rare, iridescent glow and I dished it up with the kind of dumpling that they say only a Norfolk-born woman can make. I'd managed it, though.

Kitty Thorley, whose attitude towards me, towards us, had changed as soon as she realised that we were related to *the* Mrs Spender whose gentle voice carried great weight on so many committees, was absolutely enchanted to meet Ella, face to face over a glass of sherry, over a meal. And old Fred Murray-Smith said the right thing, the wrong thing, something that made a link.

"As soon as I turned off the lane, and saw the chimneys," he said, "I knew where I was. Good God, half a century ago. I was staying with my aunt and somebody lent me a pony. The meet was held here. The first time I'd ever tasted cherry brandy. It'd be your grandfather. Marvellous old man."

"That was *my* grandfather," George Thorley said with no pleasure in his face. Perhaps that was the hunt which had ended fatally. Or perhaps he grudged, retrospectively, the lavish supply of cherry brandy. He had spoken of his grandfather as a spendthrift. Kitty Thorley, however, did relish this reference to past family glory.

We finished our meal with fruit from the wall; a kind of plum which I had not tasted since I was a child; not as ovoid as a Victoria and of a different colour. Absolutely delicious. Favourable comments were made by everyone except Kitty Thorley, and then her husband said:

"You can't buy such stock these days. When we moved down to Park, I laid out a small orchard. It's prolific enough, but nothing tastes the same as the old stuff."

Ella said, "It may be the soil. Mrs Gordon and I once went to the Chelsea Flower Show together and we both fell in love with a new rose. We both ordered a bush. I can only describe it as a silvery pink, quite entrancing and most unusual. In Mrs Gordon's garden it turned almost orange; in mine, plain salmon pink. No trace of the silvery look at all. It was most disappointing. Yes, Mr. Thorley," she went on in her sprightly way, "I know what you are thinking—that we received the wrong bushes. But Mr Gordon took it up with the suppliers. They blamed the soil."

George Thorley made the first move to go; explaining that even on Sunday afternoon cows had to be milked and he had only one man who didn't mind working unsocial hours, being a tiger for overtime pay.

Ella, the most resolute dodger of washing-up that I had ever encountered, offered to help me with the dishes. I said I was not going to bother about them just now.

"I must have a word with you. Alone," she said in a low, urgent voice.

We went into the garden.

"Jill, I did warn you about this place—and about Alice. I know, my dear, that you have a great deal to think about. It may have escaped your notice that Alice lives in a perpetual state of terror. She told me that she simply dared not go up to the bathroom alone—in broad daylight."

I had not noticed. I had told Alice to tell me if she heard a bump and we'd investigate it; but she had never mentioned the matter again. Now I was obliged to say, "No, I have not noticed." I had noticed Alice's enthusiastic greeting to her grandmother, and some long, apparently confidential talk. But Alice, quiet and docile, unless led into mischief by John, had always been Ella's—and Elsie's—favourite.

Human behaviour is a very puzzling thing. Here was Ella, very genuinely concerned for Alice, but also slightly triumphant. She had warned me; and the warning was justified. And in me, something that I had always tried to repress—I would *not* fall for that old mother-in-law, daughter-in-law syndrome—reared up. I said,

"Ella, it's just a phase. Most children go through it. I did myself." Unbelievable as it may sound to you!

Ella said, "That may well be so. I hope it is. But it is a theory susceptible to proof." For a moment I was startled; she sounded like Bob! "I would like to take Alice back with me. If she is still fearful there, then it is a phase. If not, then there is something here to which Alice is susceptible and the rest of you are not." She made a little pause and added, "Mrs Thorley was."

"Oh!"

"Yes. She was trying to explain why they had moved. She told me that from the very first the place had made her uneasy and that to be alone here was torture . . . She doesn't look particularly sensitive, does she? But she is, apparently. Never mind about that. May I take Alice back with me and see what happens."

"Of course. It will, as you say, be a test." Of what?

I did notice that Alice, asked to go back to St Giles' Square—"Elsie and I miss you all so much," Ella said—looked jubilant and then dismayed.

"I must pack," she said and stood rigid. Dear John said:

"I'll come and help you." His next words, "Rather you than me!" I hoped were not audible to Ella.

The test proved positive, from Ella's point of view. In St Giles' Square Alice ran about happily. No fear at all.

For me one of the most immediate results of Alice's going was John's demand for a bike.

He said, very sensibly, "It'd save you a lot of time, Mum."

That was true: school started at nine, the WI shop

did not open its doors until ten. If I had shopping to
do, I did it in that interval; otherwise it was a wasted
hour. Then there were the afternoons. Collect at four
o'clock. And I could no longer leave Bob to take
charge of Tony. Something that George Thorley had
said about harvesting sugar beet had sparked Bob's in-
ventiveness and, working away on something so new as
to be revolutionary, he was often lost to the world; so
Tony, often objecting loudly, must go with me, wher-
ever I went.

Having a bicycle made John much more mobile; for
the few days that remained of that summer term he
could do all the after-school things which he had enjoyed while we lived with Ella; and during the summer
holiday he and his special pal, a boy called Terry,
roamed far and wide, pursuing their newest hobby—
brass-rubbing—in such churches as still boasted
brasses. They covered a considerable territory and
found at least two churches said to be haunted; one
where, on the anniversary of the Battle of Edgehill, a
bunch of roses mysteriously appeared on a tomb.
"Edgehill," said my son who had a good head for figures, "was the twenty-third of October 1642. A bit late
for roses, don't you think? The old woman who was
scrubbing about absolutely swore that watch had been
kept. Nobody could have smuggled them in. Terry and
I are thinking of doing a bit of watching ourselves
there, this year." Another expedition took them to the
church at Salle, the place where some people believe
Anne Boleyn to be buried under an unmarked marble
slab; and from there John brought home another ghost
story. The old sexton had told them that once he had
kept watch all night, and seen only a hare which came
in through a door he'd have sworn was closed and led
him a chase and then vanished. "We might go there,
too, but it isn't until May."

"By which time you and Terry will be train-spot-
ting," Bob said.

"Likely!" That was, like "Ah," a country word capable of meaning a great deal; in this case scorn.

During that holiday I felt cut off from Alice. During term time John saw her, if not in class, in the dining room; his reports were laconic—she was there, and she looked all right. At the end of term I had suggested that Alice might like to come home—just for a little holiday. Alice threw what I recognised as a look of appeal at her grandmother and Ella said, I am sure on the spur of the moment, that she and Alice and Elsie were thinking of going to Bywater, just for a breath of sea air. What could I say against that?

One evening, towards the end of August, with just that faint hint of autumn in the air, I was in the kitchen, weighing up runner beans by the pound and slipping rubber bands over each bunch. I owed the runner beans and several other things to Mr Thorley, who had given me some plants he had to spare.

John had been out all day, taking with him a very substantial picnic lunch, but he came in, as always, hungry and said:

"Bacon and eggs! Goodoh!"

"Eggs, sure. No bacon, I'm afraid." I had in fact given up buying bacon; it was fiendishly expensive, and Bob, now settled and happily occupied, was having a bit of a weight problem. Not good for a weak leg.

"But I can *smell* it. You and Dad ate it all. Gluttons!"

"What you can smell is wishful thinking. We had a meagre, cold, salad supper."

I had in the larder what was left of a bit of boiling bacon—the cheapest of joints. I'd carved it carefully, giving Bob what lean there was, saving the fat for my hens and the bone to make the basis for a vegetable soup. The fat, carefully cut and frizzled in a frying pan, did smell rather like bacon and John ate contentedly.

Then it was September; apples and pears, the last of the plums, the last of the runner beans; the first of the self-sown artichokes which, judging by the demand for them, everybody wanted, and few people bothered to grow. And presently I should have something very rare to sell—walnuts. At the very end of the garden there was a great old tree, one of the few that had survived the eighteenth-century passion for furniture made of walnut wood. In its shade there were shrubs which seemed not to have fared too badly. One, a magnolia, was just breaking into flower and every bloom would be worth fifty pence. We were surviving. Bob had produced some drawing of a sugar-beet harvester, in which a big engineering firm in Peterborough had said—cautiously—that it was interested.

And even Miss Brewster had contributed to the general feeling of well-being; good, conscientious, grey woman she had sent me a note by John; she said that I had been right, Alice's odd drawings had simply been part of a phase; she was still drawing with exceptional originality and skill, but the macabre element which she had mentioned to me had vanished.

That autumn I had another cause for complacency; I was beginning to acquire a few private customers. My first was the proprietress of The Hawk In Hand, once an old coaching inn on the Market Square, now a flourishing hotel. She did all her own buying, and we frequently encountered one another just inside or outside the WI shop and began to exchange Good-mornings, the way people do. Then one morning she said, "I've been waiting for you, Mrs Spender. They haven't got a decent lettuce in the place this morning." It was drawing towards the end of a hot dry summer, but my garden had not suffered; I had access to the moat. Ella had kept her promise to provide a length of chestnut fencing, part of it a gate which could open and shut, all I had to do was to dip out pailfuls. Bob had promised that as soon as his sugar-beet harvester was off the drawing board, he'd devise a less laborious method of irrigation.

Then one morning Mrs Greenfield watched me deliver, and instead of going straight to the counter and buying what she wanted, followed me out to the car, where Tony sat strapped into his little seat inside the passenger seat. She said she had been thinking, how much more convenient for both of us if we dealt direct with each other; it would save her time, and me money.

Naturally the WI shop charged a commission—they had rent and rates to pay, and one or two full-time helpers were paid, too. The idea of saving their percentage was certainly attractive, but I had a somewhat sentimental feeling towards the shop which had given me my start. So I said I'd think about it, and let her know.

The stately old lady who was in complete charge, checking what was brought in for sale, scrupulously rejecting anything not up to her rather exacting standards; deducting from one's credit any perishable article brought in on a former occasion, working out what was due—and all without, it seemed—taking her eyes off what was going on in the shop itself, sat at a high desk, rather like an old-fashioned schoolteacher's. She was said to be well over eighty but she had perfected the art of doing four things at once with complete imperturbability.

Tony, who hated being confined in any way, began to drum his heels and shout, "Mummy," at regular intervals, so I had no time to waste. I asked her whether the Women's Institute would mind if I sold a few things elsewhere.

"Why should we? Excuse me. Ah, honey." She held a jar to the light and approved its clarity. "But you *must* fill in the label, Miss Crawley. Place of origin. Have you a pen? We never pretended to hold a monopoly, Mrs Spender. Of course we should still *hope* to have some of your splendid produce. Miss Wade, those iced cakes are in the *full* sun and beginning to melt. I imagine that Mrs Greenfield approached you. Not to *us* a good customer; she buys everything of the best and so much of it. Short of imposing rationing . . . What *beautiful* chrysanthemums, Mrs Yates; we'll try them at seven p. a head and would you tell Miss Barclay to reserve a dozen for me? All *pink,* please. If I may offer a word of warning, Mrs Spender; we are a nonprofit-making concern; Mrs. Greenfield is, so keep your eye on current prices and don't be done down."

Feeling slightly dizzy I felt that at least my conscience need not trouble me; and actually all my dealings with Mrs Greenfield were easy and pleasant. She could tell me what she needed and I could tell her whether or not I could supply it. Through her recommendations I found two other regular private customers, both owners of cafés; and through her I learned just a bit more about the house in which I lived. One day Mrs Greenfield produced a very faded early photograph and told me that her great-grandmother—come to that her great-great-grandmother—was thus commemorated.

It is extraordinary how the most unlikely people cling to some sort of lineage. In my days as a librarian I'd met quite a number—some cranks, of course, but some just plain, sensible people anxious to trace, eager to know something about their families. Mrs Greenfield was an eminently sensible woman, and she was plainly a Londoner, but she, and many women before her, had cherished this fading relic. The house in the background was either Gad's or some very similar building; grouped in front of it were six people. A family; mother and four daughters, and a boy; he was in Highland dress. I judged by the clothes of the young women the date to be in the mid-eighteen forties; the mother had ceased to be fashionable some decade earlier. Except for one, all the girls were of similar height and since Mrs Greenfield was pretty tall, I expected her to point out the tall one as her ancestor; but she pointed to one of the others. "She, we were always given to understand, was our great-grandmother."

I said, "How very interesting." Devoid of colour and even its brown and buff tones fading, the photograph was not very informative.

"And it is Gad's? I've been meaning, ever since we came down here, to go and take a look, but I never had time." She turned the stiff cardboard over and there in ink, as faded as the picture itself, I could read: June 1848; Gad's Glory. First Prize. Mamma; Diana, Deborah, Caroline, Lavinia, George.

I did some of my rather inexpert mental arithmetic and thought that the boy in the kilt might be George Thorley's grandfather, the squanderer of cherry brandy . . . But, given a time-slip, he was the boy the present George Thorley should have had; indeed there was a likeness.

But for that likeness, and the fact that George Thorley had no child, I think I would have borrowed the photograph; a man so wrapped up in the past would have been interested; but it might inflict a hurt.

Mrs Greenfield then said something which relieved my mind of the fear that she might show the picture to him.

"I was given to understand that there've been Thorley's at Gad's since the day of creation, till about five years ago. But my grandmother's name wasn't Thorley; she was born Osborne, and her married name was Spicer. So perhaps she," she touched the girl who looked the haughtiest, "was just on a visit."

"Very likely," I said.

The year moved on and it was time to gather and store apples and pears that would keep and fetch good prices through the winter. For such a job nobody could have better assistants than two lively eleven-year-old boys. Terry and John scrambled about the trees like monkeys all one Saturday morning. Terry was staying for the week-end. In the afternoon they were going to a football match and on Sunday they proposed to carry the baskets and barrels and buckets of fruit up into the attic to store.

George Thorley had taken Bob to a place called Foxton, where there was to be a display of the various virtues of sugar-beet lifters already on the market. I knew that Bob was in good hands. George Thorley had the dead right touch; he didn't think that a weak arm and leg and a hesitancy of speech justified treating a man like an invalid or an idiot; but I knew that if there were seats to be had, Bob would get one and his full share of what the invitation called a Fork Luncheon; and it would all be done without any ostentation.

As soon as the boys had gone it occurred to me that I could usefully employ myself by carrying fruit up to the attic so that they could gather in the morning. I'd come up against the fact that I was not quite as lively as I had once been; I often ended the day with a back-ache; nothing to worry about; it stopped as soon as I lay down; but it made me careful about lifting and carrying things. I gave myself reasonable loads as I went up and down that afternoon.

I had some thoughts about Alice. I felt that I had lost her; she should have been here now, helping to gather and carry apples, giving a little time to Tony. I felt that the way she was living was a bit old-maidish and finicky; on the other hand she was plainly the light and joy of life to Ella and Elsie. And I, after all, had spent a lot of time with *my* grandmother, with no lasting harm done, except perhaps a rather too sensitive conscience—something like a grumbling appendix. Real stoics, true Puritans of whatever sect, have at least the consolation of thinking that they have God's approval and are quietly ticking up good marks in some cosmic conduct book. Somewhere along the road I'd lost that happy assurance, but I still wore the harness while lacking the certainty of green pastures awaiting me at the end of the long pull. I was still capable of feeling guilty about Alice and another thing. I'd let Alice go a bit too casually. The other thing was different . . .

All right; if sex mattered so much—or so little— we'd all have been born hermaphrodites. Nature could easily have devised some self-fertilising, self-propagating species and saved everybody a lot of bother.

Like everybody else, I regard myself as normal; I'd certainly been fortunate in that I had never felt much urge to bed with anyone until I met Bob; then the attraction was mutual and our married life had been happier than most—and still was, though sex no longer had a part in it. A flaccid leg and arm was no insuperable barrier, I suppose, but all impulses begin in the mind, that is, in the brain, and that part of Bob's had simply gone. When he said to me once, "My poor dear, I'm afraid you're left with only half a man," he meant just that.

We'd accepted the situation calmly, and, I hope, with dignity.

Up to a point George Thorley's behaviour towards us had been the result of his devotion to Gad's; he wanted it to be in suitable hands; he was delighted to see the old things back in place; even the loan of a man to dig, and the gift of a load of manure may have resulted from his desire to see the garden in good shape again.

When I gave my little luncheon party, I had six chairs, all of the kitchen variety, and Bob sat in his swivel chair; John and Alice shared the sawhorse, which was no longer needed as a Tony-deterrent by the moatside. It looked very makeshift and odd, until everyone was in place and eating heartily.

About ten days later George Thorley, on one of his evening visits to Bob, said with his usual inoffensive directness:

"You're a bit short of chairs. I get around quite a lot, sales and such. Would you like me to keep my eye open for you?"

I said, "Yes—so long as you remember that I'm in the market only for chairs at a pound apiece. And at that price, short of a miracle, you're unlikely to find anything that wouldn't disgrace the table."

Very shortly after that he turned up with six chairs, Chippendale style which, had they been genuine, would have been worth thousands. Their drop-in seats were covered with dark brown leather, a bit scuffed but good for another thirty years.

We hadn't then advanced to Christian name terms—when we did it was at his wife's suggestion—so I said, "But Mr Thorley, I told you a pound apiece was my limit."

"Then I got a bargain; six for five fifty."

"But at Bidwell's, I saw a set exactly the same and that was eighty pounds."

"Floor space is costly now and every now and then Bidwell has a clear-out, and sends a load of stuff along to one of Staple's auctions. This lot nobody wanted; falling between two stools; not genuine antique and not up-to-date. Besides being a bit big for the houses they're building now. Here you are!" He took out and offered me a smudgy bit of paper; Lot 20, £5.50 and a receipt stamp.

He had the somewhat rare gift of receiving as well as giving gracefully. Down at Park there was always plenty of milk and he had a contract with Amalgamated Dairies; but there was often a surplus, and then one of the stockman's wives tried her hand at butter, at cream cheeses, and milk cheeses, she even ventured upon sage cheese. We could have what milk we could use; "What's over goes to the pigs—and they won't miss a pint or two." And other things he'd bring along, just for us to try. In return I gave what I had to spare: two kinds of apple which for some reason did not flourish at Park Farm, and for Kitty, his wife, some boughs of the extremely late-flowering magnolia which grew under the walnut tree. That was a Greek gift, in a way; I wanted access to the fallen walnuts and hacking the magnolia helped . . .

But the moment of truth came over—of all things—a sack of potatoes.

"I'm beginning to lift my main crop," he said. "And they look like being scarce this year. But I don't want you to go short and I'll set aside some seed ones—they'll be short too—so that you get a good start off with earlies."

The potato shortage was already making itself felt; humble spuds were ten p. a pound and the WI shop had been driven to rationing—nobody to have more than two pounds; and here was I with at least half a hundredweight. Worth five pounds.

I said, "George, I do wish you'd let me pay. For these anyway. Honestly, I can't see why . . . " I broke off because such a change came over his face. God help me, I thought for a second I'd angered him.

"Can't you?"

I blushed so hotly it felt as though my face would melt. I tried to look away, but his gaze held mine; I could only stare, helplessly, and understand and know that my eyes were betraying me, just as his were him.

He broke the spell, or the circuit or whatever it was.

"Where do you want them? Store room or larder?"

I just managed to say, "Larder, please." He lifted the sack as though it weighed nothing. I doubt whether I could have lifted an egg. But I went through into the room which, except for that one occasion, had been

Bob's exclusive domain and I said in such an ordinary way that I was astonished.

"George is here. He has brought us a sack of potatoes."

If I'd let go I could have burst into hysterical laughter. A sack of potatoes! And with two words and a look the man had offered himself to me; without saying a word I'd acknowledged—and responded as far as circumstances allowed.

Well, as somebody said—Love is a many-coloured thing. I did not love Bob one whit less. I'd still have gone through hell and high water to save him from a pang of pain or from a humiliating stumble; but I was in love with George Thorley too. And it was ridiculous to make the obvious, trite distinction between the body and the mind. Much of my feeling for George Thorley *was* physical, but I liked him as a person, too.

I'm inclined to think in generalities. Actually what is called the permissive society, wife-swapping, divorces as plentiful as hot dinners, had never appealed to me; too much squalor about it, too many children either completely abandoned or subject to what the papers playfully called the tug-of-love. In a truly civilised society, I thought, with all the taboos, new and old, done away with, George Thorley and I could have bedded together, with no hurt either to Bob or Kitty, and I'd have given him the son he wanted. And who would have *lost* anything? But that time was not yet; might never be because it demanded a rational approach and the last thing men and women will ever be is rational. They'll be saintly, or devilish, brave or cowardly, intelligent or stupid, but rational, no.

That afternoon, late in October, I went up and down with apples, thinking my own thoughts, minding my own business; making sure for instance that no stored apple touched another. Tony was in the kitchen, engrossed with a new toy. I'd got a good filling dish of mutton and haricot beans simmering away at the back of the oven, awaiting John and Terry, Bob, and George if he chose to stay. On another shelf in the oven I had some of those potatoes, baking in their jackets.

All was well—so long as George and I didn't look at each other, and we no longer did. Alice was all right. I'd rather have had her at home, part of the family, but she was happy with Ella and Elsie and they were happy to have her.

So what hit me as I closed the apple-room door and stood for a moment to ease my aching back? For one thing, utter despair. I knew that Bob would come home with the news that his invention, still under consideration, had been forestalled; I knew that I was heading for a breakdown; mentally I should go silly and do something daft; and physically my back would so cripple me that I could neither harvest what remained nor sow for next year. I thought: I have done my best and it wasn't good enough. Because from the beginning everything has been against me—against everybody. Better, I thought, never to have been born than this; brought out of nothingness, to labour and strive and back into nothingness again; a bit of fungus on the surface of a splinter of a dying star . . .

Tony yelled, "Mummy! Mumm*eee!*". . . .

Moving like an automaton I went down into the kitchen. His new toy—a gift from George—was an engine. It had a driver who when the thing was in action wagged his head, as though surveying the track; at intervals the thing hooted; it had some kind of almost extrasensory organisation because when it ran into an obstacle it would back away and take another course. It ran on batteries.

"Stopped," Tony said. "Mummy do?"

John had always been fiercely independent; Alice moderately so, but Tony was lazy. "Mummy do," had worked its way into the family's private language. Mummy do. Mummy did, remembering some spare batteries in the dresser drawer; George had even remembered to include a box of spares with his present. My hands were shaking so much that I had difficulty in dropping the little tube into the narrow groove.

As clearly and as separately as though it had been the voice of another person, something said in my mind: What you need is a good stiff whisky!

It had never been my drink, except for a dash of it in hot milk as a cold cure. At Scunwick we'd always kept a bottle in the house, mainly for guests. Now, even if we could have afforded to buy spirits, Bob was not allowed them; half a glass of sherry or a glass of white wine occasionally was his limit. But on this late November afternoon there was a half bottle in the house; Ella had kindly smuggled it in, because The Boy Friend would not drink anything else, holding that sherry was bad for the liver and gin a tipple for old hags. In the emotional and physical hustle of removing Alice, she had forgotten to take it back. I'd forgotten about it, too, and until this minute should have had difficulty in finding it. Now I knew exactly. On the top shelf of the larder with several other things not in everyday use and I felt irresistibly drawn towards it. I actually went to the dresser and took a glass.

Tony said, hopefully, "Time for orange juice?" I poured it for him, the neck of the bottle chattering against the glass. I added water and gave it to him.

"Driver first," he said, and spilled a good mouthful over the little plastic figure. I took another glass and went into the larder. As my arm reached up and my fingers closed on the bottle, I knew, in advance, how steadying, soothing and strengthening a good stiff whisky would be. With its aid I could bear with apparent fortitude any bad news Bob brought back from Foxton, realise that an aching back was a very minor affliction, and that being in love with two men not all that unusual.

And that's how drunks are made!

I'd long ago discarded my grandmother's absolute teetotalism—she was a devoted member of the British Women's Temperance Association and invariably wore the little enamelled bow that was its badge—but I seemed to see her face, sorrowful and disapproving. And then I laughed. A fine chance I had of being an alcoholic with the stuff the price it was!

Still, I didn't lift down the bottle and I had grown steadier, capable of testing the meat in the casserole, and of turning the potatoes.

John and Terry came in jubilant; their team had won. Bob and George came in jubilant; there hadn't been a machine at the demonstration anything like the one Bob's would be. A member of the Peterborough firm had been present, had talked to Bob for a long time, and there was to be a visit to the works next week.

George stayed to supper, Saturday being one of Kitty's regular bridge nights. Nothing seemed demanded of me except the dishing out of huge quantities of food. Bob was sticking to his view that rugger was a vastly superior game to soccer. The boys disagreed. George said he'd never played either game. "No time," he said. "My poor old Dad needed all the help he could get, but he was a tiger for education, too. So it was up and milk early in the morning, ride down to Baildon Grammar, scurry home, milking, feeding, mucking out . . . It was those dark evenings I told you about. A wolf behind every bush."

My logical son said, "But Mr Thorley, the last wolf in England was killed in the reign of Henry VIII."

"I knew that. Mine were imaginary wolves. A sight worse than the genuine article." For some reason that sentence seemed to be directed at me; and for the first time since the potato incident we looked at each other, calmly, giving imagination its due; its bad a sight worse, its good a sight better. It was though we had signed a treaty.

In the kind of peace that comes with convalescence, or that follows physical exhaustion, I thought about that attic floor.

Ella had sensed horror and evil.

Mrs Snell had heard bumps; so had Alice; and Alice had felt fright.

I had experienced despair; and there was a time when despair—monks called it *accidie*—was regarded as the ultimate sin, a sin against the Holy Ghost, that indefinable member of the Holy Trinity. Keep the ten commandments and you were all right with God the Father; observe the clauses of the Sermon on the Mount and in addition love thy neighbour and you should be all right with God the Son; but God the Holy Ghost was less easily pacified and because His claims were so very tenuous they must be all the more strictly enforced and reached out not to what people did, or how they behaved, but to how people thought, how they felt; and over such things who has ever had the slightest control? A thought once thought is thought, by no volition of the thinker; a feeling once felt can never be retracted.

I had felt despair, and should never forget it. Ignore it? I could try. What I could not avoid was wondering why. What had happened here? Once upon a time . . .

Part Two

WHEN, in late summer 1841, George Thorley re-married, his friends—of whom he had many, being a genial and hospitable man—were delighted. A man still in his prime needed a wife, Gad's needed a mistress, the two little girls were growing up wild. Also, considering that there had been a Thorley at Gad's Hall since time immemorial, George needed a son.

There was a little regret that he had chosen a foreigner. For Suffolk men foreigners began at the Norfolk border and the second Mrs Thorley came from Leicester. A few young women, and their fathers, a decent widow or two were disappointed, but George Thorley had always been a bit of a gadabout. He bred pedigree cattle, Durham shorthorns, and was forever going to shows and sales. He'd go to Leicester, Colchester, even London almost as casually as his friends went to a local market.

The wedding took place in Leicester and was very quiet. Nobody was invited and that was understandable; second marriages—the bride was a widow—were perfectly legal, often desirable, but not matters for much display. It was rumoured that the second Mrs Thorley had two daughters of her own, very near in age to the two Thorley girls.

Her arrival was awaited with great interest and curiosity and her actual presence a matter for speculation—and some dismay. What on earth had good old George gone and done?

At first sight, at a distance she looked rather young and pretty; close to she looked older, and worn, her cheeks rather hollowed under high sharp cheekbones, her nose thin and high arched. Beautiful eyes—if you admired them so dark as to be almost black, which nobody in Suffolk did, and a wealth of hair, so black as to have a blue sheen, like a blackbird's plumage. Her figure, though shapely, was slight.

Her older daughter was nine, her young seven and a half. Their name was Osborne. Diana Osborne. Lavinia Osborne. The Thorley girls, with their more homely names, Deborah and Caroline, fitted in between.

Women, much concerned with breeding, were inclined to think that the new Mrs Thorley might not give George the son he needed. She was not as young as she looked, and her second daughter was not—if they were any judge—healthy. Very pale, and what they called pingling.

A few hard-headed men in George Thorley's circle wondered if money might not be concerned. Cattle breeding and showing was likely to cost more than it brought in. Not one of them would have married the new Mrs Thorley, with all her airs and graces, and two girls into the bargain, without considering the financial side. And she always acted as though she had money; very high-handed. And look what she was doing to Gad's! Wallpaper, a new kitchen range. Unless the woman had money, then old George must be daft! And would he, after all, get the boy he craved?

And what kind of stepmother would she make? With two of her own?

The answer to that was: Unique! Even the sharpest-eyed critic never saw a ha'p'orth of difference in the treatment of the four girls. When one had a new outfit, so did the others; identical in quality, similar in style, differing in colour. The new Mrs Thorley once said that if she had only one apple she would divide it into four as evenly as possible.

You could tell an Osborne girl from a Thorley if you saw them close to and knew what you were looking for. Both the Osborne girls had black hair and dark eyes; the Thorleys were fairer, with light eyes. Most people soon gave up trying to distinguish between them and they were known collectively as the Gad's girls.

They all called Mrs Thorley Mamma, and in that simple word something of the change which was overtaking Gad's was foreshadowed. Ordinary people's children called their parents Mother and Father. George Thorley was subjected to some good-natured teasing from his intimates. "And how is Papa today?" It sounded a bit daft in the Corn Exchange or the market at Baildon, but George bore it good-humouredly until one day when he'd had enough of it and said, "Well enough to give you a clout on the jaw Sam Stamper if you don't lay off." And everybody could see that he meant what he said. He was a giant of a man and although nobody, least of all he, himself, knew anything about it, in his veins ran the blood of the Viking people who had come in along the Wren River a thousand years ago, bent not upon a quick raid and a quick retreat, laden with booty, but upon settlement; the acres to plough; the roof tree to build. Permanence.

And, fortunate fellow, all must admit; within a year, the new Mrs Thorley had given him what he wanted—a great, lusty boy.

Imperceptibly, by this little step and that little step, he gave her what she wanted.

None of George's old friends could honestly say that the new Mrs Thorley had discouraged them, done a thing, said a word which hinted at a severance. All his old friends were made welcome, but they dropped away.

No power on earth could really make an East Anglian farmer feel inferior—it was in the Bible; a man diligent in his business could stand before the King and not be shamed—but even a diligent man, ready to stand up before the King, though it was now Queen, could be made to feel awkward.

Awkward because . . .

Well . . . The doctor was somebody you sent for when all the home remedies had failed. The lawyer was somebody you went to to draw up your will or settle a debateable point about boundaries, fishing rights, or some such; and parsons had their function too. But meeting Mr Gordon, Doctor Taylor, the Reverend Mr Spicer and more of their kind at a table, set with too many knives, spoons and forks, that was different. That was awkward.

And wives were inclined to be bothersome after a visit to Gad's. Why wouldn't they have wallpaper, a piano, a necessary house with a contraption above the seat which poured sawdust into the cavity under the seat; why couldn't they have a new range cooker and a yellow chinaware sink instead of the old grey stone one? Why couldn't their girls go to Miss Hardwicke's Female Academy?

Women, in fact, were best kept away from Gad's, and before young George was a year old, his father's *real* hospitality was restricted to all-male gatherings after Wednesday market days, sessions where you could discard your jacket, use earthy expressions, play Blind Hookey and drink all you wanted to, trusting your horse to get you safely home.

Mrs Thorley seldom disturbed these parties; she might indeed not have been there, except that the food, solid, simple and easy to manage, was better than in the days when George lived alone; and now and then she could be heard playing the piano in what she called the drawing room, but which in their homes would have been known as the parlour.

If George Thorley ever noticed that his life was now conducted on two social levels, the fact did not disturb him. His dear Isabel was a woman of education, and naturally she preferred the company of educated people. He adjusted easily; he had the natural dignity of his breed without its prejudice against airs and graces; in fact a submerged liking for airs and graces had drawn him to Isabel in the first place. Now and again one of his new friends proved useful in a practical way. It was from Mr Walford, who owned the Sudbury Brewery that George first heard of a new kind of barley, especially suitable for malting. It was Mr Fallowfield, who owned the recently established, but very flourishing Bacon Factory, who mentioned—over the port—the public's changing taste in bacon. "I don't mean the poor," he said, "they like it fat—and they need it. But they rear their own pigs and get the bacon cured by a hit or miss method. We don't cater for them. Those we do cater for prefer more lean meat. And the way to get that is to let pigs range. Cooped in a filthy stye, a pig, however poorly fed, gains weight, which is what most people aim at. We don't. After all," he said, "what was the wild boar, once considered a kingly dish, but a pig which had had plenty of exercise?"

George Thorley was capable of taking a hint. He had inherited from his father three hundred acres of good arable land up at Gad's, two hundred and fifty acres, mainly pasture, down at Park. And the herd, which had been his father's hobby and pride, but which, as some of his old friends suspected, often proved to be a burden rather than a support. For sentiment's sake, for pride's sake he'd kept the herd together and, when necessary, subsidised it from the profits of ordinary mixed farming, and they would come down with a bump if the people now agitating for a repeal of the Corn Laws had their way.

George Thorley was glad to plant the new kind of barley in his biggest field and to turn another one over to pigs which appeared to revel in their new conditions, giving plain proof that pigs were not necessarily filthy, sluggish animals.

He profited, too, from association with Mr Gordon, the lawyer, who knew everything that was to be known about taxes.

Isabel was helpful in other ways. You'd never think of it to look at her, but she had a good head for figures and was more than handy with a pen.

No marriage—leave alone any second marriage—had ever been more successful.

It lasted for seven years.

In June 1848, George Thorley, in perfect health and high good spirits, went off to London to show his very promising young bull, Gad's Glory. The Cattle Show, which took place in Hyde Park, lasted only three days, but beasts must go well beforehand, to get settled in after the journey; careful owners saw to such things themselves, and also supervised the loading up for the homecoming. And, win or lose, there was some celebrating to be done. And a bit of shopping. All in all, he expected to be away for a week, maybe eight days.

Before he left he said to his wife, "Now, let me see, Diana'll be seventeen next month. Leaving school and putting her hair up. Old enough for ear-rings, eh? I'll have a look round. And you, my dear, what would you like as a fairing?"

She was a woman of sound good sense and she was not greedy. She said:

"Nothing, my dear. You have already given me so much."

So much! He had long ago ceased to distinguish between the girls; they were all his, as they were all hers. His little girls had lacked a mother, her little girls a father; goodwill on all sides, needs dovetailing, had produced that happy family atmosphere.

He came home in a state which his wife diagnosed as due to exhaustion and a bit too much celebrating— Gad's Glory had won a minor award.

In the morning he was worse rather than better and she sent a boy on horseback into Baildon to summon Doctor Taylor, who, a friend, a frequent guest, came immediately and for a while straddled the thorny fence which every physician occasionally faced. To tell or not to tell?

Say cholera and throw everybody into a panic?

Keep silent and put the whole household at risk?

It was some time since there had been a major epidemic of the dreaded disease in Baildon, just sporadic outbreaks in unsanitary districts like Scurvy Lane, and even they were frequently confused with what were called putrid summer fevers. There was no known specific cure, just opium to relieve the pain. There was no certain guard against the spread of infection, except isolation.

"Has George been near his father?"

"No. He was in bed when my husband came home last night. And this morning—as you see."

"Servants?"

"Our stockman, Joe Snell, brought him home, carried up his valise, and helped him off with his boots. I am the only person in the house who has been in contact . . ."

And I, she thought with remorse, attributed even his raging thirst to the effect of too much drinking.

Doctor Taylor hesitated. To ask so dainty-handed a woman to nurse, all unaided, what might be a cholera case did not seem exactly right. Perhaps the stockman, already at risk . . .

Mrs Thorley took the decision.

"I will do all that is necessary, Doctor Taylor. I spent the night with him. I have already been exposed to . . . to whatever it is."

The old doctor had always considered her charming, and a good manager; now he was grateful for her quick understanding.

On his way home Doctor Taylor looked in at the other farm. Joe Snell was at work, in his usual good health. He'd spent his nights alongside his charge; Master had put up at a hotel on the edge of the Park, very fine place, like a palace. No, he hadn't seen anybody ailing, nor heard anything about sickness being about, but of course the crowds everywhere were so thick that a man might have been dead and not able to fall down.

Giving her orders from the top of the kitchen stairs, Mrs Thorley began organising. "No, Jenny, don't come near me. Doctor Taylor does not yet know what ails your master, but we are taking precautions." A sheet soaked in vinegar to be hung outside the bedroom door; a constant supply of barley water to supply the moisture lost by the frequent vomiting and the evacuations—both of which had now taken on the appearance of water in which rice had been boiled; every hour a shovelful of red hot embers to be brought to the top of the stairs, with a good bunch of fresh lavender. The best disinfectant known.

Her main concern was for George. Six years old, very precocious and more than a little spoiled. She was, in fact, the only person with the slightest control over him, and that influence could not operate through

a third person. He'd scent a mystery, lift the vinegar
sheet, open the door. The wonder was that he had not
already done so, for he was as inquisitive as a monkey.
The explanation was most probably the new pony.
George—often called Georgie—was a most fortunate
child; absolutely idolised by his father, by his
mother—a little less absolutely, but far enough; he
was, after all, her justification, her return for all that
Gad's had given her, and a living contradiction to the
doubt which had shown itself in the eyes of George's
old friends—was she young enough? Was she able? So
in her way, she had been indulgent, too. And there
were the girls; three of them; not Lavinia. Perhaps, of
all the people with whom she came in contact, the little
half-brother, aged about two, had first sensed something different in Lavinia. The others, incipient mothers, had contributed towards the spoiling.

What to do with a spoiled little boy who must be
kept safe? Who would be better out of the house? Mrs
Thorley, making her eighth or ninth trip to the head of
the kitchen stairs, found the answer.

George loved receiving gifts, but he loved even more
giving them. This endearing quality could be exploited.

"Jenny!"

"Yes, Ma'am."

"Now listen carefully. Tell Willy to kill a fowl and
make it ready for table."

"Is Master better?"

"I cannot yet tell. The fowl is for Mrs Spicer. Listen.
I want Master George to ride down to the Rectory with
the fowl and a dozen eggs. And a note. Here it is.
Catch."

The folded paper fluttered like a butterfly.

Most fortunately, Mrs Thorley was now on Christian

names terms with the Rector and his wife and had
been able to scribble: Dear Amelia . . .

The Spicers were very poor; the living of Stonham St
Paul's was a meagre one, and Mr Spicer's passion for
buying old books would have tried even a better-bal-
anced budget. Mrs Thorley had often thought, half-ex-
asperated, that they did not make the best of their
resources; surely, between them, they could have kept
a few hens, cultivated some vegetables, let off part of
the vast rambling Rectory. She had known poverty
herself, and knew that it must be fought. The Spicers
just drifted along, he resigned, she rather plaintive.
They kept only one general maid-servant and spent
little on food. A prime table bird and a dozen eggs
would predispose Mrs Spicer to accede to the request:
Please try to persuade Georgie to stay with you until
tomorrow. My husband returned last evening feeling
very unwell, and Doctor Taylor has not yet named his
ailment. The boy has not been near him. I am sorry to
impose upon you . . .

*

"What is a Garden Fête?" George asked suspi-
ciously.

"A kind of Fair, dear."

"Roundabouts?"

"About that I cannot be quite certain. There will be
fireworks."

(In her mind, the Rector's wife defined a Garden
Fête exactly—a means of extracting money from
people; sometimes, as in her case, ill-spared money.
Yet it was for a good cause—missionary work in India—and if the Rector of a parish did not support so
worthy an effort, it would look very bad indeed.)

"That'll be after dark, Mrs Spicer?"

"Yes, dear. But in her letter to me your Mamma
gave her consent for you to stay here. So that will be

quite all right. Put your pony in the stable. Can you unsaddle him?"

"Yes. Deb—that is Deborah, you know—she showed me and made me practise. Deb—Deborah knew I was to have a pony this summer and she said nobody was fit to have a pony if he couldn't look after it."

He had mastered the principle of names used within the family and those used outside it. Diana was Di, Deborah, Deb; Caroline, Caro, just as he was Georgie. Outside was different. And for some reason Lavinia had never been called by a shortened version of her name.

"Deborah was quite right," Mrs Spicer said, forgetting for a moment that of all the Gad's girls, Deborah was the one she liked least. For no particular reason, except that there was something . . . well, call it uncompromising about the rather too tall, slightly angular girl with her clear blue-grey stare.

Because they were all going to a Garden Fête at Stonham St Peter's where refreshments would be on sale, they had what Mrs Spicer called a light lunch which George did not regard as a meal at all. Some kind of milk pudding, but not milky and not sweet, rather peppery, if it tasted of anything at all.

But for this deprivation, George made up at the Fête.

He appeared to have a pocketful of money, and, sadly spoiled as he was, he was a well-mannered little boy. He plied Mrs Spicer with sandwiches, with slices of Victoria sponge, with cups of tea, with glasses of lemonade. He bought raffle tickets, tickets for the enclosure where a pig was bowled for, and another where a little plot of ground had been dug and a treasure buried. There you planted stakes, all numbered. He spent at least two shillings on the Hoop-la, sharing the rings with her. You try, Mrs Spicer. Very little expenditure was required of her.

Mr Spicer, at the last moment, had decided not to accompany them. He pleaded lumbago—everybody knew how suddenly that could strike! He would not have let Amelia go alone, but she would now not be alone, she'd have the company of this exuberant, garrulous six-year-old. Mr Spicer knew that it was a Christian's duty to love children. Suffer little children to come unto me, Christ had said; and there was threat, too, that only those who became as little children could inherit the Kingdom of Heaven. But there it was; just as some people could not bear spiders, or cats, he could not abide children. He would not have hurt one for anything in the world, he would have saved the life of one at the risk of his own; it was their company, perhaps just the pitch of their voices, that set him on edge. Yet he had married, stood in front of an altar and heard a fellow cleric pontificate about the purpose of marriage and known all the time that he was marrying Amelia because a country parson—he had just accepted this poor living—needed a wife. A wife was cheaper than a housekeeper, or a curate. He regarded the childlessness of the marriage as a blessing. But there loomed on the horizon a long-dreaded day: if prices went on rising he would be obliged to take pupils. They would be day boys, he decided, and they would take lessons only in the mornings, five days a week.

Left to himself, George would have gone home immediately after breakfast—one egg, no bacon, two pieces of badly made toast. He would demand a proper breakfast when he reached home. He was also anxious to give his mother the prize which the Hoop-la stall had eventually yielded—a piece of pottery in the form of a cow, crude but lifelike. He'd had his eye on it from the first.

However, Mrs Spicer had several errands to be done in the village. "It is such a long time since I had somebody sensible to do an errand for me, George."

"I'll ride," he said, "then it won't take me long. And then I'll go straight home."

"Not straight home, dear. There will be things to bring back here."

Some of the errands were genuine; some concocted. Mrs Spicer was doing her duty as she saw it, and she imagined that soon some message would come from Gad's. She did not regard it as unethical to send George to ask a question of Mrs Catchpole, in whose garden the Fête had taken place: Did you chance to find a glove yesterday? She asked George to return a book she had borrowed—that was a bit of a sacrifice on her part since she had not finished it and although the Rectory contained many books they were all beyond her understanding. With the book went a little note, asking Miss Riley to detain George as long as possible; she would explain this singular request when next they met. The loaf of bread was needed, in a way, though ordinarily it would not have been bought until tomorrow.

No fewer than five gloves had been found, all left-hand ones; three white, one grey, one lavender mauve.

"I don't suppose you noticed, George, what colour Mrs Spicer's gloves were yesterday." He had not. Mrs Catchpole knew something of Mrs Spicer's circumstances and knew that the loss of a glove could be serious. No lady ever went out without gloves.

"I think it would be as well if you took them all. I'll wrap them."

She then remembered that there was lemonade left over.

Miss Riley detained him even longer. She was not

inventive, and when she had spent as long as possible
over the choice of book to replace the one just returned, and shown him how her cat could sit up, almost like a dog if a tit-bit were offered, she could think
of no further delaying tactic, except to ask him to wait
while she wrote a little note in reply to Mrs Spicer's.
She took an exceptionally long time about it and
George fidgetted. He *must* get home soon. Before he
starved to death. Since yesterday morning's breakfast
he hadn't had what he called a proper meal at all, and
although he had himself taken a good fowl to the Rectory, he distrusted what would be made of it. People
who couldn't make decent toast even! Last night, Mrs
Spicer had said that after all they had eaten at the
Fête, a glass of hot toddy would suffice. And the Rectory hot toddy bore absolutely no relationship to the
beverage served at Gad's to anyone suffering from a
cold. George was only six but he knew milk and water
when he saw it.

Nor was his concern only for himself. His pony,
Tom Thumb, was a fellow sufferer. At the Rectory
there was a stable and once it had been occupied by an
ancient horse which might have lived a little longer and
still served had anybody understood that teeth wore
down, that hay must be munched and oats champed
and that very old horses could only survive and go on
being serviceable if fed with pappy stuff.

What that long-dead horse—dying of inanition—had
left in his manger, some shreds of desiccated hay, a
few mouldering oats, had been as unacceptable to the
spoiled pony as the food inside the Rectory had been
to his young master. Tom Thumb was at the moment
better off than his master because at every stopping
place he could snatch mouthfuls of grass, managing,
despite the bit in his mouth to get some enjoyment,
some sustenance. Once let them get back to Gad's . . .

Mrs Spicer had received the expected message and

wondered whether it was her duty to break the sad news. She shrank from the task. Some eighteen, nineteen years ago she had been obliged—since there was nobody else to do it—to break the news of total bereavement to a little boy about a year older than Georgie Thorley now was. It was an experience which she did not wish to repeat. To that other little boy she had had the obligation of relationship, though he was only her nephew by marriage. To this little boy she had no such obligation. His mother was alive and the messenger who had informed her would by this time be in Baildon, telling the girls, calling them home to support their mother. So, seeing George off, Mrs Spicer said no more than, "I fear, my dear, that you will find a sad house. Be good."

*

Queen Victoria had not yet made widowhood a fulltime profession, but a year in full mourning and at least six months' seclusion from the world were rules enforced upon all but such unfortunate women as must go out and earn bread. Mourning was not intended to be becoming, and that of Mrs Thorley and the girls did not even fit, having been bought ready-made at the one shop in Baildon which stocked such low-class things. Doctor Taylor, now confirmed in his suspicion, and aware of the hot weather, had advocated early interment. Much mourned by all who had known him, George Thorley went to his grave, to lie peacefully amongst his forebears—one of whom had been killed at Crécy and brought home at a cost which had burdened Gad's with debt for two years.

By his own request his coffin was borne by four of his own employees.

He had made a will, not of the makeshift last-minute affairs which served so many of his kind. He had had the advantage of being on social terms with Mr Gordon, and Mr Gordon knew the value of a will, properly drawn and properly witnessed. George Thorley had made his will when his son was eighteen months old, and when he fully expected to live to see a riotous coming-of-age party. He had not regarded it seriously for more than the time it took to make it. But—after all even lawyers must live—once he'd settled down to it, he did, as he had done most things, very thoroughly.

That he wished to be carried to his grave by his own employees was not the only idiosyncratic thing about his will. He wanted his wife, Isabel, to be his sole executor.

"But that is most unusual," Mr Gordon protested. "Too heavy a burden for a woman."

"My wife has a head for business."

And there was nothing legal against it. By some curious anomaly, which even Mr Gordon recognised, women were nothing; everything they owned, unless carefully guarded by marriage settlements, belonged to their husbands. Even if they earned money it was not their own. On the other hand, there was something almost sacrosanct about the will of a dead man, reaching out from the grave. A will was a will, and made by a man obviously of sound mind . . .

But, taking note of other details, the lawyer wondered what exactly would be the legal position if a man, as sound in mind as George Thorley was, named a monkey in the Regent's Park Zoo as sole executor? To him it seemed almost as extreme as that, though he liked Mrs Thorley as a person and admired the way she ran her house and what could have been an awkward family.

George Thorley evidently had unlimited faith in his wife's ability. To her and to her alone, he entrusted not only the executing of his will, but, until the coming of age of his son, complete control of his estate and all his business interests. After that she was to have an income of five hundred pounds a year.

He had dealt with his daughters and stepdaughters in identical fashion; each girl was to receive five hundred pounds upon her marriage or her twenty-first birthday.

Just as, seven years earlier, there had been much speculation as to what the new Mrs Thorley would be like, so interest now centred about what she would do. The most sensible course, and the most likely, was to appoint a reliable foreman; the two farms together were too much for one woman to handle, and there were aspects to the breeding business quite unsuitable for such a ladylike creature to know about, let alone deal with.

Most of the old friends, and some of the more recent, could name a suitable candidate for the overseer's post. Almost every family had a younger son. Some fathers by pinching and screwing managed to provide farms for their second or even third sons; holdings smaller in size and generally inferior in quality to the family acres. Other boys must seek employment and the area offered few posts both congenial and suitable for a young man with farming blood in his veins. It was a district of farms rather than large estates and such of the gentry, like Lord Chelsworth and Sir Archibald Hepworth, who had more land than they cared to administer themselves, appointed poor relatives who were called agents and often very grand indeed. A good many farmers' sons, armed with what cash was available, emigrated to Canada or Australia, where land was to be had for the asking. Others remained at home, helping out and hoping that luck would bring them a bride who had no brother.

Sam Stamper made the first approach and was thus the first to hear the startling news. He began gently, commiserating with the widow and saying how greatly George would be missed by one and all. Then he said:

"I'd like you to know, Mrs Thorley, that if there's anything I can do, in any way to be of help you've only to give the word."

"That is extremely kind of you. I am sincerely grateful."

"I expect it's a bit early days for you to decide what you're going to do. I mean about keeping on the farm and suchlike."

"There is no question of decision. Naturally my husband expected me to keep everything going. Just as before."

"Well, I bin thinking about that. As you know, I got three boys. Sam'll hev the old place and I managed to set Tom up on his own. But times ain't what they were and I doubt if I can give Peter a proper start. He's talking about going abroad and that'd just about break his mother's heart."

Although Mrs Thorley had not spent much time in the company of George's old cronies, she knew how, on any important matter, they'd circle round before closing in. She guessed what was coming and said, pleasantly:

"Yes, I am sure Mrs Stamper would feel it very much. He is her youngest."

"He's the best of the bunch, too," Sam said, recklessly sacrificing the others in Peter's interest. "He's the hardest worker of the lot. More interested in animals, too. Rare stockman Peter is."

There is was, the bait plainly dangled. She had only to take it, and there they'd be, everything nicely arranged and without either one of them feeling under an obligation to the other. And that was a very important part of striking a good bargain.

She sat there, a small, fragile figure in her black which emphasised the pallor of her face and hands.

"There's another thing," something that should appeal to her.

"Peter is edjercated. He did so well at the village

school, my missus insisted he should hev two years at
Baildon Grammar."

(Behind that simple statement lay a history of
struggle, a clash of arms. By some unwritten law
farmwives like Mrs Stamper were entitled to egg-and-
butter money, their own to earn, their own to spend.
When Mrs Stamper expressed her wish to spend egg-
and-butter money on a bit of further education for Peter, her husband had protested. She had retorted by
using the underdog's only weapon: the withdrawal of
labour. Very well, if what she earned couldn't be spent
as she wished it to be, she'd give up. And you couldn't
compel a woman to make the best butter, the best
cheese, by clouting her over the head. Peter had had
his two years.)

Mrs Thorley, as fully aware as Sam Stamper of the
formalities that must be observed, said:

"It was so kind of you to think of it, Mr Stamper.
But . . . as a matter of fact, I intend to run Gad's and
Park myself."

"What?" Momentarily jerked out of rustic caution,
Sam Stamper almost shouted. Park meant the herd,
and the herd meant . . . well, a lot of stuff no female
should dabble in.

"You are surprised? I am prepared to admit that I
may not succeed. But I intend to try. Wish me luck,
Mr Stamper. I shall need it."

Nobody could know now, or, if she had her way,
would ever know, how she was once again in need of
luck, good luck. She had known both kinds.

A stormy past; pretty, pampered daughter of a
Westmorland squire, she had married young, the man
of her choice, handsome, gay, well connected.

Delighted by the match, her father had given her
five thousand pounds as a dowry. What was hers was
Stephen's, and he knew how to spend money; he also
knew, when the money was spent, how to live lavishly

for short periods of time, on credit, and how to vanish when creditors became too demanding. There were bad spells, and good ones; he was not a consistently unlucky gambler and although in the end his immediate family renounced him entirely, he received, from time to time, legacies from old aunts who remembered him as a charming boy. A great deal of the charm remained, and for years Isabel could be completely disillusioned and then reinfatuated and furious with herself for so being.

They spent some time in France; once, as a result of a legacy, in Paris, where old families were desperately trying to bring back the old days and forget that the Revolution had ever occurred, or Napoleon ever existed. France at the time was madly Anglophile; the English had sheltered members of the French royal family and a number of aristocrats. The almost legendary figure of the English milord—free with his guineas—was partially restored. That had been a wonderful time. The second visit to France—to Boulogne, where living was so much cheaper than England—was less happy.

So life had swung like a see-saw and when Isabel was widowed for the first time—Stephen had shot himself in a moment of despair—she was left with almost nothing, and with two little girls to support.

Why had she chosen to settle in Leicester? Because it was new and growing and there she was unlikely to meet anyone who knew her. That was her main concern; not to be shamed.

She set about earning a living with the poor weapons at her disposal. She could sew, draw, play the piano. All her activities must be home-based, because of Diana and Lavinia, whom she certainly did not intend to hand over to some indifferent, ignorant servant. So everything she did must be done within the confines of the narrow, hired house.

No slave ever worked harder. Anybody could sew, but Mrs Osborne could design dresses as well. Mrs Osborne, on a hired piano, taught unwilling little girls with ten thumbs to hammer out a tune. An enterprising man named Blaker started up a pottery factory and Mrs Osborne drew designs for him.

In the end it was the one asset which she had not considered that brought her good fortune. One spare room.

Just around the corner from St Martin's, an old, respectable street, stood the inn; and for the innkeeper's daughter, Mrs Osborne had designed a wedding dress of such glory that the bride's mother felt that something more than mere cash—which in any case would drift through the dressmaker—was needed. She went herself to say: Thank you . . . Mrs Osborne received her, civilly but coolly, and gave her a cup of very weak tea—sure sign of poverty in the eyes of the innkeeper's wife, who liked hers almost black. There were other signs, too. Apart from the piano there was not an article of furniture worth twopence; except for a rag rug in front of a wretched fire the floor was bare; Mrs Osborne and her two little girls wore dresses of the poorest material. Yet the innkeeper's wife knew a lady when she saw one, and Mrs Osborne was certainly a lady, brought low, but, to judge from her bearing, proud.

Praising the bride's dress and sipping her tasteless tea the kindly woman cast about in her mind for some way of helping which would not humiliate, and before her cup was empty had hit upon a possible way.

"I did come, Mrs Osborne, to thank you for helping Miss Ramsey to make that dress—it made Maggie's waist look inches smaller; but I had another reason, too. A favour I wanted to ask of you."

"Oh yes?" I am in no position to do you or anybody else a favour.

"It's like this . . . The town's so busy these days we're often fuller than we can hold. There's men that don't mind sharing a room, and others that do. We've talked about building on, but that'd cramp the yard; and we ain't always crowded. I wondered whether, now and again, you'd let us a bedroom. You're so near, you see. We'd pay two shillings a night, just for the bed. And I promise I'd only send you a nice sort of gentleman; nobody rough or drunk."

"I have a spare room," Mrs Osborne said. No need to mention that it was completely unfurnished. Two shillings was what Mr Blaker, Miss Ramsey and one other dressmaker paid for a design; and the price of a piano lesson was sixpence.

Judging by the furniture of the sitting room the bed wouldn't be up to much. Easily remedied, and again done with the most delicate tact. There were men who, while not objecting to sharing a room, insisted upon separate beds, so there were one or two double beds stored away somewhere; together with other various bits and pieces. If Mrs Osborne could find room . . .

The infinitely experienced eye had no difficulty in selecting the kind of guest who would not wish to share a room and would gladly accept the alternative—just a few steps round the corner. George Thorley, up for a Cattle Show, was such a one.

If he noticed the poor gimcrack quality of the sitting-room furniture—in such sharp contrast to the solidity of the stuff in the bedroom—he attributed it to fashion's whim and to the fact that there was no man in the house to require solid chairs and tables. He was much impressed by the airs and graces of the lady of the house, and equally by the behaviour of her two girls—much the same age as his own, who were beginning to grow a bit wild.

On the first evening of his stay he decided to turn in early, and found Mrs Osborne, whom the landlady of the inn had described as a friend who now and then obliged her by putting a spare room at her disposal in crowded times, drinking the cup of tea which consti-

tuted her evening meal. She offered him one and over
it they sat and talked.

She liked him; the deep instinct which under the
pressure of Stephen's charm had failed her, informed
her that here was a man, solid, reliable and kindly—
and, it emerged, badly in need of a wife. Somebody
had mended his shirt, so badly that in places the
stitches were breaking away. She mentioned it, offered
to make a better job of it, which she did, and he was
absurdly grateful because she had noticed and bothered; not because a patched shirt meant much; he had
brought four others . . . He also had two farms and
some prime stock cattle; he reckoned, he said, that the
bull he brought to the show, Gad's Goliath, should
sweep the board.

She liked him. Even when he showed very clearly
that his feeling for her was far warmer than liking and
she knew that she was incapable of reciprocation.
She'd known love and had seen it wear out as even the
sturdiest fabric could do, subject to friction; she wanted
no more of it. And although he offered the one thing
that she and Diana and Lavinia needed most—reasonable financial security—she was careful about commit-
ting herself. She wondered what he was like when he
was drunk; Stephen drunk had been another person
entirely.

There was the question of class awareness—quite a
different thing from snobbery. She faced it squarely;
George Thorley was not a man whom her father would
have asked to dine at his table. He had natural good
manners. No education. No sophistication. He was not
of her world—but then who was? Now? It was all too
easy, as she had proved, to move from one world to
another.

She was not deliberately acting hard-to-come-by; she
was genuinely uncertain; but the delay, through the last
weeks of June, all of July, all of August, strengthened
her hand enormously. During that time, the busiest in a

farmer's year, he had snatched time for visits, and he had written to her, letters quite touching in their naïveté. Like a schoolboy's first letters to his love. Which, in effect they were; George Thorley had married, as most men of his kind did, a neighbour's daughter; an eminently suitable young woman for whom he had felt—as a man should—respect and regard and affection. Romance had never brushed him with its extraordinary wing, until Leicester. Until Isabel.

So it had come about, and it had lasted for seven years, and now it was over and Mrs Thorley was once again facing a financial crisis. Not the acute one; not like knowing where the next rent, the next imposition of rates, the next pair of shoes were to come from, but nonetheless a crisis. She certainly could not afford to hire Peter Stamper or any other likely young man. In fact if the girls were to have their dowries, she must be active, cunning, smart.

They sat at the table, and she looked at them, and thought: *All my pretty ones*. And that was something from *Macbeth*, a play which everybody connected with the stage regarded as unlucky to quote from. She knew such things because her first husband, early in their marriage, had conceived a passion for an actress.

My pretty ones! Two pairs of sisters but with no more in common than the bloom of youth—and Lavinia lacked even that—and their ugly mourning dresses. A stranger would have taken Deborah Thorley for the eldest, she was so much taller, a long-legged, rather angular girl who already wore a look of reliability and responsibility. As she advanced out of childhood her fair hair had darkened to something perilously near sandy and her eyes were a clear blue-grey. She was very much like her father, a typical Thorley.

Diana Osborne was smaller with a figure softly rounded above and below the greatly admired eighteen-inch waist. She was very vain of her appearance and spent most of her pocket money on creams and lotions to preserve her already flawless complexion and her milk white hands. Miss Hardwicke, who believed that girls should be clean and tidy and give their serious attention to their lessons, slightly disapproved of Diana Osborne and mentally referred to her as Young Madam. Diana's conduct seldom warranted reproof, her work sometimes did and on these occasions the rebuke was received with an icy dignity which even the schoolmistress found disconcerting. The ability to look down one's nose when being scolded was rare and not altogether desirable.

Caroline Thorley should have been the beauty of the family by the criterion of colour, her hair had deepened to golden, and was curly and her eyes were deep, almost violet blue; but her nose was snub, her mouth too wide; there was something monkeyish about her face though it lacked entirely the melancholy of the simian face; she was gay, frivolous, mischievous, a bit of a hoyden. From her a rebuke evoked ready tears and earnest promises of amendment. Then, within ten minutes she'd be laughing, in the centre of a group of giggling girls; not a care in the world.

Neither Mrs Thorley, that careful mother, nor Miss Hardwicke, experienced as she was, could make anything of Lavinia. Silent, withdrawn, absentminded, unpunctual, indifferent. She had been a thin, pale child, and the years had not changed her much. George Thorley had said, in his hearty way, "The country air'll soon put the roses in your cheeks." The country air had been of no avail, nor had the good food, nor the doctor's advice or the nostrums, cod-liver oil, iron pills, sure cure for anaemia. Over fifteen now, Lavinia still had the lost-child, waif-like look.

She had inherited her mother's skill with paint brush and pencil, she drew well, but all her drawings had a touch of fantasy. Mrs Thorley had occasionally thought that if ever—which God forbid—Lavinia were reduced to making designs for pottery or for dresses, there would be no buyers.

For her younger daughter's oddity—her complete inability to make friends, for instance—Mrs Thorley blamed the circumscribed life they had led in Leicester. There they could not afford to consort with their own kind, and because there was a markedly rough element in the town she never allowed the girls to go into the streets without her. The country, George had assured her, was perfectly safe and after the move Lavinia had taken to long, solitary walks, often missing a meal, and coming home with an armful of wilting flowers and foliage. George had feared, at first, that not being country-bred, she might eat a poisonous berry, and had given a little lecture on the subject. To that Lavinia had listened attentively and at the end had said, "Thank you, P'pa," and kissed him, voluntarily. "She'll come round," George said.

At his death it was Diana, not his child, had made the most display of grief. And that, in a way, was understandable. He had been the first man in her life— her own father was only the dimmest of memories. And she was old enough to be grateful for all that he had bestowed; not least the complete acceptance of her as his own. Diana cried and cried, hardest of all when the ear-bobs, each a cluster of chains weighted down with garnets, were discovered in his coat pocket.

"Oh, my birthday present! To think that his last thought . . ."

Deborah, crying herself, but less copiously, put her long thin arm around her half-sister and said,

"Di, dear. Don't think that way. He loved buying things and giving presents."

"I shall never wear them."

"But you must. He would have wanted . . ." They leaned together, mingling their tears. One of the nicest things about this reconstructed family was the way in which the two elder girls, so different from one another, and each with good reason for jealousy, had taken to one another from the start.

Now, because of the ear-bobs they thought simultaneously of the birthday.

"We must cancel the party," Diana said, nothing of self-pity, nothing but sorrow in her voice.

"I'll see to it all," Deborah said.

Caroline had cried, of course, on and off for some days, but her spirit was volatile enough to make her complain about the ugliness and ill-fit of the mourning dresses. "We look like a lot of crows," she said; and then, pushing up the loose bodice, "like black pouter pigeons." She made a grimace which, given the slightest encouragement, would have become a smile; half-hearted and shamefaced, but still, a smile.

Lavinia had not, so far as anyone knew, cried at all. Informed of her stepfather's death she had said "Oh!" and looked for a moment quite simple-minded. Then she had gone off on one of her walks.

Mrs Thorley had been almost embarrassed by her own inability to weep. Good, kind man, cut down untimely. She felt grief in her mind, a constriction in her chest, a hard painful lump in her throat; but the relief of tears was denied her; perhaps because she had shed so many for so many reasons, in so many places when she was younger; or perhaps because, later on, she had not dared to cry, telling herself fiercely that if she once gave way she'd be done for.

She felt sorry for the girls, especially Diana, whose seventeenth birthday was to have been celebrated so lavishly; a dance in the smaller of the two Assembly Rooms' ballrooms in Baildon, hired caterers, a proper band. Now nothing.

It was not a thing about which she could speak to Diana, who would break down into floods of tears.

Without fully realising it, during the years and especially in this time of grief and confusion Mrs Thorley had come to rely upon Deb. With her she discussed Diana's birthday, saying:

"I have been thinking, Deb. Could we not mark the occasion with a small, absolutely private dinner party?"

"Why not, Mamma? It would do us all good. Actually I have been asking myself—What good does it do? All this mourning and crepe and going into purdah. It is the very last thing Papa would have wanted. He was all for life, was he not?"

That was true.

"Whom should we invite, Deb?"

"Susan Walford," Deborah said promptly. "She was Di's very best friend at school; and her brother Richard is home now. The Gordons? Doctor Taylor, and Edward, if they could both be free. Enough, Mamma?"

Enough for the present; after a meal, prepared by Jenny, fully determined to show that she could do as well as, or better than, any upstart catering firm in Baildon, the younger people went into the drawing room for a sing-song around the piano. Played by Deborah.

In Leicester, at odd times, on the hired piano, Mrs Thorley had tried to teach both her daughters, with small success. Diana tried, conscientious, labouring, no ear at all, and Lavinia made no effort. On the really beautiful piano, one of the things which George Thorley had enjoyed buying and giving, Deborah played by ear as naturally as her father whistled.

Over their cards at the gate-legged table in the living room, the bow window open and the scent of roses, stocks, and lilies drifting in, the older people heard first the sweet sentimental songs; and then a change; dance music; not merely the waltz, which in Mrs Thorley's youth had been so daring as to be almost improper, but the polka which, even more daring, far less sedate, was becoming popular.

"They are dancing," Mrs Gordon said with a look of sour disapproval.

"Why not?" her husband asked. "They're young. You're only young once, you know."

"How true," Doctor Taylor said, sorting his cards. "Youth's a stuff will not endure . . ." He liked making an apt quotation and he believed that he had long ago accommodated himself to the facts of life. People— even young children—did die, despite all he could do. Some lived to be old, getting hard of hearing, sight failing, joints stiffening, muddle-minded, fumble-fingered. He'd seen it happening, to other people, and, steeled by his training, had never related it to himself. Now, suddenly he did, thinking that the time to retire was when one still had one's faculties, and strength enough left to enjoy oneself. He'd served his time, hadn't he? Built up a good practice which Edward was qualified to run single-handed. Since Edward joined him, four years ago, they had had amiable, but vigorous arguments about newfangled methods. Nonetheless, the boy was sound. Unlike poor old Gordon's son, a rattle-pate if ever there was one; never did a stroke of work, cricket and tennis all summer, hunting, shooting, golf all winter. If Gordon wanted his business to survive his retirement, he'd need to take in a good steady partner.

"That was my ace, partner," Mrs Gordon said with some acerbity. Absentminded, she thought; getting old. Next time medical attention was needed in the Gordon household, she'd be careful to ask for Doctor Edward!

The girls did not return to school for the little that remained of the summer term. Diana was not to go back at all and Mrs Thorley told Deborah that she could leave, too, if she wished. She had a vague feeling that in the coming few months—the testing time—she would find Deborah of more help than her own daughter. Deb at least took an interest in the farm, knew the workmen by name, could tell a bull from a cow.

Caroline and Lavinia, offered a chance to curtail their schooling, would have seized it, the one with delight, the other with relief, but Deb, though she said, dutifully, that of course, if she could be of use to Mamma, betrayed her real feelings in her face. She loved her home, revelled in country life, but she enjoyed school and the coming term was one of exceptional promise. She would be head girl—and therefore Miss Hardwicke's orderly—practically a member of the staff. There was the School Concert in November; the special Carol Service in St. Mary's and then the School Play at the end of term.

"Oh no," Mrs Thorley said quickly. "I was only thinking that you and Di have always done things together."

"Di will find plenty to do without me," Deb said. When she smiled a dimple appeared in one cheek, not in the other. It gave her smile a lop-sided look, not unattractive.

As a matter of fact, they would all leave at Christmas, Mrs Thorley decided. It would save the fees and the provision of a secondary wardrobe. Miss Hardwicke did not insist upon a uniform but the clothes that found favour in her sight were such as no self-respecting girl would wear outside school. With skirts getting wider and wider, she insisted upon narrow skimpy dresses, explaining that nowhere in school, not in the clothes closets, the schoolroom benches or in the dining room, was there room for voluminous skirts or full sleeves. Collars must reach at least an inch above the base of the throat, sleeves over the wristbone. The choice of colour was left to the girls' parents—so long as they were sombre. To the best of her ability Miss Hardwicke waged the fruitless war against the most besetting fault in girls—vanity. Diana Osborne and Caroline Thorley—both as vain as peacocks—had passed unscathed through her hands. So had many others, but upon some she had made a mark and long after she was in her grave there were women who avoided any colour brighter than tan, or olive green, or a blue much brighter than cornflower. And there were others who chose brighter shades and wore them with a faint feeling of guilt.

Caroline made a great fuss about going back to school. Since this was usual, nobody took much notice until she said a rather shocking thing.

"I intended to ask Papa to let me leave. And he *would*, you know."

It was probably true. Despite her monkeyish face, Caroline had a way with men.

"Oh," said Diana, tears and handkerchief ready, "must you remind us of what we have lost?"

Deb said, "Shut up, you clown," and administered a sharp kick on Caro's ankle.

"I know just how Caro feels," said George. For what Mrs Spicer had hoped and Mr Spicer had feared had come about and George was to start lessons at the Rectory; mornings only, five days a week, to begin with. "And even when I do have to stay afternoons, I will *not* have my lunch there," George said firmly. "I've seen better pig food in my day."

"If, after all, you need me—if only for company—just let me know, Mamma, and I'll come home," Deborah said at parting. It was obvious that Diana was going to be of little comfort or support in the trying days ahead. The way she had received the news of her mother's intention to carry on her husband's activities had drawn protests from the Young Madam.

"But Mamma, what will people say? Have you thought of that?"

By people she meant her personal friends; all the nice girls who had gone to school with her; most of them slightly older; girls who should have been at her birthday party; girls with whom she meant to keep in touch now that she was also grown up. She planned a whole round of visits. She could just imagine them saying: Is it true what I hear?

"I know exactly what they will say, Di. And I'll be the first to say it." Deb gave her stepmother a brief hug, a glancing kiss. "You're a damn brave woman!"

Mrs Thorley said, "Thank you, my dear. I accept the tribute . . ." The unspoken words, while deploring the language, hung in the air. When Mrs Thorley first came to Gad's, Deborah and Caroline had used very bad language; words far worse than damn.

"Surely, Mamma," Diana said, "you could be in control but hire a man to do, well, you know what I mean, the—the unsuitable things."

"I could, but I do not intend to." Mrs Thorley looked her elder daughter in the eye and said something that she had never said to George. He'd never guessed how welcome the life-raft offered had been. "I have done unsuitable things before, Diana. In Leicester, you may not remember, but I earned a living for us all. What I have done once, I can do again."

But secretly she admitted to herself that seven years of easy living, of being looked after, had softened her fibre. Ahead of her lay things she dreaded.

It would have been idle to pretend that the wives of even prosperous farmers did not work, but in their own homes, dairies, yards, they did not conduct business in the full view of the public. The news that Mrs Thorley intended to do so caused a sensation, the more so because of her la-di-da manner and the fact that she was not even country-bred. The general opinion was that she would make a fine mess of it, as well as being a laughing-stock.

The Corn Exchange at Baildon was a huge Gothic building, lighted from above, so that samples showed up as clearly as in the open. Regular buyers had their own stands; desks on tall legs with the owner's names painted on their fronts. Corn merchants, maltsters and millers were the élite of the assembly and held themselves a little apart from those who plied subsidiary trades, men selling agricultural implements or insurance, or beer.

It was so strictly a masculine preserve that even legal wives, tired of waiting towards the end of market day, never set a foot inside it. Little boys hung about the door, anxious to carry a message for a ha'penny. Usually politely phrased messages about the lateness of the hour. Sam Stamper's wife had once sent an arbitrary one: Will you go tell my husband—he's up there at the bar, with his hat on the back of his head—that if he doesn't come at once I shall drive home and he can walk.

Not to be endured; if Sam had budged then he'd never live it down. He gave the young messenger a penny: Nip out the back way, boy and tell them at the livery stables not to harness up till I come.

Women should be kept in their place!

Mrs Thorley, stepping out of hers, walked into the Corn Exchange on one of the busiest mornings; the third Wednesday in September. In black from head to toe, to her very finger tips, she looked small, pitiable, and there was hardly a man there who, properly asked, would not have done the bargaining business for her. A hush, beginning at the door, spread like a ripple as, moving as calmly as though she were in her own parlour, she made her way to the stand bearing the name Carver and Son. Son Carver, being of a younger and more flexible generation, would probably have handled the situation more easily; his father was so embarrassed that he stammered, stepped down from the little eminence behind his desk and said:

"Mrs Thorley, there was no need for this. Just a

note and either I or my son would most gladly have called upon you."

She said, "Thank you, Mr Carver. I came to you first because my husband often dealt with you. But, you understand, I must sell on a competitive market. Look at it . . ."

From the black velvet reticule she carried she took one of the little sample bags, tipped its contents into her black gloved palm and held it out.

From the rear of the hall a slightly drunken voice said:

"Good for you, lady! Beat the old bugger down."

Visibly sweating, Mr Carver said, "Mrs Thorley, you see to what you are exposing yourself. Allow me, please, to conduct you to the door. I will come, tomorrow . . ."

She said, "Mr Carver, I am quite impervious to bad language." And that, God knew, was true. During the bad times with Stephen; low-class hotels, sleazy boarding-houses. Had she wished, she could, she knew, have outsworn any man in the building—and in two languages.

Amongst certain of the élite there was an inner ring made up of shrewd buyers who realised that it was better to cooperate than to compete. They communicated by signs; like bookmakers on race courses.

Mr Carver, stung by her remark about a competitive market and by her refusal to be conducted to the door, almost automatically made the sign which meant: Don't bid against me; we'll do a deal afterwards.

Mrs Thorley was aware of the hush and of the fact that Mr Carver had not made her an offer, and she thought: So that's it! There is a conspiracy against me! She knew a sinking of the heart, and then a mounting anger. Neither showed in her voice or manner.

"Very well, if nobody here wishes to buy the best barley in Suffolk, I can take it elsewhere."

A loud, somewhat strange voice called:

"Spare yeself the bother, ma'am! Fetch it across to me. I'm from Ireland meself."

He was not in the ring, being the rankest of rank foreigners. Buyers from Burton-on-Trent or from Chelmsford could just be tolerated, business making strange bedfellows, but even they were not admitted to the secret enclave. This pushing fellow did not even hire a stand for the day.

"Mrs Thorley, I have not *refused* your barley," Mr Carver said, mopping his forehead. "I'll give you . . ."

He was so demoralised that he named a price, sixpence a bushel above the very highest tacitly agreed upon beforehand by members of the ring. It would have been all right had he not inadvertently made that sign; in theory everybody believed in free trade and an open market; but he had made it, and now he would rank with Judas! Even his fellow Freemasons, sworn as they were to brotherly love, would be cool towards him. It was not just as though he had bid against that damned Irish fellow, that would have been permissible, laudable. He would appear to have taken advantage of a privilege; just as Mrs Thorley had—he now saw it—taken advantage of her sex. Had he not been so concerned about her he would have kept his head better and had she been a man that damned Irishman would not have interfered so swiftly. Everybody knew the Irish weakness for the underdog, and momentarily, so small and black-clad, she had seemed to be one. But she was not; she was a damned shrewd woman and his brief encounter with her had cost him money, and, what mattered more, his reputation. She was a brazen bitch, and George Thorley, decent man, must be turning in his grave.

A woman might conceivably be—had indeed proved herself to be—brazen enough to walk into the Corn Exchange, but no woman with a shred of decency, leave alone pretensions to gentility, would go near the

Cattle Market, which thronged with drovers, renowned for their drunkenness, rough manners and foul tongues. Even poor old women who had managed to fatten a pig or a couple of geese for sale in October would get some man, relative, friend or neighbour, to deputise for her in the Bedlam of noise and stench.

George Thorley had kept what he called a Cattle Book. A rough record which bore about as much relevance to the real state of the Gad's herd as a record of royal weddings might bear to the state of the countries concerned. It was with this which Mrs Thorley, who could write more quickly and in a smaller, neater hand, had helped him most. Stud fees were proudly recorded—any bull which did well at a show was desirable as a sire. But the truth was that a stud bull—in the hands of a man like George Thorley—cost more than he earned. Horses were different, a good pedigree stallion could be led about, keeping appointments with mares ready for mating. Bulls were more dangerous and the cows must come to them. And then George would offer hospitality . . . supper, bed, breakfast. A loss.

There was also the question of the calves born to the pedigree cows. Nobody knew exactly how they might turn out; no breed was absolutely stable; no calf immediately showed promise. It all took time. A true Durham shorthorn developed a colour called roan, red and white hairs blending into a kind of shimmer. That took time and some never attained it; so there were other pages in the Cattle Book, headed Ordinary Sales, which contained lists of what were virtually failures—butcher's meat.

When it came to this culling of the herd, Mrs Thorley was willing to take her stockman's advice.

"That'n," he said, pointing with his thumb, "should've gone three months ago. We ain't in the fattening business. He never did shape up right. Now that'n," he indicated another and shook his head,

"Master had hopes of but look at him; white as a whitewashed wall. Good lines to him, but we ain't breeding Ayrshires, are we, ma'am?"

He was whole-heartedly with her now, having had doubts at first. There was a breed of man that didn't mind taking orders from a woman, footmen, butlers, dancing jackanapes. A good, experienced stockman was not of that kind. And there'd been the teasing—coarse to say the least of it. Most of Joe's kind recognised only two forms of humour: something ridiculous happening to somebody else, like slipping in a cow pat and falling face downwards into a neighbouring one; or something randy, meaning sexual. And a breeding herd was very closely related to sex. Joe had borne quite a lot. Questions beginning: What'll you do boy, if she arst you what that owd bull is up to, clambering about on top of that pore little cow?

The idea of working for a woman had been repugnant, but he couldn't let her down all of a sudden while she was in sorrow, could he now? He was a recognised good stockman and attempts had been made to coax him away from Gad's. One such offer had included a new, brick-built house and a rise of two shillings a week. And that had been in Master's day. But there were arguments against any move. He'd liked Mr Thorley, who'd always treated him well and handed over any money prize; always been, in fact, fair and square. There was also the fact that in Stonham St Peter's, and come to that, Stonham St Paul's, there was a close network of relationship; nearly everybody was at least second cousin or aunt by marrage to everybody else. So he had stayed, helped carry the Master to his grave; lived on edge for fear that a woman, most unaccountably left in full charge, might sell out. Or put somebody else—a hired fellow—in charge.

Instead she had said, "Joe, my husband depended upon you, I know. I shall depend even more. So you must be remunerated." She had then upped his wages by two shillings a week; and he was her man, life and limb.

Now she was relying upon him to cull the herd, and she took his say-so about the two animals doomed for butchery. But when he said:

"That'll be all right then. I'll take them into Corby's, come Wednesday," and she said, "I'll see you there," he was shocked. He knew that she had ventured into the Corn Exchange, but a cattle sale . . . Leave alone everything else, think of the filth! Frightened animals lost all control of their bowels and bladders and since there was so much to be swilled down at the end of the day, a lot of men weren't too particular either.

"You can't do that, ma'am. And why should you, with me ready to stand in? I'll take the creatures in, see 'em sold, collect the money. You can trust me. Surely?"

"I trust you absolutely, Joe. But—well, I made a kind of promise to myself—to take my husband's place as far as possible. And that includes the market."

"But Mamma, I do beg you think again. Would Papa have wished it? Why, even two streets away one can hear the noise. And the smell! Ugh! Let Joe go for you."

"Joe is an excellent stockman, dear, but I doubt whether he'd be a match for those who might take advantage of his ignorance."

"You are inexperienced yourself, Mamma."

"True. True. But I am capable of learning."

"What is there to be learned from an auction?"

"That I don't know. Maybe nothing. But I propose to find out."

The delicate wild-rose colour in Diana's cheeks deepened to scarlet. She took a long breath.

"I will come with you."

"That is very sweet of you, dear. But it would be most unsuitable. And it would disappoint poor Susan."

The adjective, coupled so often with Susan's name, bore no relation to money. Mr Walford had taken over the Sudbury Brewery and by sheer hard work and attention to business made it into a flourishing place. His wife—the pampered only child of the former owner had felt herself neglected; her father had always found time for his family. She then convinced herself that Mr Walford had married her simply to get his hands on the brewery. To gain the attention she craved, and also to retaliate, she took to invalidism. Nerves; impossible to define exactly; impossible to cure. Hired attendants could be afforded, but she never felt happy without one of her family within call. Mr Walford, though less busy than in the early years of his marriage, was busy still; Richard must go to school; so the burden fell upon poor Susan, who for years took lessons with a visiting governess, in Mr Walford's dressing room. It was not until Doctor Taylor detected symptoms of a genuine nervous breakdown in the daughter that she was allowed to go to school. By that time Richard was back from school, and supposed to be learning the brewery business, but his lessons were as often interfered with as poor Susan's had been and finally Mr Walford saw that the boy's only hope was to get away; so he sent him to Burton-on-Trent. And that meant recalling poor Susan from Miss Hardwicke's.

Amongst the many things which made Mrs Walford's nerves much worse, brought her in fact to the verge of collapse, was noise of any kind; so hospitality was impossible in the big brick house, built and furnished with lavish entertainment in mind. People went about on tiptoe, spoke in muted voices. Mrs Walford was not bed-ridden, except on occasion; the further end of the big bedroom had been made into a kind of sitting room, a wide, comfortable sofa, one easy chair, one not so comfortable and a Pembroke table. And of course any of dear Susan's friends were welcome to take tea there; always provided that they were quiet and allowed Mrs Walford to do the talking, in her weak, I-am-about-to-die voice.

Very few visited a second time and Diana Osborne was one of the few. Under the vanity and the strong self-preservative sense, Diana was capable of pity; she was genuinely sorry for poor Susan. (Miss Hardwicke had often noticed that girls paired off in pattern; every pretty girl's *best* friend was a plain one; lively girls seemed to prefer dull ones, and so on, through all the combinations and permutations which a limited community allowed.)

The mention of poor Susan settled the argument; Mrs Thorley set off for Baildon driving the tall horse in the trap, leaving the sedate pony and governess car for Diana.

The noise and the stench were terrible; and just at the entry of Mr Corby's saleyard, a man stood relieving himself against the wall.

"Button up," another man said. "Ladies present."

"You drunk this early? Ladies?" With a short, rude word the man with the unbuttoned breeches described what should be done to all ladies.

"S'Missus Thorley, you fool." Buttoning himself the man said what should be done to Mrs Thorley, who passed by, seeing nothing, hearing nothing. Against stench she had taken the precaution of sprinkling her handkerchief with lavender water. Holding it to her nose she took her place in the ring of people, gathered around the space where terrified animals were harried about.

Mr Corby sat on a platform, much higher than the ones in the Corn Exchange; his clerk sat beside him.

Mr Corby was a man with two distinct personalities. The private Mr Corby lived in a nice house, with a nice wife, and was devoted to his nice garden. He was a churchwarden at St. Mary's, a past master of his Masonic Lodge, a member of the Board of Guardians.

That Mr Corby was precise of speech and fussy of manner. He could not have sold an ice-cold drink in a desert. The other Mr Corby was quite another man, loud-voiced, aggressive; a mixture of clown and entrepreneur who could have made Satan put in a derisory bid for hell. He never missed a bid, his eyes flicked about and in a voice that penetrated to the very edge of his saleyard he kept up a constant patter.

Somewhere in her checkered past Mrs Thorley had seen and enjoyed a ventriloquist's act and she was reminded of it now, but had no time to examine the thought.

The first of her calves trotted in, frightened, wild-eyed, and Mr Corby rattled off his pedigree. Somebody said, "Ten bob."

Mr Corby said, "You want me to die laughing? Ten shillings; eleven: Yes, I see you. At the back there: Thirteen. Fourteen. Shillings not guineas you there in the corner. Fifteen. Sixteen. Are you all dead on your feet? All wearing blinkers? All got cotton wool in your ears? Yes, sir, twenty. Against you. You'll regret it. Thank you. To my right; twenty bob . . ."

Mrs Thorley admitted to herself that this was all too quick for her. By comparison the Corn Exchange was a garden party. But she was rallying herself and had noticed you-there-in-the-corner, a man who bid just by raising his hand. Something, the stubborn streak in her which had refused to admit that her first marriage was a dead failure, and that she had been left, very poor, practically destitute, now sprang up again.

Ordinarily, like Mr Corby, she had a quiet voice, but it had a carrying quality.

"Twenty-one," she said. A few people laughed.

Mr Corby had noticed her and been less surprised than he might have been, for the news of her preformance in the Corn Exchange had spread. He now perceived how she could be made use of. One of a good auctioneer's aims was to keep—and if possible maintain—the goodwill of the crowd, and there was no surer unifying factor with any crowd than a common hostility. He deliberately paused, feigning astonishment too deep for words, and then looking at the roof of a nearby shed, said:

"We appear to have with us somebody ignorant of the rules. In this saleyard, bids over one pound advance by half a crown; those above three pounds by five shillings. With that understood, we will resume. One pound I'm bid, gentleman in the corner. Any advance on one pound?"

"Twenty-two and sixpence," Mrs Thorley said.

"Twenty-two and a half," Mr Corby corrected her.

"Twenty-five."

"Twenty-seven and a half."

Joe, greatly agitated, elbowed his way to her side. He saw and approved her intention, but at sales inexperienced people tended to get carried away.

"Don't go above thirty bob, ma'am. He ain't worth more." He had told her yesterday that with luck they might get thirty bob for each calf.

"Thirty bob."

"Thirty bob, I'm bid. Gentleman over there," Mr Corby said, and made a joke about the high price of veal. Joe was jubilant. Home and dry—and all thanks to her. But for her intervention the too white calf would have been knocked down for a pound. Then, foolish woman, she said:

"Thirty-two and a half." There was no further bid and here they were, landed with their own calf, an animal with no future—except appetite.

Mrs Thorley realised the same thing; a little pang of dismay; on her own thirty-two-and-a-half bid, for her own calf, she'd have to pay Mr Corby's ten per cent charge. She'd be out of pocket. But that feeling lasted no longer than a second; it was money well expended, for it had bought experience. She'd had to be informed, in a nasty sarcastic way, about the stages by which bids rose; she'd learned that; but also another thing. More important. Up to a pound the bidding had been brisk; then Mr Corby, who, after all, made his living by extracting the maximum possible price, had seemed willing to sell for twenty shillings to the gentleman in the corner. After that, she and that finger-raising man had been the sole bidders; and her eyes, anxious, yet curious, and not nearly so able as Mr Corby's at flicking about, had seen Mr Corby finger his neat little greying mustache and the gentleman in the corner had turned away after bidding thirty shillings for a calf which, had she not been there, would have sold for twenty. Another conspiracy?

She stood, thinking things over, and making no bid while her other calf, the one that never had shaped up to standard, was sold for eighteen shillings. To the Baildon butcher from whom she bought her meat. No veal, she thought, for a fortnight; I should feel like a cannibal!

She turned away, but near the entry of the yard was intercepted by a man with a broad red face.

"Mizz Thorley," he said, shifting his hat a fraction of an inch. "If you and me could hev a word . . . That whitey calf. Did you buy him back to set the pace like?"

"No, Mr . . . Mr . . ."

"Hopper," he said.

"No, Mr Hopper. I am, as perhaps you understand, not very experienced. But as that calf went round I saw a kind of glint on his coat. He may well be roan after all. I saw my mistake—and bought him back."

"You take three pound for him?"

Something—and it was difficult to say exactly what—made her say, "No. I think that as a potential breeder—not in the show class, of course, but a good sire to an ordinary herd, he is worth . . . five at least."

"Four's my limit."

"Very well, Mr Hopper. Five is mine."

Another man, and he might have been twin to the other, strolled up and said, "Getting yourself a bargain, Tom?"

Mr Hopper spat in a very uncouth manner indeed, hardly bothering to turn his head. Then speaking as though she were not present, he said:

"Offered her four. She's sticking out for five."

"I'll go four five," said the newcomer.

"Four ten."

"Four fifteen."

"Five. And sod you, John Borley!"

Mr Corby's ability to hear and see everything at once had reached such a peak of perfection that without missing a bid or hesitating for a second in his patter, he was fully aware of what was going on. The damned woman, in addition to her other misdemeanour, was now conducting a private transaction in his saleyard, a place he owned and upon which he paid high rates.

Her other fault had been to take up the bidding just as he was about to knock down the white calf for a pound to his own henchman. All the habitués of the market knew that when Mr Corby's man bid and Mr Corby paused in just that way, it was best to keep silent; for he had a way of getting back at those who broke the unwritten rule. He could refuse to accept your animals at all, saying that his pens and his lists were full. Then you had no choice but to go along to Larkin's, an inferior place in every way. Or he would accept your entry and then conduct the sale in a half-hearted way, making it seem that the beast wasn't worth selling, leave alone bidding for. Both these punitive measures would seem to be against Mr Corby's own interest, but buying in, at practically his own price, through his own agent more than compensated him for such trivial losses. For what he bought in, dirt cheap, Mr Corby had outlets unknown to the ordinary fellow; places far away where money was plentiful and prices high. Nobody really approved of the practice; he should have been content with his ten percent without extorting a form of blackmail as well. But in this world you had to take the rough with the smooth and Mr Corby, when he tried—which was most of the time—couldn't be matched.

Mr Corby went home to his nice house and his nice wife in what she called a mood; a state she attributed to his digestion. On busy days, like this, market day in October and everybody wanting to get rid of surplus stock, he paused only for the most necessary purpose; a dash across to the back of the public house, the Market Tavern, whose back wall was part of his boundary. There he visited the necessary house, decently screened off, and had a sandwich. New bread. That was the trouble. Ninety-nine of the Market Tavern's customers liked sandwiches cut from new almost spongy white bread; Mr Corby liked them, too, but they did not always agree with him. This was one such time. Good, accommodating wife that she was, she changed the supper menu from steak and onions to a coddled egg. A change which did little to restore his temper. Having eaten his egg without appreciation or enjoyment, he said, "I have a letter to write, my dear."

He was handy with words. He could afford to forfeit the Gad's Hall trade; it did not amount to much; pedigree stock was almost always sold privately; and he did not mind if no animal from that place, belonging to that woman, ever came under his hammer again. He must vent his spleen.

Madam,

I am aware that you are ignorant of market etiquette. I feel it my duty to enlighten you. There is, of course, no law against any seller buying back stock offered, but it is a waste of time and money.

I must also point out to you that it is unethical,

if not positively illegal, to conduct, as you did this morning, a *private* sale, on the premises of a *public* auctioneer. A few steps would have taken you and the men who were bidding against one another, out of *my* yard and into Woolhall Street where any activities in which you cared to indulge, would have been acceptable.

There, he thought, signing his letter with a flourish, that should take her down a peg or two; arrogant bitch!

Having written it, stamped it, hitting the stamp as though he were smiting Mrs Thorley, he felt a great deal better and, emerging from the little room in which he did his writing and kept accounts, asked jovially, "What's for supper, Bella?"

*

The year ran downhill. For some reason Mrs Thorley always saw the year, in her mind, as an ascent, beginning with snowdrops, mounting steadily to June with its roses. Then a little plateau; summer; June, July, much of August, and then the decline into the trough, with Christmas the only bright spot. This year, so extraordinary in many ways, followed the pattern. The girls came home. And Joe Snell, who by this time not only accepted Mrs Thorley, but downright admired her, mentioned the Christmas party which had been part of the Gad's Hall routine for as long as he could remember, and his father, his grandfather, before him.

"I reckon, ma'am, you 'on't want to be heving the Barn Party this year?"

"But of course, Joe. Didn't I always say that things should be as usual? You see to the decoration and I will see to the food."

She thought on the periphery of her mind that now the girls were home for good and approaching marriageable age they should all learn the fundamentals of cookery; one never knew what the future held and when hard times had struck her her ignorance had been a great handicap. The trouble was that Jenny disliked having anyone—even Mrs Thorley herself—in the kitchen and made no secret of her feelings.

In former years the Rector and his wife had always been present at the Gad's Hall party for employees on Christmas Eve, but this year, like Joe Snell, they had assumed that there would be no such jollification and had engaged themselves elsewhere. When Mrs Thorley came to proffer, in person, her invitation, Mrs Spicer said, with the utmost sincerity:

"Isabel, dear, I am so extremely sorry. Arthur will be too, I am sure." The Rector, on such occasions, said grace, ate heartily and then retreated to the quietude of the house and a glass or two of good sherry. "Miss Riley's brother, his wife and family are spending Christmas with her this year, and on Christmas Eve she has asked us to join them for tea. And that in a way is awkward for me, since I have a guest arriving sometime in the afternoon and I can hardly suggest taking him with us; Miss Riley's accommodation is so limited. You will excuse me if I go on with my knitting? Christmas always seems to catch me unawares."

If only her circumstances had been easier Mrs Spicer would have been delighted to go about the parish distributing tea and sugar, tins of biscuits, yards of flannel; as it was, the best she could do was to take advantage of a firm in Bradford who early each year advertised four-shilling bundles of assorted wool, colours which had proved unpopular, odds and ends, discontinued lines as they called them. She was always pleased with her bargain and derived some pleasure in sorting and assigning the many colours, thinking a contrast better than an ill-match. She knitted shawls and scarves, stockings, mittens, and this year had ventured upon a garment known as a hug-me-tight, far more practical than a shawl for women who wanted the full use of their arms. It was not unlike a half-sleeved waistcoat with tapering fronts which crossed over and fastened behind the wearer's back. Such a garment took less wool than a shawl, but it demanded more attention.

As she resumed knitting, Mrs Spicer thought: After all, I obliged you by taking George last summer when his father was dying . . .

"If your afternoon guest would care to come to Gad's . . ."

"Oh, I am sure he would. How very kind. A little lively company . . . Poor Everard, he's had rather a sad life. He's Arthur's nephew. Arthur's brother and his wife were both missionaries, in India, and when he was six he had to come away. He was to go to a school intended for the children of those who labour in the foreign field. Poor little boy, he was actually here when we were informed that both his parents had died in some dreadful epidemic. I was obliged to break the news to him." Mrs Spicer, tapering off the hug-me-tight, recalled the scene which had made her averse from informing Georgie that his father was dead, began on a new line of stitches and a new part of the story.

"Arthur and I could never quite understand why Everard's parents chose Mr Everard as his godfather. He was a merchant, in India, and very rich, but not an educated man. He was still in India, then, but he chose the school to which Everard should go, and for which of course he paid, and for a while Everard spent his holidays here. Then Mr Everard retired and came home and bought himself an estate in Buckinghamshire. Naturally after that, Everard spent his holidays there. He was at Eton." She turned the knitting about and began on another decreasing line.

"So far as anyone knew Mr Everard had no children. To speak of expectations . . . I always think it rather squalid, but it certainly looked as though Everard . . . However, it was not to be. When Mr Everard died he left his estate and quite a considerable fortune to his illegitimate son and to Everard just enough to see him through Cambridge and to qualify as a lawyer. Nothing more."

Mrs Thorley said, "That must have been a great disappointment. But a good education is always a sound investment."

"I trust it may prove so. At the moment Everard is with Mr Gordon, and I must confess that I find it significant that he invited himself *here* for Christmas. The Gordons have a big house and three maids. I have a suspicion that they regard Everard as a kind of office boy."

"She could hardly do that," Mrs Thorley said soothingly. "Not with such qualifications. I expect she thought that having you so near . . ."

"That is possible," Mrs Spicer conceded. Then she sighed. "What makes it the more awkward is that Arthur was hurt and angered when Everard chose law instead of the Church. For one thing the Spicers have always been a clerical family and for another he regards all lawyers with some suspicion. He has never told me why, and naturally I have never asked, but I think he must at some time have had an unhappy experience . . . You may have observed that when they are both guests under your roof, Arthur's manner towards Mr Gordon is somewhat . . . reserved." She turned her knitting again. "Of course what you say, dear Isabel, about a good education never being wasted *is* true to some extent. Poor Everard was finding things very difficult; it is hard to get established when one is without money or influence, when he met James Gordon at some kind of reunion. I think it was to do with their preparatory school. That is how Everard happened to come to Baildon. I think he was offered some hope of a partnership, eventually, but to be honest, judging from Mrs Gordon's behaviour, I have doubts.

Everard has looks and manners that would grace any dinner table."

"Well," Mrs Thorley said, feeling that she had wasted enough time, and getting to her feet, "he will be very welcome to our rather rustic festivity. I have things to do."

The idea of match-making was the farthest thing from her mind. Diana was only seventeen and a half, the others ran down the scale of age in a manner impossible with four girls borne of the same mother. And, moulded by her own experience, Mrs Thorley was opposed to early marriages. Girls simply did not know their own minds—she had known hers, been given her head and suffered from it. She wanted all her girls to be about twenty before forming a permanent attachment.

She had told Joe Snell that all should be as before; that he should see to the decoration and she would see to the food. The holly and the ivy, evergreens which symbolised survival through the darkest time of the year. And there was the tree, a custom introduced by Prince Albert.

The barn, into which so much greenery and presently so much food were to be dragged, was very old; far older than the house. It had been the first hall, reared by one of the successful invaders, Creek men, Vikings, so long ago that nothing remained of them even in memory except a few beams carved with Thor's hammer, and his name. Thursday was Thor's day, and Thorley, Thorsby, Thorson were all well-known names. In this place the winter solstice had been ceremonially observed for a very long time before Mrs Thorley came in to assure herself that this, her first Christmas Eve of full responsibility, was in order.

All was as before; and she spared a thought for George, who had so greatly enjoyed this kind of thing.

All along one side of the barn, trestle tables set end

to end, and covered with glistening white table-cloths, overlapping. At one end an urn ready to dispense tea, milk jugs, sugar basins, tea-cups. At the other end a cask of ale. In between mountains of food, all prepared by Jenny, helped by Katie, who could be ordered about as the young Misses could not—which was why Jenny did not welcome them in the kitchen. Sausage rolls, sandwiches, salt beef or ham, take your pick; mince pies—made in the old way, with real minced beef amongst the fruit and spices—fruit cake cut into wedges, sponges cut into triangles, buns, biscuits.

All as in former years.

"Mamma, may I light the candles now? It is getting dark."

"Yes, darling. Be careful of the tree."

Christmas trees must be illuminated; tiny candles in little candlesticks which clipped on to the boughs. There had been accidents, but not here, and Mrs Thorley intended that there should not be. Willy, the odd-job boy, stood ready with a bucket of water and a long-handled mop.

The girls came in—Di, Deb, Caro and took their places behind the long table.

Lavinia was not with them. Late as usual, Mrs Thorley thought; and then, with a flash of impatience: She might have made an effort for once.

They looked very pretty, for Mrs Thorley, while intending to remain in mourning for a full year—but not forever, as some widows did, since it was so unbecoming—had decided that for girls so young, six months was sufficient. Diana wore the muted pink, known as old rose; Deborah a soft green, and Caroline a silvery blue, all dresses which had hung unworn since the disaster, and only Deborah's had needed any alteration; it had been lengthened by the addition of a deep hem of velvet, and in order to avoid the contrived look, bands of the same stuff had been let into the sleeves and around the neckline. No doubt about it, Deb was going to be taller than average, which was rather a pity. Men did not like very tall girls.

Mrs Thorley did not think of herself as an ordinary match-making mamma, and certainly she did not wish any of her girls to marry before the age of twenty; but marriage must be the ultimate aim since there was no alternative except miserable spinsterhood. Deb was clever and bookish, she might conceivably become a governess, a most unenviable fate. And it was difficult to imagine Deb, so forthright and outspoken, in a subordinate position . . .

How stupid to worry about that now! Dear Deb had only just had her seventeenth birthday.

Lavinia drifted in, wearing her old black dress. For once she volunteered an explanation, not an apology. "I had no time to change. I was busy."

Then Everard Spicer arrived. He was an extremely handsome young man, with bright brown curly hair and eyes of almost the same colour. His manners were polished and his voice exceptionally pleasing, deep and resonant. Mrs Spicer had said that her husband had hoped that Everard would become a parson, and certainly the voice would have been an asset in a pulpit—but equally so in a law court.

She introduced her daughters in order to seniority. Then she said, of Jenny, in place by the tea-urn, "And this is Jenny, who is responsible for all these good things—helped by Katie, of course."

And then she knew, by the way the young man eyed the food, that he was hungry. In bad days the windows of English cook-shops and French *patisseries* had reflected her own face with just that look.

"Let us make the most of our opportunity," she said. "Help yourself, Mr Spicer."

"As a matter of fact," he said, "I missed my lunch. I was offered a lift and could not choose my time."

He chose a good solid sausage roll and Mrs Thorley reflected that on a farm whatever economies must be made, one need not stint on food. She took a biscuit and gave Deborah a look which she—far and away the most perceptive of them—instantly understood. Diana and Caroline looked at her as she took a substantial sandwich and felt identical pangs of envy. Deb's figure, of course, was not ideal; her waist was twenty inches, her bosom and hips rather small by comparison, but she could eat anything, anywhere, at any time.

George, a smouldering taper in his hand, hurried up, indignant.

"Mamma, you told me not to *touch* anything. And here you are, *guzzling!*"

"This is my son, George," Mrs Thorley said with justifiable pride. George was handsome, too, and looked very well in the sailor suit—that echo of Trafalgar which formed part of the wardrobe of every boy who was not actually poor—and it had infiltrated to even lower levels, since kindly people often gave out-grown clothes away. "And this is Mr Spicer." At the name George recoiled a little; it stood for everything he disliked; long lessons in a room that smelt of musty old books; long dreary sermons. But this Mr Spicer was different; he said genially:

"It's not too late, George. You come and guzzle, too."

And while George ate a wedge of the fruit cake, and Mrs Thorley nibbled her biscuit and Deborah munched her sandwich, Mr Spicer disposed of two more sausage rolls and a mince pie. George thought: Greedy.

Then Joe Snell, master of ceremonies, came in and said:

"Ma'am, we're ready."

The women with few exceptions wore black. With families so intermarried and so numerous, everybody had to go into mourning once or twice a year, so the best dress might as well be black; and degraded to ev-eryday wear, black had the advantage of not showing the dirt. Just a few young women wore lighter, brighter colours. The women clustered about the tea-urn, the men about the cask of beer, manned by Joe. The children ate, staring at the lighted tree. Ready, presently, to sing carols.

There had been a little argument about one of the old carols.

"We can't sing God bless the master of this house, Joe. Not with him laying down in the churchyard."

"There's the young master."

"Wouldn't be right, would it, to put him afore his mother—and she taking such trouble to keep everything as it was."

"Then how about God bless the mistress of this house, likewise the master, too?"

"Don't sound right, somehow."

"Leave it out then. There's others."

"But that'd be different; and she been very particular to keep everything as it was."

"Then let's keep it like always . . ."

Everard Spicer, standing between Diana's end of the long table and the beer barrel, said, as the carols ended and the gifts from the foot of the tree were distributed, "How delightfully feudal!"

For the first time in her life she regretted not having paid a little more attention to lessons. Feudal? She had the vaguest memory of somebody talking about the feudal system, but for the life of her she could not remember what it was. However, he had called it delightful, so she felt safe in saying, "Yes, is it not?" which seemed to be a completely satisfactory reply.

And this year, although the aim was to keep everything the same, there was a difference. When Mrs Thorley had distributed the gifts—all good useful things which had cost money—Joe Snell stepped from behind the now empty beer barrel and said:

"Ma'am, this year we got a little token for you. We hope you'll accept of it, with best wishes from us all."

Many men, she knew, were handy at what they called whittling—using knives and skill on wood, making spoons and bowls and clogs and buckets, handles for axes, spades, forks—but the thing which Joe handed to her was out of this utilitarian class. It was a small wooden model of a Durham shorthorn bull; horns, genitals. It was not painted, somebody had chosen exactly the right wood, the real roan colour. And it was not Gad's Goliath, getting a bit old and thick now. It was one of his progeny, Gad's Glory, a young bull of which George had had high hopes.

A few tears now, she felt, would be appropriate, but their source was still dammed. She had that old, known lump in the throat, but it did not affect her voice. As clearly as it had sounded through the Corn Exchange and the Cattle Market, it said, "How very beautiful! I thank you all. I shall treasure it forever. And so will my son. And now—Happy Christmas."

"And to you, ma'am. Now—God Save the Queen," Joe said.

Every public gathering ended with the National Anthem, at least where decent people were concerned; for the goings-on in France had been simply shocking again this year . . .

The long table in the dining room was already set for tomorrow's Christmas dinner, so the family and their guest ate what was called a simple supper at the gate-legged table in the living room. A huge log fire burned on the hearth and the simple meal consisted of thick ox-tail soup, the same ham and salt beef from which the sandwiches had been cut, some of Jenny's green chutney and an excellent cheese.

It was the first really *family* meal Everard Spicer had ever shared. There had been India, very vaguely remembered, his parents always busy; he'd had an ayah, of course; ostensibly a Christian, otherwise she would not have been employed, but she would not eat meat. He had never really shared a meal with her. Then England and school. Terribly cold. He could remember his first chilblains—he thought he had leprosy! Holidays at the Rectory, where a whole egg was presented as a favour. Another school. Holidays with Uncle Everard; good food there but no family feeling between him and an aging man, often a little drunk. Cambridge. Baildon, where the only thing that could be said of his lodging was that it was cheap.

Here he was in the very heart of a family and he revelled in it.

Caroline was the lively one; very sure of herself.

She said, "Mamma, I think they are all slightly confused between you and Her Majesty! I thought to myself while they sang:

"God save our gracious ma'am,
Giver of cakes and ham,
God save our ma'am.
Thy richest gifts in store,
On her be pleased to pour,
So she can give us more.
God save our ma'am."

Mrs Thorley showed no sign of being offended; she said, "You have a gift for parody, Caro."

"If only you could carry a tune," the tall one, Deborah, said.

Diana said, "Really, Caro, you are *awful!*"

George came to the defence of his favourite sister. His preference was quite irrational. He should, he knew, have liked Deb best—he'd inherited her pony and she had taught how to ride it, how to care for it. He loved her, and Di—and Lavinia, of course, but Caro was *funny.*

"I don't think Caro is awful, Di. I think she's deuced clever."

Deuced he had discovered—feeling his way about

the world—was an acceptable word; he knew about twelve that were not.

Mrs Thorley had brought the model bull and set him, on his solid plinth, in the centre of the table. Now as the meal ended, Lavinia, generally so silent, leaned forward and touched the broad head between the short horns. She said:

"For well-wishing a name should be given." The family were all accustomed to such apparently irrelevant remarks.

"It is Gad's Glory, I think," Mrs Thorley said.

"Wait until tomorrow and you can baptise him, Lavinia. In good red wine," Deborah said.

It was true. Possibly because Gad's Hall was largely surrounded by the moat, it had no cellar. Just across the passage it had a good store room, and although George Thorley had left far less in the way of money than could have been expected, he had left, in that store room a very respectable cellar.

"What a dry stick," Caro said on the landing. "He never cracked a whole-hearted smile."

"It may be," Diana said, "that you are not quite as funny as you think you are."

"Spare me! You sound like Miss Hardwicke. And I've done with her, thanks be to God."

"That'll do, Caro," Deborah said, opening the door of the room which she and Diana had always shared, just as Caroline and Lavinia had shared the one next door. Mrs Thorley, being tactful, tentatively feeling her way, had thought that perhaps the sisters—two pairs—might have held together, but age seemed to count more than blood kinship; Diana and Deborah had linked up; Caroline and Lavinia, more or less thrown together.

"What I do think," Deborah said, inside the bedroom, "is that he's *greedy*."

"He had no lunch, Deb. He said so."

"So he ate four sausage rolls and three mince pies and two slabs of cake. Then he came in and had two helpings of everything."

"He was hungry."

"Not after all he ate in the barn. Nobody could be. What would you bet me that he is now gorging one of the Rectory rock buns?"

Mrs Spicer's tea-time offering, more rock than bun as Caro had once said, was a long-standing family joke, and when now it failed to elicit even the shadow of a smile, Deborah looked at Diana sharply.

"I do believe you're sweet on him." Every nice girl believed in love at first sight as firmly as she believed in the Creed; yet, in case the attraction should not be mutual, it was wise to conceal one's feelings until some sign of favour had been shown since nothing made a girl look more ridiculous than seeming to be sweet on a man who was not sweet on her. However, with one's best friend—or one's half-sister, one could be frank.

"Well, I do think he's the nicest young man we know."

Two remarks: We know very few; and: We don't really know him, must be resolutely repressed. Any kind of dissension within the family must be avoided.

"You may be right. Anyway you'll see him tomorrow. That reminds me, we shall need an extra place at table. And I intend to put up my hair tomorrow. Christmas dinner has always been more or less my birthday party."

"Yes," Diana said, momentarily diverted. "Not high, Deb, you're tall enough already." Not: Too tall, which would have been offensive. "I think drawn back, and dressed low, Deb. A chignon. Oh, if only we had some chenille . . . But net would do. Let me see."

Anniversaries are absolute *hell*, Mrs Thorley thought, remembering how, last Christmas, George had been here. She had decided that everything must be as it had been, but there were times when even the routine procedure, apart from a hitch now and then, soon overcome, tended in a way to decry the dead. Take a bucket of water out of a pond, and no hole shows. Not a nice thought. We are all expendable.

Christmas Day was following its usual pattern. Presents.

Bracelets for the girls; gold; no pinchbeck stuff or fake stones. Mrs Thorley, in one of the hard times, had learned what a life-buoy something genuine could be. She hoped with all her heart that none of her girls would ever be reduced to selling a trinket; but just in case, she bought gold.

They gave her presents, too. Deborah and Caroline, working away during the time which Miss Hardwicke allocated to free activities, had made her a petticoat with so many tucks and insertions of lace that it could practically stand up on its own. Diana had made a matching corset cover. Lavinia had given her a picture; slightly more odd than those which Mrs Thorley had received in the past. It portrayed a field of poppies; quite beautiful until one saw in the centre of each flower, a face, ugly, unfriendly. How could Lavinia *know* that the men in the Corn Exchange, in Mr Corby's saleyard and various other places, had appeared just like that; red, alien? Then look again, at a slightly different angle, and it was just a field of poppies.

George was still at an age where he gave what he would wish to receive and hoped eventually to share; chocolates; peppermints and a delicious new sweet called brandy-and-butter-balls. For his mother he presented something he could not share—a little flask of lavender water. And from her and from his sisters he had received a number of very acceptable gifts; best of all a clockwork toy; a miniature railway engine.

The railway had not yet reached Baildon, but it was coming; it was almost at Sudbury and should be through to Bywater next year. Everything about it was new and exciting and George was so pleased with his little model that he could not resist smuggling it into church where presently, when Mamma, Di and Deb had gone to the altar rail, he found himself alone with Caro, who had not yet been confirmed. Lavinia had excused herself from church; her back ached from standing at the Barn Party, she said.

Only with Caro would George have dared to do it. With a mischievous, conspiratorial glance, he took the toy from his pocket and pushed it gently along the pew towards her. She made a face of mock reproof, but pushed it back towards him. It was not wound up and he was not yet familiar enough with it to know that the hooter on it was worked, not by the winding mechanism but by the revolution of the wheels. The noise sounded much louder than it had done at home. Mr Spicer almost dropped the silver cup and Caro laughed! Quite as unseemly a noise as the hoot in the hushed church.

"That was extremely naughty of you, George," Mamma said as soon as they were outside. "Give the thing to me. You will not be allowed to play with it until tomorrow." Occasionally she had to make a show of strictness; widows' sons were notorious, and George had in addition four—no, three, for in this as in everything else, Lavinia must be discounted—doting young females around him. Even now Diana was saying:

"I blame *you*, Caro, more than George. To let him do it. And then to laugh!"

"Caro didn't know, nor did I that it would hoot without being wound up."

Mrs Thorley pushed the toy into her sealskin muff; and even that tiny friction was enough to make it hoot again; a muffled, derisory hoot at which even Mrs Thorley smiled. Diana preserved her look of offended dignity. Deb knew why. Diana had always been oversensitive to what-will-people-think; and Everard Spicer had been one of that startled congregation. Without actually sharing Di's feeling that the Thorley family had disgraced itself, she understood. And the immediately comforting words, A good dinner will put us right in his sight, must not be spoken. She had already almost imperilled a long friendship by using the word greedy last night.

Christmas dinner at Gad's had been much the same for six years—it had taken Mrs Thorley a year to organise her campaign. The Rector and his wife, for whom Christmas was such a busy season; Doctor Taylor, and presently his son, for whom it was anything but a busy season; unaccountably, few people felt like dying on Christmas Day. Susan and Richard Walford—their father always did duty on such occasions.

They'd always had turkey, the biggest available; and George had always carved, lavishly but untidily. This year Doctor Taylor said, "May I?" and carved with a surgeon's skill. And that was not the only difference. Everybody had aged by a year. Or more . . . or more. Once, really looking at herself in the glass, Mrs Thorley had been ridiculously startled to see silver streaks in her hair. Had they appeared overnight? And once, looking into a shop window, as in the past she had sometimes looked and seen a hungry face, she had seen another and had time to ask herself; Who is that ferocious-looking old woman? in the blink of time that it took to realise that she was confronting herself.

Now the young were beginning to pair up; and doing it badly, as the young always did. As she had herself done.

Take Edward Taylor, that serious, dedicated young man, where in the world could he find a more suitable mate than Deb, so sensible herself, so ready to be dedicated, and so practical. Mrs Thorley was reasonably confident that if Deb were alone, except for a servant, in the big old house in St Giles' Square and somebody rang the bell and showed a thumb hanging by a thread of flesh, Deb would have dealt with it, undismayed. But the silly young man had eyes for nobody but Caroline, who was frivolous, amusing and quite useless in an emergency; once, sharpening a pencil, she'd nicked her own finger and thrown a hysterical fit.

Richard Walford was just as silly, wanting Diana, the last person to settle down to a household geared to the requirements of an invalid. There was in Diana what her mother recognised as a good healthy streak of selfishness. Richard Walford, too, would have done better to direct his attention to Deb.

In any case Richard had lost Diana, at least for a time. Mrs Thorley, having been through the process herself, and suffered thereby, knew love at first sight, recognisable as measles. Diana was offering to drive Everard Spicer back into Baildon on the day after tomorrow.

Driving home to Baildon, Edward Taylor said:

"You know, it's time we did something to return Mrs Thorley's hospitality."

"We mustn't upset Hattie, dear boy."

Hattie was their Treasure; a member of the firm as it were. Be late for a meal, as doctors so often were, and there it was, ready, waiting and never spoiled. Be called out in the night—and for some inexplicable reason all babies who came reluctantly and needed more than the ordinary midwife's attention were born between three and seven o'clock in the morning; and more people died then—come back at some unearthly hour and there was Hattie, in her red flannel dressing gown with a good, heartening hot drink. Never a grumble.

"I shouldn't dream of upsetting Hattie. The Angel does a bit of outside catering. And the rooms just need a good going over."

Dining room, drawing room, all shrouded in dust

sheets for the last ten years; ever since Mrs Taylor died of influenza.

"That would mean work for Hattie."

"She needn't lift a finger. I can find a dozen women in Scurvy Lane who'd be only too glad of a day's work."

"Hmm," Doctor Taylor said, expressing his disapproval without saying a word. The younger man thought: He's got into a rut, medically and in every other way; it's time he was shaken out of it. Taking his father's consent for granted, he said, "The piano will need tuning."

Driving home to Sudbury, Richard Walford said:

"Really, you know, Sue, we can't go on accepting invitations, and never asking anybody back."

"I don't see what can be done about it," Susan said gloomily. "You know how Mamma is . . ."

Mrs Walford's hearing was almost uncanny. Her bed-sittingroom was at the front of the house, the kitchen at the back, but let so much as a saucer drop and she heard it. Both Richard and his father had, on very rare occasions, tried to offer the merely token hospitality of a drink and a cigar in the snuggery, also at the back. Entering stealthily as burglars, by the side door, muting their own voices, hoping visitors would imitate, somehow they were always discovered and sent for.

Richard felt sorry for Susan—it was worse for her; he and his father did get out and about, they saw people all day long. Poor old Sue was beginning to look dim and miserable and old. Compare her with Diana Osborne, only a few months younger.

"I know what we could do. And I'll do it. Hire the Victoria Rooms. The whole place, restaurant and all, for an evening. Ask everybody. Have a proper dinner and dance afterwards."

"I'm not sure about dancing—if you're thinking of

Diana. And Deb and Caro, of course." She knew that his thoughts were with Diana. "I mean, they're still in mourning."

"They didn't look like it today! Besides, we danced on Diana's birthday."

"That was different. Both times they were in a private house."

"The Victoria Rooms will be private; *our* house, just for one evening. Don't *you* begin waving wet blankets. There're enough of them about."

"I wasn't. I was just thinking. When would it be?"

"How about St Valentine's? That'll give you time to get a new dress. A nice cheerful colour, eh?"

"I know. I have been letting myself go. Everything is so difficult. I do sometimes feel that nothing's worth the effort."

"A lovely poppy red," Richard said, following his own line of thought and naming the colour which was most men's favourite; a fact recognised by bad women, and, in a negative way, by good ones, too, in that they tended to avoid it. But poor Susan did need livening up; her hair was fair, but a dim kind of fair, no sheen to it. There were things that could be done to liven up that kind of hair; and also that kind of complexion, the unhealthy pallor that came from too much confinement to stuffy rooms.

As a young man, with plenty of money, serving a purely nominal apprenticeship, Richard Walford, during his time at Burton-on-Trent, had acquired a good deal of knowledge about women who did things to their hair and their faces, wore dresses brighter even than poppy red and did not demand to be called Miss Whatever-it-was for more than five minutes after the introduction. But he had settled, in his mind, for a good girl, dignified, pure, possessor of every virtue, every grace—Diana Osborne.

Diana, who was saying to Everard Spicer:

"Mr Spicer, did I hear you say on Christmas Eve

that you had been given a lift. Have you been offered one back?"

"Unfortunately not. But I think that once I am on the main road . . ."

"I will drive you. With pleasure."

*

Mrs Thorley, infinitely the most experienced person at this, or any other local gathering, recognised, in her own daughter, her young self; infatuated, head over heels in love; and despite all her sophistication, she was surprised to feel a slight dismay; a hope that this would not come to anything. Why?

A young man with everything to commend him; respectable family connections; good looks; beautiful manners—Eton had stamped its own; an honourable profession which, while not very remunerative at the moment, held prospects . . . Mr Gordon must retire at some time and James would shrug off the yoke. Gordon and Spicer, perhaps, and who better fitted than Diana to take on the role of a leading citizen's wife?

So, why am I not delighted?

Oh, so silly to think—he has a mousetrap mouth! Yet, in her time, battling against the world, Mrs Thorley had learned that mouths, rather than eyes, were indicative of character.

The fact that the young man was a trifle too solemn was not a disadvantage; Diana, though vain, was far from frivolous.

And in any case, why worry, *now?* Everard Spicer would not be in a position to marry for quite a while yet; Diana's infatuation might not last. Her own had done so, but that was nothing to go by.

*

Plans for both parties went rapidly ahead; Mr Walford cooperating fully; deciding that Mamma should be told nothing until nearer the time and declaring that just for once he'd try to get away himself. Some long-buried streak of conviviality stirred within him. What with having had to work so hard, and then Viola becoming such a sad invalid, he'd had little chance to enjoy himself, but the capacity to do so was still there. The champagne should flow, and although February was a poor month for flowers, there was a man on the outskirts of Sudbury who grew hothouse carnations all the year round. He'd order twelve dozen—all red.

Edward Taylor's preparations went far less smoothly. Hattie, though assured that she need do nothing, absolutely nothing, was affronted. "I know I'm not as spry as I once was, Doctor Edward; and the girls I get to help nowadays ain't much good. But I could've managed a nice little dinner without calling in people from The Angel. You'd only to ask!"

As for the women from Scurvy, words failed her. Dirty, dishonest. Did Doctor Edward imagine that she was going to allow them the run of the house, all amongst his dear dead mother's things? And they so dead ignorant. Why, in all her years she's only once hired a kitchen help from the Lane and believe it or not the girl didn't know what an oven was.

"I can well believe it, Hattie. Only three or four houses in that area have ovens. It's an absolute disgrace."

He also was a rather solemn young man; concerned with social problems, in a wider sense than his father was. Doctor Taylor was *kind* enough; he'd treat the poor free of charge, push a shilling or sixpence into a grimy hand—a little contribution towards the extra nourishment needed; always carried sweets in his pocket. But he accepted the state of affairs, not gladly, but with resignation. Edward was not yet resigned.

Doctor Taylor was not resigned to what was going on in his house. Hattie upset, women from the Lane, glad to snatch at an hour's employment—the children left to the care of a grandmother or a neighbour, rushing about with buckets and mops and dusters and Hattie yapping round them like a sheepdog. His comfortable life was being disrupted and the opening of the disused rooms had disturbed him; the worst disturbance coming on the day of the piano tuner's visit. The piano had not been touched since Emily died . . .

And all this, Edward's father knew, for the sake of Caroline Thorley, the one he liked least of the three—except as a patient and a most unrewarding one—he, like everybody else, discounted Lavinia. Diana, Osborne, not Thorley, was tolerable, a bit vain and what he called set-up-with-herself, but these were the faults of youth. Deborah, less pretty and therefore less vain, had good common sense and—a thing a man should take into account when choosing a mate—bounding good health. Caroline was another cup of tea altogether. Altogether too ready with her tongue.

She had offended him—not for the first time, but for the worst time—at the dinner table at Christmas, at Gad's. He'd been saying—not for the first time—that the time had come for him to retire; when a woman had come to the surgery and insisted upon seeing the *old* doctor. He spoke of this in a self-deprecatory way which was entirely false; everybody within hearing should have said: But you are not old; or: What in the world should we do without you? Caroline Thorley had forestalled these tributes to his vanity and, leaning forward, cracked one of her silly jokes. "But surely, that was a compliment! The time to retire will be when somebody demands the Young Doctor."

It was, of course, true and none the more acceptable for being true. And what had made Edward choose Caroline, Doctor Taylor would never understand. Face like a monkey; tongue like a wasp. Still, it was Edward who would have to live with her; he himself would be far away . . .

His little hints about retirement had never been intended seriously. Playfully, in order to evoke dismay and contradiction; or angrily when he and Edward had an argument about medical procedure; now amidst the bustle he found himself thinking more and more often of a little village in Hampshire where he had once enjoyed a fishing holiday. He had a friend in the neighbourhood, still in practice in Andover. He could help him a bit, keep his hand in and not there be known as the old doctor, for his friend was at least three years older.

He visualised life in a quiet small house, not quite a cottage, something betwixt and between, big enough to accommodate himself and somebody like Hattie. Why not Hattie? Why not? Now he came to think about it, Edward had never shown a proper appreciation of Hattie. Let him learn. Find a woman from Scurvy Lane.

Yet despite all, willing as he was to disturb Edward's domestic life—as Edward for a fortnight had disturbed his—the professional sphere was another matter. He could not, with a clear conscience, leave Edward single-handed. But that problem was easily solved. Get a well-qualified man installed at the hospital, now, thanks to a legacy, well able to afford such expenditure. He brought the matter up at the meeting of the Hospital Committee, which took place two days before Edward's party. He said they must look ahead, "I am not growing younger." A protest then could have swung the balance, but Lord Stanton said, "Who is?" And Mrs Bosworth, whose annual garden party raised a substantial sum for the hospital's upkeep, asked what the Committee should *do*. "Hire a young man. Well qualified and strong as a horse," Doctor Taylor said.

Edward—flesh of my flesh, bone of my bone—said the most damaging thing of all.

"Well, in a way, I'm in favour. Nobody should die in harness. But are you sure? It has now and then occurred to me that men around sixty go through something equivalent to the menopause in women."

"Absolute rot!"

"Is it? Think of the men you know who at sixty, give or take a year, change completely. In women the state, admitted it comes earlier, is politely called change of life, and that is an exact description. It is a change. Men alter their wills, marry their housemaids . . . I think this decision to throw in your hand. It's premature. Take a holiday by all means, you've earned it, God knows, and I can manage. But don't make a hasty decision . . . Bear in mind I *am* in favour, but only when you've thought it over."

Edward was content with his party; he had done what he aimed to do—show Caroline the house of which she would be mistress if she married him; the lofty, spacious rooms with their swags of plaster flowers below the cornices, the solid, yet elegant Georgian furniture, now gleaming from the recent polishing. He had even managed to get her to himself for a little time and at the same time show her that he was not a dull dog, though often in her company he felt like one.

In the short passage which led from the house to the surgery there hung some posters which his mother had considered unsuitable for any other part of the house.

"Look at this," he said. "It was an election poster. Less than twenty years ago. It'd be considered libellous now." The candidates' names had invited caricature. Mr Hogg was depicted as a grossly fat man with a pig's face, guzzling in a trough labelled Votes; Mr Nunn, in veil and wimple, was on his knees, hands in prayerful attitude, and eyes raised to the sky across which the word Electorate was scrawled. Another poster advertised a long-past Baildon Midsummer Fair one attraction of which had been a competition—a hat for prize—for the best grin through a horse collar. For the benefit of those who could not read there was a man, apparently with horse's teeth, grinning through a horse collar.

Oddly, Caroline did not break into the merry laughter which he found so attractive. Of the election poster she said, "What unfortunate names," and of the toothy grin, "How ugly!" It occurred to him that perhaps his mother had been right in banishing the posters to this obscure passage. That no woman—even Caroline— would find them amusing. That perhaps he had been wrong, a trifle coarse, in showing them to her. While he entertained this thought, Caroline gave an exaggerated shiver. "This is a cold passage," she said. Then because she could never resist the flirtatious gesture, "Feel my hands." He took them in his own warm, competent ones; perhaps a little too closely, with too eager and expectant a look, for almost instantly she pulled away and said:

"Edward, we must go back to the others. Our absence will be noticed."

To the besotted young man this was not at all a discouraging speech. For one thing it placed him and her apart from the others. And it proved that gay and carefree as she might appear, she was properly conventional.

On the way back to the drawing room, he said happily:

"It is the Walfords' party next week. Dancing! Will you dance with me? A lot?"

"But of course."

If twenty personable young men had sprung out of the ground and made the same request, she would have given each the same answer. She was only just out of the schoolroom, but she knew all the tricks; had been born knowing them. She'd cut her man-handling teeth on her own father. He had been generally indulgent but if ever he said No to Deb—or later to Di—they had only to say, "Go on, Caro. You ask." Nine times out of ten it had worked.

Any kind of gathering in the area had many constant elements, for the social structure was as neatly striated as a layer cake. Mrs Thorley was the only one to have broken through from one layer to another, and she actually could have gone further, had she wanted to. Her maiden name, and even that of her husband, reprobate as he had been, would have opened doors to her, doors closed to those whom she had chosen as friends. She had taken refuge in being Mrs Thorley of Gad's Hall because the so-called "County" families comprised a closely knit network of people who moved about far more than ordinary people did; they inter-married; they went on visits and exchanged letters and gossipped quite as freely as lesser people did. And she wanted none of it; no faint echo of the calamitous past.

So, having established herself firmly in the middle class, pulling George with her, she was content to re-main there and to hope that the girls would make sen-sible, respectable marriages within the circles which of necessity overlapped a bit. The Walfords' circle was naturally wider and based on Sudbury rather than Bail-don.

Mrs Walford could not be kept in ignorance forever. Once enlightened, she accepted the revolutionary idea with such amiability that Mr Walford wondered what exactly he had feared; and why, in God's name, had he not launched such a venture before. She actually showed some interest in the list of guests invited; in the proposed menu; in Susan's dress. Of that she was criti-cal. She said in her die-away voice:

"Such a harsh colour, my dear, and so unbecoming. You should have consulted me."

"I was reluctant to bother you with such a triviality, Mamma."

"So I suppose you consulted Diana. Now with her black hair and clear complexion, she would look well in scarlet . . . But it is too late now. What with that, and your hair . . ."

In her own bedroom, preparing for the first proper dance of her life, Susan had been delighted by her own image in the glass; the camomile rinse—how did Richard know about such things?—had brightened her hair, and although the red dress nowhere touched her skin, having a deep, creamy lace collar, called a berthe, and falls of the same lace from the elbows, something of the warmth and glow of the colour had been reflected in her face. For once in her life she had looked almost pretty; and here was Mamma, destroying it all! As she would destroy the party!

In a blinding flash, Susan knew what would happen. Mamma was only pretending to acquiesce in the idea of being left alone for some hours with only Nurse Hardy and three servants. As soon as the party got under way somebody would come running. Oh sir, oh Master Richard, oh Miss Susan, the mistress is having one of her attacks . . .

Even if Papa insisted upon bearing the brunt and told her and Richard to stay, the whole thing would be blighted. Who could dance with a light heart while their host's wife was having an attack?

(It was over Mrs Walford and her attacks that Edward Taylor and his father had had a dispute. The older man was tolerant. "She *is* frail, Edward; and her heart is flabby."

"Keep a prize-fighter confined to one room and in bed much of the time for how long? Fifteen years. And he'd be frail and have a flabby heart." This was direct criticism of Doctor Taylor's treatment and there was an edge to his voice as he asked:

"And what would *you* advise?"

"A normal life. Not necessarily violent exercise; but walks on fine days; drives in a carriage; cheerful company."

"And what about her attacks?"

"I've never witnessed one. What form do they take?"

"Her heart goes nineteen to the dozen."

"That could be fibrillation—not necessarily a sign of a weak heart. The contrary, in fact. A resistance symptom. It occurs in hysteria, too."

"Text-book jargon, my boy."

One day an opportunity came for Edward to try his hand. Mrs Walford had an attack and Doctor Taylor had influenza. Even with a good fast horse it took a little time to cover the distance, and when Edward arrived the fibrillation had ceased. He could see, though, that she had been frightened and that her state was not helped by the fussy concern of her family, all pale and sticken around the bed. He drove them away and made a painstaking examination of the patient.

He had none of his father's bedside manner, but he took pains to assure her that there was nothing to be frightened about; her heart was sound enough. He made ludicrous suggestions about going for drives, and when the weather improved, for walks. He also told her a method—so ridiculous as to be insulting—which *might* curtail an attack. At the first sign press her fingers hard on her neck, just below the ears. He promised nothing, but had, he said, known cases where it had been effective.

He upset her so much that before he was halfway home she had another attack. She did not try the suggested cure; nor would she have him recalled. He was quite useless; worse than no doctor at all. She said much the same, in milder terms, to Doctor Taylor next time she saw him, thus flattering his vanity. And he continued to prescribe nostrums for her; mainly placebos, but two things of proved worth; a mild decoction of digitalis for her heart, and a mixture containing morphine for her insomnia. He also advocated a glass of sherry before a meal to stimulate her appetite.)

The pretty bedroom must not be cluttered; so all the

medicines stood on a silvery tray in Mr. Walford's dressing room. Alongside them stood the sherry and a bottle of apricot brandy of which Mrs Walford was very fond. It rounded off a meal nicely, she said.

"If you cared to drink your sherry now, Mamma, I could sit with you while you drink it. I am early."

"That is thoughtful of you, dear. For me it will be a long, lonely evening."

Not if you are asleep, Susan thought, the red taffeta rustling as she went into the dressing room. She tipped in the opiate with a reckless hand. Let her sleep! Let Papa and me and Richard have just this one evening.

Mrs Hardy, the hireling of the moment, liked to be called Nurse, though she had had no training except that of experience. Many nurses were slatterns and drunkards—but they were not hired by people like Mr Walford, to occupy a post which in some ways was very easy. Mrs Walford didn't really need a nurse at all; it was just that she demanded constant attention. Nurse Hardy was sober, honest, reliable. Not, Mrs Walford felt, entirely sympathetic; she had once opened one of the windows. . . .

This evening, aware of the momentous occasion, she bustled in carrying the imaginary invalid's dinner herself. A tenderly poached salmon steak—the first of the season and small new potatoes, imported at God only knew what cost. Tipsy cake, piled high with whipped cream.

Goodnight, Mamma.

Goodnight, my dear. We'll come in very quietly.

"I shall hear you, my dears. I never sleep when one of you is out. Tonight, all three. . . ."

You'll be asleep, Nurse Hardy thought; I'm not going to have you sending for them; making it look as though I couldn't manage! I'm happy here; I'm Nurse Hardy; I don't eat with servants; and there's nothing messy or unpleasant. When Miss Susan takes over, I'm free, to walk in the woods and pick primroses.

You're going to sleep, my lady, Nurse Hardy thought, tipping, with a hand as reckless as Susan's, a good dose of the opiate into the apricot brandy.

It was a wonderful party. Mr Walford was making up, with a vengeance, for the lack of hospitality he had shown in the past. The atmosphere was so care-free; the company so mixed. Mr Walford had spread his net very wide and even Lavinia. . . .

At first Lavinia had not wished to come. She said so, emerging from her vague ineptitude to make a definite statement. Very well, she need not. She'd be perfectly safe at Gad's with Jenny and Katie. Then, in her awkward, unpredictable way she had decided to come after all and appeared to have fallen in with somebody with whom she was in accord.

"Mr Walford," Mrs Thorley said, catching him by the sleeve and making him jump because he'd known all evening that he was enjoying borrowed time. "So many people were introduced, I did not catch all the names. There, under the palm tree, with my youngest daughter. Who is he?"

"Oh. Virtually a stranger. Mr. Fremlin. Old Mr Fremlin died a while back. This Mr Fremlin inherited Abbas Hall. He's a nephew. He's been in India all his life and seemed rather—friendless and as I'd met him in the way of business . . ."

There was no need, Mrs Thorley thought, for the half-apologetic way he spoke. Mr Fremlin appeared to be entirely presentable. He was in fact the most elegantly dressed man in the room, and although he was old—between forty-five and fifty—one of the most handsome. His face was tanned—India accounted for that—and his hair was silvery, thick and glossy. His smile revealed splendid teeth. It struck her as slightly strange that he should seem to be friendless, for old Mr Fremlin had definitely been "County" and the county people usually looked after their own.

Still, no matter! Obviously he had the ability—unique in Mrs Thorley's experience—of getting on with Lavinia. Her eyes were not looking through him, or beyond him. She was smiling. With something of a shock Mrs Thorley saw that in an animated mood, Lavinia was positively pretty; perhaps the prettiest of the four. It struck her for the first time that some of Lavinia's shyness and awkwardness was due to her place in the family. She was only slightly younger than Caroline, but Caroline was old for her age, poised, socially adequate, whereas Lavinia was immature and shy. Maybe, Mrs Thorley's mind took an unusual flight of fancy, any crowd, to a shy girl, looked like that poppy picture with the hint of unfriendly faces half revealed, half hidden. Lavinia would feel at ease with a man old enough to be her father. Perhaps he was telling her about India; she seemed to be engrossed. Or she was telling him about her drawings; she was now sketching something on the air. And possibly Mr. Fremlin was the first person to show an appreciative interest in her talent.

Contentedly, Mrs Thorley turned her attention to other people. Poor Susan appeared to be enjoying herself wildly. Like Mrs Walford, Mrs Thorley thought the colour of the new dress a trifle too bright. She would have opposed such a choice by any of her girls. Yet Susan looked pretty tonight; the champagne had coloured her pale face and brightened her eyes. Even her hair looked different. It might be the lighting. This room was often let for dancing and the people who ran the place understood the value of pink shades on the lamps which stood on brackets around the walls. Far kinder than the overhead lighting from the many-candled chandeliers in the older and more gracious Assembly Rooms at Baildon.

Richard Walford had determined that Susan should have the evening of her life; and since it was an unbroken rule that any man who could dance must dance at least once with the daughter of the house, he had invited every young man he could think of, including Everard Spicer, whom Edward Taylor had driven over. Doctor Taylor had not come, for although the Hospital Committee had advertised for a resident doctor and were now comparing the applications, no decision would be reached until next week.

Diana never lacked partners, nor, despite her extra inches, did Deborah, whose musical ear made her a good dancer and who was liked by men, though she was not a girl to inspire romantic feelings, even during the most dreamy-tuned waltz. But, as always, at any kind of gathering, Caroline was the centre of attraction. Close your eyes and you could generally tell whereabouts in the big room Caroline was; she could dance and talk at the same time, and there'd be a boom of delighted masculine laughter, and Caroline's ripple of merriment. Mrs Thorley noticed, with slight disapproval, for despite her unconventional way of taking to business she was conventional over smaller things, that Caroline was dancing rather too often, and in a manner far from sedate, with one of the young men a stranger until this evening.

She had no need to be reminded of his name, for Susan had made that introduction, with a faintly proprietorial air. "My cousin, Mr Frederick Ingram." Shortly afterwards, across the carnation-laden table, Mrs Thorley had heard that young man say, "I'm Freddy to my friends." Innocuous enough in the circumstances, he was with his relatives and their friends; but something jarred; there was a touch of that false bonhomie which she had experienced in the past, in the bad days, when some of Stephen's friends had been, to say the least, dubious. Now she encountered it occasionally in the commercial travellers who sold cattle food.

Once, taking a corner, Freddy-to-my-friends swung Caroline clean off her feet; some petticoat showed, and more of a white lace stockinged leg than was seemly.

And not long after, in another dance, Caroline, with that same young man, had stopped to laugh, leaning back against his arm.

Well, he was only a transient. And there, she presently learned from Mrs Gordon, she was wrong—though she had been right about the commerical traveller aura. Frederick Ingram did represent a wine company—a very respectable firm, Hodge and Baker; and because he was some kind of relative and very successful, Mr Walford had commissioned him to sell, at the same time, the product of the Sudbury Brewery.

Edward Taylor drove Everard Spicer home, feeling rather sorry for him, plainly as set on Diana as he himself was set on Caroline. But the poor chap had nothing to offer. No house, no conveyance, and only the most mediocre job. Edward, apart from his feeling for Caroline Thorley, was a hard-headed fellow and could see that the Gordons were not treating Spicer as a putative partner; had they been doing so they would have offered him a lift.

About his own position Edward was being equally rational. He had danced with Caroline several times, and laughed a lot. He saw no serious threat from Freddy Ingram. Caroline attracted men as a candle attracted moths, and she was so gay, so careless. And she was having her fling before marriage—surely the better way.

After some deceptively mild weather, primroses studding the banks, hazel catkins nodding yellow and the birds mating—which was the real, ancient significance of St Valentine's Day—the weather had changed. Frost-sharpened stars sparkled in the sky and the wind blew cold.

"If I might suggest," Mr Fremlin said, "my carriage is here. Miss Lavinia tells me that she feels the cold very much and that Miss Thorley can drive; so if you would allow me to convey Miss Lavinia and yourself it would give me much pleasure."

Lavinia was not susceptible to cold; she spent hours in the unheated attic which she now called her studio; she took her long lonely walks in all weathers.

"A very kind offer, Mr Fremlin, but it would take you at least six miles out of your way."

"Nothing to horses habitually overfed and little exercised."

"I will accompany Lavinia, Mamma," Diana said.

"Very well, my dear. Deborah, what about you? If you fancy a drive in a carriage . . . I am not nervous."

"Thank you, no," Deb said with some emphasis.

A carriage with its own coachman always took precedence over a mere trap and it was some minutes before Mrs Thorley's was brought round.

"Let me drive, Mamma, *please*. We'll show *them!*"

Deb had a way with horses; she'd never struck one in her life, not even the light, half-playful flick of whip that was so usual. She talked to them in a peculiar language that they seemed to understand; and since the horse which drew the trap was making for home, and those which drew the carriage were, by their reckoning, going in the wrong direction, at what in Suffolk was called a hill, a slight rise out of the flat land, they overtook the carriage and once it was behind Deborah ceased her chatter to the horse, the Oops there, get along; Ya, best foot forward; hup, yup! Now and again glancing over her shoulder, to see that she was well ahead, Deb said:

"Isn't he—Mr. Fremlin—a bit odd?"

"I had no opportunity of judging, Deb. In what way, odd?"

"There's something—well, to me almost repulsive about him. Slimy. The voice. Insinuating. Did you not notice?"

"How could I? He was introduced to me and then I

had no speech with him until he offered to drive me— and Lavinia—home."

"Well, I did. As a matter of fact I thought Lavinia had got stuck with him. And she isn't very good yet at managing, so I took James Gordon across. He's such a good dancer; he could dance with a barrel of beer, and Lavinia must learn sometime. You can't sit out forever . . . James did absolutely the right thing; he asked Lavinia to dance; and Mr Fremlin asked me. And I told a thundering lie. I said I'd ricked my ankle and would like to rest for a bit. So we sat and talked. There was this, oh, I don't know how to explain it, Mamma; something about him that repels. Some people feel that way about cats, or spiders." She did not name the things which she most abominated, went, in fact, quite senseless about.

"It is unlike you, Deb, to be so fanciful."

"Well, we all have our little weaknesses," Deb said. And then, Oops, boy, pick your feet up!

Mr Walford's hiss, *Shussh* as they approached the house, was completely unnecessary; they were all moving like mice. They'd all had a wonderful time—the host, who had just for once broken out of and let himself go; Richard, who had danced five times with Diana, and Susan, who had danced every dance and had a quite dazzling party.

The house was curiously silent. Dead. Separately or in pairs they had absented themselves and always come back, if not to a welcome, at least a fretful recognition of the fact that they had been away and were now back. Tonight nothing stirred. Thankfully they tiptoed away to their beds. Mamma was asleep.

Mamma was asleep forever, they learned in the morning.

Everything had been absolutely as usual, Nurse Hardy said. Mrs Walford had enjoyed her dinner, been made comfortable and dropped off to sleep. A lovely way to go.

*

"There you are," Doctor Taylor said, triumphantly to his son, "I knew her heart was weak."

A letter for Mrs Thorley, written on very thin paper, with very black ink and in a hand as plain as print.

Dear Mrs Thorley,
  My son had recently the privilege of meeting you and your daughters. Were I not so infirm, I would have called upon you.

Something slightly wrong there, Mrs Thorley thought; it was for the earlier resident in a district to call upon the newcomer. But perhaps living in India explained that.

  I should however, be delighted to make your acquaintance and if you could spare time for a short visit on any afternoon convenient to you I should be most deeply obliged. I could send the carriage should you wish it.

Yours sincerely,
Penelope Fremlin.

Mr Walford had spoken of the friendlessness of Mr Fremlin; and now Mrs Thorley visualised an old woman—she must be old to be his mother—in some way afflicted, yearning for contact with her neighbours. Also, she admitted to herself, she was curious, so she wrote back that she would call, at three o'clock on the following Monday and that she would drive herself.

"Am I not invited, Mamma?" Lavinia asked,

showing a natural emotion—disappointment. "Mr Fremlin mentioned the pictures at Abbas and promised that I should see them."

"Only I am invited this time, my dear."

Abbas Hall was even more remote than Gad's; it was invisible from the road, standing at the end of a half-mile-long avenue of elms. It had been built on the site of, and partly from the stones of, an old nunnery. Some ruins remained, a line of arches, some piers of stone, rearing up from smooth green lawns. So far as one could see approaching the front of the house, there were no flowerbeds, and Mrs Thorley, who cherished her roses and her herbaceous borders, thought that this lack combined with stone to give the place a cheerless appearance. To look out of any window on this side of the house must be rather like looking out over a graveyard.

She was expected; before she had reined in a man appeared to take charge of her horse and trap. His clothes were those of an ordinary English stable-yard man, but his face was dark. He had not merely been in India, he was Indian. And so was the man who opened the door before she had mounted the three semicircular steps.

The hall was wide and high and very grand. Beautiful rugs lay on the marble floor; stags' heads and other trophies of the chase decorated the walls, interspersed by old weapons, pieces of old armour, and a few dark pictures. She had time only for one glance.

The servant said, "If you plizz, madam, this way."

Certainly Mr Fremlin had pictures; the corridor, as wide as a room, and lighted by several windows, all looking out onto the grass and the ruins, was lined with pictures, brighter and more colourful than the few in the hall. To her, walking past, they were merely flashes of colour, but she thought that if Mr. Fremlin kept his promise and invited Lavinia to see them, the girl was in for a treat.

But mainly, as she advanced, Mrs Thorley was conscious of the smell of the place; something heavy and spicy, half attractive, but only half; under the sweetness lay something else which for the moment Mrs Thorley could not find a name for . . .

Another door.

"Mizz Thorley, Mem."

It was almost as though he had opened the door of an oven. An enormous fire blazed on the hearth and there were, in addition three lamps, necessary because heavy curtains were drawn across the windows. The room was no bigger than the general living room at Gad's, and it seemed to be full of flowers, great bowls, not only of the carnations which could—as Mr Walford had proved—be obtained, even in winter, but lilies.

Near the fire two large winged armchairs were placed; and one was occupied.

"It was kind of you to come, Mrs Thorley. Please excuse me that I do not rise. I am somewhat lame."

The lamps were so placed that only the firelight shone on the occupied chair and what sat there might have been a heap of cobwebby lace, for even in this overheated room, Mrs Fremlin was all wrapped about. Out of the bundle a hand was extended; not a hand, a bird's claw, so delicate, so frail. And despite everything, cold.

"It was kind of you to invite me," Mrs Thorley said. Except for the suddenly oppressive weight of her sealskin coat, she was perfectly at ease. She had been born into a class absolutely sure of itself, married well; been dragged down, survived. Many another woman, she knew, passing through that impressive hall and the picture gallery, ushered into this inner sanctum and invited to sit down—but not to remove her coat—would have sat there, sweltering. She did not. She said, "I will take off my coat," and did so, laying it on another chair. The bundle said:

"You find the room warm? Personally I find the English winter insufferable. I am never warm." It was a firm, positive voice, with a lilt to it. Mrs Thorley remembered the lilt in Mr Fremlin's, almost undetectable, yet there. In his mother it was far more marked.

"Coming to East Anglia from India you must notice the cold very much."

"I am not only from India. I am *of* India. I wished you to see for yourself. Before I requested a favour of you." The two incredibly delicate hands moved, pushed back some of the enshrouding lace, and Mrs Thorley's eyes, now adjusting to the dim light, saw a face, old, but still of cameo clarity, and pale: paler than Lavinia, always suspected of being anaemic, paler than Susan Walford, who until last week so seldom went out-of-doors; but it was a different pallor. Mrs Thorley could find no word for it; but nowhere, not even in the polyglot communities of Continental watering places, could Mrs Fremlin have been mistaken for a woman of purely European origin.

"You are shocked, Mrs Thorley?"

"Of course not."

"Most people are," Mrs Fremlin said drily. "The more so because I am not pure Indian. You know what is said of mongrels—of both breeds the worst qualities and the good ones of neither! Then I compound the fault. I had beauty when I was young, and I married an Englishman. Of good family, but no wealth. No expectations that he knew of. Ah! You will take tea?"

Very pale tea with a faintly floral flavour; jasmine? mock-orange?

Having poured it into cups of the utmost delicacy, the old woman took up her tale, bridging some years in silence.

"I have been truly blessed in my son. Of the dead let no ill be spoken; but had the inheritance fallen to my husband, he would have come alone. And he would have been wise. Johnny refused to do that. Unless I came too, he would not come. And I, wishing him to take his proper place in the world, came. A mistake indeed. There is more prejudice here than in India."

"I am sorry," Mrs Thorley said, shouldering the fault of her countrymen. She was not conscious of feeling any prejudice herself; yet her thoughts slid away to Deborah, whose response to Mr Fremlin had been blindly instinctive; a bit odd; slimy; insinuating; she'd avoided dancing with him; refused to ride in his carriage.

The old woman had spoken of asking a favour and Mrs Thorley decided to grant it if she could and immediately, upon that thought, ran full tilt into the prejudice which she had not recognised with herself.

Not marriage!

What small information she possessed about India had drifted to her through missionary propaganda; if only enough money could be raised, enough missionaries found, the Indians would stop worshipping cows and burning live widows with the bodies of the husbands; Indian men would give up their harems where wretched women lived in purdah. That kind of thing. And if Mr Fremlin had conceived the mad idea of marrying Lavinia, she would oppose him with all her might, without actually understanding why.

"What I wished to ask of you, Mrs Thorley is that your daughter—the youngest, I think—Lavinia? should be allowed to visit. My son was greatly impressed by her. She has talent. We both feel that it should be fostered. As you see, this house has many pictures; the ceiling of the drawing room was painted by Angelica Kauffmann. My son felt that your daughter should see such things."

"How can he know that she has talent?" A natural question enough, for he'd never seen any of Lavinia's work.

"From her talk—they spent much time together. Mrs Thorley, could anyone have spent an evening with William Shakespeare and not recognised genius—without seeing a word he had written?"

For Mrs Thorley an unanswerable question. She had never made any pretence at intellectualism; as a child she had been introduced by her governess to the Lamb's *Tales from Shakespeare* and enjoyed them moderately; in later life she had seen performances of the plays, and to be truthful, found some of them boring; of William Shakespeare and his effect upon a person meeting him casually, she could make no mental image at all.

"Lavinia is very young," she said.

Mrs Fremlin, pulling the lacy wool, the woolly lace closer about her head, said:

"Mrs Thorley, I understand. Any kind of—alliance is quite out of the question. So much misery has been caused . . . We intend to stay here only until the estate is disposed of. We may go to Brazil. There, my son says, colour is so much in the melting pot, and wealth so important . . ." She left that sentence unfinished and stirring a little amongst her wrappings said, "So you see, if your daughter wishes to see one of the best collections in private hands we have no time to waste. Also—one's own wishes should be subsidary, of course—my son is often absent and I should much welcome the company of a girl young enough to be free of prejudice; and with talent. You, I understand, have four daughters; imagine having none, and the prospect of a grand-daughter somewhat remote."

Mrs Thorley gave the matter her most serious consideration and could see nothing against the proposition. Lavinia had always, by her very nature, been lonely, and here was a woman made lonely by circumstance. And her one fleeting suspicion—inspired by missionary talk about the poor little child brides of India—had been set at rest by Mrs Fremlin's remark about any kind of alliance being out of the question. Besides, Lavinia was so immature; if Mrs. Thorley had understood the missionary lectures aright the child brides of India, young as they sounded, were at least nubile.

And she rather liked Mrs. Fremlin, felt sorry for her. She said warmly:

"Of course Lavinia may visit you. It will be most pleasant for her. She will probably wish to bring some of her pictures. I hope you will not be disappointed in them. I find them rather—strange."

"And you are an artist yourself?"

How did she know that?

"I never made such a claim. I drew a little, at one time, in a purely conventional way."

Patterns, she thought; for potters and dressmakers; a commerical exercise which had made her unwilling ever to touch pencil or paint brush again.

"This is Monday," Mrs Fremlin said. "Johnny will not be back here until Thursday at the very earliest. Would you allow her to come tomorrow. I would send the carriage."

They'd all, of course, wearing decent black, attended Mrs Walford's funeral and now Diana was comforting poor Susan, helping her with mourning that was not downright ugly; Deb was occupied in the garden, pruning the roses and Caroline was rearranging the bedroom which she had delightedly seen cleared when Lavinia moved her painting things up to the attic. Caroline, too, was planning some alleviation of the Walfords' mourning. "After all, Mamma, if you remember, we had Diana's small private party. I think to ask the Walfords who could never get out together, and Freddy Ingram—who is after all, related—would be only kind."

They all, except Lavinia, were enmeshed in ordinary life. And when the carriage came, delivering a great wide basketful of carnations and lilies, and collecting Lavinia, who had taken the smallest valise in the house, just enough for night-clothes . . . but under her other arm a bulging portfolio, Mrs Thorley thought: Yes, she will have something, too.

So it began.

For Richard Walford and Edward Taylor that spring would have been a halcyon time but for the existence of Everard Spicer and Freddy Ingram, who kept cropping up. Not unnaturally. So far as possible all good hostesses liked to keep some kind of balance between the sexes, and Susan and Deborah must be provided for; yet inevitably Everard and Diana seemed to pair off, and Freddy and Caroline. Constituting no *real* threat, since neither had much to offer. Richard and Edward were alike in many ways and it was significant that even now, brought into close and frequent contact, each respected the other, while privately thinking him rather a dull dog. Yet, after each faintly unsatisfactory gathering together, both solid young men entertained the same thought. Richard's apparent rival was little more than a lawyer's clerk, and lived in lodgings; Edward's was no more than a commercial traveller, and lived in lodgings.

Susan had once suggested that Freddy should be invited to live in the big house, which, now that Mamma had gone, did seem empty at times; but Mr Walford had repudiated that idea, looking rather slyly at his son.

"I think we should wait a little. Richard may be thinking of marriage, the house would not be too large then."

Mr Walford was one of the men who heartily admired Mrs Thorley and imagined that he saw many of her qualities reflected in her daughter. Little money or none! Knowledgeable men had agreed that George Thorley, for all that he'd lived in style, couldn't have left *much*, otherwise his widow could have sat back and folded her hands; and in any case Diana was only his stepdaughter. But that did not matter; Richard had the brewery behind him. And Susan would have two thousand pounds as well as shares in the Light Suffolk Railway, which navvies were already hacking out towards the coast.

Edward Taylor was in an equally sound position; in

fact he had the whole beautiful house in St. Giles' Square to himself. If anything, too much to himself, for his father had taken Hattie with him and so far Edward had not been able to replace her. He was cared for, after a fashion, by a series of women from the Lane who could only spare odd hours, and cooked— when they did cook—like the devil. To his own dismay he found himself ceasing to make excuses for them; a woman who had nothing but an open fire, a saucepan and a frying pan to work with should, one might have supposed, be able to boil a dumpling, fry an egg. But they couldn't, and a horrible suspicion was dawning upon him—they lived in the Lane because they were unfit for any other place. And proper, competent housekeepers avoided taking service in doctors' households where hours were so irregular. He now realized how right his father had been in calling Hattie a treasure and in persuading her to go with him.

Edward now took his main, mid-day meal at The Angel, and there was trouble if he were late. All this, all that, had been eaten, he'd have to make do ...

Look on the bright side, he admonished himself. He now had more free time because the hospital doctor, young, strong, eager, was prepared to work, day and night, and take his free time in a block of forty-eight hours. He had a home—his own or his parents' he never revealed—in Bermondsey and liked to catch the up train at four o'clock in the afternoon of Friday. Down trains on Sunday were fewer and slower, but starting at two o'clock, he was back on duty by seven.

"She's a gonner," Joe Snell said, looking with disgust at what had seemed the most promising heifer of the herd, struggling, painfully and ineffectually, to give birth to a calf which was presenting itself hind legs first. It was a rare, but not unknown condition, and it was always fatal. Any young animal, in the ordinary way, came almost egg-shaped, head first, front legs, or paws, neatly tucked under; they slipped out. The occasional one went wrong, backside and hind legs blocking the passage. And there was nothing anybody could do about it.

Mrs Thorley dead ignorant, said, "We must do something, Joe."

"What, ma'am?"

"Help her, poor thing." The heifer struggled and moaned; with each pang and thrust the hindquarters and back legs of the calf were made visible. Then there was the retraction.

Mrs Thorley was making her routine visit in the bright morning light. She never failed. She trusted Joe absolutely, he knew that, but if anything she was more conscientious—more often on the spot—than Master had been.

Now she pushed back her sleeves almost to the shoulder and set her face; the calf's hindquarters, awkward legs, presented themselves at the next thrust and she grabbed, pulled firmly but gently, moved her hands inwards towards where the main body lay; and there the calf was, safely delivered on to the clean straw. And a heifer into the bargain.

"You're a masterpiece, ma'am, if I may say so," Joe said. "Now, if you'd just come across to my place, there's always a kettle on the hob."

"I'll manage with a bucket, thank you. You see, Joe, I'd prefer nobody to know about this . . . operation. I have enough nicknames, without being called a cow midwife."

He wondered how she knew the things that were said about her now that the novelty and the faint respect that mourning evoked had worn off. Coarse-minded, coarse-tongued men put the worst possible construction upon her leaving Mr Corby's saleyard for Mr Larkin—Larkin was a notorious womaniser. To some extent, Joe, when he encountered such jibes, had pretended to be in accord: Well, she'd upped his wage and had his cottage rethatched. It didn't do, in a small community, to seem different, or to have any regard for other than things you could touch and handle. Now, seeing her dowse her arms in a bucket of cold water and dry them on a bit of sacking, he thought: Next chap say a disrespectful word about her, I'll knock flat.

All that spring and summer Lavinia came and went between Abbas and Gad's. Sometimes simply to keep Mrs Fremlin company, sometimes to meet people—all with difficult foreign names. Contact with this wider world had done little to change her behaviour at home.

Once, coming back with a portfolio even more bulging than usual, she'd almost dropped it and some pages slipped out. Mrs Thorley caught a glimpse of some very strange drawings; figures with an unnatural number of arms, legs, breasts; but before she could really observe them, Lavinia snatched them away and said that Mrs Fremlin had drawn them. For it seemed that Mrs Fremlin, before age had quenched her, had been an artist, too.

Then, in late May, Mr Fremlin had taken one of Lavinia's pictures to London, and sold it for fifty pounds.

To whom?

Some dealer in Bond Street or somewhere.

Fifty pounds! It seemed a vast sum of money to Diana and Caroline, who never had enough to spend on their wardrobes; and to Deborah, who was slowly and painfully saving up to buy a proper hunter, one day; and to Mrs Thorley, who had sold what she still thought of as proper drawings for such pitiable sums. Lavinia was entirely unimpressed.

"I would like to keep about ten pounds for materials," she said. "You can have the rest, Mamma."

"I shall bank it—your name, my dear." For there was always the possibility that a girl so undeveloped of body, so withdrawn in the company of ordinary people, might not find a husband.

"Oh, Mr Fremlin thinks he can sell others," Lavinia said with the utmost indifference.

That evening Mrs Thorley looked again at the picture of poppies, and at some of Lavinia's earlier gifts to her. All, by her reckoning, a little queer, out of proportion, out of perspective, and some in colours untrue to nature; but the hostile faces which seemed to come and go in the hearts of the poppies were strangest of all—a talent developing rapidly; and one could not, in view of the fifty pounds, say on the wrong lines. Perhaps what Lavinia did was to set the imagination to work. Twice before the poppy picture had seemed to Mrs Thorley to have an inner meaning; once the faces of men in the Corn Exchange and on the Cattle Market; once as all faces appeared to a shy girl; and now they had meaning again, calling to mind the imminence of the South Suffolk Cattle Show, where the young bull, Gad's Glory, was to make his debut, and where she would appear, the first woman, the only woman to take her place in the enclosure reserved for exhibitors. A worse ordeal than the Exchange or the Market, because there would be thousands of faces, many of them those of competitors, and if Gad's Glory did what was expected of him, there'd be plenty of hostility . . .

She had done a lot of arithmetic and a good deal of heartsearching about the business of exhibiting cattle and decided upon half-measures. Distant shows she would avoid; they brought renown but little monetary return; she decided to enter and attend only those within easy reach, enough to keep the herd's name alive and George's memory green.

By this time Everard Spicer was almost one of the family. Diana's infatuation had increased rather than lessened. The Gordons, she felt, were most unfair to him, making him keep the office open every Saturday until noon. And his lodgings, found for him by Mrs Gordon, intent upon doing a good turn to an old acquaintance living in much reduced circumstances, were truly deplorable. Diana had forgotten that in Leicester her mother had sometimes let a room, or even two, and spoke harshly about amateur landladies.

"People who do things just for pin money never do them properly. Everard would be far better off at Mrs Bolton's."

"Is there any reason why he should not move?" Mrs Thorley asked. Something about the words amateur and pin money stung a little.

"Only the cost, Mamma. Believe it or not Mrs. Bolton now charges fifteen shillings a week. The railway men have sent prices soaring. And Everard is trying to *save*."

A sudden hot blush ran up from the base of Diana's neck to her hair-line. It receded just as quickly, but Mrs Thorley had read the message.

"Well, my dear," she said, bringing this conversation back to where it had begun, "by all means fetch him, bring him back and give him a few good meals. Food, thank God, is one thing we are not short of."

So, almost every Saturday Diana with the small pony and trap waited outside the office and transported Everard to another world. He was not actually short of friends; a young man with the right clothes, manners, voice had entry to many homes, but he had never chanced to meet a girl half as attractive as Diana, or half as fond and undemanding. By June he was as much in love with her as he could be with anyone and had enough faith in his love to ignore something which James Gordon let slip. Quite out of order, unprofessional, unethical. "There's no real money there, old boy. Five hundred apiece, so the will read; and I rather doubt whether, if they all got married tomorrow, the ready cash would be available."

Everard said, "Oh," in a noncommittal voice; but he looked disgusted and he had a face singularly suited to take on an expression of disgust. The look was provoked, not as James Gordon imagined, by the small size of the dowry but by the breach of etiquette committed by the mention of such a confidential matter to one who was not even a member of the firm. Yet!

"Now Susan Walford—I bet her papa would come down with something handsome," James said.

In Everard anger flared; he longed to say: You and your family chose to lodge me with an old woman who has forgotten what a square meal looks like; you and your father choose my work—always the dullest and dreariest; I'm damned if you shall choose my wife! But he restrained himself and said stiffly:

"I happen to prefer Diana."

"So does somebody else we know of," James said with a mischievous grin.

Everard had been half aware of Richard Walford as a rival and now that he came to think about it he perceived a real threat. Diana was often at Sudbury, sometimes, since Mrs Walford's death, staying overnight. Ostensibly visiting Susan; but who knew?

He took stock of the whole situation. In July, Diana would be eighteen. She could afford to wait two years; but would she? With Richard able to marry her this year? Mr Walford would approve; he always spoke very highly of Diana, saying how faithfully she had made visits and cheered Susan when she was so tied. And he seemed to expect Richard to marry soon. That had come out in some casual talk—in Mrs Thorley's crimson-papered dining room. Something about having the big old house at Sudbury completely redecorated. Better wait a little and see, Mr Walford said, people had differing tastes and the lady of the house should be able to give her choice full range. And his glance—yes, his glance had slid slyly about, linking his son with Diana. Susan must be taken into account, too. A girl's best friend often had influence . . .

Look into the future; see it at its least promising; by staying in his uncomfortable—but cheap—lodging and saving every possible penny, at the end of two years he would have saved enough to hire a small but decent house and buy the absolutely necessary furniture. Diana would have at the least twenty-five pounds a year, which would buy her clothes. One could not expect her to scrub and scour, but cleaning women could be hired very cheaply.

They could manage.

They would have no need to manage! For before two years were out the half-promise of a partnership would have materialised. He was already doing most of James' work, as well as his own; and he had the queer idea that the Gordons were trying him out, making him serve, as it were, an apprenticeship.

And in a way being engaged would mean not only security, but economy. A girl firmly betrothed and with an engagement ring on her finger was allowed some latitude; she could, for example, attend a concert in the Assembly Rooms, or a matinée at the theatre without a third person in attendance. Mrs Thorley was usually lenient in many ways, strictly conventional in others—rightly so, of course—and never yet had he and Diana appeared in public, *à deux*. Having no home in which to entertain, unable to afford a hired place, he had done his best to make some return for hospitality, and it had invariably meant three, even four seats at any entertainment.

Early on the Monday morning before the South Suffolk Cattle Show, which always took place on the first Thursday in June, Diana, delivering Everard at the office, just as the clock in St Mary's church tower struck nine, said, "Here we are, dead on time. Everard, do try to get away on Thursday afternoon. Nobody will do business that day. And Mamma needs support. Nobody would believe it, but she is nervous about some things. And this is her first show. And if that young bull—Gad's Glory—does any good, we'll have a wonderful party afterwards. I do so want you to be there."

"I will try. You know . . . I'd do anything within my power to please you, Diana. Dear Diana."

Nine o'clock on a Monday morning was not the best time for romantic speeches, but something kindled.

"I know. As I would for you, darling Everard."

All that had lain, suppressed, shrouded, leaped into the full light of morning, unashamed, triumphant. Moved by a mutual impulse they leaned forward, kissed.

Now, fully committed, they could speak of marriage. Would she mind waiting two years? Two years! She was prepared to wait forever; gladly, gladly. And of course, by all the rules that governed such an occasion, he must ask her Mamma's consent. To that Diana could say truly that Mamma, not being blind, knew how things were going and, had she disapproved, would have shown it long before now.

"And if it could be arranged," Diana said, "I mean asking Mamma is only a formality . . . the party after the Show could be our engagement party. Wouldn't that be wonderful?"

Not only wonderful, but fitting, for of her little group Diana was the oldest member—except poor Susan—not to be yet betrothed. Barbara Catchpole, Charlotte Anderson, Margaret Agnew, all engaged, wearing with pride their engagement rings and saying: You next, darling. Now it had happened.

"It would be wonderful. But dearest, I shall not be able to ask your Mamma's consent before Thursday—even if I get away then. And even about that I am not sure, yet."

"You could write."

"Yes, I could do that." And some things were more easily put down on paper than said face to face.

"And even if you can't manage to get to the Show—but oh, I do so hope, you can . . . I'd pick you up here at six o'clock."

Unnoticed, the hands of St Mary's clock had crept forward, reached the end of its first quarter circle; boomed out the time; fifteen minutes past nine; and Mr Gordon, who prided himself on his punctuality, rounded the corner.

He was getting on in years—he'd married late and there had been two little boys before James; one had succumbed to the croup, and one to scarlet fever; James had survived and, merely by surviving, earned more indulgence than many men showed towards the one who was to succeed them. James could be very clever when he chose, but he was a gadabout. Why not? Mr Gordon could afford, and was indeed proud of, a gadabout son. And he had accepted Everard Spicer to do the donkey work. But he did not like him; hadn't from the first. Too superior; too much inclined to look down the nose which was so perfectly shaped for looking down upon. Many people, wishing to make a will, or driven by this or that dispute to seek a lawyer's services, felt strange, a little nervous; they needed the reassurance of the hearty, hail-fellow-well-met manner which Mr Gordon could assume at will, and which came to James as naturally as breathing. Everard was always the lawyer, correct, formal. He was a very good lawyer, and they were lucky to get him so cheaply—the prospect of a possible partnership had been the lure there; but he'd have to wait a long time . . . perhaps forever.

Mr Gordon would have liked young Spicer more had the young man been open to correction or rebuke, but his work was always faultless and if an argument arose over any point, he could always prove himself right.

However, this morning, just for once he'd put himself in the wrong.

Approaching the little trap Mr Gordon raised his hat and said:

"Good morning, Miss Osborne." He was one of the few who could always distinguish Osborne from Thorley. "Morning, Spicer." There was a marked change, a departure from geniality in his manner. He glanced up at St Mary's clock, took out his watch and ostentatiously checked it. Inside the office he said sourly, "Since when has the week-end extended well into Monday morning?"

Everard's manner remained respectful:

"I'm sorry, sir." But his look showed clearly what he thought of such pettiness.

That so small a lapse should have been noticed, let alone rebuked, was very irksome; but he soon forgot about it as he composed in his mind the letter he would write to Mrs Thorley—and thought about the ring. Diana deserved, and must have a ring which she could display with pride; but how could he afford one? He gulped down his luncheon—an egg that had been too old to poach well, on a piece of sodden toast—and went into the High Street, to study the window of the only jeweller in Baildon.

There were rings to suit most purses except very deep ones; Mr Collins did not cater for the rich; in his display there were only two rings priced above twenty pounds, one at twenty-two, one at the twenty-five, and frankly neither of them was worthy, though both were as much, as far out Everard's reach as if they had been a hundred.

He realised that he had been very rash, very premature. He had not given the ring a thought. He had no-one from whom he could borrow. He had a few things which he could sell, or pawn; all presents from his godfather; a gold half hunter; cuff-links and studs and the signet ring he wore on his little finger. People who sold things because they needed money quickly never got a fair price, he knew that; about pawnshops he knew nothing at all. He'd never seen one in Baildon—if one existed it would be in the Lane.

He might gain a little time by saying that Collins hadn't a ring good enough, and ask Diana to wear, as a token, a temporary substitute, the one from his own finger. But the only point in gaining time was to have some attainable object in view. Being poor was the very Devil and he regretted having let his feelings run away with him.

In a dejected state of mind he sat down to write to Mrs Thorley; his disciplined mind came to his aid;

well-composed sentences expressing all the correct sentiments, flowed smoothly. It was a model letter.

"I imagine you know what this is about," Mrs Thorley said, having read it with approval.

Blushing, Diana said, "Well, Everard did intimate . . ."

"I consider it very sensible of him to suggest waiting until he is more established."

"That was understood, Mamma. And two years is not long. But if you do approve, I thought it would be pleasant—and an economy—to combine our after-the-Show party with the announcement of the engagement."

"We're not yet sure about Gad's Glory, my dear. I was proposing only a spur-of-the-moment celebration, if he won. But you are quite right. We must, in any case, entertain Mr van Haagen."

Mr van Haagen was Dutch, and some weeks earlier had written a letter to a dead man—George Thorley—from whom at some time in the past he had bought a young bull and a cow. He wrote, in perfect if rather stilted English, that his experiments in cross-breeding of Durham and Friesian had been completely successful. He had not come hastily to this conclusion; it had taken some years. He hoped that Mr Thorley remembered him after so long a time. And he was sure that Mr Thorley would be interested in what he had learned about cross-breeding; which was that the dam had more effect upon the offspring than the sire. "Bearing out the truth of an old saying, my dear Mr Thorley; a jackass could sire a race horse should the mare be good enough. So I come to buy cows."

Mrs Thorley had written back, explaining that her husband was dead, but that since she had kept the herd together, she could offer Mr van Haagen a choice of promising young cows. And as his proposed date for the visit coincided with the South Suffolk Cattle Show when accommodation would be difficult to find in Bail-

don, invited him to stay at Gad's. He might find the
Show interesting.

On Tuesday, quite early for him, James Gordon
strolled into the wretched cubby-hole which was Everard's office. He perched in a negligent way on the
edge of the desk and said:

"I'm taking the day off, old boy. Newmarket. I'd
only two fixtures. See to them for me, will you?" He
slapped a scribbled paper on to the desk.

"Of course," Everard said, thinking: Oh how enviable; to be going off, care-free, heart-free to Newmarket
Heath on a sunny June day.

Swinging a leg, James said, "All right then," and felt
a pang of compassion, almost of self-reproach. Not
that he was to blame. His father had kept saying things
like, "Well enjoy yourself while you can," and "I can't
last forever, you know," and, "Honestly, what you'll
need, dear boy, is a reliable partner."

So, by chance, he'd met Everard again and seen in
him the best possible future partner; and it was not his
fault that things had gone a bit awkward.

Trying to make up for all that had gone awkward,
James Gordon said:

"Tell you what; I'll put five bob on the favourite for
you. Reward for virtue; dealing with old Mrs. Rorke."
He tapped the paper.

Something very near to mental derangement fell
upon Everard. He said, "Thanks, James, but I'll make
my own bet. Have you a list of runners?"

James hauled a piece of printed paper from his
pocket.

Like every inexperienced punter Everard went by
names. And one struck him. Laurel's Lad. Laurel;
Daphne; Daphnis, taught by Diana. The connection
was as tenuous as a connection could be, but it was the
only one.

He reached into his pocket and took out a precious
half sovereign.

"Put this for me on Laurel's Lad."

"Hell's afire, Everard! A rank outsider. Couldn't win a sack race."

"It's the only one I fancy."

It was already as lost as though Everard had thrown it into the river. But James did as he was told, put Everard's ten shillings on Laurel's Lad, and then, keeping his promise, remembering Mrs Rorke, five shillings for Everard, two pounds for himself on the favourite which did win, but odds against so that the gain was minuscule. In a later race Laurel's Lad appeared to stroll home.

"Old boy," James said, scattering sovereigns on the tidy desk. "You must have access to a crystal ball! I'll consult you before I make another bet." He then added a wise and well-meant warning—in Everard's case unnecessary—about not letting beginner's luck go to his head and turn into a real gambler.

Fifty pounds. And the best ring on offer in Baildon was the one at twenty-five pounds which he had despised when it was far out of reach. And tomorrow was Thursday. Well he'd just have to tell Diana that Collins had nothing good enough, but that he was having a selection sent down.

Mr Collins showed no resentment at being told that what he had in the window was not good enough for young Mr Spicer, who though occupying a pretty humble post at Gordon and Son was in every other respect a toff.

"I don't put everything in the window, sir. I only display what I can afford to insure. I have superior articles. If you would just come through." He led the way into a room occupied by a work-bench—for he mended clocks and watches—and a safe.

"May I ask what kind of ring you had in mind? Up to what price?"

"Forty pounds." And that would leave ten towards the house rent, the furniture.

"Umm," the jeweller said, a trifle disappointed. Neither quite one thing nor the other. People who despised a twenty-five-pound ring should, he thought, be prepared to go to fifty and over. Still, forty was something. Indicating that Everard should sit on the stool by the work-table, Mr Collins fiddled about with the door of his safe and then, keeping his body between his potential customer and what was in the safe, he groped about inside it.

There was nothing dishonest in this side of his business. There was in fact, working at the back of the network, great delicacy of feeling. Everywhere, all over the country, there were ladies—like Everard's landlady, come down in the world, anxious to sell a trinket, but not to advertise the fact. So jewellers in quite distant places made exchanges. In addition to the ladies who were feeling the pinch of rising prices, there were the French who time after time had been obliged to flee their native country in what they stood up in—and their jewels.

Living as he did in a quiet, small country town Mr Collins' part of this network was that of collector, rather than distributor; he bought what he could, very cheaply, exchanged for new goods; sold hardly anything directly. He was in fact awaiting the arrival of his London contact.

Burrowing like a mole he came out with three rings.

"Not new of course," he explained, laying them on the workbench amongst the entrails of clocks and watches. "Secondhand and with the added value of antiquity. Forty; forty-five; fifty. And every one of them worth ten times as much."

They were all beautiful, a vast improvement of the best in the window; but only one was Diana's, matching the red stones which danced at the end of her ear-bobs. Red stones, and diamonds alternating, a great flashing half-circle.

"That one," he said, so firmly that Mr Collins, who had lain the things out in order of merit, felt justified in saying, adjusting slightly:

"Ah. The fifty-pound one. Rubies are rarer now than diamonds. A very wise choice, if I may say so."

"I'd like it in a case," Everard said.

Some shows shifted about, but the South Suffolk always took place in Lord Stanton's park, a bit up river from the town. The ring was a great oval. At one end, under an awning and on padded benches, sat the very important people, including, on this exceptionally beautiful June day, a minor foreign royalty. At a slightly lower level along one side of the oval was the judges' stand, not much occupied since they moved about, conscientiously studying animals, even touching them. Next in grade came the stand for those exhibiting animals—they must be considered since without them there would be no show; then a stand for those who were willing to pay a shilling for a seat. And at the far end of the oval the gateway through which animals entered and left. The other side of the oval was for those who wished to watch, but could not pay.

There had been a little trouble about Mr van Haagen, who had surprised everybody at Gad's; they'd thought of him, coming up out of the past, as fairly old, Papa's contemporary—and perhaps because of the roundness of Dutch cheeses, they had visualised him as plump and red-faced. In fact he was tall, lean, young-looking, handsome; and although his spoken English was less perfect than his written, he had so much charm that Mrs Thorley was angered by the fact that some blockhead at the gateway of the exhibitors' enclosure had refused him admission. All seats were booked.

Deborah said, "Mr van Haagen can have my seat, Mamma. I'll go and pay my shilling."

"But no, my dear young lady. Easily, I find a seat." With surperb self-assurance he walked away, over to the enclosure of the important. And there, because he sounded un-English and might well be in some way connected with the honoured visitor, he was admitted without question. From his privileged position, he called and smiled and waved his programme of events and entries, making, Mrs Thorley felt, her and her family more conspicuous than they were already, which was conspicuous enough, for she had decided that since the thing must be done, it should be done in style. She and all the girls were wearing new dresses. Her own was half-mourning, a dark lavender colour with black velvet bows. It would serve as her best summer dress for several years, purple bows presently replacing the black ones. The girls were all in muslin, in varying shades of rose colour, and George wore the Highland dress which Queen Victoria's fondness for Scotland had made fashionable.

All the preliminary judging had been done earlier in the day; only potential winners were paraded now. Gad's Glory was amongst them, but victory was not yet sure. Lavinia emerged briefly from her self-absorption and said, "There is no need to worry, Mamma. He will win."

(Because I have willed it! I am only a novice yet, barely initiated; but I know the feeling of power. I have touched the ritual.)

"If he should, George, you know what to do."

"Yes, Mamma." But George had his secrets, too.

The animals paraded. Gad's Glory, Mrs Thorley reflected, was not behaving very well. He was going to be one of those bulls that needed two men, each gripping a pole, linked into the nose-ring to control him.

Diana looked about. Everard had not been able to come; Mr Gordon and James were there—at the very front of the shilling stand. They had in their selfish way left Everard to mind the office.

A man to whom Nature had given a good, resonant voice, now amplified by a wide, lily-shaped horn, shouted the judges' final decision. Gad's Glory, for all his restive behaviour, had won the coveted red ribbon and the prize of five pounds.

Every woman present and some of the men had

wondered what she would do, how she would look, crossing the space, all dung-spattered, in her dainty shoes and a dress at least twelve yards wide around the hem.

There was a little dutiful clapping; and somebody stood up in the seats of the privileged and shouted, "Goot! Goot!" Then George Thorley stepped out. He bowed to the flower-decked stand where the important sat. That he had been told to do. But he turned about, bowed to the people in the shilling stand, and then God bless his little heart—to those pressing against the rails. He took the five shining pounds in one hand, the red rosette in the other. He slipped the money into the pocket of Joe Snell's beautifully laundered smock and then took two sideway steps which made his kilt swing, to face the bull, its great head tossing and turning.

Mrs Thorley said, "Oh God," and put her hand to her mouth. But it was all right, George chose his moment and slipped the red ribbon into the head harness. Then, unharmed, thank God, he turned and made another bow, towards the place where his mother and sisters sat.

It was a perfect performance, and all but the most envious recognised it. Timing, daring style. The crowd rose to him and his course was set for the next sixty-eight years. Be bold, play to the crowd. In that one sunny afternoon was the embryo of a reckless old man who did not feel very well, whose body would have preferred slippered comfort by the fire, whose purse was thin; but who must dispense cherry brandy as freely as water, and ride a young, untried hunter.

The party at Gad's that evening was hilarious. Diana had collected Everard and he had given her the ring. Congratulations all about and Mr van Haagen saying, "Ah yes; goot! In Amsterdam are the best diamonds, so I am knowing. Is a beautiful ring and the finger worthy of it. I am happy to be sharing so happy an occasion."

It was an occasion for champagne. For little backward glances. Poor George, how he would have enjoyed the double celebration; how proud he would have been of his son. Diana thought that Papa would surely have approved of Everard. Deborah thought how Papa had always predicted great things for Gad's Glory and would have been delighted by the victory.

Susan spared a thought for her brother. Diana had confided in her as soon as Mamma had given her consent and to Susan had fallen the duty—doubly distasteful—of breaking the news to Richard. Of all the girls she knew she would best have liked Diana as a sister-in-law, and although Richard pretended not to care, saying: Well, I'm not surprised, are you? she'd seen his hurt and shared it. He was not here this evening. And despite herself Susan's heart lightened, for it meant that Freddy would have to drive her home. Edward Taylor was absent too for the lovely summer weather had produced the usual outbreaks of summer fever in the Lane.

Still, they could have danced a little, had Mr van Haagen been a dancer; but he was not. "Much to be regretted, but an art I never acquired."

Very well, they'd sing. Unfortunately that was another thing Mr van Haagen either could not do, or did not care for. "For me, no. I will sit with Madam. Not for business. That is finished this morning. With much satisfaction."

But he was their guest; something must be done to entertain him.

"Do you play cards?" Mrs Thorley asked.

"The whist? Not goot." He seemed to realise suddenly that he was being a rather unsatisfactory guest. He looked glum. Then he remembered something, and with the radiant smile which displayed his splendid teeth, he said. "With the cards I can tell fortunes."

It was not a skill which he was called upon to use often, for the circles in which he moved were composed mainly of men who were not interested in such things. He had learned to read cards from his grand-mother during long winter evenings in a lonely farm-house within sound of the sea. She had taken the business very seriously, was sometimes consulted by women, both young and old, and had made some sur-prisingly accurate forecasts. In earlier days she would probably have been accused of witchcraft. To the boy it had been a form of entertainment, rather like learn-ing another, simpler alphabet, but he, too, had occa-sionally made predictions that had been startlingly fulfilled.

The girls were all agog; the two young men re-mained aloof, politely sceptical.

"In order of age, please," Mr van Haagen said, hap-pily taking charge. There were strict rules about the whole busines; one being that to attempt to read one's own fortune was absolutely forbidden.

"Oh, don't bother about me," Mrs Thorley said. "I've had more than half my future. Besides, I must confess, I have no belief in such things."

"So! But you have not tried me yet. I am goot!" He had a brief, very brief moment of self-doubt; it must be three years since he had read the cards. Very accurate then. He could have lost the knack. No matter; all that most women wanted was something happy. He had never cheated yet because cheating was as forbidden as reading one's own fate.

"It is private," Mr van Haagen said, taking the pack of cards which somebody had produced and shuffling them expertly. "Go and sing! You, Madam, please, cut into three." He took the top card of each pile and laid it away, gathered the pack together and said, "Please, again." She did so; and again until there were nine cards in the smaller heap. Then with a flick he spread the remainder into a wide half-fan.

"Select three further. Anywhere, Madam." She obeyed. He put her twelve cards together, pushed the rest away.

He turned them over, her chosen cards, and studied

them, as one might study a page in a book. He made little adjustments to the pattern; four lines of three; three lines of four; a zigzag shape, a cross, a hollow square.

And something seemed to have happened to him. He was a different man from the rather prosaic cattle dealer with whom she had done business earlier in the day, and the cheerful stormer of privileged places in the afternoon.

"Such hard times," he said at last. "And such grief, the little boy dead. Very sad."

It was something to which she had deliberately shut her mind. The first hurt and disillusionment, the real- isation that Stephen was not only silly about money but unreliable in other ways as well. The shock had ended her lactation and made the baby dependent upon cow's milk; and milk drawn from cows kept in dark, under- ground byres was known to be bad for children. There were, however, some cows kept in Hyde Park, eating green grass, enjoying the sunshine. A long trudge every day, but she'd made it. Uselessly as it proved. The little boy had sickened and died.

"There is more trouble. You will overcome it, using good sense and moderation . . . That is to be remem- bered, Madam; moderation in all things, working, eating, drinking, all things." He shifted two cards. "Of money, plenty. Much successes, as today's. Yes, of success plenty." He bore down on that point because he could not see for her the serenity of old age. He shifted the cards again and said, "A thing to decide, Madam. Yes, a decision of the most momentous. Of family, not business." He moved two cards and looked puzzled. "It is with this as with all things, just so much and no more. The decision and a time of," he lifted his hand and made a see-sawing motion in the air. "But all will be well, with moderation. Money, goot. Health always with moderation—goot. And that is all they say to me, for you, Madam, this evening. Thank you."

"Me next," Susan Walford said. "I'm older than Diana."

Unobtrusively Mrs Thorley moved to another chair, well within hearing distance. Mr van Haagen's mention of her lost child had dented her scepticism and if he said anything likely to upset any of the girls she was ready to intercept at once.

Susan went through the preliminary of cutting the cards and Mr van Haagen, a kindly man at heart, was pleased to see that her immediate future was bright.

"Ah, for you a courtship. How am I to say it? Of the whirlwind? Yes. And marriage soon. Most happy." He shifted a card or two and did not like what he saw. But he adhered to his old grandmother's rule—Tell the pleasant, but not the untrue; tell the true, but not the unpleasant. "Of money you will not lack," he said, and then fell back on repetition. "Yes. An early happy marriage. What more can I say?"

"Happy ever after, Mr van Haagen?" Susan spoke with a sprightliness new to her; glanced at Freddy Ingram and wished Caroline Thorley out of the way.

"That is so." Something impelled him to give a hint of a warning. "Have a care for your health."

Susan made a slight grimace. She'd had enough of caring for health—not her own, her Mamma's.

Diana next, slightly disdainful. With Everard's ring on her finger she felt that her fortune was already assured. Still, now that she and Everard were now practically one, Mr van Haagen might tell her something about Everard's prospects. Not that she really believed much in fortune-telling. And Mr van Haagen's first words bolstered her disbelief.

"London," he said, very positively. Diana recoiled from the thought; she hardly ever thought of Leicester, which she had left at the age of ten, but that city had left her with a distaste for life in towns, noisy and smelly and lonely. Also, because they had been poor in Leicester, town life had an association, in her mind, with poverty. Besides, she liked her own little circle, where she was regarded as a belle, a setter of fashion, one whose advice was sought on what to do about unruly hair or freckles.

"Three children," Mr van Haagen säid inexorably. "Girl, boy, girl, I think. Of money, well enough. Moderate means is the word, is it not? Health, goot." He hesitated, for here again was the combination which spelt a momentous decision, a little less wrenching than the one he had foreseen for her mother, but still a decision and a little trouble. Hardly worth mentioning. And now he saw something which would surely take that displeased look from her face. "You are to be married, not suddenly, but sooner than you think. Within a year."

And that was palpable nonsense, for she and Everard had agreed to wait two years, until he was established, and earning more.

"Thank you, Mr van Haagen," Diana said, coolly, dismissingly. He had told her nothing that she wished to hear and two things at least which displeased her. He was a charlatan and she did not intend to give his rubbish another thought.

Rising she called to Deborah at the piano.

"Deb, your turn next. Come and hear what horrors the future holds for you."

That young lady is annoyed with me, Mr van Haagen thought; yet I left out what would have displeased.

To Deborah he said as soon as the cards were sorted:

"Horses. So many horses. My dear young lady, with horses you will spend your life."

"Nothing would suit me better." She gave him her one-dimple smile.

"Other things, too. Marriage, soon, and one child, a boy. Much money."

Damn! It sounded like Simon Catchpole, the only

man who had ever shown her any serious attention and for whom she had no feeling at all.

"Someone I know, Mr van Haagen?" At least she was taking it seriously.

"No," he said, having moved some cards about. In the process he uncovered another clue. That decision again and with this young lady something alien to her nature. It would change her, which would be a pity, for she was very nice as she was. And how sad, in the four futures so far inspected, so little of positive happiness.

Perhaps with this third of the Gad's girls, Caroline with the merry, rather monkeyish face and the dancing eyes.

Oh no! If anything worse. Many tears! He made some slight rearrangement. More tears. A calm; a scandal; then two children, boy and girl and many good works. Sort that out into something acceptable.

"I see marriage within a year," he said. "A decision to be made—you will act wisely. You will have a husband of the utmost devotion. Of money more than enough. You are generous by nature and will be able to afford to be charitable, and charitable you will be. Renowned for good works."

Caroline thought: If only I can be married to Freddy, of course I shall be charitable and do good works. I shall be so happy that I shall wish to share it with everybody. Mr van Haagen was by her standards old, and until he offered his one parlour trick he had seemed dull; but he was a man and she gave him one of her her gay, mischievous, flirtatious glances as she thanked him.

There remained of the young ladies only Lavinia, who, as usual, had retreated to a corner. Diana, Mr van Haagen noticed, took no part in urging her sister forward, but Susan Walford and Deborah and Caroline said, "Lavinia, you must join in." "Lavinia, he's marvellous!" "Lavinia, do for once join in."

In the ordinary pack of cards, half are black, and even in the black suits the court cards have some colour. So the odds against choosing twelve completely black cards were long. But Lavinia's were all black.

Mr van Haagen said, "We will try again." He shuffled the cards with vigour; and although the odds against all the chosen cards being dead black for the second time must be about a million to one, black they all were.

He wished, heartily, that he had never started this bit of foolishness. He felt a little shiver run down between his shoulder blades. Only one combination of cards said anything ordinary—flowers, but flowers in completely wrong context. He did his best; he said, "Many flowers. You like them, Miss Lavinia?"

"Yes."

"Are you afraid of the dark?"

"No."

He said, almost violently, "Then you *should* be. You should beware of the dark, of anything dark. Stay in the sunshine, Miss Lavinia. You make pictures, is it not? In stitching? In paint?"

"I paint."

He had now exhausted any ordinary line which the black cards offered. Of the rest he could not speak.

He always tried when speaking a language not his own to *think* in that language, but now in his native Dutch, he thought: Oh my God, help me! She is so young!

"I am not speaking of the dark of night, or the light of sunshine. Rather the influence of dark things. Such as melancholy . . . You understand?"

He looked at her and saw something flash behind her steady, blank stare. No warning, however plainly, even brutally expressed could help now. She was already lost. He said, and even to himself he sounded fatuous:

"Hold to the bright side, Miss Lavinia. Paint pleasing things. There is in this world much of beauty."

He began to gather the cards together and she did

not ask as any ordinary girl would have done: Is that all? No husband? No future? No children?

Mrs Thorley, who had listened, and heard nothing amiss, thought that she understood the omission of all the usual things from Lavinia's future. Nothing more detracted from a girl's chances of marriage than eccentricity. Most spinsters were eccentric and most people attributed their eccentricity to their unmarried state. But that was to put the cart before the horse. Lavinia would, as her mother had long ago felt, remain unmarried and the advice to paint pleasing things was sound.

It was a little difficult to imagine Diana in London, living on limited means with three children. If that should be a true prophecy I must help as far as I can. Caroline doing good deeds, unlikely as it might appear to a superficial observer, did not appear so to Mrs Thorley. Caro was flippant and now and then her wit had a caustic touch, but she was wildly generous. Once, Mrs Thorley remembered, Caro had given all her pocket money to a beggar, purportedly blind, and then cried half a day because she had thus forfeited a pair of real silk stockings.

Abruptly Mrs Thorley resumed her role as hostess.

"I am sure, Mr van Haagen, that after all that you need a drink."

He would have welcomed a heartening draught of schnapps, but accepted whisky as a substitute. And never, if he lived to be hundred, would he try that parlour trick—which was no trick—again.

Mrs Thorley said, "Come to a more comfortable chair, Mr van Haagen." She looked towards two near the wide-open window.

"Thank you, I do well where I am, Madam." But he did not look comfortable on the rather frail upright chair; in fact he seemed to sit with a curious rigidity and his voice had lost some of its friendliness. It occurred to her that he might be offended because of her eavesdropping. She was willing to explain.

"Until this evening I had little faith in such things,"

she glanced at the cards, "but your mention of my other child half convinced me. I thought I should listen."

"In case I said something amiss?"

"Let us say rather in case there was something for which I should be prepared or could prevent."

"There never is. Of course the cards do not tell everything, but in my experience what they speak is with a true voice."

Deborah was back at the piano. Horses and money for her. The only likely person in the neighbourhood was Simon Catchpole, for whom she had shown no liking; but she might change. Mrs Thorley hoped she would not marry anyone far away, for although she loved all her girls and took great pains to treat them all alike, she knew that Deb was the most dependable and the most capable.

And I really must speak to Caroline, Mrs Thorley thought; she is too old now to behave with so little dignity. She and Freddy Ingram were sharing a joke and Caroline was lolling—there was no other word for it, against him, and he was holding her by the arm.

"I think," she said, coming back to the cards and their veracity, "that in one respect they were mistaken. Marriage in a year. Diana is engaged, but she and Everard agreed to wait for at least two years and I am old-fashioned enough to think that the eldest should be the first to be married."

"It is also my experience," Mr van Haagen said in that same distant way, "that it is unwise to hold—what is your word?—inquest on such things." He stirred and winced and said:

"I beg you to excuse me, Madam. Sitting so long at the Show, on narrow bench, has provoked in me the lumbago."

On the Continent it had another name—the witch strike; and Mr van Haagen knew just when, and why, it had struck him.

Instantly everybody was all concern. Deborah ran to

the stable for the liniment, a fiery lotion used indiscriminately on animals and humans alike. There wasn't much to be done for lumbago, with warmth and rest it vanished as suddenly as it came. Everard and Freddy practically carried Mr van Haagen to his bed and Freddy applied the liniment with more vigour than discretion.

When she was alone in her bed and drifting towards sleep, Mrs Thorley jerked into full wakefulness, seeing for the first time, and wondering why she had not seen it before, a connection between Mr van Haagen's warning about the dark and Lavinia's visits to Abbas, where Mrs Fremlin, for all her pallor, was not white, and sat in that dimly lit room, and Mr Fremlin looked tanned, even in winter, and all the servants were very dark indeed. The cards do not tell everything. Mr. van Haagen had said, but tonight they could have conveyed a warning. About the carriage? Black as a hearse, drawn by black horses, driven by a black man. An accident!

Oh, what nonsense!

Yet care must be taken. Lavinia must not ride in that carriage again. How to prevent it? Well Lavinia must drive herself in Diana's little pony chaise.

And that would bring about what Mrs Thorley had always most sedulously avoided—dissension in the family; for such an arrangement would lead to trouble if Lavinia and Diana both needed the pony chaise at the same time.

Lavinia's visits to Abbas were always sudden. There'd be a letter from Mrs Fremlin, written in that very black—there you are, that word again—ink, asking that Lavinia could go to Abbas and spend a night, two, three, because Mr Fremlin would be away and Mrs Fremlin needed company, or because there was to be a guest at Abbas, an artist, somebody who knew about pictures, or a writer whom Mrs Fremlin wished Lavinia to meet. And the carriage would call for her. This afternoon. First thing tomorrow morning.

Diana would resent her own far less haphazard programme being interfered with. She made many afternoon visits to her friends and she went, at least three times a week, in to Baildon, taking a picnic meal to share with Everard in some shady, secluded corner of the Abbey ruins. Often on Saturday she stayed on and went with him to a matinée at the theatre and then drove him back to Gad's for the week-end.

No, Mrs Thorley decided, rising up slightly in her bed and giving her pillow a thump, that arrangement could never work. Lavinia must have a conveyance of her own. After all, I always believed in treating them alike and a pony, in the country, costs very little to keep.

Her mind darted off at a tangent. If it came about that Diana did go to London and have only moderate means . . . Even a pony cost a great deal to keep in a city where there was so little space and all fodder must be bought. And then it struck her, there alone in the dark, that to not one of her daughters had Mr van Haagen promised happiness. What a singular omission!

*

Mrs Thorley had delayed what she called in her mind her serious little talk with Caroline about her behaviour in general, and with Freddy Ingram in particular, and when at last she was forced to it she made a rather tentative approach. With Caroline one never knew; she could make a flippant, yet waspish retort, she could collapse into a flood of tears.

"Caro, dear, I know that you are very popular and it is very pleasant for a girl to be so. But I feel forced to say that you are making yourself conspicuous by your behaviour with Freddy Ingram. Twice in this last week you have driven home with him—alone in his gig—when other transport was available."

"Dear me! What is Mrs Grundy saying?"

Caro was going to be flippant. Easier to deal with than tears. And it was easier to take a stern line once this mythical arbiter of morals had been mentioned.

"I think you must know, Caro, that I have never paid much attention to Mrs Grundy. In fact I have allowed myself and all you girls, a good deal of freedom from the Mrs Grundys of this world. What concerns me is your happiness. You are doing yourself damage."

"In what way?"

Very well, hit hard!

"By behaving as though you were engaged, which you are not. And by showing such open preference to one young man, you lay yourself open to humiliation later on."

The shot went home. Caroline had known Freddy almost as long as Diana had known Everard, and there was Diana, stiff as a poker, prim as a dish, safely engaged, a ring on her finger. Bloody unfair. Hurt made Caro jaunty.

"Then I must seek safety in numbers. I'll go with Edward on one of his long dreary rounds. I'll coax Simon Catchpole—Deb doesn't want him. I'll ride with Phil Ambrose. If necessary I'll stand in the road and beg lifts from any passing gig. If riding in a gig means so much."

"Caro, you know perfectly well that I was merely referring to one thing. You are being evasive." Hit hard again! "If after all this, Freddy should choose ... elsewhere, it would leave you ..."

"I know! Money! Filthy lucre. That's all anybody thinks about nowadays. God be my judge, if I stood in Di's shoes would I wait, ticking two years away? I'd go and live in Scurvy Lane, I'd have a stall on the market, I'd take in washing, or scrub steps ..."

George Thorley, Caroline's father, had been a very amiable man, but he was capable of losing his temper and now in the vehemence and the language of Caroline's outburst, Caro showed her breed. But, oddly, also something of Mrs Thorley, no blood kin to her. Mrs Thorley thought: That is exactly how I felt about Stephen and look where that landed me!

In her gentler voice she said:

"What I was trying to say, my dear, is that it is not always wise to show preference too obviously. It sometimes defeats its own purpose. There is something in that old saying about not wearing one's heart on one's sleeve."

Caroline took up another evasive position, completely contradictory.

"I wasn't talking about hearts, Mamma. If I appear to prefer Freddy's company it is because he's the only man I know who can tell a joke from an Act of Parliament. He amuses me; I amuse him . . ."

It was true, but it was only a fragment of the truth.

"So long as you don't make yourself conspicuous," Mrs Thorley said, coming back to her starting point.

"In gigs! Perhaps I could persuade Freddy to exchange his for a covered wagon." What a mistaken thing to say. Oh God, oh God, for the privacy, the intimacy of a covered wagon, with Freddy, even in the wilds of America about which there was so much talk these days.

"Just remember, my dear, a little discretion. That is all I ask. After all, you are young, and I am responsible for you."

Caroline went away, flung herself on her bed and cried; and Mrs Thorley was left with a sense of failure.

*

"I s'pose, Miss Diana, you forgot the matches again," Jenny said.

"I'm afraid I did, Jenny."

Being in love did make people forgetful, Jenny knew. She'd been in love three or four times herself. And Miss Diana was not only in love, she was very busy with making a table-cloth; linen, with crochet edging about a foot wide, and insets.

"Then what'm I gonna to do?"

It was one of those summer evenings, dark purple clouded that held a hint of darkness coming earlier. Mrs Thorley was doing her paper work at the desk in the window embrasure; Diana had just folded her work. Deborah and Caroline and—for once—Lavinia were there, waiting for supper.

"There must be matches somewhere," Mrs Thorley said a trifle crossly, for she too had forgotten the matches.

"There was," Jenny said. "And I've borrered one here, one there, and all out of the spare room. Now there ain't one in the house. And I let the stove out, it being so hot and me counting on Miss Diana."

"I'll go down and borrow a few from Mrs Spicer," Deborah said.

And then Lavinia spoke, tentatively.

"If we all concentrated," she said almost playfully, but testing herself—and them. "Just for a moment, think about, wish for, matches."

They'd all seen it done, but only as a game called Think of a Word. One of the company—or several— went out of a room and these within whispered, choosing a word; then the other, or the others, came in and in perhaps seven out of ten times did hit on the chosen word, or one very like it. Speculate could be spectrum, or accumulate; coffee could be toffee, or coffle. It was a hit-or-miss game and it dealt only with words. Deborah was the one to point out the absurdity. She said:

"So we all think about matches and a box falls from the ceiling."

Lavinia said, "Just think."

Nothing happened. Outside the wide bowed window the sky lightened and the evening bloomed as the dark cloud moved. Light enough to make candles unnecessary on the supper table. Deborah ate hastily, her errand to the village foremost in her mind.

"Better take a box with you," said George, who had noticed his tutor's wife's parsimonious ways. "Mrs Spicer won't have a spare box."

"Wise boy," Deborah said, and went into the kitchen. Jenny and Katie were at the door, outside which stood a little man, a flat cart and a very poor-looking donkey.

"He've got matches," Jenny said. Apart from that the pedlar's cart was disappointing; nothing pretty; no ribbon, no lace, or tawdry ornaments. All plain household stuff.

Deborah viewed the outfit with a different kind of dissatisfaction. To begin with the flat cart was too big for the donkey and it was loaded with rather heavy things.

She said, "Wait!" and hurried up the back stairs and snatched from a drawer the old cigar box in which she kept her small hoard—her savings towards the hunter she wanted.

"I'll have that, and that, and that." She stood by the cart and made a haphazard selection of all the things that looked heaviest; a big iron preserving pan, several saucepans, two flat-irons, some of the coarse thick crocks used in dairies. The little man danced around the cart, ecstatic and garrulous.

" 'S'marvellous thing, lady. I bin on this road regular and never thought to turn up your lane afore. Tonight it come to me. Somebody might live along there, I thought to myself. Somebody might be wanting a thing or two." But not this much, he thought, more than he usually shifted in a week.

Jenny and Katie hovered about, taking the purchases. Jenny with surprise and disapproval. "But Miss Deborah, we *got* a preserving pan. Better than this. Real copper." The purchase of several yards of chain and a bundle of iron stakes amazed even the pedlar. Extraordinary things for a young lady to buy; and not, he somehow felt—for he was an experienced man—done out of any kindly feeling for *him*. Every time her glance met his it was cold and hard and unfriendly, though he smiled his most ingratiating smile.

On the kitchen table there was a basket of apples, the first real sweet ones of the year, clear crimson all over and scented.

And if I give him those, he'd eat them himself, Deborah thought.

"How much is all that?"

"Now, let me see." He pretended to check over, though he knew to the last penny. "Three pound, two shillings and seven-pence."

She paid that without a qualm and then said again, "Wait."

She ran across the yard, vanished, and returned with a good armful of hay which she placed on the cart. He can't very well eat that, Deborah thought almost viciously. She darted into the kitchen and brought out two apples—not for him—for the moke!

Well, she was a curious one all right. And despite the unfriendly looks and giving the donkey what a man could have eaten, not ill-disposed.

"You say you make this round regularly? What day?"

"Monday's my day for the Stonhams, lady."

"Then include us in your round. I can't promise to buy this kind of thing regularly, of course. But matches and candles, hairpins . . . That kind of thing."

She disliked him for ignoring the fact that wheels out of alignment, leaning outwards or inwards, and axles ungreased made pulling twice as difficult as it need be. Next week she'd be ready for him . . . A good bran mash for that poor creature and some suggestions about the cart.

"What on earth?" Mrs Thorley asked, drawn towards the kitchen by the noise, feeling guilty, for she has also had forgotten to buy matches and without a candle, in the kitchen which faced away from the sunset, Jenny and Katie might be dropping things or blundering into one another.

"It was a kind of pedlar, Mamma. He had matches." Suddenly Deborah reverted to the angular awkwardness of her early adolescence, all arms and legs. "He also had household things, very cheap and since Di is thinking of setting up house . . ."

Diana, who had followed Mamma into the kitchen, had great difficulty in holding back an exclamation of dismay. All such cheap, horrible things!

She seldom, looking forward, thought much about her kitchen and when she did she visualised it in romantic rather than practical terms. Everard had said that it would be two years: Mr van Haagen, although on the whole he had displeased her, had spoken of a shorter period, which, accepting the pleasant, discarding the rest, she had convinced herself meant that Everard would get his partnership, and she her house. A kitchen with copper pans, all matching, of different sizes; dishes and bowls all pleasantly blue and white; all kept in order by a neat maid who could cook, answer bells in proper fashion, wait at table. All these clumsy, ugly, cheap articles shattered her dream. Only for a moment. And it was impossible to be cross with Deborah, always so well-meaning.

"It was a kind thought, Deb. Thank you."

Then there arose the question of where the things should be stored. On the attic landing, it was decided. From this operation Jenny exempted herself; the stairs, she said, were as much as she could manage when she had to. The others were lively. George deliberately putting off his bedtime; Katie thinking that if Willy would only come to the point, how glad she'd be of such a wedding gift; Caroline teasing, "I bet, Deb, that pedlar was short of a limb, or had a squint." Lavinia, silent and withdrawn again, glad that nobody, in the confusion, had seemed to connect the thinking about matches with the arrival of them. Secret was best and secret she would be, but the sense of power was there, was growing. One day she would be able to . . . able to . . .

*

The corn harvest promised to be heavy and Mrs Thorley decided that she needed another work-horse. It would, naturally, be of the breed known as Suffolk

Punch and it would, naturally, come from Mr Bridges'. He bred the best; some for show purposes, some for ordinary sale. He lived at Foxton, just across the Norfolk border; an area of heath and breckland but containing, as a desert was said to contain oases, a few pockets of rich land.

She wrote, explaining what she required, not a show animal, just a young strong working horse. Foxton was only about twenty miles away and she expected to have the creature within a week.

Instead she had a visit from a youngish man who bore a strong resemblance to the animals he bred. Big, strong, mild-mannered, and amber-brown all over, from the tip of his riding boots to the crown of his gleaming head.

He said, after the polite preliminaries:

"The point is, Ma'am, I never sell a horse without being pretty sure it's going to a good home."

"Very admirable," Mrs Thorley said, slightly annoyed. "If you wish, you may look around my stable and you will see that my horses are well cared for."

Deborah, who by chance was present, and, "But Mr Bridges, how can you know? I mean . . . you could sell a horse to what looked like a good home and it could be sold next day—to a bad one."

"Not with one of mine. I don't aim to have one of mine sold into slavery. They weigh around a ton, Miss; and properly treated they can pull their own weight, and be guided on a cotton thread. And they're not going dragging more than they can and work to death and end up at the knacker's."

"But, Mr Bridges, how can you prevent it?"

"Easy. Anybody buys a horse from me signs a legal document. No selling, except back to me. See? Condition of sale. It's worked against me a time or two and I've got quite a few old horses ending their days in peace at my place."

Deborah said with great feeling, "How perfectly wonderful."

"No credit to me. I can afford it."

He was very rich; from his father he had inherited a thousand acres and from his mother a prosperous pottery factory.

"As I said, you may inspect my premises, Mr Bridges." Mrs Thorley's voice and manner were cool. For some reason which she could not exactly define she found herself rather disliking him. There was nothing to which one could fairly take objection; manner, clothes, even voice, perfectly ordinary and when he said that he could afford to indulge a whim, he said it without boastfulness. A flat statement of fact.

"I'll just take a look round," he said. Flat; set in his ways; and, yes, a bit arrogant; not taking her word for the fact her horses were well treated.

"I'll show you," Deborah said, eagerly.

"There is no need for that," Mrs Thorley said. "Will is somewhere about the yard."

"But Mamma, I'd like to show Mr Bridges our horses. And see his . . ."

His was a splendid animal; more chestnut than amber-coloured. It stood, untethered in the yard, placidly waiting, but alert. Deborah remarked on this and Mr Bridges said:

"Oh, it'd take a fire to shift Peter if I'd told him to stand." He dived into one of the capacious pockets of his tweed jacket and produced a little irregular lump of white substance.

"Like to give it to him? It's salt, not sugar. A lot of people make that mistake. All right in winter, helps keep 'em warm. But in summer, they sweat and lose salt."

She offered the tit-bit rightly, flat on the palm of her hand. Peter took it with soft, gentle slobbering lips.

"I need a pretty big horse," Tim Bridges remarked. "I'm heavy."

"I outgrew my pony."

And that linked up with that reckless disbursement of savings, and she found herself telling him about the

pedlar's donkey. With one part of his mind noting that
the Gad's Hall stables, hay stores, water trough, green
pasture were all satisfactory, a suitable home, enough
of it ran free to make conversation possible.

"It is," he said, "a problem. I've faced it often
enough. I mean, buy that poor decrepit beast and put it
to pasture. The man'd simply buy another and treat it
the same way. The money isn't minted that could save
'em all . . ."

"I do think," Deb said when he had gone, "he's one
of the very nicest men I've ever met."

Mrs Thorley gave her a sharp look and said with
some asperity:

"I hope you are not going to fall in love with him
simply because he cares for his horses. Most men do,
after all."

"You didn't like him, did you? Why not?"

"I did not dislike him. In fact I had no great feeling
about him either way. Except that to come, and actually *inspect* . . . And to make people sign what he
calls a legal document. It smacks of presumption."

"I think he's absolutely right," Deborah said. Her
voice was mild enough but she looked stubborn. Mrs
Thorley thought: Oh dear me; I've made a mistake!
I've probably planted the idea in her head. Just because something about the man ruffled my temper.

She hastened to make amends. "Of course, my dear,
you are right. And so is he. It was just that I was annoyed at being as it were under suspicion of not
treating my animals properly." She restrained herself
from adding that she thought there was something
slightly uncouth about Mr Bridges; to say that would
simply make Deb stick up for him more. In any case,
why worry? They were unlikely to meet again. For although any enlightened person would have hotly denied it, the gulf between Norfolk and Suffolk was almost
as firmly as it had been a thousand years earlier when
two different tribes settled and divided the bulge of

East Anglia between them. County families met, mingled, intermarried, but for ordinary people the invisible barrier was there. Mr Gordon, for instance, would not be consulted by any client living North of the border; any Norfolk man needing a lawyer would choose a Norfolker who might live more than twice as far away. Mr Walford found a readier market for his beer in Cambridgeshire, or even Bedforshire, than he did in Norfolk. To anyone like Mrs Thorley, coming from a wider world, the dialect of speech of the two countries was identical, but at shows and some markets—events which flung frail bridges over the gulf—the true Suffolk man either did not understand or pretended not to understand the one from Norfolk. There was a strongly held belief in Suffolk that nobody in Norfolk could cure a ham properly; a matching belief in Norfolk that no Suffolk woman could make a good dumpling.

So Mrs Thorley could dismiss Mr Bridges.

Who turned up two days later, just as they were sitting down to their mid-day meal. Katie announced his arrival as she brought in the food.

"It's Mr Bridges, Ma'am. With the horse."

"Very well," Mrs Thorley said. "Call Willy. And give the man something to eat. And a glass of beer."

Katie was not very clear-spoken, and the difference between Mr Bridges' man and Mr Bridges, ma'am, was slight. Even Deborah did not imagine that Mr Bridges would deliver, in person, a cart-horse.

Katie went out and reappeared, slightly flustered.

"It's Mr Bridges hisself, Ma'am. And he want to talk to Miss Deborah. Important, he said."

"I'll come," Deborah said.

It was himself. And what he had brought was not the cart-horse that was expected, but an animal, a mare, of such breath-taking beauty . . . Deborah said, remembering how she had confided to him her grief about the outgrown pony and her hope of a hunter—one day; the day deferred by the loss of three pounds

two shillings and some odd pence, "But Mr Bridges
. . . It is kind of you, but I couldn't possibly afford . . ."

"Affording isn't concerned, Miss Thorley. I want
you to have her. I mean, she's useless to me. Bred for
racing and she failed one of their daft tests. She was
dragging a coal cart . . . And useless to me. I'm too
heavy to give her exercise. So I thought. You'd fit together. If you'd accept her."

And it was not, Mrs Thorley thought, that, brought
in by Deborah, given a place at table, he was awkward
with knives and forks. But the word *uncouth* could not
be avoided. Any man who knew anything must surely
know that for a girl to accept such a present was absolutely unheard of. Stupid? Arrogant because he was
rich? And uncouth; for to force upon a woman something too difficult to explain was uncouth.

She said in her light la-di-da manner, "Run away, all
of you. Mr Bridges and I must have a little talk."

She was absolutely brutal.

"Are you not aware, Mr Bridges, that no decent, respectable young woman could possibly accept a gift
worth at least fifty pounds? A few flowers perhaps. I
believe that nowadays a small flask of lavender water
or even a fan. But a horse, Mr Bridges. Quite unthink-
able!"

He said in that way, something that had angered her
before, a practicality impervious to anything but itself:

"Where would be the harm? There's the mare, useless to me, and there's Miss Deborah with nothing to
ride. Why not bring them together?"

Even the term, nothing to ride, was subtly offensive.
It must be explained.

"My husband had a good saddle horse; not the most
easily handled of animals. My daughter was still at
school, so who was to exercise him? My stable-
lad"—almost unthinkingly she promoted Willy—"was
afraid of him. So I sold him. As a matter of fact I have

been on the look-out of a suitable mount for my daughter."

His silence, his look asked: And in a year you found nothing? Aloud he said:

"Well, now it's here. Suitable as could be."

"Entirely *un*suitable," she said shortly; irritation swept her again. "Surely you must see that." Suddenly the exact word for him occurred to her. *Thick*. Thick-headed. Thick-skinned.

Outwitting her again, he said:

"You're thinking about how it'd look? Well, for one thing, I'd have thought you of all people wouldn't bother about that. For another, who'd know?"

She saw a solution.

"It could all be settled very easily, Mr Bridges. I be-lieve you satisfied yourself the other day that this was a fit home for a horse. So I hope you will allow me to buy the mare."

"That wasn't what I had in mind. But if you'll feel happier, all right. Thirty shillings."

"Don't be absurd. I haven't seen the animal but my daughter says it is a pedigree race-horse. Tell me the proper price."

"Thirty shillings is what I gave for her. You find that difficult to believe? You shouldn't, being a cattle dealer. Things you breed that don't come up to stand-ard go to the butcher's, don't they? It's the same with horses—especially race-horses. Some miss their mark and go to the knacker's. Or worse."

"Very well." She went to her desk near the window and wrote the cheque. Let that be the end of that!

It was not.

"While I *am* here," he said, standing tall, solid, stolid, "I might as well mention another thing. I've had no chance to try out how Miss Deborah feels about me, but I'd like your permission to find out. I know how I feel about her. She's the girl I've been waiting for all my life."

She fenced, feebly. "But Mr Bridges, you have only seen my daughter twice."

"Once was enough. I knew that first day." To some women his artlessness would have made an appeal; and to many mothers what he said would have seemed like an answer to prayer.

"I'm thirty-two," he said. "I'm not well known—except for my horses—in this part of the country, but where I am known, my name is good, I hope. I never fooled around. As regards this world's goods I'm well set up. And within ten minutes of our meeting, I took a great fancy . . . I mean I realised that Miss Deborah and I were meant for one another. I thought it only right to speak to you first."

Another case of love at first sight. Like Diana and Everard. Like—but that was lost in the mists of time—herself with Stephen Osborne, and then George Thorley and herself. Who could decry it: Who fight against it?

And why should one?

No answer to that. All she knew was that she had had slight misgivings about Everard and had even more about this.

Am I one of those possessive mothers, anxious to keep my girls with me, resentful of all suitors?

No! I am not. I want all my girls to be happy. And I am resigned to Everard. To this man I don't think I can ever be. And yet against him—nothing.

"Certainly you should be old enough to know your own mind. Deborah is very young. I am growing old and am inclined to think that hasty decisions are often regretted. And choosing a partner for life on the strength of two meetings seems to me to be the height of folly."

He said with the patient air of one attempting to explain something to a child, "That was what I was getting around to. I know my mind, but she can't know hers until we're closer acquainted. I'm telling you my intentions are honourable and asking permission to see her."

It was her feeling of helplessness, of being up against

some power much stronger than herself, that made Mrs Thorley say:

"And suppose I withhold it?"

"I should be sorry. I prefer things open and above-board. But I should see her nonetheless. I mean to have her—if she'll have me."

And Deborah, in so little time as it had taken her to show him around the stables, had decided that he was the nicest man she had ever met.

Another weakening was that memory of Mr van Haagen's prophecy for Deborah. Horses. Wealth. Possibly some things were inevitable.

"I also prefer things to be above-board, Mr Bridges. Let me think . . . In a few days' time my eldest daughter will be celebrating her eighteenth birthday. Just a gathering of young people. If you would care to join us."

"I would indeed. Thank you."

Diana's birthday actually fell on a Thursday, but was kept on Saturday for the convenience of Everard.

Richard Walford was no longer one of the little group. Only Susan knew why he had decided to return to Burton-on-Trent almost as soon as Diana became engaged to Everard Spicer. He'd made business his excuse; some process in the making of beer about which he wished to know more.

Edward Taylor must be asked, if only because— poor boy—he never had a decent evening meal these days; Freddy Ingram; James Gordon, who might—just divert Caroline, being just as much of a wit and flirt as Caroline was; but with far more behind him than Freddy Ingram had. Simon Catchpole towards whom Caroline had threatened to relent.

Mr Bridges in this company looked old and somewhat odd. He said, "I am a teetotaller." Deborah ran and fetched lemonade—and drank it herself. Mrs Thorley, watching, thought: That took courage; he is a strong character; so is Deb and if they ever come into conflict . . .

Freddy-to-my-friends was the catalyst; in no time at all calling Mr Bridges Tim or dear boy.

Tim didn't drink, didn't smoke, didn't dance, but he could play the piano. Surprising considering the size of his hands.

In the little space left before harvest began, Tim Bridges wasted no time. He invited Mrs Thorley and Deborah to visit his home. In size and style it was much like Gad's, but no modernising hand had been laid upon it, and the room in which they took tea was called the parlour. Mrs Thorley, looking around with critical eyes, saw that while there was no ostentatious evidence of wealth, everything was solid and good and well cared for, by, presumably, the one servant, a woman of great age who somehow managed to convey, without speaking, her disapproval of the visitors. Mrs Thorley wrongly interpreted this covert hostility as fear of coming change. Actually it was directed at the flounces and bows which mother and daughter revealed when they removed the thin dust coats they had worn in the gig. The old woman—her name was Emma— wanted to see her master married and settled, and if possible a father, before God called her to heaven; but if this was his choice—after all the good, quiet, *homely* girls he could have married—then it was a pity. A thousand pities, for no doubt about it, the master had fallen victim to the lust of the eye. And acting silly!

"It's not much of a garden," he said. "My mother grew flowers. I've had no time. It's got out of hand."

Emma heard this shred of conversation and was more resentful than ever, for the garden, thus spoken of in such derogatory terms, was extremely productive of vegetables, of herbs. It just went to show . . .

Showing off his useful but not very decorative garden, Tim Bridges said, "I've been thinking; twenty miles here and twenty back . . . Suppose you took my gig-horse, Ma'am, and left yours. Then, the day after tomorrow, I'll bring yours back and collect mine. Would that be agreeable to you?"

Another meeting. A further erosion. Something else to think about in the night.

She began to dread the night. Go to bed tired, ready for sleep, and wake as suddenly as though you had been shaken. Reach in the darkness for the matches, light a candle, look at the watch. Always a quarter to three, or three, or a quarter past. Within the half hour it could vary a little. But the roundabout of thought did not vary at all.

All about the girls; her own; and those whom she had made her own.

Curiously, George never walked down the dark corridors of her sleepless hours. His course ran straight and clear. Mr Spicer was drilling him for entry to Biddle's, the school to which money alone could not ensure entry. Biddle's favoured bright boys and Mrs Thorley favoured Biddle's because it was fairly near. The only school nearly approaching its quality was in Felstead—far away in Essex. She wished to do for George what she had done for the girls, deliver, collect, attend any ceremony. And George was so teachable, so observant . . . No need to worry about George.

The girls? Yes.

Diana, who should really be learning to cook, instead of doing so much fancy work. Mrs Thorley herself had never learned to cook until harsh necessity forced her to do so—and sometimes with little to cook with. She wished her daughter to face the world better armed. So she must speak, must insist, and Diana would be daintily, scornfully resentful.

Deborah. And what was wrong *there* even the wakeful mother could never hit upon. Deb and the man who was plainly set upon marrying her had things in common—a love of horses, a love of music. She'd have a house very much like the home she was leaving; a husband who would certainly allow her a free hand in the garden. And Deb's nature was not only practical, it was cheerful—she was the only one of them who had accepted the discipline of school life happily. What was there to worry about?

Caroline. Plenty to cause anxiety there! The little talk had been quite unavailing and Caroline was still making a spectacle of herself with Freddy Ingram. Even worse, perhaps, since some of the young men who had danced attendance on her in the past, enjoying her gaiety, seemed to have been discouraged by her marked preference for Freddy, and had fallen away. And Caroline herself had changed. There seemed to be something a little feverish about her gaiety at times, and some of her quips had more sting.

The tall-case clock on the landing would boom four strokes as Mrs Thorley debated the wisdom of speaking again, not to Caroline this time, to Freddy. Fathers often demanded to know what a young man's intentions were. Surely a widowed mother was entitled to do the same. But Mrs Thorley shrank from the idea; it would seem to be making too much of the matter. Freddy simply hadn't a serious nature and the idea of being taken seriously by a match-making Mamma would vastly amuse him.

Then there was Lavinia. She no longer rode in the black carriage. Mrs Thorley had acquired, at a reasonable price, a quiet skewbald pony and a miniature carriage. Consciously or unconsciously she had heeded Mr van Haagen's words and was pleased that the pony should have so much white about it, and that the little carriage was largely composed of pale canework. Lavinia still came home laden with flowers—and with exotic fruit; there was a pineapple house at Abbas. Except to say that Mr Fremlin had sold another of her pictures—a hundred pounds this time—she seldom volunteered any information about her visits to Abbas. Asked direct questions she gave short answers. Yes, thank you, she had enjoyed herself. No, Mr Fremlin was not there. Yes, Mr Fremlin was there, so was a gentleman from Brazil who wished to sell some property near Rio de Janeiro. Since the child always went so eagerly to Abbas and seemed to enjoy herself there, one would have expected her to mention the prospect of losing her friends with some change of voice or expression, but Lavinia gave no sign.

Because they had asked her to go with them?

Now that I should never *allow! Never!*

There might lie Mr van Haagen's hint of warning. Mrs Thorley's missionary-inculcated ideas of such places were horrifying; all very dark people and the cannibal pot never far away.

Sometimes, when sleep failed to return, and the clock had struck five, Mrs Thorley rose and went softly down to the dining room and poured herself a small measure of whisky. No decent woman drank spirits of any kind except when suffering from a heavy cold; then a tablespoonful of whisky in a glass of hot milk was permissible. And sleep often followed such a dose. Sometimes, but not invariably, it worked for her, and if she did not actually sleep, her thoughts took a more cheerful tinge. At first she felt guilty about such indulgence, but that feeling wore off; it was medicine, wasn't it? And she was at an age where women who had led far more sheltered lives, done less work, had fewer worries, often had little ailments and resorted to doctors. And after all it was her whisky and cost her nothing. George had liked his whisky and laid in a good store; in casks, each plainly dated, since, unlike some beverages, whisky improved as it aged.

Then it struck her that it was foolish to make this almost nightly excursion, soft-footed through the silent house; far more sensible to keep a supply in her wardrobe, on the top shelf, behind the hats.

A golden, beginning-of-harvest morning and a letter from Susan Walford, in whose life Caroline had now replaced Diana. The friendship between Diana and Susan had been understandable; Diana had been sorry for Poor Susan and Poor Susan had been grateful to

Diana. Then Diana had become engaged and naturally had less time to spare. Also to be considered was the fact that between the girl with an engagement ring on her finger and the girl who had not there was a little divergence of interest. For Caroline's stepping into Diana's place in Poor Susan's life, Mrs Thorley could only assume the most unworthy motive—to keep in touch, through Susan, with Freddy. Caroline had no reason to be sorry for Susan and often, indeed, made rather barbed remarks about her. A friendship of convenience.

It was a longish letter and Caroline read it with darkening eyes and whitening face. Then, never one to control or conceal her emotions, she flung it away, folded her arms over her hardly touched breakfast plate, put her head down and began to cry. Not the easy crying to which they were all accustomed, but racking sobs.

George was the first to move, leaving his own breakfast half eaten. Of them all he liked Caro best and to see her in such misery distressed him, though he had no notion of what it was all about. He went round to where she sat and patted her head, her shoulders. "Don't cry, Caro. Please don't cry. Whatever it is, we can put it right."

It was nothing that anybody could put right.

It was a letter from a happy girl—a girl, Mrs Thorley thought, reading it, either blind or insensitive. Susan wished her best friend to be the first to know; she and Freddy were to be married; Papa had missed Richard so much and was now so happy to take Freddy into the business. She and Freddy were prepared to make their home with Papa, and Papa was happy about that. There'd be an engagement party next week and an Easter wedding; would Caroline be her chief bridesmaid?

Diana asked a question with her eyes and Mrs Thorley nodded. Diana then looked smug. Deborah put her arm around her sister and said:

"Freddy? Damn him to hell!"

"Yes," George said understanding nothing except that somebody, Freddy? had made Caro cry. "Damn him to hell."

"That will do," Mrs Thorley said sharply. She had always known that no good would come of that flirtation, had tried to warn Caro, was slightly surprised that Poor Susan should be Freddy's final choice—and then not surprised. Freddy was in fact doing very well for himself.

She wished she could say to George: Run along, dear, you'll be late for your lessons. But Mr Spicer kept strictly University terms; when students at Cambridge went down for the long vacation, young George Thorley was set free. The best she could do now was to invent an errand for George.

"Caro is all right, George. Run and tell Willy to get the trap ready. I have to go to Baildon. You can come with me. And ask Jenny to fry you another egg . . ."

As soon as the innocent looker-on had gone, Mrs Thorley could say, kindly, but firmly:

"Come along now, Caro. It *is* a blow. We all understand. But you must pull yourself together, my dear, and make light of it. It is the only way."

Caroline lifted her head and showed her stricken face, more monkeyish in its complete despair than it had ever been in sorrow or merriment.

"There's as good fish in the sea as ever came out," Deborah said. "Come and lie down. You'll feel better soon."

Caroline did not feel better soon. She lay on her half of the bed which she shared with Lavinia, and cried and cried; shedding the many tears which Mr van Haagen had foreseen. She wouldn't eat, wouldn't talk, wouldn't listen. The absolutely obligatory letter had to be written by Diana, who had social sense: We all, she wrote, offer our very best wishes to you and congratulations to Freddy; and we look forward . . .

Perfectly in order; Diana was socially adept.

But the day of the party crept on, soft-footed.

"I can't, I can't," Caroline moaned. "Say I'm ill. Say I'm dead. I wish to God I were . . ."

"But you are not," Mrs Thorley said. "And now, just for once, Caro, you must listen to me. Unless you come this evening, to Susan's party and act as though nothing had happened—nothing that you cared about, be as gay as ever you were—there will be talk. Do you want that?"

Mamma had spoken about *talk* before—but talk of the right kind, admiring, envious, spiteful because envious.

Into her sodden pillow, Caroline said, "No. Not that."

"Then you must get up. An egg shampoo and a vinegar rinse for your hair . . . My dear, I know exactly how you feel. I have taken some blows in my time and learned that wounds should not be licked in public. So far only we—your family—know what has happened. And if you rouse yourself and behave as usual, nobody outside this house need never know."

As gay as ever you were. Over a heart, shattered and frozen, curls could dance, mischievous glances flash. Oh, it might as well be Edward—they're all one to me now, Caroline thought, giving Edward Taylor a smile that dazzled him and everyone else within range. When she chose Caroline could always be the centre of attraction, and since Susan had chosen to have her celebration party in the form of a dance, Caroline had a wonderful time. And a horrible time. It was a waltz—one of their favourites; sentimental, slow, and Freddy Ingram, stupid young man that he was, having done his duty with all Susan's friends, and with Susan, thought that this . . . this he might despite everything be allowed, with Caroline, something to remember forever.

She knew that if he touched her the brittle thin surface of gaiety would crack and she would be crying again, helplessly, hopelessly, and forever. So she said, very clearly:

"Freddy, you have a short memory! I told you at Di's party, I'd never waltz with you again. Fallen arches I just dare not risk."

Inside her the wound which must be concealed bled and the tears which she had been fighting off almost had a victory as she danced the waltz, their waltz, with Edward. He was not a bad dancer, a bit heavy, a bit inclined to talk, seriously. She heard her own voice in an empty, echoing cave, saying: Yes. Yes of course. She was halfway home before she realised to what she had committed herself; to become one of the Friends of the Hospital and to help with Mrs Bosworth's garden fête, the proceeds of which went to that good cause.

"My first good deed," she said, some irony mingling with the forced gaiety, "will be to suggest roundabouts and swings instead of all those knitted egg-cosies."

"I hardly think Mrs Bosworth's garden is large enough."

"Then we'll borrow the meadow next door."

"A splendid idea," Mrs Thorley said. She was pleased with Caroline's show of spirit. She had learned herself that a pretence at confidence could lead to the real thing; and cheerfulness might be the same.

*

Mr Bridges appeared to think that he had been missed, and opened his interview with Mrs Thorley by explaining that he had been busy harvesting. His harvest had been splendid; he hoped hers had.

"Very good. Quite exceptional," she said. Her irrational dislike—no; perhaps that was too harsh a word—distaste, reared itself.

"I wrote to Miss Deborah, though."

He had indeed been a most faithful correspondent, and Deborah had seized upon and read his letters with an eagerness which showed that her feelings for him were never in doubt . . .

"So now," he said, "it's time for a serious talk, Ma'am. I'd like to ask her today and get married any time between now and Christmas." Now was the first week in September, for the good weather which had fostered the wonderful harvest had continued and ensured that the gathering in went forward without interruption.

Not without a flick of pleasure, Mrs Thorley proceeded to put Mr Bridges—she could never think of him as Tim, though everybody else did—in his place.

"That," she said, "is quite impossible, I am afraid. You may think me very old-fashioned, but I am one of those who regard it as desirable that the elder sister should marry first—if at all possible." It had once been a rule, broken only when the older girl was so unattractive for this or that reason, that it must be disregarded; it was still desirable.

"I thought Miss Deborah was the oldest."

"Many people make that mistake. Deborah is in fact six months younger than Diana, and since Diana is already engaged . . . And the time for her wedding more or less fixed—a twelve-month next June, I certainly should not wish Deborah's wedding to precede it."

"I call that silly. Mind you, I can understand the need to wait in their case. Not much of a job yet, and no house . . . But why should *I* wait? Can you tell me that?"

She wanted to snap out: Because I say so! She restrained herself; open hostility must be avoided. Yet it was there, a steady current below the surface ripples.

"It may simply be that I like things done in order."

"With *some* things," he said. "Were you thinking of order when you went into the Corn Exchange here at Baildon, where never any female except a scrub-woman had ever set foot? Or set Corby's saleyard upside down? The last thing in the world I'd want to do is to be offensive, but there it is. You can't very well defy convention, or fashion, or whatever you call it, on the one hand and stick to it on the other. You have to be—consistent."

"I try to be." She recognised the threat he held and the weakness of her own position. Fathers could forbid marriages for their daughters who were under age. Presumably mothers had the same power. But stepmothers? Unsure of her ground, she offered a compromise. A double wedding, next June not the June after next. Bracing her shoulders, she thought: I'll manage it somehow.

The rocky man said:

"You mean in church?"

"Naturally. Where else?"

"I'm Methodist," he said. And then she understood all. Non-conformity explained his abstention from alcohol and tobacco, his plain speech, his invariably dull clothes and even self-assurance. She had come into contact with several of his kind during her time in Leicester and knew that they all regarded themselves as being in direct touch with God, and provided they followed what they regarded as *His* will need fear no man. Very admirable, of course, but it made them intractable to deal with. She thought: Poor Deb. He would, of course, be a good husband, unlikely to fritter away her money or run after other women but . . . But dull, set in his ways, and always sure, in any argument, of God's full support.

The only Methodist Chapel she knew of was a wretched little building on the road to Sudbury and she certainly was not going to have Deb married there.

"We," she said, rather pontifically, "are Church of England and I wish all my girls to married according to its rites." Not in some place not even licensed for marriages; a place where a wedding, in order to be legal, must be witnessed by the local registrar.

"Well," he said, amiable and unruffled, "we won't

quarrel about *that*. Though my mother would turn in her grave." His mother had brought her form of religion, and her money from the Midlands; she had built a chapel at Foxton, and he largely supported it, for most of its members were poor. It was, he understood, different in the North. "Standing up to be married by a parson will do me no damage," he said. "But I wish you'd be a bit more accommodating about time. Next June is a long way off."

"Ten months," she said crisply. "A short engagement by ordinary standards. And I have already been extremely accommodating—bringing Diana's wedding forward by a whole year." And with, as yet, not the slightest notion of how it could be managed.

"Yes," he said, "I realise that. But it's all right if I ask her and give her a ring? I brought it, in case." He felt in his capacious pocket and produced the ring which he had brought in case, not in a case, but carefully wrapped in tissue paper. With a gesture which, now that she understood him, she found rather appealing, he offered it for her inspection.

"Not new," he said—quite unnecessarily. "But precious in its way. My mother's father gave it to her when she settled on a Norfolk man."

It was a curious ring, wide, gold, with an oval of blue enamel, and on the blue, in more gold, a word: *Mizpha*.

"It's a word with meaning," he said. "It means: The Lord watch between thee and me, when we are absent one from another."

"So much in five letters? Very concise," Mrs Thorley said.

On the whole she had, once she understood, relented towards him. What she had always felt—that slight animosity—was fully explained; and Deb wore the extraordinary ring with as much pride as Diana wore hers. Time slipped away, and Mrs Thorley went house-hunting.

"I may have been precipitate, Everard," she said, "but it did seem to me a chance not to be missed. I do a certain amount of business with Mr Larken, as you know, and he drew my attention to it. Houses for rent, especially in such a nice area, are rather rare and when he mentioned it to me, I thought it worth a look. I took a week's option and—wait—I would like to give you the rent for the first year, as a wedding present. That is, of course, if you and Diana approve of it."

As who could not? A lovely little house, one of six, three aside, facing each other across a cul-de-sac which ended in a wall, topped by high trees from the gardens of bigger houses—one of them Edward Taylor's—in St Giles' Square. It was called Friars' Lane; and its open end just turned the grey bulk of St Mary's church. It was near the wide market square and the streets leading off it.

Ideal for a young couple. Perversely, Everard Spicer felt that he was being hustled. So far no sign of a partnership; old Gordon was still remarkably spry for his age, and James was frivolous as ever. Between them they managed well, unloading any job they didn't fancy on to him. He'd been with the firm a full year now; they'd had time to see his worth; to realise that he was conscientious and reliable and knew more law than the pair of them put together, yet there had been no mention even of a rise in salary. And he sensed something distant and cold in Mrs Gordon's attitude towards him; he was, after all, supposedly James' friend, yet Mrs Gordon asked him to the house only when she needed a man to keep the numbers even—and he greatly suspected, had been let down by somebody. Never casual, never friendly.

His insecure childhood had rendered him oversensitive, and at the same time greedy. Now, looking back, it seemed as though he had always been dependent upon somebody's favour; and now he was going to be dependent upon Mrs Thorley's. If he allowed her to hustle him, and pay a year's rent.

Of course Diana was the dearest, sweetest, most adorable girl in the world; and of course he was anxious to marry her—but in his chosen time. The extra year would have given him time to be certain of Mr Gordon's intentions; or to look around for some more promising opening. With a wife on his hands, and a house he'd be tied down. Perhaps forever.

He set about looking over the little house as moodily as Diana was ecstatic. He said things like: "It's very dark, don't you think?"

"Not in itself. It's the dark paper and so much brown paint. Easily remedied."

"Redecorating costs money. Then there's the furnishing. I have saved very little, you know."

"But dearest, I shall have some money. Five hundred pounds that Papa left me. It isn't a fortune, but it will be enough." She was so busy planning, the nest-making instinct so active, that she was oblivious to his lack of enthusiasm; even when, at the end of the inspection, he said:

"Well, darling, what do you think?" in a voice which almost defied her to give a favourable answer.

"I love it already. Wasn't it clever and kind of Mamma?"

"Lord love us," Deborah said, "we could do most of the work ourselves. I've never yet papered a room, but I'm willing to have a try."

The quiet little house in the quiet cul-de-sac, until lately occupied by a quiet old woman, became a centre of activity. Diana and Deborah drove into Baildon almost every day, taking with them first one of Jenny's picnic meals and then, as the weather grew colder and the kitchen range was back in working order, with materials for a proper meal. All that the range needed was the attention of the chimney sweep—the quiet old woman had for a long time shirked such an upheaval and the flue was blocked; she'd boiled her kettle and her egg on the sitting-room stove.

"I must master cooking," Deborah said. "I don't much like the look of Tim's Emma and I'm sure she loathes me. I may have to cook if she leaves, as I think she will."

It was Deborah who ordered a ton of best household coal, and paid for it, since she now had no reason to save. With something in the oven, or simmering away in one of the pedlar's pots, she soaked and stripped off wallpaper, pasted and hung new paper, splashed paint about. Disasters in the culinary line—they grew fewer—or in the paper-hanging, were greeted with hilarity. Everard came every day when he knew the girls would be there, had a meal and did a little work, though Deborah limited his activities: "You can't do that, Everard. You mustn't go back to the office looking like a whitened sepulchre."

Deborah's mare must be exercised, and as the year ran downhill so that there was no evening, Deborah often rode in, and sometimes Caroline shared the pony carriage. Edward offered the hospitality of his quite extensive stables. Edward fell into the habit of dropping in to share the rather makeshift meal, and if time allowed he would work for an hour or so.

At Christmas Edward asked Caroline to marry him and she agreed, wondering why in the world he had been so slow to read the signals she had been sending out ever since that terrible, terrible time in the summer.

Caroline was the only one of them actually to choose her own engagement ring. Mr Collins, the jeweller, was, perforce, one of Edward's patients and when Edward said, "Get half a dozen down on approval," Mr Collins gladly did so. Caroline, confronted with such richness, chose, not the dark sapphire which almost matched her eyes, but an emerald, with green upon green in its depths. Green was the colour of envy, and she knew that however long she lived, however much she was pampered and favoured, she would envy Poor Susan.

It would be not a double, but a triple wedding, and

in the end a saving, Mrs Thorley reflected; since most of the guests would be the same and one wedding feast served for all. And she would design, and largely make, the white satin dresses which would conform to the rule laid down long ago; equal, but not uniform.

It was March, the daffodils dancing; and Mrs Thorley had spent some of her sleepless hours thinking about veils for brides. She had held on, through all vicissitudes, to her own, which had been her mother's and her grandmother's. By every right, Diana's, but that would be to make an invidious distinction, for no such lace, fine as a cobweb, was obtainable now. So each girl must have a third of it; the thing divided and eked out; the sturdier English lace at the top, taking the weight, the filmy less substantial stuff stitched on, under a band of white satin ribbon which would hide the seam.

Happy, practical thoughts which should have induced sleep, but did not. She saw the dawn invade, despite the curtains, in fragmented shafts of light. She heard the clamour of the morning chorus of birds. And from the purely feminine business of bridal veils, so easily settled by a slash of the scissors, her mind moved to money. The girls must have their small dowries . . . Gad's Goliath must go; and not enough! Several cows, some calves. She was arranging these things in her mind when Caroline opened the door and said,

"Mamma—will you come? Lavinia is ill. She's just been dreadfully sick."

Lavinia *had* been dreadfully sick, and there was Caroline, who in three months' time would be a doctor's wife, vulnerable to worse emergencies, looking very sick herself.

"A glass of hot water, with a good pinch of baking soda in it," Mrs Thorley said, struggling into her dressing gown and thinking that they'd all eaten the same food yesterday, and although Lavinia had always been pale and frail, subject to backache, headache now and again, she's never been bilious; possibly because she ate so little.

But sick this morning she had been and now, very pale and exhausted, she lay on the soiled, disordered bed. Mrs Thorley put her hand on her daughter's forehead. And on her neck. Thank God, no fever; on the contrary, rather chilly and clammy.

A curious thought occurred to her. She said:

"You'll be all right, dear. I can't think why you should be sick, unless—did you lick your paint brush or hold it in your mouth yesterday?"

It was the only explanation she could think of; some paints did contain dangerous colouring matter.

"No," Lavinia said, cold; hostile.

Caroline pattered in with the faintly cloudy glass.

"Come along," Mrs Thorley said, slipping her arm under Lavinia's sharp-boned shoulders, "drink this, and if you don't soon feel completely better, we'll send for Edward."

"I'm all right. I don't need Edward. I'll just lie flat for a little while."

"A clean sheet and pillow-case, Caro," Mrs Thorley said. "Don't stand there looking as though it were the end of the world."

Two seconds later she faced the end of the world.

The bulge was all the more conspicuous because Lavinia's body was still that of a child.

Mrs Thorley clapped her hand to her mouth, holding back the terrible cry which had almost escaped her. She felt sick; she felt dizzy; she felt faint. Yet she rallied sufficiently to pull the soiled sheet over the bulge as Caro came in with the fresh linen and her voice was astonishingly calm as she said:

"Take your clothes, Caro, and dress in another room."

While Caro, glad to be dismissed, collected her day's wear, Mrs Thorley had time to think: How ridiculous! This is not a thing that can be hidden.

Then she had another thought. Had she jumped to too hasty a conclusion?

There was the remarkable case of Lady Flora Hastings, a lady-in-waiting who had appeared to be pregnant. The Queen's own doctor had declared that she was. Gossip had even named the putative father. Then the poor lady was found to be suffering from a tumour of the liver—and had died of it.

Better something like that in this case?

Yes! To think thus was terrible. But the thought remained. Illness, early death were tragic, but not shameful. Besides, medicine had advanced . . . Diagnosed soon enough . . .

Caro went out, closing the door softly, and before Mrs Thorley could speak, Lavinia said in a cold, remote way:

"There is no need to worry. I am going to have a baby. But not here. Somebody is coming for me on Lady Day."

That was the 25th of March and only five days away.

"Who? The Fremlins?"

"Does it matter? I shall be fetched and nobody need know anything. Just say nothing for five days."

"Don't talk such rubbish, Lavinia. How could I possibly let you go—into the blue—with people who are . . . who have proved . . . so untrustworthy. Do you realise what you are saying. A baby, and no husband."

It struck Mrs Thorley that Lavinia didn't realise; she'd always been odd—some people said a bit dimwitted; living in a world of her own; a dream world. Of her innocence, ignorance, immaturity, somebody had taken most cruel advantage. She asked, as any mother in her place would have done: "Who was it?"

"I am not going to talk about it."

As Mrs Thorley had suppressed her cry of horror, so she repressed an impulse to take the girl by the shoulders and *shake* her, make her come into the open for once and behave as any other girl, caught, disgraced, shamed, would have done. But even had she given way to the impulse, she knew that she could not have performed the action. Another wave of weakness swept over her; she clutched at the bedpost and almost fell into a sitting position at the foot of the bed.

"It should not have happened," Lavinia said. "I meant nobody to know. I have been sick before and always managed to get out. This morning I was caught unawares. But if there is no fuss, no questions . . . Just for five days, everything will be all right, I assure you."

Mrs Thorley wanted to say: How? How can everything be all right? But even the power of speech seemed to have deserted her. Everything of strength, authority and reason was concentrated in the pale girl on the bed.

The door opened. "Anything I can do?" It was Deborah, of course. And it was Lavinia, not Mamma, who said:

"No, Deb. Thank you. I'm all right now."

Something in Mrs Thorley tried to call out: Help me! But it was like a nightmare in which one screamed and made no sound, or tried to run and made no progress.

"Five days," Lavina repeated, not coaxingly or persuasively, but with an absurd, though unmistakable air of authority. "Then I shall be gone and you can explain it in any way you like. Until then I shall sleep in the studio."

Not one word of apology, or of regret, not even a hint of explanation. Incredible behavior. Mrs Thorley could hardly believe that what was happening was happening. Her own feeling of utter helplessness was understandable, she had had a severe shock.

In a vague way she recognised that the suggestion of Lavinia's sleeping apart was sensible. All the girls dressed and undressed in a modest way, removing and replacing underclothes within the shelter of their night-gowns, but even so it was amazing that Caroline, sharing a bed, hadn't noticed. But no more amazing than that she herself—always a woman to meet an emergency with action—should be sitting here, passive, dumb and seeming to agree to keep the secret for five days. It was though she were under a spell.

"I'll dress now and begin moving my things," Lavinia said.

It was a dismissal and Mrs Thorley accepted it summoning from somewhere the strength to get to her feet and walk away.

Outside her own bedroom door she became very conscious of the whisky, hidden away there behind the hats; but it was too early, one really must not give way. She went on, down the stairs, and joined the other girls at the breakfast table.

"She said she was all right," Deborah said. "Is she?"

"Oh yes. Just a bilious attack." Odd, she could now speak normally, even with composure. "She realised that it wasn't very pleasant for *you*, Caro, so she's going to move up into the studio."

"Good," Caro said. "So that old chaise-longue of hers will serve some purpose after all."

Five days sounded so short a time, but for Mrs Thorley they were endless, partly because they were aimless. She had plenty to do, but was completely unable to give her mind to anything. Against all the arguments of good sense, she found herself believing that someone would come on the 25th and take Lavinia away. Then what should she say: That Lavinia had gone to Brazil, invited to stay with the Fremlins? That would surprise no-one, but it would be entirely unsatisfactory at another level. After all, Lavinia was her daughter; still very young; pregnant and singularly lacking in good sound sense; maternal responsibility could not be shuffled off so easily. But she was incapable of following that line of thought to any conclusion;

she was up against something she could not handle. Something for which there was no precedent.

Lavinia reappeared at the family table and seemed to eat heartily. Mrs Thorley found it almost impossible to address her directly, and tried to avoid looking at her.

George once touched on dangerous ground, saying pontifically,

"Anybody who's been bilious shouldn't eat cream, Lavinia. You'll be sick again, and get fat. Once when I was sick I couldn't face cream for a week."

Diana, always so correct, said, "George that is hardly a subject for talk at table."

"And you are wrong," Caro said. "Once after I had been unmentionably indisposed," she shot one of her mocking glances at Diana, "I ate like a horse for three days."

Once, alone with Lavinia, Mrs Thorley did manage to say, "What are you taking with you?"

"Just what I took to Abbas. Enough for the night. And my pictures."

And on the 25th the little overnight valise and the bulging portfolio were there in the hall, inconspicuous, but ready to hand.

That was the longest day of all. One of those warm, premature summer-like days which March occasionally produced.

Diana and Deborah and Caroline had all gone into Baildon; two to work on the little house, and Caro, in the afternoon, to present a handwriting prize at the Ragged School. As she lightly said, one good deed led to another; she was now a member of the Committee of the Friends of the Hospital; a patron of the Ragged School, "and unless I am very careful I shall end up in charge of that place for unmarried mothers!"

George had decided to go with them and Gad's settled down into a waiting silence. Nothing happened.

Nothing had happened when they all came back, ready for supper.

"It's as well," Diana said, with just a touch of spite in her voice, "that Caro is marrying a reasonably well-to-do man. What do you think she did today? She gave every child in the school a currant bun and a packet of sweets."

"Well, there were only two prizes, both dreadfully dull. Ten-shilling vouchers for boots! Not that they aren't needed. And I felt sorry for the losers." A loser herself! "I must say, though, that all through the ceremony—that was dreadfully dull, too—I kept asking myself what would Miss Hardwicke say? *Me*, a judge of handwriting."

"I know what she would say," Deborah said. "That one need not be a hen in order to tell a good egg from a bad one."

Through the chatter and the laughter Mrs Thorley was listening, as she had listened all day, for the sound of wheels and hooves on the gravel. One of her furtive glances at Lavinia informed her that the girl showed no agitation. Placid, confident, she sat at the table. The day died in splendour, hyacinth blue, apple green and daffodil yellow in great swaths across the West. George went to bed. Deb said that she must wash her hair, despite all precautions it was spattered with whitewash. Caro went with her, but Diana moved to a chair near the lamp and took up the now almost-completed table-cloth. Lavinia sat idle, waiting, but without any sign of anxiety or impatience. Mrs Thorley went to her llttle desk in the window embrasure and stared at pages which conveyed nothing to her mind, which was busy with what she would say to whoever came.

Finally Diana said, "Well, that is finished. Hardly worth starting anything else now. Goodnight, Mamma." The ritual exchange of kisses. "Goodnight, Lavinia."

Presently the clock on the half-landing struck eleven. Mrs Thorley wanted to break this unnautral silence, to say something, anything. She tried to mention the lateness of the hour, to ask if Lavinia were sure of the date.

Lavinia said, "Whoever comes, please, no reproaches! It would be most unwise. Nobody was to know."

Mrs Thorley thought of all the heated exhortations she intended, the promises she meant to extract knowing all the time how futile it would be because she would not be able to use the ultimate weapon. She could not, in the circumstances, refuse to let Lavinia go . . . Oh God, what did I ever do to deserve this?

On the first stroke of twelve Lavinia stood up, rigidly attentive, poised, ready to go. Mrs Thorley rose too. The clock seemed to take an extraordinarily long time to complete the marking between March 25th and the 26th, and when the last boom had died to nothing, Lavinia fell to the ground.

Mrs Thorley had seen people faint before, but not like this. Lavinia did not crumple at the knees and subside, she fell prone as a sapling would at the final stroke of the axe. She lay on her back with her eyes open, wide and staring.

Dead?

A feeling of relief, of which she was instantly ashamed and which she regretted for a long time, shot through Mrs Thorley. Nothing now to hide. In the same instant she was thinking: Smelling salts, none handy; cold water; wrist slapping; head between the knees. All effective for faints, but this could be a fit. About them she knew nothing at all.

Feel the pulse. Alive, thank God! She pulled Lavinia into a sitting position, her back against a chair, and proceeded as for a faint, pushing the head forward and down.

"Oh, my dear . . ." The first endearment she had used, even in her thoughts, since her discovery of the girl's position. The nearest she had come to tenderness was pity; poor child, poor innocent, poor deluded girl.

And even such thoughts could only be entertained when out of Lavinia's presence. Now she could say, "We'll manage . . . somehow," which in the circumstances was gallant. "Come, let me help you into the chair. I'll get you a little brandy."

"I'm all right," Lavinia said, and as though to prove it, stood up. Physically she *seemed* to be all right, strong on her feet anyway. She still looked blank and stunned—and who could wonder? She'd been so confident, had such complete trust in somebody . . . And now there is only me, Mrs Thorley thought. Released from the kind of trance which had held her passive and dumb for five endless days, she was the more aware of the absurdity of it all. Whoever the guilty man was— and the first suspect was Mr Fremlin—was it likely that he would come? On a date so specified that when the day ended, Lavinia had had a kind of fit.

Lavinia went to bed. She moved in a rather curious way, a bit like a clockwork toy well wound up, but still, part of Mrs Thorley's mind noted, not a word of regret, or explanation, and not a tear. Mrs Thorley went with her to the foot of the attic stairs and said, in a muted voice:

"Try to sleep, Lavinia. We'll think about things in the morning."

You will think about things now, Isabel Thorley, and drunk as you may be, you will try to think straight.

A miscarriage. Lavinia has had a shock and a fall. Miscarriages have been brought about by lesser causes. And she was always delicate, the one who had to be coddled along with cod liver oil and iron pills. A miscarriage would be the most desirable solution.

But not to be counted upon. What then? You have the others to think of. Of the three only Caroline might escape from the resultant scandal unscathed. Edward Taylor, a doctor with a trained mind, might not feel that in marrying Caro he was marrying into a family afflicted with leprosy. But Everard, so cool and precise and ambitious, and Mr Bridges, so Puritanical . . . Strange to think that on the rock of an unprecedented scandal, Diana and Deborah, who loved most, would suffer most.

Think of yourself for a moment. Yes, with what zest would those who regarded her business activities as un-womanly pounce upon this, proof that she had neglect-ed her family, failed to exercise the supervision girls needed. And the coarse jokes about letting the wrong bull get at her heifer.

Of course there were places like that to which Car-oline had made such light-hearted reference, Lying-in Hospitals, Shelters for Fallen Women. But so far as Mrs Thorley knew, they offered only temporary shel-ter, and what kind of women would be there? Could she possibly consign Lavinia to such a place. And would Lavinia, who seemed to have no sense of guilt, or shame, connive at the only possible alternative—to go away to some distant place and pretend to be mar-ried and widowed cruelly young.

Oh, what to do? Where to turn?

Just hope for a miscarriage, after the shock and the fall.

It was almost daylight when the whisky and utter ex-haustion threw her into the abyss of unconsciousness.

"It is unlike Mamma to be late," Deborah said as she set the dish of eggs and bacon on the table.

At Christmas, Katie had brought Willy to the stick-ing point—and not before time. Mrs Thorley had not replaced her; her wage had been small, but there was her keep to be considered; a tiny saving, but it all counted; and while the girls were here they could help; when they went surely Jenny could manage to cook for one woman and a boy. Jenny had accepted the change with resignation, simply saying that running about could not be expected; not at her age, and not with her legs. Most of the resultant running about had been done by Deborah.

"I'd take a tray up," Deborah said, "but honestly I think a bit of extra sleep would do her more good. This last day or two I've felt that she had something on her mind. She's been unlike herself."

"Yes," George agreed. "So quiet." He looked at his half-sister and his two stepsisters with slight reproach. "Three weddings all in one is rather more than most mothers have to deal with."

Halfway through the meal, Deborah said, "By the way, Di, I shan't be coming in this morning. I must prune the roses here."

"Oh, Deb," Diana said, dicontent in her voice and on her face. "With so much to do in Friars' Lane! And I thought one pruned in the autumn."

"I did. But with this warm spring they've made a lot of new growth and if I leave them, and a frost comes . . . "

"Oh, well," Diana said with a resigned shrug. "You coming in, Caro?"

"I might as well. Not to whitewash, though."

George saw and seized his opportunity.

"If you like, Deb, I'd exercise Foxy for you."

Why not? The mare, despite her name, which was a contraction of Foxton, was anything but foxy by nature, the gentlest thing alive, and every time Deborah thought of her, pulling a coal cart, she felt something like adoration for Tim, who had noticed and saved her from that fate. Also, George, trained by Deborah herself, was a good rider and he was rapidly outgrowing his pony.

"All right," Deborah said. "But no jumps, mind."

Mrs Thorley woke from what was rare for her, a beautiful, happy dream. In it she had been young, very young again, in Westmorland, playing with an assortment of dogs, not a care in the world.

She woke, realised from the way the sun lay across

her bed that she had overslept, and that, waking, she was one of the most care-ridden women in the world.

She rose quickly and was immediately aware of last night's excess taking its toll; inside her head a cannon ball rolled about, but she put on her slippers, pulled on her robe and went towards the attic stairs. Had it happened, the thing which would deliver them all?

Apparently not. Lavinia lay on the chaise-longue which was now her bed, sleeping, curled up like a kitten. She looked peaceful and very young. Once again Mrs Thorley's mind cried out in rebellion; Oh God, *why?* How *could* you allow such a thing to befall us all, through such an innocent instrument?

Downstairs, two cups of strong coffee cleared her head a bit and from the other side of the room the papers on her desk reproached her. Forms to be filled in, giving the pedigree of every animal that she intended to enter for various shows. Awards in themselves were of little monetary value, but they promoted sales, and whatever happened within the family one certainty was that she would need money.

She approached the job with reluctance, but it was one which demanded concentration, and although her personal problem was not banished from her mind it receded a little as she filled in space after space with the neat copperplate hand which George Thorley, himself a scrawler, had admired so much.

A commotion in the kitchen disturbed her. Jenny screaming, Willy's voice, some shuffling sounds and above all Deborah's voice, clear and authorative, "I can manage."

Jenny stood with both hands clenched to her chest, a knife in one, a half-peeled potato in the other. Willy stood gaping by the door which opened upon the back stairs, and four or five steps up Deborah was dragging Lavinia, roughly. Water steamed from them both.

"She ain't dead, Ma'am," Willy said. "Miss Deb got . . ." But Mrs Thorley was already on the stairs; in time to see Deborah free a hand and slap Lavinia hard across the face. There was some blood. After that there was less resistance and within a minute they were on the attic landing and into the studio. There Deborah released Lavinia with a push and said, "You bloody fool! Do you want everybody to know?"

Mrs Thorley took charge.

"Deb, go and get into dry clothes. I'll see to Lavinia."

"I don't like leaving you. She's mad! She *bit* me." Deborah held out her hand, blood oozing from punctures on the inside and outside of the thumb.

"I can manage," Mrs Thorley said, secure in the authority which she had exercised for so long. Without being told she knew approximately what had happened. Lavinia's father, faced with a crisis out of which neither charm not influence could help him, had shot himself. Lavinia had tried to drown herself. It all fitted.

That terrible thought again: If only Deb had let her! Instantly she refuted it, giving as much care to see that Lavinia was not chilled as she had last evening to see that she did not die in a fit.

"Strip," she said; and although Lavinia still looked blank, she obeyed.

An idea, forming like a bubble on an about-to-boil pan, came to the surface of her mind. It might be just possible, with a vast deal of contrivance and connivance.

"Now," she said, "if you try that again—or anything else—you will go into a lunatic asylum. You know what that means? But if you do *exactly* what you are told, you shall have your baby and bring it up, not as a bastard. You understand me? Of course you do. You're not an idiot. You're trying to hide. I know you are there, Lavinia, and I am speaking to you. It's this or an asylum—and I promise you, a strict one."

Most were. The idea that lunatics—at any rate the harmless ones—should be kindly treated had been promulgated by a few humane doctors but it had gained little ground. Whippings, starving and violent purging were still in vogue . . . And of course one could not hand over one's own daughter, flesh of one's flesh, bone of one's bone, to such a régime, any more than one could consign her to the company of women—all rough and most of them prostitutes, in places which took in unmarried mothers.

Lavinia looked sullen but she said nothing.

"Mamma, I know it is a shocking thing to say, but you should know . . . Lavinia deliberately tried to drown herself. I know, I was there. I was pruning the roses. She couldn't see me, but I straightened up, just in time to see her *jump* into the moat. And she resisted me. She looks so frail, but thrashing about in the water . . . and she bit me. I yelled and Willy . . . But for him we could both have drowned. I tried to make it sound like an accident. She is so absent-minded, stepping back to get a better view . . . But it was intentional. You may not believe—wish to believe it, but it is true. And on the stairs I simply had to hit her, because of Jenny and Willy. I mean most people, just rescued wouldn't have been so . . . so awkward."

Mrs Thorley remembered that she had somewhere heard, or read, that bites from a human being could be more dangerous than those from an animal. Carbolic soap was supposed to be good for wounds which might fester, and so was alcohol. Try both.

Submitting to treatment, protesting that the little punctures didn't warrant any fuss, it was just the idea of biting which was so horrifying, Deborah added:

"And she may try again. Mamma, I hate saying this, but she always has been a bit odd. We must admit that. She never had a friend, except those people at Abbas. Now they're gone and all of us . . . I mean there is only three months' gap between Caroline and Lavinia, and Caro is to be married in June . . . Being so left out . . . I think it turned her brain."

Speaking shortly but with a distinct feeling of sharing her impossible load, Mrs Thorley told Deborah the truth—so far as she knew it.

"My God!" Deborah said, and clapped her hands to her face and stayed so still that for a moment or two Mrs Thorley feared that she, the most reliable, most sturdy one, was about to give way. But when at last Deborah dropped her hands, the face revealed was calm, determined and older.

"Then she must be locked in. A suicide calls for an inquest. We should have a double scandal."

"I threatened her, very severely. I said . . . I said that if she didn't behave she would go into an asylum."

"I doubt whether she understood. And if it came to the point who would want to marry into a family with insanity in it? Leave it to me. She must be kept safe until we have time to think."

Deborah was handy with tools and knew where to look for what she wanted. It took her very little time to fix two staples, a length of chain and the padlock. Then she stood, hesitant, thinking of Jenny, who slept in the neighbouring attic and must surely notice. She went into Jenny's room and knocked out the window frame, not a difficult thing to do, the wood was old and rotten. There was no crash, for the whole thing fell on to a tough rosemary bush.

Jenny's wardrobe was not extensive, one good armful. Deborah carried the clothes down and laid them on the bed of what was always called The Little Room. Then from her own room she fetched a hat-box, carried it up and placed in it Jenny's rather pitiable collection of treasures—silhouettes of people cut from black paper, pasted on white and held in tin frames, a few fairings of coarse pottery and some bits of finery, mainly things which Mamma and the girls had discarded. The room was soon cleared.

"Jenny, something rather awful has happened. The window of your room has blown out. I've brought all your things into The Little Room."

And what was awful about that? Answer to prayer, rather. That top flight of stairs was steep, the final trial for legs at the end of a day.

"You shouldn't hev bothered about my stuff, Miss Deborah." She was the only one of them who would have done. "I could've managed them stairs just that one more time." A way of saying that once settled in The Little Room, Jenny did not intend to be relegated to the attic again.

"S'funny thing. Katie was allus whimpering about noises up there. And I allus towd her it was winders or doors. So now we know."

"Miss Lavinia will have a tray. I'll take it up, Jenny. The sousing gave her rather a shock."

"She never was very strong, was she? How did it happen, Miss?"

"I can only think that it was the peach tree. She was stepping back to admire it—perhaps planning to paint it; I don't know. She just stepped back and fell into the moat."

That was to be the story—for the time being.

Deborah thought about windows, how easily the one in Jenny's attic had fallen out; how easy it would be for Lavinia, always a bit demented and now with every reason to be more so, to throw herself out.

Over the meal called lunch, substantial when everyone was present, at other times rather skimpy, and one for which neither Mrs Thorley nor Deborah had much appetite, Deborah said:

"I have been thinking about that window, Mamma. Could you bear to come up and keep an eye on her, while I put up some bars. I must work from the inside because otherwise Willy will notice, and I can't lock the door from the inside."

Deborah's reaction had been exactly what might be expected; helpful, practical. What would that of the others be? Cold disgust from Diana? Hysteria from Caroline? Or—with girls one never knew, perhaps the dead opposite.

Lavinia's attic, into which until today no member of the family had set a foot, was, though furnished with odds and ends, better than some bed-sitting rooms which Mrs Thorley had occupied in the worst days. It occupied the centre of this remote gable end and was quite spacious. There was the piece of furniture to which Caroline had referred as that old chaise-longue of hers, now made into a bed so that its upholstery, silk but tattered, was largely hidden. A wickerwork chair, slightly lop-sided, but still comfortable-looking. An oil lamp on one of the high wooden stools used by clerks in offices, but painted bright lacquer red. Near the window was the proper artist's easel which Lavinia had bought when she sold her first picture, and a trestle-table laden with the tools of the trade. Into one corner fitted a triangular washstand. The floor was bare, except by the bed where the, oak planks, some of them eighteen inches wide, were covered by a rug, old and faded but still beautiful. And one wide sweep of whitewashed wall Lavinia had used to paint upon. A confusion of brilliant colour and strange shapes.

Lavinia was at the easel when Mrs Thorley and Deborah entered. Deborah had said, "We might as well make one errand of it," and had carried up the tray. "It's cold anyway, so time can't matter." She now set the tray down rather roughly at one end of the trestle-table and went on to deal with the window. Rather more of a problem than the door, because up directly under the roof and in an exposed gable, air would be necessary. It was a casement window and she must arrange it so that one half at least could be opened, but so that the opening would not be wide enough for Lavinia to squeeze through.

As she worked Deborah brooded over her inability to feel really sorry for Lavinia. Naturally she had been annoyed with her for making the rescue so difficult, and nobody enjoyed being bitten, but when she knew the truth, surely her first thought should have been: Poor little Lavinia! Surely any girl seduced and abandoned should be pitied. But all she had felt—after concern for the scandal—had been repulsion. And she could trace its origin. She assumed Mr Fremlin to be the man concerned, and from the moment she had first met him she had been repelled by him. Now something of him was in Lavinia. Loathsome thought! Her instinct had been right—she had refused even to ride in his carriage. He was evil. And look what calamity he had brought upon them all. Lavinia had always been eccentric, but harmless; now here she was, out of her mind and pregnant, being locked in, barred in. And taking no notice at all, working away at one of her silly pictures as though her life depended upon it. And who ever saw a goat with four horns?

Mrs Thorley, standing by the door, had addressed Lavinia and said, "Eat your lunch, Lavinia."

Without looking round Lavinia said, "Presently."

Dared one still hope for a miscarriage? The shock of disappointment, a fall, a drenching in the moat—water was cold in March. Any one of those would have ended a *wanted* pregnancy, in a strong girl, Mrs Thorley thought bitterly. But not this one! No. Not this.

"Mamma, I think the girls should be fortified. I'll get some sherry."

Neither Diana nor Caroline was in a good mood. Deborah, who could be relied upon to do some decorating and make a decent meal, had let Diana down. Diana had made no attempt to continue whitewashing the ceiling, she had painted a skirting board and somehow managed to break two of her cherished nails. Then she had gone to the cook-shop and bought a meat pie, which Everard had eaten, hungrily, but without much enthusiasm. And who could wonder at that? He could have bought a meat pie and eaten it in his office. Because she was so much in love she had apologised for the meagre meal, and smiled so sweetly that Everard had thought: Of course she couldn't be expected to slave in the kitchen. But could they afford a cook? In three months' time? Just because Mrs Thorley must be so hasty, and so managing? What he worried about and resented was reflected on his face and Diana had interpreted it as dislike of the pie, and justifiable, the meat tasteless and rubbery, the pastry like cardboard.

Caroline had endured criticism of another kind.

She had gone to lunch with Mrs Bosworth, who was entertaining all the Friends of the Hospital, and of course Edward was there and he'd administered a rebuke, mildly, kindly, but still a rebuke.

"Darling, I heard about yesterday. How generous you were with sweets and buns . . ."

"You should have seen their faces!"

"I know. But I'm not sure that it was wise."

"Why not?"

"Well, old Miss Meadows was there . . ."

"Naturally. She is one of the governors."

"Darling . . . it's just that she is so deadly poor. She would have loved to give buns and sweets, but she hasn't a penny to rub against a key. The best she can do is cadge bones from the butcher in cold weather and make a little soup for the neediest."

"Then wouldn't you think she'd love to see them gobbling buns?"

"Darling, people's minds don't work that way. She would feel . . . diminished."

"God love me! The things you think of!"

"I was only suggesting that it would have been . . . well, a little more tactful to have left the buns and sweets for the master to distribute. Afterwards. And while we are the subject . . ."

"Yes?"

"Well, darling, there are people who don't like to hear God's name taken lightly."

God love me! I'd love to tear off this ring, throw it at him, say: To hell with tact and schools and hospitals and *you*, Edward Taylor, and all the deadly dreary things you stand for.

She knew she could not afford such a gesture. She had just escaped—by Mamma's advice—looking as though she had been jilted by Freddy. Break her engagement to Edward and talk would be virulent. A near engagement, and a proper engagement broken off. Something very wrong with Caroline Thorley . . . No, she must hold on, at least until they were married; then she'd show everybody, including Edward.

The sherry did something to soothe ill-humour, and supper was not noticeably different to Diana and Caroline, and George, all young and self-engrossed; Mrs Thorley and Deborah tried to keep up a front, for George's sake and Caroline introduced a subject of perennial interest by saying that having had a huge lunch at Mrs Bosworth's, she must be careful about supper or she would have trouble with her waist. Eighteen inches was the ideal for girls who wished to be admired and both she and Diana occasionally slipped over the limit. Severe tight lacing helped, even if it hurt. Caroline would sometimes say that her stays were killing her, she could hardly breathe; then within half an hour she could be dancing, talking, laughing, all at the same time. Deborah was enviable; although she was taller than either of them, she was so naturally slim as hardly to need lacing at all.

That subject exhausted, Caroline gave a list of the guests at Mrs. Bosworth's. "Lady Norton was there. As usual she looked as though her clothes came from a jumble sale, but I must say she has a sense of humour."

"Which means that she laughed when you cracked a joke," Diana said. She had always thought Caroline too flippant, and now there was envy as well. Diana, the belle of her circle, slaving away painting skirting boards, while Caroline, over lunch, met Lady Norton. There was envy at another level, too—only half recognised. Diana felt that if Caroline had offered Edward a dog biscuit for lunch he'd have eaten it happily and said that it was the best lunch he had ever had. Not that Diana would have exchanged Everard for Edward, never in a thousand years!

What I must do, Diana decided, is to learn to cook, just a few simple dishes, a guard against an emergency such as today's.

Nobody mentioned Lavinia or her absence from the supper table. Her comings and goings had always been unpredictable.

Pushing her food around and making a pretence at eating, Mrs Thorley thought: And now I must tell them, because they must connive.

She said, "George dear, go to bed."

"Mamma! It's so early."

"Well, go and find something to do. We have something to talk over."

"Oh, I see." Women's talk about the wedding to which he was greatly looking forward because for him it meant new clothes and a chance to shine, socially. And he would be host, after all, he was the son of the house.

Mrs Thorley said, "I have something terrible to tell you," and told them, as briefly as possible.

It was Caroline who said, "Oh, poor Lavinia" before beginning to cry.

Diana said the completely conventional thing.

"Whoever he is he must be made to marry her. At once."

"If he could be found. Mr Fremlin—I suspect him most strongly—is now in Brazil; most of the other men she met at Abbas were foreigners and she refused to tell me . . . So what is called a shot-gun marriage is out of the question. But I have a plan. To carry it out I shall need all your help . . ."

She outlined the plan which had begun as a mere bubble in her mind. Lavinia had fallen into the moat and for a few days could stay in bed, suffering from the resultant chill. That would give time for an invitation to arrive, inviting her for a long, long visit. It must involve a long journey too, to give Lavinia time to find a man and be married aboard ship—sea-captains were authorised to perform marriages. Lavinia would then be widowed, have a baby and bring it home. But of course, all the time Lavinia would really be up there in the attic.

"If you see any flaw in this arrangement, say so. You are the ones most intimately involved."

Caroline—the only one to have uttered a word of compassion—mopped her face and took hope.

"Mamma, can we be sure? She never even . . . Well, you know, the curse, the female benefit . . . Lavinia never had it, so how could she be . . . pregnant? Don't you think that Edward should give her a thorough examination?"

"Lavinia herself said that she was going to have a baby. And I promised her that if she did exactly what she was told, she should have it, without any shame or scandal."

Deborah said, "It might work, if we were sure of her cooperation. But she might do anything, at any time. And think of the endless lies. I think she should be put away. After all she is mad."

And bad. She must be, to have anything to do with Mr Fremlin.

Diana, who had not cried, but who had turned whiter than the table-cloth, said:

"Will it affect the wedding?"

"Not if we work together."

Deborah said, "While we are here . . ."

And though that had an ominous sound, in the main things worked very smoothly. India must be Lavinia's supposed destination—a great number of girls went to India and found husbands. It must not be a well-known place, not Bombay, Madras or Calcutta, because even in their small circle almost everybody knew somebody, or was related to somebody in those areas. Deborah's atlas contained a patchwork map which showed spheres of influence, English—through the East India Company, some French still, some Portuguese. They chose a seemingly untouched native state —Killapore.

Everybody said, "Oh, what a pity. I cannot even write a letter of introduction."

But everybody accepted the story. Lavinia Thorley—no, Osborne—had never attracted a suitor here where girls were ten a penny, what more natural than that she should accept an invitation to stay with one of her mother's relatives in Killapore, where men were ten a penny. For even into the so-called native states, white men were moving as military or financial advisors, or as bridge builders.

And of course, the invitation coming so suddenly, there was no time for farewell parties such as usually preceded a departure. Lavinia simply vanished and even George didn't wonder why she had not bothered to say goodbye. She'd never behaved as other people did.

Food was a problem, made a little worse by George in his innocence. Jenny served so much for so many and however Mrs Thorley and the girls tried to spare—Lavinia must be fed—George was almost sure to say, "If nobody wants this, I'll eat it."

Mrs Thorley was driven to ask Jenny to cook rather more.

"Ah," Jenny said, "Master George he do eat like a team of horses, but bless his heart, he's growing."

Since the girls cleared the table anything that chanced to be left over could be scraped into a bowl and hidden in the chiffonier until Jenny's whereabouts, and George's, were certain; it would never do to be caught carrying food towards the attic stairs.

There were times when Mrs Thorley was forced to

rely upon what she called shop food. It was good
enough, thousands of people never ate anything else,
but she distrusted it as nourishment for a girl at a time
when she needed the very best. She had herself eaten a
good deal of such makeshift stuff when she was carrying Lavinia and that might account for her poor
physique. Almost imperceptibly, Mrs Thorley began to
think of the coming baby in a proper grandmotherly
way. It was misbegotten, but it must have every
chance. Poor little thing, it was not to blame. Linked to
this thought came the problem of exercise. Everybody
now agreed that in the early stages a little gentle walking in the fresh air was beneficial. The only possible
time for Lavinia to emerge from the attic was on Sunday afternoon when Jenny went down to the village
and Deborah would take George riding, he on Tom
Thumb, she on Foxy, but with a promise that at some
point he should be allowed to change the saddles and
ride the mare. Then it was possible for Lavinia to come
down and take a brief airing. But that meant no week-
end visits and that brought a protest from Diana:

"Everard did so enjoy his week-ends. And after all it
is not his fault that we are in this dreadful position."

Caroline could not resist the quip:

"Wouldn't it have simplified everything had he
been?"

It took Diana a breath-space to sort that out; then
she said:

"Don't be so disgusting!"

The word echoed in Mrs Thorley's mind. For there
was a disgusting side to this secret incarceration. A living body had other needs . . .

Like every well-appointed house, Gad's owned a
commode which had been housed in The Little Room.
It was now upstairs in the attic and Mrs Thorley was
obliged to act as a night-soil remover. About this, as
about food, she was conscientious and in what had
been Jenny's room she kept a bucket, or rather a slop-
pail with a lid. Nothing offensive was allowed to stay in

the occupied attic for long. Every night, when the house was asleep, she moved softly about, carrying her lantern. Water carrier, too, since Lavinia's ewer must be filled. Everybody must *wash*.

And never, for any service, a word of thanks. Lavinia appeared to be entirely oblivious. She seldom spoke; sometimes she lay on her bed, staring at the ceiling; sometimes in her chair, looking into the garden; or she was painting, at the easel, at the table, or on the wall.

She had cut herself entirely and her mother was cut off, too. She dared hardly leave the house. In a moment of the hopelessness she wrote and cancelled all her entries for shows. But the wedding must take place, that triple wedding, planned before all this begun. It sometimes seemed extraordinary to Mrs Thorley to reflect how active and resourceful she had been, so little time ago, and how now there was nothing left but to go round and round, like a blindfolded donkey turning a mill-wheel.

The problem of laundry was solved by Diana. There had opened recently in Baildon an enterprise called the Hand Laundry, most conveniently anonymous. Each new customer paid threepence down and received a coarse linen bag, stamped with a number. Diana's was 408. This number was then printed in marking ink on every article sent to be washed. One handed in the bag of soiled stuff, preferably on Monday or Tuesday, and called for it on Thursday or Friday. Nobody there in the steam and heat noticed or cared how the amount of laundry compared with the size of the household as would have been the case with Jenny and the village woman who since Katie's going came up to help with the Gad's washing.

Having seen to the laundry and the shopping for ready-to-eat food, Diana felt that she had done her duty, beyond occasionally asking, rather perfunctorily: How is she? She felt the whole business to be disgusting and degrading, just when the preparations for the wonderful wedding should have been going forward so happily. Caroline was more sympathetic; for her Lavinia had not ceased to exist as a person. She sometimes bought chocolate or fancy cakes—without Di's knowledge—and would then offer to take up the smuggled supper bowl. Alone of the four, she felt how Lavinia must miss all contact with growing things; she'd been so fond of walking in the woods. Caroline sometimes took flowers, too. But she always came down in a state of distress.

"She wouldn't even look, leave alone speak. How terrible it must be to be in such a state of mind. Poor, poor thing!"

She, too, had known despair, the feeling that life was meaningless, that she did not wish to see or speak to anybody, ever again.

On such occasions, Deborah, the kindly one as a rule, showed that she shared Diana's attitude.

"If you must cry for anybody, Caro, cry for Mamma. She is the one to be pitied." Or, "If the sight of her upsets you so much, keep away." Or, "Caro, you're just being sentimental."

Deborah had had what was, literally, an illuminating experience. From the first, when she was certain that Lavinia was mad and bent on self-destruction, she had insisted that Lavinia should have no lamp, no candle. She was quite capable of setting the house on fire. But one evening in April, carrying up the supper bowl in order to spare Mamma one journey, Deborah had found the attic lighted. Lavinia had rearranged things. The finished picture on its easel, had been pulled close to a cleared space on the trestle-table, and on that space, not in sticks, but fixed to the table by their own grease, there were two candles. And they were black. Between them stood a vase containing a posy, wallflowers and a few narcissi. It was, in fact, a travesty of an altar.

For a girl of her time and class, Deborah was, if not

perfectly educated, better read than most, for during her last months at school Miss Hardwicke had given her the run of her library, which had contained many interesting and curious books. She was horrified by what she saw, and half recognised, yet her response was practical. She said:

"Don't you realise that a light in this window can be seen for miles?" She blew out the candles and in the twilight asked:

"Where are the rest? And the matches?"

Lavinia made a little whimpering sound, but that was no answer.

"Then I must search. Sit down in that chair and if you dare move a finger, I'll knock you silly."

Lavinia did not speak. She stood still, and for a moment, in the dusk, her face assumed something of the leering, sneering look of the four-horned, half-human face of the goat in the picture. A battle of wills, of forces, ranged, momentarily, the heavy battalions on Lavinia's side. Deborah, the strong, the logical, practical one, felt something of the slackening of fibre that had made Mrs Thorley almost fall to the bed on that bright March morning. And what came to her rescue was not, oddly enough, her orthodox religion, or anything she had read: it was something remembered from early childhood, when she and Caro had shown every sign of growing up wild, associating with work people and village children. Without thinking she crossed her fingers and said, "Keep away from me, Owd Scrat!"

Lavinia sat down in the chair and Deborah remembered that under the bed was the traditional hiding place. She reached into the shallow space between the chaise-longue and the floor and found several other candles, all black, and a box of matches.

She went down the back stairs, into the garden and flung them all into the moat. She said nothing to anyone, but she spoke with urgency to Mamma.

"There *must* be some place where such people are cared for. It would be expensive, of course, but

Mamma, I don't need my legacy. Tim is well-to-do. You must think of yourself. It's bad enough now, you're worn to the bone. And have you *thought* about what it will be like when the . . . the baby comes? We shall be gone. You'll be left with George . . . And you can't tell a baby to keep quiet. Honestly, Mamma, it is an impossible situation and I'm sorry that I ever connived. She must be put away." It sounded terrible, but it must be said.

Mrs Thorley skirted around the main issue.

"Naturally, Deb, I have thought of the future. About George I have already made my decision. We cannot count upon his gaining entry to Biddle's—the examination is *very* competitive. I have applied for a place at Felstead and he will go there at the commencement of the autumn term."

Just what Mamma did not want; George the well-beloved out of driving reach. Poor Mamma! What a bloody, bloody, devilish mess!

"George's going to Felstead may ease things, Mamma, but only for a time. He'll be home for Christmas . . . And there's Jenny. Oh, I know you made this plan on the spur of the moment and we were all shocked out of our senses and agreed. But it isn't feasible. Look, let me go to London. I could ask about there, amongst doctors. Nobody would know me."

"And what of the child? No, Deborah, I must stick to my plan. And you can help me there, as you did about Lavinia's mythical voyage. How soon may we announce her sudden engagement and decision to be married aboard ship?"

"You are the most pig-headed woman. But quite the dearest," Deborah said. "All I hope is that you will never have cause to regret . . ."

Once, on one of those so-carefully-manoeuvred Sunday afternoons, Mrs Thorley had Lavinia in the garden, her hand like a gaoler's on the girl's elbow, and reaching the place where the view across the moat was unblocked, saw two people. Not locals. No country people would trample about in a field of young wheat. She was past being startled, even the knife-edge of apprehension had its limits, but she was angered. She called, in the voice that could carry without shouting, "What do you think you are doing?" She felt the relief which she knew to be idiotic, of letting free the anger that smouldered inside her.

The couple answered her placatingly. They'd come for a drive and let their little dog out for a little run; and he'd run into the field. Even as they spoke, in another part of the field a pheasant whirred into the air and the woman cried, "There he is! Charlee! Charleeeee!" Trampling more wheat they both ran towards the scene of the disturbance. Mrs Thorley found herself shaking; a tremor that began in the marrow of her bones and spread outwards. It just didn't do, she thought, to give way to anger. For a moment her hold on Lavinia was so shaky that if, as Deb said, she would try again, she could not have controlled her. So she hustled her in, away from the sunny, cuckoo-loud out-of-doors and back into prison. Then to make up for it, cooked bacon and eggs and carried the dish up, still almost sizzling.

A good hour later Deborah and George came in from their ride and George sniffed the air, looking puzzled.

"Who's been having fried bacon in the middle of the afternoon?"

"Nobody!" Deb sounded quite snappy. "It's simply your imagination. You think of nothing but food."

Everybody was short-tempered these days. It was the wedding, George supposed. Why marry if it made you so edgy? He gave Deb a reproachful look and she thought: It's not his fault!

"If you're really hungry, I'll cook you some. With eggs?"

Ships bound for India could stop briefly at the Canary Islands to take on fresh fruit and vegetables. And from there passengers could send letters; and the sooner Lavinia's mythical romance began, the sooner it could end. The news must be broken, with simulated surprise and pleasure.

Mrs Spicer, one of the first to be informed, said:

"Oh, but my dear; I hope she has not made a rash choice. She is so very *young*."

"In fact a mere three months younger than Caroline."

"Of course, but the difference always *seemed* much greater. Did you say his name was Harrington? Now, oddly enough it was a Mr Harrington who wrote to inform us of Everard's parents' death. Or it could have been Harrison. I don't know about you, Isabel, but I am growing forgetful. Is this Mr Harrington in the mission field?"

"No." It had been decided, in a family conclave, which, Caroline thought, would have been comic had it not been so serious, that Mr Harrington must not belong to any network which in India linked people over unimaginable spaces. He must not be employed by the East India Company, either in a military or civil capacity; he must not be a missionary or a doctor or an engineer. It was, of course, Deborah who came up with the word anthropologist.

Mrs Spicer accepted Mr Harrington's profession without question, the mention of Caroline Thorley, to be married on the third Saturday of June, caused her mind to go off at a tangent. Wedding presents. Absolute bugbears to a woman of position and not much money. With the humble it was fairly easy; when, for instance Willy Snell, who worked at Gad's, had married Katie Snell, who also worked there, and Arthur had sighed and said that there should be law against in-breeding, Mrs Spicer had been able to buy from the pedlar with a donkey cart a tea-pot, shaped like a beehive, and cheap at sixpence-halfpenny. It would never be used for teamaking, it would be an ornament, a bit of colour in a drab home. But for the Gad's Hall girls more was needed and Mrs Spicer was plying her needle, embroidering pillow-cases for Deborah and Caroline. To Diana and Everard, since Everard was related, Mrs Spicer proposed to give a different present, six silver teaspoons in a case, given her when she married, but seldom used because what domestic help Mrs. Spicer could afford was always hasty and heavy-handed and the spoon handles were of filigree, delicate as lace.

Well, Mrs Thorley thought, driving home after a cursory look in on the herd, and Joe Snell, disappointed over the cancellation of the shows, disappointed in fact with Mrs Thorley, who had seemed so different, and was now showing herself to be, after all, just a female, so wrapped up with the coming wedding as to have no time or thought to give to real business—I've told Mrs Spicer and within twenty-four hours everyone will know. As good as hiring the Town Crier.

Diana told Everard. To him the word anthropologist had meaning. It implied an independent income, the most enviable thing in the world. Foot-free in India! Everard's memories of that country were distorted, glamourised. He could hardly remember his parents, but he still had a clear mental vision of his ayah, a silver ring through one nostril, who had spoiled him inordinately. Of the uglier side of life in India he had seen nothing. He knew better now, of course; his godfather had been free with his reminiscences, blind beggars who looked as though their eyes were filled with milk, lepers with no noses and only stumps of fingers, diseases, such as the cholera which killed Everard's parents—and countless, literally countless, nameless other people. Mr Everard, safe with his fortune in Buckinghamshire, had no illusions about the country in

which he had made his fortune. "It's the same with
West Africa, my boy; there's a jingle, but with truth in
it—Beware, beware the Bight of Bemin; Few come
out, though many go in—and India is boiling up for
something. I may not live to see it, I hope I don't, but
there's a bloody bloodbath pending."

Nonetheless, Everard had cherished memories of his
childhood fairyland and envied Mr Harrington,
whoever he might be.

Of Lavinia he had only the faintest recollection. She
had never seemed to be part of the family.

Edward was more concerned. When Caroline told
him he said:

"She always seemed so immature. Let's hope she
hasn't fallen into the hands of some crapulous old man.
They have a weakness for young girls."

"Crapulous? Edward, what does that mean?"

"Drunk, darling. Just not temporarily but as a way
of life."

He realised that as usual he had said the wrong
thing. And been stupid. Except that he himself had always found Lavinia unattractive, there was absolutely
no reason why a Mr Harrington—perhaps young and
handsome—shouldn't have fallen in love with her. And
now he'd gone and put a clumsy foot wrong again and
made Caroline serious. He hastened to make amends.

"I have had an idea, Caro. My wall forms the end of
the cul-de-sac. If I made a gateway in that bit of wall,
you and Diana would be practically next door neighbours. She wouldn't have to go round the church in order to use my stable, and if, say, I knew I had to be
away at night, you could slip across to Di's, or she
could slip across to you."

So very kind, well-meaning and *dull*. If I had to be
away at night . . . Freddy would never have given
such a contingency a second's thought. He'd have said:
We're off to London, Paris, Timbuctoo . . . We!

It could never happen now, and Caroline had made

her bargain. Behind her stretched a long line of Thorleys who had made hard bargains, shrewd ones, but never a cheating one. So Caroline mustered a smile and said that Edward's thought about a gateway in the wall was wonderful and so kind.

Edward, much encouraged, said, "And perhaps we should begin to think about our honeymoon. Where would you like to go?"

"Oh, London, of course," Caroline said. Just for once Edward had surprised her. The honeymoon, in the sense of a holiday, of going away to stay somewhere, was not yet common practice among ordinary people.

"London it shall be," Edward said, happy to be able to indulge her.

Tim Bridges, told of Lavinia's engagement, was momentarily at a loss. Lavinia? Lavinia? If he had ever seen her she had made no impression upon him.

"My half-sister," Deborah said, well aware that last year at this time she would have said: My sister.

"Oh yes. A bit sudden, but we know how sudden such things can be, don't we? I hope she'll be happy."

Dear Tim! If you only knew the truth.

For the first time in his life, Timothy Bridges was concerned about what to wear. He'd always been, in his own opinion and in the eye of all beholders, well dressed. His breeches were made for him by a man whose name was known far beyond the bounds of Norfolk; so were his tweed jackets. He had two dark suits for formal wear, Sunday clothes. All a man could want. They'd last a lifetime, unless he grew fat, which was unlikely, leading the life he did. No Methodist went in for what Tim called fancy dress; and if Tim had been allowed to marry in his own time, and in the place of his choice, one of his dark suits and his good real beaver hat would have been adequate. But he, like Everard, felt that Mrs Thorley had imposed her will upon him. He was to stand at the altar with Everard Spicer and Edward Taylor, both men whose professions demanded what was known as a frock coat; dead black, worn with striped, or lighter-coloured trousers and a hat at least five inches higher than Tim's good beaver.

Expense did not come into it. Tim could afford whatever he wanted, but to be dressed up like that, just for one day, went somehow against his principles. On the other hand he did not want to let Deborah down. So now, quickly dismissing Lavinia from his mind, he tested his ground.

"You're all going to be dressed alike, eh?"

"Not really. That is where Mamma is so thoughtful. We all, always, had the same clothes, but different. That sounds a contradiction, doesn't it? But it is true. All our wedding dresses are made from the same roll of white satin, but they are different. And she was marvellous about her wedding veil. She'd kept it all those years and then cut it so that we should each have a piece."

Abruptly Deborah remembered how Mamma had said that if she had only one apple she would cut into fair quarters. She had cut her delicate lace veil into thirds, because Lavinia . . . Oh dear!

In the blunt way which Mrs Thorley considered uncouth, Tim said:

"What do you want me to wear?"

If she had been explicit, the element of resistance in him would have been fortified, but Deborah said, at once understanding and indifferent:

"Oh. Frock coat and topper? Don't bother. It's only for an hour, anyway."

That decided him. And while Deborah was thinking about the hour—God send it would not be longer—an hour while the house and the secret would be left unguarded, and how could Mamma possibly manage when that hour's ceremony had dispersed them and left her single-handed, was thinking that there actually was Biblical justification for his decision to conform; the person not wearing a wedding garment had not been made welcome.

There was another mention of a wedding, the one at which Our Lord had turned water into wine. Total abstainers like himself argued away that discrepancy by saying that times were different then, it was *because* of the evils of the present days, the gin-palaces which were centres of immorality and the public houses from which men reeled home to their starving wives and children, that a Christian must try to set an example by eschewing alcohol altogether. Tim's mother had had a first-hand story of a young man, the rich inheritor of a brewery and a chain of public houses, who had been so shocked by the sight of poor ragged women and children waiting outside one of his public houses, hoping that the bread-winner would emerge with just enough left to buy a loaf, that he had closed—not sold—all his businesses, given away all of what he regarded as tainted money and gone to work in a factory that made buttons. Not surprisingly such virtue had been rewarded. His employer's only child, a daughter, had fallen in love with him, he'd discovered some new way of speeding up the manufacture of buttons and ended by becoming rich again. "As it says in the Good Book," Tim's mother had pointed out, " 'I have been young and now I am old, but I have never seen the righteous forsaken, nor their seed begging bread.' "

Such stories and homilies had made a great impression upon the boy's mind; an impression deep enough to resist the possible erosion of a reasonably good education—three years at Baildon Grammar School, where he had borne some teasing—weak ale was still then served for breakfast, being cheaper than tea or coffee, and occasionally a little mild persecution. The teasing he had suffered with that deliberate, cultivated indifference which had hardened into stolidity; the persecution he had resisted with his fists. Who is on the Lord's side? Smite the enemy hip and thigh! That obstinate rockiness of character which Mrs Thorley had recognised, without approval, had begun early.

Tim did not approve of Mrs Thorley. She was unwomanly, and she was worldly. And she had foisted this kind of wedding upon him. Not without a certain complacency, he noticed that she was not doing very well. No cattle on show this year! To Timothy Bridges, who exhibited his great amber-coloured horses every year and studied all show catalogues carefully, the omission of any mention of the Gad's animals was eloquent. Various explanations. She hadn't been able to maintain the standard—and what woman could? Or there might be some sickness in the herd. Tim was not very well informed about bovine diseases—Foxton kept only two cows to supply the needs of the house; but he knew that there was something called foot-and-mouth, a form of consumption and a bovine typhus. Any owner of any herd in which a symptom of such diseases had shown did well to keep out of the public eye. For the first disease there was a cure, slow, not completely certain, and Tim, for all his dislike of Mrs Thorley, who had delayed his marriage by a good eight months, was conscientious, willing to do his duty by his neighbour, worldly though she might be. So he broke off the discussion about the wedding and the wedding garments by saying with characteristic lack of preliminaries:

"If it's foot-and-mouth, it isn't lethal. Tar on the feet, sulphur and treacle in the mouth can cure seven out of ten."

For a second even Deborah's nimble mind was at a loss. Then she caught up and said:

"Oh, the herd! All in rumbustious health. Mamma withdrew from all the shows this year because she had other things to think of."

"The wedding?" Typical of a woman, frivolling about in business!

"Yes," Deborah said. She was an unwilling liar and it hurt particularly to lie to Tim, who, she was sure, had never told a lie in his life, and who was so kind and anxious to be helpful—as his last remarks showed.

"Dear George, you are too young."

"And that is where you make your mistake, Mamma. Before I spoke I asked Mr Spicer and he said there were no age limits, provided, of course, that the giver-away could stand up and say I do, when he says who gives this woman? And Mr Spicer agreed with me, I am the girls' nearest male relative."

In the case of Deborah and Caroline this was literally true. Their father had been an only son, and so had his father been, so they had no uncles, no cousins. Away up in Westmorland there was—unless he had died—a man who was Mrs Thorley's brother and therefore Diana's uncle. There were cousins, too. But Mrs Thorley had severed herself from her family forever when her brother—fresh come to his inheritance—had refused absolutely to spare a mere two hundred pounds to save Stephen from the threat of gaol for debt.

She had been considering asking Mr Walford to give the brides away but George had forestalled her.

"Well, it is most unusual, but if you are sure that Mr Spicer agrees . . ."

"He did, Mamma. You can ask him yourself, if you can't believe me."

In his own way, George was clever with words, *don't believe* would have implied a passive inability, *can't believe* implied wilful disbelief.

"Of course I believe you, darling. You shall give your sisters away."

She had an irrelevant thought: George would take up less space than Mr Walford, who, since his wife's death, had grown stout. And in a church such as that at Stonham St Peter's space was extremely limited. It wore its history in its structure.

When, comparatively late, the Angles in the area had been converted, they had built a church, somewhat smaller than a hall in which people ate and slept and entertained or a barn in which stuff was stored. Then the Normans had come, replacing wood and thatch with stone, but although they had enlarged the church slightly much of the extra space had been occupied by the solid rounded pillars, so it was still a very small church. And never, Mrs Thorley thought, had skirts been wider than they were this year. A slender, nimble giver-away was all to the good.

Not without some difference of opinion, it had been decided to dispense with bridesmaids.

When the triple marriage had first been suggested all the girls had been pleased; Diana and Deborah because they were in love and wanted to be married, Caroline because to be married so soon after what had been perilously close to a jilting would show Them—Freddy and all the old cats who had criticised her behaviour. However as the great day came nearer, some doubts had crept in. Diana felt that a girl's wedding day should be *her* day and hers alone. She would have preferred to go to the altar in solitary glory, attended by her four best friends. And she would willingly have waited another year. Though she was not markedly percipient, she could hardly fail to notice how often, over quite small things, Everard drew attention to the fact that financially he had been taken unawares. He said things like, "Darling, I have saved so little. I *had* hoped that by next year . . ." When he said such things, Diana could always say that, thanks to dear Papa, she would have five hundred pounds.

Deborah only regretted the triple ceremony because she knew that Mr Spicer would make the most of it. He was inclined to be High Church but he was also inclined to be lazy, and if she and Tim had had a simple, quiet wedding, he would have been unlikely to have taken much trouble over the things which would certainly affront Tim's nonconformist taste. As it was, she suspected—rightly—that Mr Spicer would rise to the occasion and go digging about, or making his wife dig about amongst the mothballs. Deborah was as willing to dispense with bridesmaids—just one more bit of show—as Diana was anxious to have them. And when the matter was under discussion, Caroline discovered, with a jolt of surprise, that she had no *best* girl friends. At any gathering she'd always been surrounded by a laughing crowd, but the girls were there only because the young men were. Truth must be faced.

The best-man problem had been settled neatly—largely due to Edward's good nature. Everard had chosen, for reasons of policy, James Gordon to stand by him and produce the ring at the right moment. Edward had intended to ask the new young doctor at the hospital to perform the same office for him; and that left Tim odd man out. All his close friends were Methodists and would think he had gone off his head, dressed up like a shopwalker and being married in such style, to say nothing of the reception afterwards with all the spirituous liquors! He said he reckoned he could manage to look after his own ring. Then Edward said, "Why not let James serve for all?"

Everard, in his secret heart had hoped that the marriage might bring a partnership as a wedding present. Old Gordon was not stupid, he must realise that as a married man, and a householder, Everard would need more than his present meagre salary. He was marrying a girl of whom Mr Gordon surely approved, the daughter of a friend. Not that anyone could possibly disapprove of Diana. Nor, indeed, could anyone look at her and imagine her as a poor man's wife. No word was said on the subject, however; Mr and Mrs Gordon expressed their goodwill in a pair of majolica vases of supreme ugliness, and James contributed a handsome carving set with handles of deers' antlers.

Diana and Caroline, helped by Mrs Spicer, decorated the church with lilies and roses and mock-orange. Mrs Thorley and Deborah were to see to the flowers in the house, but Deborah gave most of her attention to something which, though flowery in appearance when completed, had a utilitarian purpose. Today, for the

first time since Lavinia disappeared into the attic, the
house would be unguarded and it would be full of
people. There were the village women who had come
up to help Jenny, and there would be the guests. Deborah had never found a use for the iron stakes she had
bought to lighten the donkey's load; now they served
perfectly. She wedged three of them through the bannisters at the foot of the attic stairs, and then twined
them with green stuff and flowers, choosing as far as
possible, plants of a prickly kind, wild roses, black-
berry brambles in full flower, heads of the decorative
thistle which many people grew for winter decoration.

Everybody agreed that it was a most wonderful
wedding. A good many female guests shed a few tears,
daintily dabbed away with lace-edged handkerchiefs.
Mrs. Spicer wept for Arthur. In full regalia, and for
once exerting himself, he looked and sounded so impressive that he should have been a Bishop—and now
it was too late. Mrs Gordon wept because James
showed no sign of settling down and giving her grandchildren. Miss Riley's tears were self-pitying. Unappre-
ciated, unwooed, she had withered on the bough—and
now it was too late. Some people cried because it was
the correct thing to do at weddings.

Tim Bridges had always suspected that there would
be something more like a theatrical performance—not
that he had ever seen one—than a simple ceremony; in
his mind he called it a lot of monkey business. At the
crucial moment Mr Spicer enfolded the hands that
were to be joined in the end of his stole . . .

Outside the church there was a demonstration of
what Everard had once called feudalism. Children
throwing rose petals for the brides and their men to
walk upon. Then, up at the house, a proper wedding
feast, with the last of George Thorley's champagne, a
wine which did not keep indefinitely. And, of course,
the interesting inspection of the presents, each guest

looking out for his own and thinking how much better it looked than any other.

It was a wonderful wedding.

Edward Taylor made the first move towards breaking up the merry party. He and Caroline had a train to catch. Tim was anxious to be away, too. A time for goodbyes, though each girl avoided the finality of the word.

Diana said, "I shall come, twice a week, Mamma. Caroline, too."

Caroline said, "We shall be away only four days, Mamma."

Deborah said, "I hate leaving you . . . But I'll come at least once a week. I promise. That barrier I put up, Mamma, I unhitched it and pushed it halfway down the kitchen stairs. Willy can remove it tomorrow." It was typical of Deborah to think of such a practical thing!

The peculiar silence that overtakes places lately fully occupied and then left, deserted or underoccupied, a ringing hollowness with something sinister about it, settled down on Gad's.

But at least the girls were all now reasonably safe, whatever happened. But what could happen? The Lavinia of the story was already married, possibly pregnant. Sudden widowhood might well precipitate a birth. But juggle as one might there were still months to go. And a lot of guess-work to do. Lavinia had been as dumb about *when* as she had been about *who*?

Mrs Thorley could only judge by size. By this rough reckoning she thought it might be August.

"Everybody said I did well." George's voice held a slight challenge.

"Darling, you did magnificently. Nobody could have done better. If I have neglected to say so, it was because I was so busy."

"I know," George said. "It was lovely, but I do feel a bit tired."

I must not tire. Nor feel deserted. I have my duty to do, and my promise to keep.

A good stiff whiskey, and another and she was ready for action again.

One of the things about which Lavinia was difficult was over the business of taking a proper wash. To get the hip-bath up those stairs was palpably impossible, but as Mrs Thorley knew from her times of privation, it was quite possible to keep clean with a wash-bowl. Lavinia would dabble her hands, run the wash-cloth over her face and seemed to think that that sufficed. At first Mrs Thorley had thought that her reluctance to strip and have a proper wash was due to modesty, belated and ill-placed. So she would put the clean underclothes on the bed, the can of water by the little stand and say, "Have a good wash, Lavinia," and then go away, sometimes no farther than the landing. That Lavinia had not obeyed her—though the water had been transferred from can to slop-pail, was proved by the cake of soap lasting so long, and presently by a kind of odour—nothing to do with the commode about which Mrs Thorley was so scrupulous. Nothing to do with ordinary, healthy perspiration, either; but then how could it be? The poor girl never did anything to provoke sweat. But despite the clean clothes, the regular changing of bed-linen there was in this attic a curious scent, difficult to define, half sweetish, half rotten. Having sought any other source, some bit of food overlooked, or vase of flowers not removed in time—stocks, so sweet in themselves, were particularly offensive—Mrs Thorley decided that the scent emanated from Lavinia, and tonight—oh, the irony of it—she had a powerful bribe: a bowl of leftovers from the wedding feast.

Of that she had not counted the cost, for it was obvious that in a way she was getting off lightly; one wedding instead of three. Tonight Lavinia's evening meal consisted of several dainties, and a slice of rich fruit cake from which Mrs Thorley had thoughtfully

removed the white icing. Lavinia appeared to have retreated into herself, but one never knew.

At first she had been indifferent to food, then she
had shown the precarious appetite said to be a sign of
mental illness; finally she had become avid and tonight
Mrs Thorley had no scruples about showing her the
food and saying firmly, "But you must strip and have a
thorough wash first. And I shall see that you do . . ."

*

Edward thoroughly enjoyed his short honeymoon
and saw nothing ominous in the question which Caroline asked on the second day:

"Edward, do you know no-one in London?"

"No. I didn't train here, you know, Sweetie; I'm an
Edinburgh man."

And if he had had a hundred contemporaries and
acquaintances he would not have wished to make contact with them. He had attained his heart's desire: Caroline, all to himself. He had unaccustomed leisure and
money to spend. The hotel he had chosen, just off the
Haymarket, was extremely comfortable, even luxuri-
ous; for two plays and one concert he had obtained the
very best seats. He could afford to hire a hackney cab
to jog round so that Caroline could see the sights of
London; they went by river to Hampton Court and
lunched under the apple trees in the garden of the ancient Mitre Inn.

Most girls would have found it an idyllic honeymoon, especially as Edward as a lover was gentle and
undemanding and not altogether inexperienced. He was
easily satisfied because, despite his medical knowledge,
he clung to the delusion that nice girls were different.
In Edinburgh he'd had a hired woman from time to
time and had been left with the idea that unless you
had some feeling for the woman in the bed the whole
thing had no more significance than an evacuation of

the bowel. Now he had his beloved Caroline and his feeling was so intense that it was enough for two.

For Caroline the four days were days of unmitigated boredom. Nothing but Edward, day and night, night and day. His dullness, his literal-mindedness laid a dead hand on every outing, every entertainment. The comedy he had chosen was innocuous, its humour largely dependent upon the misunderstandings which resulted from one character being deaf. It amused Caroline, but Edward said, "Why should deafness strike everybody as so funny? Nobody would laugh because a blind man missed his way, would they?" Caroline thought: You should have married Deborah! She would enjoy such talk. I don't.

And alongside the boredom, in fact contributing to it, was the anonymity. Caroline, the popular girl, had never joined any company and not been greeted by smiles, waves of the hand. Here nobody noticed her. Her talent for amusing people, the light quip, the eloquent grimace, the mocking imitation, could not be used with only Edward for audience. Nobody even gave her a glance of disapproval—in London there were dresses far more décolleté than any she owned. She simply could not wait to get back to Baildon, even if it meant the dullest committee.

They were due to go back by the morning train, but when Caroline said, "I am quite looking forward to going home," Edward, eager to please, said, "Would you like to go this evening?" He looked at his watch. "We could just about make it."

"Well, possibly Miss Humberstone may be feeling lonely."

Miss Humberstone was the treasure for whom Edward had been searching ever since his father had taken Hattie away. He was genuinely thankful that this elusive quarry—a competent cook-housekeeper—had been run to earth before his marriage, so that Caroline would have a cushioned life.

Miss Humberstone was one of that all-too-numerous

tribe to which Mrs Thorley had herself once belonged, a distressed gentlewoman. She could have become a governess, but her spelling was highly idiosyncratic, her grasp on arithmetic poor; also she could not play the piano, and had forgotten any French she ever knew. She was further handicapped by the fact that she owned a few pieces of furniture and two cats to which she clung obstinately. She could cook and claimed to have some nursing experience, having done everything for her father until he died. Edward had heard of her through a patient who knew somebody who knew somebody who knew Miss Humberstone.

With two casual helpers, poor women from Scurvy Lane, one to do the laundry, one for cleaning, Miss Humberstone managed very well, and on her knees, every night, thanked God for bringing her to such a haven. She'd seen Caroline and knew that she was no threat—a butterfly creature.

Mrs Thorley, when she first took on her mixed and potentially difficult family, had tried to insist upon thought for others as a rule of life. So to poor Di, who had no honeymoon, Caroline did not elaborate upon the pleasures of hers.

"London was so hot, Di. And dusty and noisy. I'm truly glad to be home."

For the first time since he had encountered her, Everard approved of his sister-in-law. Had she come back exuberant, he would have loathed her. Such a contrast! With an extraordinary lack of consideration, Mr Gordon had not even offered Everard a day off; a day which added to the Saturday half day and all Sunday, would have made a long week-end at Bywater a feasibility—though very expensive. In fact June was the month least likely to bring Everard any leisure since James was playing cricket most of the time.

"You have made it pretty," Caroline said, glancing around the sitting room, small in size, but furnished in the latest style, mitigated slightly by Diana's innate good taste. The majolica vases, for instance, were not on display; but they were handy. When Mrs Gordon came to tea, or the whole family came to dinner, they would occupy the place of honour on the mantelshelf.

Neither Diana nor Everard knew that Caroline envied them and was thinking how happy she would have been in a house far smaller than this, in a tent, if only ... No use thinking about it; think of something else.

"Have you been back to Gad's?"

"No. I was waiting for you and I didn't expect to see you until tomorrow."

"Shall we go tomorrow."

"We could. I have a tea-party in the afternoon, but Mrs Wedgewood comes in the morning."

Mrs Wedgewood was not quite the treasure that Miss Humberstone was, but Diana realised that she had been very fortunate to obtain even her limited services. Mrs Wedgewood had started her working life at the Mount, Lord Norton's big house. There she had learned to cook superbly. She'd married the estate carpenter, an ambitious man, and a Radical. He'd set up on his own and was finding things a bit hard. He had no objection to his wife earning a bit, so long as it did not interfere with his comfort. On both market days, Wednesday and Saturday, she went to help at The Hawk In Hand; she and her skills were on call for balls, weddings dealt with by the catering firm; very occasionally she went back, in an emergency, to the Mount. But she had some spare time, and a little job in Friars' Lane, only just round the corner from the woodyard, suited her well. So well that she was happy to make, alongside the lunch, three days a week, dishes which young Mrs Spicer had merely to heat up, for supper on this day, or lunch the next.

The pony was fresh and thought, so far as he was capable of thought, that he was headed for home. So he rattled along at a good pace.

"I wonder has Deborah been," Diana said.

"She said once a week—and it is not a week yet."

"She may even be here today."

Despite their diverse characters, Diana and Deborah had paired off, and Diana thought that it might be *just* possible to ask Deborah, lightly, whether she liked being married. Deborah, so quick to understand, would know what the question meant. Nothing to do with being Mrs or proudly wearing a broad gold wedding ring, and ruling one's own household. There was another side to marriage and Diana loathed it. She loved Everard dearly, would have followed him round the world, and she knew, in theory, what marriage meant. But she'd deliberately looked away, just as she had looked away from cooking and making ends meet. The reality had simply been . . . messy, one of the most condemnatory words in her rather limited vocabulary. It had not been in accordance with the pretty night-dress—the finest cambric with tiny tucks and lace on its collar and cuffs, or with her hair, brushed smooth and made into two shining plaits, each tied with white ribbon, or with the fresh bed-linen, or indeed anything in the dainty bedroom. Diana had hated it, and then wondered if she were alone in this feeling or was it shared by all the married women in the world?

It was not a subject to discuss with Caro, who never took anything seriously, but she could have asked Deb.

With Caro one was always safe on the question of parties. Mannerly people made calls upon brides and issued invitations. Then hospitality must be returned.

"You have no need to worry," Diana said, a tinge of acid in her voice, "but I'm in rather an awkward position. Even in summer one can hardly serve a totally cold meal and nobody can play hostess *and* cook at the same time."

Caroline spared a thought for life as-it-might-have-been. Married to Freddy. A lot of happy people sitting about—on the floor if necessary—eating sausage rolls or wedges of pork pie and drinking beer if wine could not be afforded. She put the thought aside.

"Why shouldn't we give a *combined* party, Di? I have space enough. We know *almost* the same people and I'm sure our dining table could take twenty."

For the rest of the journey they discussed, happily, the form the party should take.

Deborah was not there, nor had she been. Tim regarded Deborah as a brand rescued from the burning and he had no intention of allowing her to go back. He sounded reasonable and kindly.

Deborah said, "I have a few things to fetch, Tim. Some books and sheets of music."

"There are good shops in Thetford. Buy what you want, my dear."

Deborah said, "But I promised. Mamma must be lonely, losing all three of us at once."

"She still has George. And the two girls within easy reach."

Deborah was in no state to argue against him, for if Diana had been able to ask her question: How do you like being married? Deb's answer would have surprised. Bliss undreamed of. Two healthy, untried bodies, untroubled by any physical or mental reserve, had come together and attained a shattering climax.

"No," Mrs Thorley said. "Deborah hasn't been, but I had a letter from her yesterday."

A very sensible letter, too, and one that proved that Deborah, within so short a time of her wedding, had spared some thought for Mamma. "George will now have nothing to do on Sunday afternoon. Could you change Jenny's half day and let her have Saturday instead; then George could go shopping in Baildon, or even to a matinée at the theatre. L could then have her little walk."

It was matter of indifference to Deborah whether Lavinia had a walk or not, but it was one of things Mamma worried about.

"Unfortunately, Jenny did not take kindly to the

idea," Mrs Thorley said. "I quite see why. Sunday is the only day when everyone is free. I then suggested that she should have Saturday *and* Sunday, and that brought up the question of how much walking Jenny's legs could be expected to do."

"I could always have George for a week-end," Caroline said. She could foresee week-ends of such tedium that even a young brother's presence would be a relief. Edward did not have a surgery on Saturday evening, and as he had once told her, very few people fell ill on Sunday—they waited until Monday when a week's work loomed ahead and a *bona fide* excuse, what they called a sustifcut, signed by Edward, would entitle them to a few shillings from one of the Friendly Societies, or from a pub club.

Diana wished that she could make the same offer, but it would entail making another bed, emptying more slops, washing more dishes. And then there was the food! George was a prodigious eater.

"I suppose it is not having seen her for five days in a row," Caroline said as they drove back to Baildon, "but I thought Mamma had changed. So much more white in her hair and her face looked thin, yet puffy at the same time."

"My hair is so like hers. I hope mine doesn't go so soon. Of course, it's this ghastly worry . . . Deb had the right idea, you know. She should have been put away, from the start. We should have insisted."

Diana thought of bag 408 wedged into the back of the little carriage alongside produce from Gad's, the last asparagus, the first new potatoes, eggs.

"It will be worse, after August or whenever it is," she said gloomily. "Babies make a lot of washing, too—things that can't wait for a week."

That was another aspect of marriage from which she had averted her thoughts. Of course everybody wanted a baby, and she was no exception; but until this moment she had thought of a baby as a pretty, living doll, ignoring the messy part. And even now she skirted it, thinking that by the time she had a baby, Everard would surely be better off. He might, at the moment, compare unfavourably, from the financial angle, with Edward Taylor and Tim Bridges, but he would achieve heights to which neither of them could aspire. She hoped very much that what she thought of as the messy side of marriage would not result, too soon, in an even messier baby.

Think of something else. Talk about the proposed party. Whom to invite; what to wear.

Just across the border, Foxton was preparing for an annual event called a Camp Meeting. *Real* Methodism had begun in a field because John Wesley, the founder of the movement, and whose intention was not to break with the Church of England but to reform it from within, had been barred from all orthodox pulpits. As a memorial to that open air meeting, Camp Meetings had been instituted. They took place after the hay was in and harvest not yet begun.

"Many of them travel miles, and sleep out," Tim explained to Deborah, who knew nothing about such gatherings. "And I always give them a good tea."

"Oh, I know the kind of thing, Tim. Food without plates."

Emma, at first distrustful of the frills and furbelows, and then dubious because the young Missus had taken more notice of the horses and outside things than of those inside the house, was totally won over when Deborah rolled up her sleeves and set to work.

"Our cook, Jenny, taught me a trick with pastry, Emma. Not the plain wooden rolling pin, a bottle filled with the coldest water you can get."

Willing to learn, too, Emma noted with satisfaction as she in turn showed Deborah a trick or two, mainly concerned with making lemonade a nutritive as well as a thirst quencher. One version which contained an oatmeal mash, just on the ferment, and a quantity of yeast, struck Deborah as not too far removed from being alcoholic, but she was wise enough to say nothing, and to herself Emma said: She'll do! and began to prepare herself for partial retirement. She had no intention of leaving Foxton, having nowhere to go, but she'd ease off gradually, leaving things in Deborah's competent hands. She'd be here and ready and willing to help with the baby which she hoped would arrive within a year.

At Gad's, though each day might seem endless, time slipped away. Furtively Mrs Thorley prepared some baby clothes. Of George's layette upon which she had lavished much time and care, only a few things remained, preserved through a mixture of sentiment and the thift which hard times had inculcated—anything might be useful, someday. But she had kept only articles impervious to moth and now must make woollen vests and flannel binders, and diapers.

Diana and Caroline were very good; they did all the necessary shopping and came, as promised, twice a week and Caroline's offer to have George any weekend, or indeed any time, still held. It was George himself who rebelled against it. Caro had always been his favourite and his first week-end in Baildon, which included an evening visit to the theatre, had been enjoyable, the second had been very boring or something rather worse. The Friends of the Hospital had spent some money on providing little treats in the way of toys and rag books—washable—for sick children and Edward, in all innocence and goodwill, had thought it would be appropriate for a child, George, to make the presentations.

George was horrified by what he saw. It was his first encounter with that side of life. In Stonham St Paul's there was an old soldier who stumped about on a wooden leg, and always at the corner between Baildon Market and the High Street there was a blind beggar—part of the scenery. But to see children, most of them younger than himself, grey-faced, jaundice-faced, crippled or maimed, splintered, bandaged, made him feel sick. And helped to shape his attitude towards life. Afterwards he said to Caro:

"We can't help these horrible things, can we? It's not our fault, is it, Caro? And making ourselves miserable doesn't do them any good, does it?"

"No. Being miserable does nobody any good," Caroline said, and then, only then, George realised that Caro understood misery, too. She had not changed colour or been crippled or lost a limb, but she had changed.

And really, Mrs Thorley reflected when George refused to spend another week-end in Baildon, it did not matter much, for he was bound for a longer stay, in another place; he was going to stay, with Deborah, at Foxton.

Tim had agreed readily to the suggestion. He regarded his young brother-in-law as spoilt, cheeky and precocious. A stay, over harvest-time, in a God-fearing household, would do him a power of good. Himself born and bred to what he regarded as the one and only faith, Tim was sufficiently aware of the fact that potential recruits were caught young.

"Of course," he said, "he can come and be welcome. Let's see, now . . . I'm free on Tuesday. We'll drive over and fetch him."

It was not the visit that Deborah had intended, but better than nothing. And to be honest nothing was all that she had been able to offer as a dullish, wettish July sped away and August came looming up. Mamma had said that she thought August . . . And if only Deborah could have gone, just for one day, on her own, she could, she felt, have done so much to help; but every attempt she had made to get to Gad's on her own had been neatly countered. So neatly that even Deborah had not seen the motive behind it.

And now, when at last she was back here at Gad's, she had hardly a moment with Mamma alone. Just time enough to notice, as Caro had done, that Mamma looked terrible. Just time enough to exchange a few hasty words; most of them used by Mamma, explaining how she was getting rid of Jenny.

"She is going to stay with Diana. I must admit that I never thought of it, but Jenny has never had a holiday in her life. It sounds incredible but she has never been in Baildon. Now she can go and have the time of her life. Even the Lammas Fair . . ."

"And you will be completely alone?"

"Yes, my dear. That is how it must be. How I wanted it to be. Not knowing *when* makes everything more difficult; but it must be soon . . . And with George going back with you today, and Jenny going with Diana tomorrow, things will be so much eased. I can manage now."

"I wish to God," Deborah said, and checked herself. It would be completely dishonest to say that she wished herself unmarried. But she did wish, vehemently, that she were free to come and go, to stand by Mamma, to help. "I wish I could be of more use."

"My dear, in taking George off my hands you are being the greatest possible help. Don't look so worried. I know exactly what to do."

Now she was completely alone in the house and could do what she must. Drag up a mattress and a pillow; two lamps, one to be lighted, one in reserve. Stoke up the stove so that water in its side boiler was always hot. Towels, scissors, fine white twine, all in neat order. And of course the whisky, now a necessity. Without it she could not sleep at all, and even with its aid, slept lightly, alert to the slightest sound. And then in the morning, only a good stiff whisky made her able to face the day, go shakily down to open the back door so that Willy could put milk from Park, or bread on the kitchen table.

She was never, she thought, drunk; but she had moments of hopefulness. Lavinia, once the child was born, *might* return to sanity. She was very young and the dumb madness was possibly the result of her condition.

"I practically stole it," Caroline said, holding out what had been a scent bottle. "Some poor woman had a . . . a very difficult confinement and Edward had to . . . to help her. He gave her some of this to ease the pain of it. So I thought . . . I hope you won't need it."

"So do I, most devoutly. It was very thoughtful of you, Caro."

August came in with sweltering heat and the attic floor, close under the tiles, was very hot, though Mrs Thorley did her best to mitigate it. Livinia's half-casement was open, and by night so was her door, with the mattress placed just outside it. The window in the other attic had never been replaced, the door there stood wide, as did the door and window of the apple room. The ghost of old apple scents was sometimes perceptible on the landing but it was overriden by that mysterious, corrupt odour from the occupied room, though it and everything in it was as clean as human hands could make it.

Each night Mrs Thorley undressed as far as her corsets which she loosened slightly but did not remove for she would need to be active and corsets gave some support. She dared not drink enough whisky to ensure a sound sleep but she took small quantities steadily. She would lie on the borderline and review what she had done in order that life should seem ordinary.

Harvest buns, for example. Hitherto Jenny had always made them, light dough buns with currants and raisins and chopped peel. This year she asked Willy to order two dozen from the baker and bring them up each morning as soon as harvest began. Willy had thought it a bit odd that Jenny—for the first time in his memory—should go off on holiday just at this minute; on the other hand, one woman alone in the house didn't want much looking after.

She had remembered the beer, too, but this year the casks were not inside the house in the store room, but in the barn. She did not want Willy with a trayful of mugs clumping in and out of the kitchen at odd moments. Nor did she want Willy to come and sleep in, as he kindly offered to do when he realised that she would be alone in the house.

"It's very thoughtful of you, Willy; but I'm not in the least nervous." Joe Snell made the same offer and received the same answer.

In fact being alone in the house was such an enormous relief that she planned to get rid of Jenny. It would, of course, be ideal, if Jenny liked Baildon so much that she decided to stay with Diana. Otherwise she must be pensioned off. Four shillings a week? And free milk from Park?

The Felstead term commenced early in September and there was every chance that George would stay with Deborah until the end of August at least. Horses were his passion, too.

Then her thoughts would veer to the immediate present. Was everything ready? The baby would have no cradle. The one which belonged to the house, the one in which Deborah and Caroline and George had been rocked, had been lent—not given—to Willy and Katie when the myth that Katie's baby had been a bit premature had first been propagated. One couldn't ask for its return, nor, very well, go buying a new one; but a drawer served perfectly well. It was ready. Everything was ready—except, apparently the baby itself.

Mrs Thorley hoped that it would be born at night—most babies were. Harvesting had begun in what was known as Top Field, only just across a bit of garden and the moat. It would be quite possible to toss a stone from Lavinia's window into that harvest field, and in this still hot air sound carried. So if it is by day and Lavinia screams, I must close that window. Yes, I have thought of, am prepared for everything.

She had said, "Call me. Do you understand? I shall be nearby. Just call."

But it was not a call that woke her from her half-doze. It was a whimpering moan. Instantly alert and upright, Mrs Thorley took the lamp and went in.

∗

The pony carriage bowled along between fields where men scythed corn and women bound and stooked sheaves and children ran about picking up stray, broken-off ears, or even a single fallen grain of corn. Harvest was harvest indeed. Men got extra money, women earned too, and the clothing for winter, in all but a drunkard's family, was thus assured. Really active or specially aggressive children could, in the course of a harvest, glean enough to provide a sack of flour.

"I wonder what we shall find today," Diana said.

"I don't know. I really am worried now, about Mamma. I would offer to stay so that she could get a proper night's rest, but I know what it would mean. Edward would want to come too, or he'd be looking in at odd hours. The *last* thing Mamma would wish."

"The last thing," Diana agreed. She had never contemplated such an offer. She was in fact enjoying having Jenny, who, after an afternoon at the Fair, a morning in the market, and an evening at the theatre had seemed at a loss for something to do, and had gladly agreed to a series of little dinner parties. The big, communal party had been a huge success, but it had, Diana felt, lacked the intimate touch. She could and would do better.

At Gad's there was nobody in the yard, even Willy was harvesting, but the pony, back again in what he still regarded as his home, stood, while bag 408 was lifted out and carried into the kitchen.

The big jug of milk stood on the kitchen table. Unusual. Ordinarily it was transferred to the cool larder.

They called, in their light, girlish voices, "Mamma! Mamma! We are here." Silence, heavy, absolute, dead.

She looked dead when they found her on the living-room settle, to which she had made her blind way. Her face, in profile against the crimson pillow, was the colour of a candle, the one visible eye sunk in a dark hollow, her mouth sagged open. On the thin cotton blue and white wrapper she wore there were irregular blotches.

They stood aghast, staring in silence until Diana said:

"Dead?" and turned to Caro for an answer. Caro, for all that she was a doctor's wife, had no more experience of death than Diana. Because of the suspicion, the near certainty, that their father, stepfather, had died of cholera, they had not been allowed to view his body. But the brownish blotches were recognisable as dried blood.

Murdered?

Crime was rare in this quiet countryside, but not completely unknown and harvest-time did bring strangers in. A woman, alone, in an isolated place and with wages money in the house, could have been attacked and robbed.

Caroline tried to speak, but her teeth chattered so violently that she could not bring out a word. It was left for Diana to reach out a reluctant, fastidious hand, and touch the death's-head face. It was warm.

Up, up, up, from the deepest depths of unconsciousness, up through infinite layers of darkness, the entity known as Mamma came to the surface. She opened her eyes, and closed them again against the blinding light, sharp as a sword. Then, shielding them with cupped hands, she opened them again and saw two of her pretty girls, in their pretty summer muslins and their pretty flowered hats, staring at her. And looking frightened. Her head felt as though somebody were splitting it with an axe, her eyes were full of gravel and her mouth full of fur, but she managed to say, "I'm all right. It's over. They both died."

Diana and Caro shared a thought: The best thing that could happen! Neither of them said it, however. Mrs Thorley pulled herself into a sitting position, rubbed her grit-filled eyes, wished she could cry, but all her tears had been shed, long ago. And now, roused from the stupor of exhaustion, shock, and whisky, she began to think again. There was still much to be done, and neither of these . . .

"I want Deborah," she said.

"It's Diana," George shouted. Of all the girls the one he liked least, but never in his life had he been so glad to see anyone. Diana had retained enough presence of mind to realise that the pony carriage, though ready, would be slow, so she had called Willy and he had harnessed up the dog-cart. Driving as though in a race, Diana reached Foxton just as the mid-day meal was ending.

It was taken in the kitchen, for as Deb said it saved so many steps. And Tim sat down to table in his shirt sleeves. Quite unknowingly, Deborah had reverted to a way of life which had ruled at Gad's, until Mamma had taken over.

George saw only the familiar horse and cart, and Diana. Come to deliver him. He was first to the door and then, close behind him, Deborah.

Driving in a high dog-cart and at full speed was very different from driving in the pony carriage; Diana's hat had blown backwards, held on only by the ribbons which tied under her chin, and her usually smooth hair was ruffled. Deborah stepped forward briskly and Diana had just time to say, "Over. Both dead and Mamma is asking for you," before Tim was there, asking: What is it?

"My sister Lavinia, is dead," Deborah said, "and Mamma is asking for me."

"You can't do anything about it." A dead girl, half a

world away. "I'm sorry enough," Tim added, a shade too late, "but I can't see what you can do."

"I can *go*. I want the gig and a fresh horse. Will you harness up for me?"

"I can't see what all the flurry is about." The horse, overdriven, lathering and heaving; Diana always so prim and proper, looking as though she had been through a whirlwind, Deb ready to rush off, because news—months old at that—had just arrived.

A Deborah he did not know, somebody whose existence he had never suspected, said:

"Will you harness up, or must I?" Tim turned towards the yard. The girls had a second together.

"What happened?"

"I don't know. Mamma was in no state . . . She just said they were both dead. And asked for you."

Then there was George, his gaping valise in his hand. Diana, climbing out of the dog-cart, said, "No. I came for Deb, not for you, George."

"Then I'll walk." He wondered why he had not thought of this simple expedient before; but he knew the answer. If he ran away, Deb would be blamed as she had been for every mistake he had made during his stay in this horrible place.

Unlike the dog-cart, the gig had no seating accommodation at the back, so George sat between the girls, a great hindrance to conversation.

Deb said, "When?"

"Last night. At least I think so."

"Is Caro there?"

"Yes. Let's hope she had sense enough to make a cup of tea!"

It sounded to George as though Mamma might be ill.

"Is Mamma ill?"

"She has had some distressing news and is greatly upset," Diana said in a manner which did not encourage further conversation.

The gig was high-wheeled, built for speed, and the horse was fresh. The miles sped by. Presently Diana, having pushed back her hair and rearranged her hat, said:

"The bother is, I have a little dinner party this evening. I can't cancel it now, can I?"

"Why should you? I had a Prayer Meeting!" Something in Deb's voice informed George that she enjoyed this weekly gathering no more than he had done. He sat quietly and reviewed his hateful visit.

It had not begun badly. There'd been a Sunday School treat in one of Tim's meadows, and both Deb and Tim had told him to join in and be friendly. So he had; he'd won the sack race, the egg and spoon, and with a lump of a girl, a handicap if ever there was one, the three-legged. Then he was told to stand back and give others a chance. No word of praise!

Then he found that he was expected to work. Tim Bridges was altogether too fond of saying, "When I was your age . . ." Well, all right, George thought rebelliously, you had a horrid childhood and boyhood, but why keep harking back, and inflicting the same thing on me?

Then there were the Bible readings; every day, before breakfast, which was shockingly early, and after supper. Tim had a special Bible, divided into portions for each day of the year, and George's visit had coincided with about the worst of the Old Testament in the morning and of the New in the evening. Who cared, who could be expected to care about somebody who begat somebody who begat somebody else? And who knew or cared about Amphipolis and Apollonia, which had to be passed through before St Paul could reach Thessalonica?

So far from making a recruit, Tim had given George a distaste for anything that smacked of religion.

Deb, driving fast, knew why she had been sent for. Both dead! And what did one do with the body of a girl, supposedly on her way to, or just arrived in, India? She thought, half-resentfully: I made a sensible suggestion at the very beginning—she was mad and should have been put away. And now, though Mamma sent for me and is relying upon me, when I make the obvious, simple suggestion, she will choose something more complicated; possibly a leaden casket, presumably shipped from Bombay . . . I gave in once, but that was before I knew the whole truth. Now I do and if Mamma says anything about a decent Christian burial to me, I shall speak out.

She spoke out to George, "Look, Mamma is unwell. And she is not expecting you. You can go in and kiss her and then make yourself scarce. Find something to do."

"That," George said with dignity, "will be very easy. I shall exercise Tom Thumb. He must have missed me."

Caroline, of whom nothing much was expected, had risen to the occasion, made, not tea, but strong coffee, stirred the kitchen stove into activity, prepared a bath. And George said exactly the right thing. In later years when his success with women was notorious, he attributed it to telling them what they wanted to hear, holding up the flattering glass. But on this day his tribute was spontaneous.

"Oh, Mamma, how nice you look. How nice you smell. And you can't *think* how *glad* I am to see you again." Mrs Thorley hugged him and then Deborah. Over her mother's shoulder Deborah jerked her head at George, who said, "Excuse me, Mamma. I must see Tom Thumb."

"Why," Mrs Thorley asked of Deborah, who usually managed all things well, "did you bring him back?"

"He was prepared to walk," Deb said. "We had no choice. At least we know where he is."

Caro came in with a tray of tea; no cake. She wondered idly why it was seemly to drink when bereaved, yet almost indecent to eat. Not that this was really a bereavement. It was a relief and once Deborah had solved the immediate problem, the whole thing could be forgotten.

"What happened, Mamma?" Deb asked, taking charge of the tea-pot. Mamma was calm enough but all of a shake.

"I can't go into details. It was all so horrible." Mrs Thorley closed her sunken eyes and shuddered. "I did my best. My dears, you must believe that. I couldn't have done more if it had been one of you. And it was a beautiful baby—a boy." She knew in her heart that the continuance of her plan, culminating in Lavinia's return with the baby, would have meant months more of secrecy and connivance and apprehension; nevertheless the loss of the child grieved her. She would have to tell Deborah something of the truth, of course, because of the state of the attic. But Deb only.

The suggestion of a leaden casket shipped home from India came up inevitably, and from Diana.

"It can't be done. One of my friend Barbara's cousins—he was a soldier—was brought home in that manner."

"Perhaps you know somebody who could make a leaden casket, seal it and ask no questions," Deb said. She spoke gently, almost casually, and yet with such venomous sarcasm that Diana looked at her in amazement.

"Well, no. It was just a suggestion."

"The time has come to face facts, damned unpleasant ones, too. Lavinia is supposed to be on the other side of the world. But she's up there, dead, and her baby with her."

"I know. I can face a fact, Deb, as well as anyone."

Never an unpleasant one, Deb thought.

"There is only one thing to do. Bury them. In the garden." It sounded harsh; all the worse because Deborah spoke so coolly, as though speaking of planting out wallflowers.

"And who would do that?"

"I will."

Deborah had been keeping half an eye on Mamma and saw that she was having trouble with her tea. She had made two attempts to get the cup to her lips, failed both times, and there was now as much tea in her saucer as in the cup. Deborah reached over, tipped the tea from the saucer into the slop-basin, dried the saucer and the base of the cup on her sleeve, and said, as to a child, "Try again."

Mamma had made no protest against the garden burial and Caro sat silent.

"Listen," Deb said. She had already in her mind surveyed the terrain. "It must be under the walnut tree . . . Nobody is likely to dig *there*. It's still early. I'll get hold of Willy and ask him to dig, ready for some shrubs and things which Mamma has admired in *your* gardens and which flourish in the shade. Bring them in tomorrow morning."

Let Deb do it. Through Mrs Thorley's exhausted mind a thought flitted—in olden times people like Lavinia would have been buried at a crossroads, with a stake through the heart.

Willy said, "Oh, Miss Deb, I mean Mrs Bridges, Ma'am, I wasn't looking to see you."

"I want you to do something for me, Willy."

"Anything. Anything you like to ask."

He'd adored her for years, almost as long as he could remember. Hopeless, of course, like adoring the moon, but if she had asked him to gnaw through an iron bar, he'd have done his best. As it was, in this late sultry afternoon, what she asked was easier than labour in the field. In the dense shade of the walnut tree it was comparatively cool and the soil, about six inches of it, dry and powdery.

"It needs to be deeper, Willy. Some of the new plants are deep-rooted; they must be set very deep."

So that was all right. Now for supper.

The pony carriage jogged along, the pony reluctant. He still thought of Gad's as his home.

They mentioned the catastrophe, sidling around it.

Di said, "It was the only way, really," and Caro agreed. "It is over now—or at least it will be—tomorrow. God love me, I was sorry for her . . . in a way . . . while she was alive; but what future did she have?"

What future do I have? Years and years and years of boredom, of every light remark being misunderstood, or met with flat reason. Better dead? Well, why not? She had access to Edward's dispensary.

She brooded on this for some minutes while her volatile spirit, in decline now ever since Freddy chose Susan, reached rock bottom, rested there and then bounced, began to soar upwards. The planes of her monkeyish face shifted a little, and Diana, seeing the change with a sideways glance, thought: Yes, that is all I need now, a fit of hysteria from Caro! To forestall it she said sharply:

"I don't know what there is to grin about!"

"Was I grinning? I just struck me that all you had to do to stay alive was to stay alive."

What a stupid statement! Diana flicked the pony.

"We're late already and I have things to see to. I have the Gordons this evening; I must get out their presents. And Phoebe Mayhew gave me a kind of table-centre, quite hideous, but it must be on show."

"Match-making?"

"That is rather a crude way of putting it. But I happen to know that Mrs Gordon is simply longing to see James married. And she likes Phoebe."

"She's far more likely to get that red head from the tobacconist's shop in Whiting Street."

"How do you know?"

"Edward buys his tobacco there. He believes in patronising small struggling shops." Almost unconsciously Caroline's voice mocked, imitated; serious, pedantic, well-meaning.

"And he has seen James there?"

"Oh, often."

"Well, I know nothing about that. I merely thought that a nice little dinner . . . I mean James can't very well talk exclusively to his father and mother, or to Everard whom he sees every day—and he never liked me much. It would give Phoebe a *chance*. And perhaps please Mrs Gordon."

It was essential to please Mrs Gordon. Diana, far from being dim-witted within her own sphere, had recognised the fact that Mrs Gordon was the power behind the throne and stood in the way of Everard's promotion because she was jealous. Everard was so much better looking, so much better qualified than James.

"I wish you luck," Caroline said, "but don't be disappointed. You'll be busy, and anyway, you haven't much in your garden. I'll see to the plants. For tomorrow."

"Oh yes. Nine o'clock?"

Trust Edward to put the damper on, saying the wrong thing while doing the right one, or vice versa.

"But Sweetie, this is not the right time to move shrubs."

His mother had been a great one for the garden and had bought several things not yet common in English gardens. Neither Edward nor his father had had time to spare; Hammond, who saw to the horses, pumped water into the cistern which enabled the house in St Giles' Square to have the first proper water-flushed closet, the first proper bathroom in Baildon, did a bit of pruning from time to time. Edward knew the principles; shrubs should be transplanted in their dormant season; not in blazing August.

"Never mind. Why I want them tomorrow is for Mamma's sake. She heard this morning that Lavinia was dead—and of course buried. And since, well, we couldn't send flowers to India, Deb and Di and I thought, something flowery for the garden."

"My poor dear," Edward said. He put a would-be comforting, sustaining arm around Caroline. His memory of Lavinia was vague; she'd never looked healthy, but she'd never seemed to ail, never his patient. And she'd gone to India, notoriously unhealthy. "What sad news. So young, too."

"Three months younger than I am."

As a doctor Edward knew that Death was no respecter of age, or class, climate. Golden lads and girls all must, like chimney sweepers, come to dust. That Edward accepted, a fact of life, but suddenly Caroline seemed doubly precious, because so vulnerable.

"You must have had a horrible day. Have a little sherry . . . Would you like to go back? Would your mother like to come here? She shouldn't be alone, perhaps."

"She isn't. Deb is there."

Then everything was all right, Edward thought, and leaving Caroline to rest, feet up, after what must have been a tiring day, he went out to *dig*. He thought that the idea of flowering things, planted in the garden where Lavinia had played as a child, a charming idea and he was sorry that at first, not knowing the circumstances, he had seemed to oppose it. After all, a shrub couldn't tell August from November; dig deep enough, and wide enough, slip each rooted clod into wet sacking and some at least would survive.

Diana bustled into her pretty little house and immediately smelt cooking. A small house was undoubtedly convenient in many ways, but doors should be kept closed. What guest wanted to walk in and know immediately what awaited him for dinner? She went along to the kitchen door at the end of the short passage, closed it firmly and then turned into the dining room, which had a communicating door with the kitchen, a fact which made serving a meal so easy that Jenny had never once mentioned her legs.

Everard was at the sideboard, a bottle of wine in one hand and a corkscrew in the other.

"Hullo, darling. I'm rather late. Mamma greeted us with such sad news. Lavinia is dead."

"Oh. I am sorry." The words were correct, but perfunctory; Lavinia had made no impression on him at all and had been gone since March.

"Mamma was quite overwhelmed. She wanted Deborah so I had to drive all the way over to Foxton to fetch her."

"You must be exhausted." Everard put down the corkscrew. "I think that in the circumstances we should not entertain, darling."

He had no faith at all in this intimate little party. There was no point in trying to please the old devil, his wife or his son. James was still friendly enough, but not in a manner that meant anything. Any real goodwill would have surfaced, in a practical manner, long before this. And no good would come of this well-meant, intimate little party. James had once confided in Everard about the tobacconist's daughter, who had made it quite clear that dalliance was not for her. "And I'd marry her like a shot, old boy, but there'd be an almighty row, and they'd hold it against Sylvia as long as they lived. Whereas, in another year or so, they'll be so anxious to hear the patter of tiny feet, they'll greet Sylvia with three rousing cheers." So why should Diana exert herself and put him to the expense of providing an expensive meal?

"Oh, I'm all right," Diana said. "A wash and a change, and I shall be as good as new."

"I was thinking of the bereavement. I'll just walk round and tell them. They'll quite understand."

"Phoebe will just about be starting now. It's eight miles. Besides, darling, it isn't as though Lavinia . . . I mean she must have been dead quite some weeks ago. And after my dreadful day, I need something cheerful."

"You may be right," Everard said, and unwillingly, he withdrew the cork. Life with his godfather had taught him about wine, and a decent red wine should breathe for an hour.

During this brief conversation the door to the kitchen had stood open and Jenny had been listening. Although she had indulged, over a long period of time, in a subtle bullying of Mrs Thorley, at heart she was fond of her, a shade fonder than she had realised. Nobody would miss Miss Lavinia much, but she was Mrs Thorley's youngest girl; quite overwhelmed, Miss Diana had said. And she'd sent for Miss Deb; *that* was understandable; if anything went wrong Miss Deb was the one Jenny would have wanted, too. But how long could she stay? Only one hasty visit since the wedding, just to fetch Master George.

Such thoughts were mere froth on the crest of a wave of emotion which had been welling up in Jenny since the first days of her so-called holiday. By that time she had exhausted what delights Baildon had to offer and had become both homesick and bored. Going to the Fair, to the theatre, to the market, looking into shop-windows—all very dreary when you were by yourself. She'd tried to be friendly with Mrs Wedgewood on the days when she came, but nothing had come of that. Try to talk about cooking, the one thing they should have had in common, and the bitch reeled off a lot of outlandish names. Offer to help and you were reminded sharply that you were supposed to be on holiday. Jenny said, "I reckon I came to holidays too late in life." Mrs Wedgewood retorted that she had never had one, never expected to. Jenny positively welcomed the little dinner parties where at least she could exercise her skills. No dishes with highfaluting names, but good sound cooking.

In fact Mrs Wedgewood was suspicious of Jenny and apprehensive about her nice little job.

"I don't want to offend Deb," George said, casting a wary look at his half-sister, "but it is all rather peculiar. They don't have proper preachers, you know. Nobody like Mr Spicer. Anybody can preach."

"There is one minister and a circuit of about twelve chapels," Deb explained, "so we depend upon local preachers. Tim is one."

"I never heard him," George said, being fair. "But that man who said 'er' at the end of every other word. I don't think he was really cut out for preaching. Honestly, Deb, do you?"

"He has this unfortunate impediment," Deb said. "What made it worse was that his watch seemed to have stopped."

That was more like the old Deb. Encouraged, George elaborated; he had, like Caroline, a gift for mimicry, which for once fell flat. And then Deborah turned the tables on him and said:

"I think—er, you—er, should—er go to bed—er."

"That," George said, delighted that Deb had shown the right spirit, "is exactly how that man talked, for a whole hour!"

When he had gone, the dismissal softened by a kind of jocularity, Mrs Thorley said:

"My dear, I have not been honest with you. The truth was so awful. And I behaved in such a cowardly way. When I saw . . . Deb this is so horrible . . . I know you never liked whisky, but there is some brandy; take a little . . . Deb, at the end it was so awful, I just ran away." There were still things which could not be said, things that nobody would believe; but something must be told.

"Deb, I delivered her safely. A beautiful little boy. As you know, I had always held to the belief that once delivered she would recover her senses. And it seemed so. She said she would like some chicken broth. And I had it, ready. So I came down, it hardly took me five minutes. And in just that time, Deb, she'd smothered the poor baby, and slashed her own wrists."

"God!" Deborah looked so aghast and turned so pale that for a moment Mrs Thorley feared she might faint. And if simply hearing about it had such effect, what would the sight of it do?

"Deb, you must drink this. As medicine."

"I'm all right," Deb said, accepting the glass nonetheless. "How terrible for *you*!"

"So was my own behaviour. I failed completely. It happened just after four . . . I kept steeling myself to face it. To go back . . . To begin cleaning up. I had time, and I thought that if I drank enough . . . Twice I got halfway up the attic stairs. I failed. I simply could not bring myself . . . I could not enter that room alone."

The question was, could she manage it now, with Deb as support? It was just possible, for she felt better. The hand which had been so shaky on the tea-pot was quite steady on the bottle. Yes, she was better now and would spare Deb the worst. She would go in first. She had told Deb part of the truth, but not the whole. Not by a long way. Nobody would believe her; they'd say like mother like daughter and think her mad too.

"She was mad, Mamma. Not responsible for what she did." With great delicacy of feeling Deborah refrained from saying things such as: I told you so. I knew it. I said so from the first. She *bit* me.

And Mrs Thorley made no mention of the ordeal which had preceded the birth. Lavinia suddenly garrulous. "They promised no pain. They promised to come for me. I was the Maiden."

In actual fact it had been a short labour, but Lavinia had resented every pang. She had cried out to the picture on the easel. "I kept faith! I never said a word! Help me. You promised!" She knelt, moaning and praying in the most blasphemous terms.

Mrs Thorley, not a woman given to fancies, was aware of another presence in the room; something evil. And once it seemed to her that face of the goat-human changed, the leering, sneering expression intensifying into one of supreme mockery. The unpleasant odour increased.

She had kept her head—then. Apart from pulling Lavinia by the arm, calling her by name, and saying, "Stop, Lavinia, stop!" she had done nothing. There was an impulse to lift her and put her on the bed, but she resisted it. Lavinia would struggle and that might hurt the baby. Also the worrying days and the long night vigils had so sapped her strength that she doubted her ability to perform the action properly.

Then Lavinia's moans and petitions changed into cries of rage. She got clumsily to her feet, seized a brush, squeezed tubes of paint, one after the other, and defaced, first the picture and then the wall-paintings. That done she became calm, lay down on the bed and submitted, like any ordinary girl, to Mrs Thorley's midwifery. Mrs Thorley said all the things that had been said to her: Bear down, dear! Go with the pain! Ah, that was a good one; it won't be long now. It was not long; a natural easy birth with no need of the opiate drops. And despite all, a perfect normal baby, better-looking, in fact, than most, not red and creased and bald as all Mrs Thorley's babies had been when she first saw them.

Lavinia said, "Thank you, Mamma," which proved that she was, as Mrs Thorley had always hoped might be the case, back in her own mind. Incredible as it might seem in the circumstances it was with a feeling of happiness that she placed the baby in his makeshift cradle. The worst was over now.

Then Lavinia said she was hungry.

"I can manage," Deborah said bravely. "You go to bed."

"I've shirked enough for one day. Will you bring the lamp? Both those . . . up there, will have burned dry. I'll bring the linen."

The first Mrs Thorley had brought to Gad's—as all daughters of decent, substantial families did—enough good linen to last a lifetime and beyond, if carefully treated. Mrs Thorley had thought about giving some of it to the girls when they married; but the linen cupboards at Foxton and in St Giles' Square were equally well supplied, so she had compromised, thinking: The Thorley linen should stay at Gad's. And for Diana she had bought new. Nothing like such quality.

Now Lavinia, not a Thorley, and always an outsider, was to go to her grave wrapped like a mummy, in such linen as money could not buy nowadays.

On the landing, Mrs Thorley weakened again. I cannot re-enter that shambles and it was wrong of me to ask Deb.

She said in a weak voice, "Couldn't we just lock the door and leave it? It's no sight . . ."

"Mamma, you know what a stench one dead rat under a floor board can raise. Look, put the linen down outside the door and sit on the stairs. I may need help in getting . . . it . . . them down, but I intend to think of it, and you must, too, just a bundle of laundry."

It sounded harsh, but that was how she must think, how Mamma must think. Lavinia as Lavinia had ceased for Deborah with the discovery of those black candles, and all the rest of it, but Deborah, with uncounted generations of people close to the earth behind her, knew the healing virtue of soil. It accepted the most revolting things and by some miracle transformed them. Into crops; into roses.

The heavy, blood-satiated bluebottle flies, disturbed by the light, rose lazily and buzzed.

Lavinia looked like marble, dead white in carved immobility, and the blue look which Mrs Thorley had recognised as a sign of death, irreversible, when she snatched the pillow away, had faded from the baby's face. There was a singular, almost frightening resemblance to the statue of the Virgin and Child that stood in a little niche in St Paul's church in the village. Stonham St Pauls was so small and so obscure that it had

escaped the attention of those two arch-destroyers—
Henry VIII and Cromwell. And the man who had
made the statue had had nothing to work with except
chalk, the subsoil of this area. Making the best of what
he had, he worked; even Mary's fingernails on the
hand which cupped the Child's head were perfectly
wrought.

Willy had worked well, too. Miss Deb had asked
him to dig deep, and he had done so. Through the
summer dust, the dark compost of many years of fallen
leaves, into the chalk. No plant would need to set its
roots deeper than that.

Deb dug slightly deeper, relieved to find that below
a certain level, even chalk became friable.

It would have been easier to put everything else—
everything Lavinia had ever owned or touched—on to
a bonfire, but, as she had once reminded Lavinia, a
light at Gad's could be seen for miles, and even in the
middle of the night one could not be certain that everybody was dead asleep. A man, full of harvest beer,
might go stumbling out to ease his bladder, a child
might wake with toothache. A fire at Gad's, in this hot
dry weather, would mean only one thing, a fire in a
cornfield and the age-old principle—help your neighbour because tomorrow you may need help from
him—would go into action. Once the alarm was given
everybody would come swarming, most to help, a few
to watch. No bonfire. All the soiled clothes and bed-
clothes, and the rug which had taken the brunt of the
gush of life-blood, went into the chalk and was
stamped down. The horrible picture, too, with others,
less positive, but all tainted.

"There's nothing more we can do now," Deborah
said at last. "I'll give the place a good scrub out in the
morning." And splash about with some whitewash, she
added to herself. Mamma—and thank God for it—had
seemed to miss the significance of what Lavinia had

painted. Mrs Thorley thought—and thank God for it—that Deborah had not realised the full truth.

"Share my bed," Mrs Thorley whispered, "no other is made up." The whole business had been made just that little more difficult by the need to move softly, speak low, or not at all for fear of waking George.

George, back in his own bed, had slept soundly, lulled by the knowledge that he was home, where the first thing in the morning was breakfast, at the civilised hour of eight o'clock. Nobody here was going to demand that he should rise at six and take part in feeding the horses, or say, as Mr Bridges had done, that early to bed and early to rise made a man healthy, wealthy and wise; or that one hour before breakfast was worth two after it. In that aphorism George thought there might be a grain of truth since an hour before breakfast seemed twice as long as any other hour of the day. But it cut both ways: an hour before breakfast, in bed, half awake and half asleep, was not only twice as long but twice as enjoyable.

Lolling, he surveyed the future and the possibility that early rising might be the rule at school. Hideous thought! He shuffled it off. Mamma might change her mind again. First of all he had been bound for Biddle's, which meant a very stiff examination—next year. Then he was bound for Felstead—slightly easier to get into—this year. But he was all Mamma had left now; and if cajolery and cunning worked, George might possibly continue to jog down to the Rectory, learn a little and be home for lunch. A boy could only hope.

The clock, like all old things, was slow and a bit wheezy. George knew that if he jumped out of bed at the first stroke of eight he could be washed and almost dressed by the last.

Eggs, just as he liked them. Turned in the pan. It was one of the ridiculous things about Foxton that any such small preference was denounced as fanciful, the result of being spoilt. Mr Bridges liked *his* eggs cooked open-eyed, so that at the touch of the knife yolk ran about and stuck to the bacon like glue. He liked his meat half-cooked, too, bloody, red juice seeping out and sullying the potatoes and peas. Nobody, in the stress of the time, had noticed, but George, during his short stay at Foxton, had lost weight. The food in itself was excellent but not to George's taste. Take ham, or salt beef, both thoroughly cooked, and of the best quality, but carved with an absolute disregard for individual preferences. Mr Bridges said people should learn to take the fat with the lean—and be grateful. When George left the fat on his plate, he was rebuked for wasting good food, and when George argued that the chickens would eat it, that was called answering back. Such little episodes, too slight really to be called differences of opinion, always brought a look of pain to Deb's face, so after a day or two he did his best to avoid them.

Over breakfast, cooked exactly to his liking, George was prepared to be cheerfully garrulous, but neither Mamma nor Deb was very responsive. They weren't cross or disapproving, merely glum. Then, of course, he remembered, Lavinia was dead. They were sad. He set his wits to work to think of a way of cheering them up a little. Gifts! All women liked gifts.

"Well, I'll get on," Deb said, rising and beginning to roll up her sleeves.

Anxious to ingratiate himself, indeed, if possible to make himself appear indispensable, George asked if there were anything he could do to help.

Mamma said quickly, "Not here, dear. I have a few errands to be done in Baildon. I'll make you a list."

"I was thinking of riding there this morning. Is there anything you want, Deb?"

"I don't think ... Yes, a jar of Fuller's hand cream."

She went out and began clanking about in the kitchen.

George said in his precociously adult way:

"Mamma, would it be possible for Deb to stay here for a week or so? I think she needs a holiday."

"A holiday? Darling, she has hardly been married two months."

"I was there less than a fortnight and I was anxious to get away. Foxton is a horrible place, and Mr Bridges is a horrible man. In fact, if I'd known how he was going to treat Deb, I wouldn't have stood there and said: I do, when Mr Spicer asked: Who giveth this woman?"

Mrs Thorley would have said that the events of the last day or two had rendered her immune to shock, but she felt a pang. She remembered that she had never really liked Timothy Bridges.

"What do you mean, George?"

"Well, for one thing Deb is a kind of servant. There *is* a servant but she leaves all the hard work to Deb. There's a piano, but only for hymn tunes. You know that pretty hat Deb had, with the yellow roses? I asked Deb why she had taken them off. Do you know why? You can only wear plain clothes for chapel. They live in the kitchen, with the servant, and only go in the parlour when they have visitors. In all the time I was there I only got two rides on Foxy. And Deb is not going to be allowed to hunt. Mr Bridges says foxes are vermin, and he shoots them on sight. I took *Gulliver's Travels* with me to read and Mr Bridges said I ought to read *Pilgrim's Progress*, and he's the same about what Deb reads." George reeled off the list of things which had displeased him and finished off with a remark characteristic of him. "There's a text on the wall. It says, 'Christ is the Head of this house,' but it's wrong. It should read, 'Mr Bridges is Head of this house. So look out!' I hated it all, and I'm sure Deb must."

"She probably does not feel as you do, George. You see she fell in love and chose to marry Mr . . . to marry Tim."

There and then George Thorley made a decision that was to keep him a bachelor until he was fifty.

Marriage was a thing to be avoided as long as possible.

And now that he was thinking on the subject, he wasn't sure about Caro, either. He'd never said anything to anybody, because really there wasn't much to tell, but it was curious . . . On the second of his week-ends there, the one which had ended with the horrid visit to the hospital, there'd been on the Saturday a party. In the middle of it he had felt the need to go to the lavatory and had gone along to the one near the surgery. That took him through a passage and there Caro and Freddy were looking at the funny pictures. They stood close together as two people looking at the same picture must do, and they were laughing. When he came back, Caro was alone, and she wasn't laughing, she was crying. He'd said, "What is the matter, Caro?"

She said, "Nothing. Why?"

"You're crying."

"Only from laughing. Honestly, every time I see these pictures they seem funnier." And it was on the next day that she said being miserable did nobody any good It now struck him that Caro, though her husband was very different, and her life far more comfortable, hadn't found married life quite all that she had hoped.

"Can you take me back this morning, Miss Di? I am all ready."

"No, we cannot," Diana said, a bit sharply. "With the two of us and the plants we shall have a full load."

Jenny sensed displeasure. Two offences. Miss Di was now Mrs Spicer. And Jenny was cutting short her holiday.

"It ain't that I ain't been happy here. But with the bereavement and all, I don't reckon Missus should be there all alone. She'll need a bit of looking after."

"Next time we go, Jenny. It is quite impossible to-day."

Diana was in no mood for trivialities. She hurried out, through the gateway which Edward had so

thoughtfully made in the wall, and there was Caroline
and the pony carriage, the rear of it looking like a
greengrocer's shop.

"Well, and how did the party go?"

Ordinarily Caroline was about the last person in
whom Diana would have chosen to confide, but she
simply had to talk to somebody.

"It was *dreadful*. James absolutely ignored Phoebe
and she hardly opened her mouth, except to put food
into it. Mr Gordon talked almost exclusively to Everard, business, of course—all about something up at
Lowestoft. And all Mrs Gordon could talk to me about
was the food. How delicious and what was the recipe?
It wasn't quite ten when Phoebe said she couldn't keep
her driver waiting any longer. And you know how it is,
with an unsuccessful party, once one person leaves,
they all do."

"I know. What a pity. But I never actually thought
that Phoebe Mayhew . . ."

"I know. You said so. And Everard said we should
cancel the party altogether. I wish I had." Diana gave
the innocent pony a rather sharp flick of the whip,
though he was once more doing his best, headed for
home, and Edward must have dug up a great weight of
soil in his anxiety to please and his determination that
all the things—even the dogwood—should have a
chance to survive.

"And that wasn't the worst of it," Diana said. "Everard—after they had all gone—talked seriously of
looking for other employment. He came to bed raging.
He said decent men didn't talk business at table, and
that this thing at Lowestoft was pushed on him because Mr Gordon was too ignorant to understand it
and James was off to play cricket. Caro, Everard really
said some terrible things—they'd always imposed upon
him and now felt more free to do so because he was
married and anchored down; tied to a house in Baildon. And he said he would apply for something he had
had his eye on. In London . . ."

"Di, you'd hate it! I did, and I was on holiday. To live there . . . I saw streets and streets—I don't mean slums. I mean houses much narrower than yours, all squeezed together, and not a green thing in sight. Di, you must take a firm stand and refuse to go. I would. I mean that if Edward got such a crazy idea into his head, I should simply say: All right, you go but don't expect me to come with you." And God! what a release that would be!

"And then what would you do?"

"Go home. Back to Gad's, I mean."

"Don't be silly! You're married. Mamma could be sued for harbouring you, or . . . or something called aiding and abetting."

"Is that so? Well, with me the question is not likely to arise. And you must talk Everard out of it, Di. You could say—and it's absolutely true—living in London is very expensive. So even if he earned more he wouldn't be better off." Caroline knew one of Everard's weaknesses. "Look at what we bring back from Gad's . . ."

Deborah set to work methodically. First everything out. Nothing associated with Lavinia must remain in this house. Nothing was heavy; even the chaise-longue was a light structure, much of it canework. She pushed it, the trestle-table and its stands, the easel and the wickerwork chair on to the kitchen stairs. Later she'd ask Willy to take them away and make them into kindling.

There were splotches of blood on the floor, around the place where the rug had been, and where it had soaked through. She tackled them; soda in the water and strong yellow kitchen soap. Later, when she had whitewashed the wall, she would do the whole floor.

Whitewash, often called lime-wash, was always available on any well-run farm; it was held to have purifying qualities, a guard against foot-and-mouth, glanders, swine fever, fowl pest. It had a good clean

smell. She splashed it about liberally, trying not to look
at what she was obliterating; some very hideous things,
some beautiful. Don't look! Don't think! It is over and
done with.

Funny! Last night had been enough to nauseate anyone, and she had felt sick, but had not actually been.
As a matter of fact she could remember being sick only
once in her life and that was long ago; something to do
with mushrooms which weren't really mushrooms.
She'd never fainted, either, though most girls at school
had done so at one time or another and Miss Hardwicke had said that it was all nonsense. Take a deep
breath and concentrate on something. Deborah now
took a deep breath and concentrated on what she was
doing. But the I-am-going-to-be-sick and the I-am-go-
ing-to-die feeling came upon her, and she had only just
time to get to the window. There she was far more indisposed than a slice of toast and a cup of coffee would
have seemed to warrant, but she gulped in some fresh
air, wiped her face on her rolled-up sleeve and
thought: Now I know what a cold sweat is.

Back to work.

The patches of floor that she had scrubbed were
drying out, but the dark marks still showed.

Deborah had read about—but never seen—blood
marks which were irradicable. Wasn't there one in
Holyrood Palace where Mary Queen of Scots' Italian
secretary had fallen, clutching at her skirts?

I'll see about that, Deborah said to herself, attacking
the dark spots with more vigour, more harsh yellow
soap. They should be removed if she had to scrub
down half an inch.

"Miss Deb; Mrs Bridges, Ma'am."

Willy's voice on the kitchen stairs.

In complete control of herself, and of the situation,
Deborah went to the top of the stairs and across the
jumble piled there looked down on Willy and said,
"Good morning, Willy," in the special, friendly way

she had. A way that made you free and equal and put daft ideas into your head.

"The Missus said something about you wanting something moved. Is this it?"

"Yes. I'm clearing out what Miss Lavinia called her studio. We had kept it, but now she will not be coming back."

"So I understood. I'm sorry."

"Thank you, Willy." God damn all to hell! Miss Deb had only to say his name and something came over him. Something Katie had never managed. "The thing is, they have woodworm and that can spread. It could get into the rafters. I think they should be chopped up and used for kindling."

"I'll see to it."

Despite the fact that standing there, looking up, Willy Snell was the victim of one of the most romantic forms of love, he had .sense enough to see that the chair was all right; basket work, and whoever heard of woodworm in a basket? Nobody wanted a board, all paint and tallow, and the couch thing was too long for any ordinary house. The chair though—just the job for Katie's mother.

Katie's mother did not think highly of Willy as a son-in-law. Not because he'd got Katie in the family way before marrying her—that was commonplace— but because Katie should have done better for herself, married a stockman, a groom, a gamekeeper, somebody with a bit more about him. So in order to forestall what he called ructions in the family Willy was committed to a long course of placatory gestures. The chair, though a bit lopsided, was more comfortable than any in his own home, but it would go across the village street to Katie's mother. Willy did not foresee that the chair would have a curious peripatetic future. Katie's mother accepted it with a pleasure she was careful to conceal, and for a day or two it was admired and envied by her neighbours. She gave it away to one of them, explaining that she couldn't rest in it, it didn't

fit her, or it creaked or something; she'd never had a
good sit-down in it. The neighbour passed it on even
more hastily. She knew better than to give her real reason, which was that one evening, just at twilight, she'd
seen a light in it, very similar to the will-o'-the-wisp
sometimes seen over the marshes. She said the chair
was too low, once you were in it it was difficult to get
out of, and when something happened, like a saucepan
boiling over, you needed to be on your feet in no time.
With this excuse and that, all plausible, the chair
moved about until it came to rest with the old soldier
with the wooden leg. He said, rightly, that it was the
most comfortable chair he'd ever sampled.

On this hot August morning, ear-marking the chair
for Katie's mother, Willy looked up again and said:

"Miss Deb, Mrs Bridges, Ma'am, I bin giving a
thought to them plants. I reckon a good barrerful of
muck, maybe two, wouldn't hurt."

Deborah had already gone out and taken a look at
her work. The long trench looked just as Willy had left
it.

"That is a splendid idea, Willy. Leave it for a little,
though. Mrs Spicer and Mrs Taylor will be here with
the plants, shortly, and then you can put in the manure
and help me to plant at the same time."

She was reasonably sure that neither Di nor Caro
would wish to go near the spot.

She turned back to the attic. The floor showed no
marks now. The wall was not entirely satisfactory. A
few dark shapes showed, very vaguely, through the
whitewash. But they might vanish as the wall dried.
What was really needed was a second coat, but that
could not be applied until the first had hardened. And
she had no time. She must get back to Foxton; for she
had come here in Tim's gig, pulled by his swiftest
horse, and left with the heavier vehicle, the older animal, he would have just cause for complaint.

She emptied the pail of scrubbing water out of the

window, pulled the half-casement close and latched it. Scurbbing brush, jar of soda, yellow soap back in the pail, and then, because the whitewash bucket was a size smaller, put that in, too.

Some instinct made her fix the chain again, turn the key in the heart-shaped padlock and put the key into the pocket of her print dress. Now, when the shrubs were planted, it would be all over.

She'd always been the strong one, the tireless one, but out on the attic landing, just as she was about to pick up the buckets, weakness, weariness, struck at the very marrow of her bones. Leaning against the wall, she knew herself incapable of lifting a cotton thread. Her mind was still active, however, and rational. It had been an ordeal, something few women were called upon to do.

There might be another reason, too. She, always as regular as the moon which controlled such things, was late this month.

I am going to have a baby!

In any other circumstances, in any other place, a most joyful thought. Too joyful, in fact, to seize upon too easily. She had explained the lateness to herself in various ways; anxiety about what was happening here at Gad's and then the small, unimportant but constant friction between Tim and George. George wasn't perfect—what boy was?—but he was anxious to please; just as Tim was anxious to criticise and rebuke.

My son is not going to be reared in that bleak, narrow-minded fashion! It'll mean a fight, long and acrimonious and all about such silly, trivial things, but I shall fight it to the last.

Gradually, as she stood there, leaning against the wall, strength flowed back. Happiness should have come with it, but did not. She had thought Tim Bridges the nicest man she had ever met, but now the inner voice asked: How many men had she met and what, really, apart from his right attitude to horses, had Tim to commend him? Look the thing squarely in the face;

why shouldn't a merry tune be played upon a piano?
What sort of God was it who objected to a wreath of
yellow roses on a hat? Was there any particular virtue
in acting as scullery-maid as well as cook? With
women all about so anxious to be employed.

Diana and Caro arrived with the load of things to be
planted. As Deborah had foreseen, neither of them
wanted to go near the place. Everybody knew, Diana
said, that Willy was dim-witted, but surely he could be
trusted to plant a few shrubs. Caroline agreed with her.
But Mamma was stalwart. She said:

"The things are supposedly a present to me. I must
help to see them properly installed."

Once that was done, she would never go near that
end of the garden again. At the moment she held the
shrubs upright while Willy and Deb used the spades.
She did not notice when Deborah slipped the key from
her pocket and buried that, too.

Going back to the house, Mrs Thorley said:

"Deborah, you have been marvellous. Without you,
I doubt if I could have managed."

"*You* are the one who has been marvellous. I mean
no disrespect to my own mother . . . I hardly remember her; but I often wished that I were your real
daughter. And never more so than now . . . I should
like to think that I had inherited your . . ." guts was
the word, the truly apt word, but Mamma disliked
coarse expression ". . . strength of character."

"But you were born with it—not through me. In
your own right. Deb, you just paid me a great compliment. I return it. I also wish you were my daughter.
Years ago, when you were at school . . . I was always
so proud of you. I had to remind myself, quite sharply,
that nothing of me had gone to your making."

Now who would have suspected that behind the
calm, if-I-had-only-one-apple attitude such a thought
could have lurked?

"But for you, Mamma, I should never have gone to

school at all. Caro and I were so wild . . . I don't know what would have happened to her; she's pretty. I should probably have married Willy!" From what deep layer of unacknowledged knowledge had that thought come?

"How absurd!"

"It's not absurd at all. If we'd got the ordinary kind of stepmother who wanted us out of the house as soon as possible."

Indoors Caro, with a vague intention of doing something that looked useful, offered to make tea. Every bone and nerve of Mrs Thorley's body was crying out for whisky, but she must wait a little. She suggested sherry. Not that sherry served the same purpose; not that she even enjoyed it any longer. She had once heard somebody say that once you took to spirits you lost your taste for wine. Deborah accepted her glass without demur and they were all sipping, as ladies should, when George walked in, and instantly looked dismayed. He had not expected to find Di and Caro here. For Mamma and Deb he had bought cheering gifts. A bottle of lavender water for Mamma and one of Eau de Cologne for Deb. All women liked scent. But he had been so reared in the tradition of treating all the girls exactly alike that now to single Deb out was impossible and his generous gesture must be delayed. If only he'd known he could have bought four small bottles instead of two large ones.

From the parcel he carried he produced the pot of hand cream.

"This is what you asked me to get."

"Thank you, George. Mamma will pay you. I haven't a penny on me."

Both Diana and Caroline noted with approval that Deborah had not—as appeared at first sight—lost all pride in her appearance. That print dress was positively servant's wear, and Diana remembered how De-

borah had appeared at the kitchen door at Foxton with
a great smear of flour on her hair.

"And who do you think I saw on the road?" George
asked, brightness returning to his face. "Jenny! Walking home, hoping for a lift. I tried . . ." he broke into
laughter. "You never saw anything so funny in your
life. I tried to heave her on to Tom Thumb and he just
went round and round. He . . . he waltzed! I had to
leave her to wait for a cart."

"I am so glad," Deb said, "that you will not be
alone, Mamma."

In fact what would have been embarrassing forty-
eight hours ago was now good news.

"Mamma would not have been alone in any case,"
George said, staring off on the path which he hoped
would lead him to his goal. "I am home now."

And here, with cunning and a modicum of luck, he
would stay. He sensed that Mamma had never really
been in favour of Felstead—it was all Old Spicer's
fault for saying that George wasn't ready for the examination for Biddle's yet. George felt that if he promised
to work *much* harder this year and *hope* to be better
prepared next year, Mamma could be persuaded. And
he wouldn't be ready for Biddle's next year. Nor any
other year. And it should not be too hard to make
Mamma see that the money would be better spent on
replacing Tom Thumb.

Jenny, thinking: Thass right! Thass just like you,
putting plants afore people! Deciding to walk if necessary; not that it would be; on the road decent people
recognised other decent people and offered lifts; had
not been far wrong. Within minutes of being left by
Master George, Jenny was picked up by a decent man
who said he had business in Nettleton and would therefore pass by the opening of the lane that led to Gad's.
In the kitchen she paused only long enough to remove
her bonnet and exchange her cruel decent shoes for the

old, down-trodden, shapeless ones which she kept at the bottom of the dresser. Then she presented herself.

"I'm home, Ma'am. I just had to come, hearing of your grief."

"I'm glad to see you, Jenny; but you shouldn't have cut short your holiday . . ."

Diana thought: So back to heating up what Mrs Wedgewood leaves ready, or cooking on my own! She was never at home in her kitchen. She wore a dainty, frilled muslin apron and truly tried to please Everard, but nothing ever went quite right; saucepans would boil over, she burned her fingers, and once her arm on the oven door. She always kept the doors to the kitchen closed—she and Everard would never eat in the kitchen as Deb and her husband apparently did, despite their wealth. But sometimes the smell of cooking—and that was different from the smell of the dish itself—seemed to enter with her. And there was another thing which made kitchen work so unsatisfactory. It was never done. Plan a piece of needlework or embroidery, and stitch by stitch it grew, moving towards completion. Something to show. Make a meal, however successful—and she had had successes as well as failures—and what were you left with? A sinkful of dirty dishes.

Jenny said, "I had enough holiday, Ma'am. As I said, I was sorry to hear . . . And now, what'll I cook?"

George came triumphantly into his own.

"Fish!"

He had not been commissioned to buy fish, but he'd just been trotting past Harper's when the fresh fish was being laid out on the marble slab. To George, as to most country dwellers, fresh fish was a treat; nobody hawked it around villages because it could go off, and stink by the end of the day: so apart from what market-goers brought home, fish was dried or smoked.

"I thought," George said, happily smug, "that a

piece of nice fresh fish would tempt Mamma's appetite."

"Oh, George! You humbug!" Caro almost smiled. The atmosphere lightened, became more like that which George liked to have about him. And of course two minutes' thought had solved his problem for him. He knew how to give Deb her present without making what Mamma had once called invidious distinctions.

"I bought this for you, Deb. For having me to stay." The correct thing would have been to add that he had enjoyed himself, but he could not bring himself to say the words.

Back in her teasing mood, Caro said, "I had you to stay. Twice."

"I know. But you have so much, Caro. Scent, I mean. At least a half pint that Edward bought you in London. French, too. Rêve d'Amour," he explained for the benefit of those who had not seen Caroline's store.

Mention of lunch had reminded everybody of the time.

"I must get back," Deborah said.

"So must we."

"Oh, but Di! I was counting, I mean I hoped that you'd come with me and bring back the dog-cart."

"I can't. I have a tea-party this afternoon." And there would not be, as she had hoped, Jenny to cut the tiny sandwiches, carry in the tray, wash up afterwards.

Her ungeneralised grievance against things focussed for a moment upon Lavinia. Alive a nuisance, dead a nuisance; it was because Lavinia was dead that Jenny had hurried home; it was because of Lavinia that now they must wear black for at least three months. Diana agreed entirely that one could not go around saying, "My sister is dead," and wearing gay colours, but while admitting the necessity, she'd grudged it. Money ill-spent, since black was not her colour and there was nothing to be done afterwards with a black dress—except hang it up and wait for another dismal occasion.

Any other coloured dress could be dyed . . . It was all very well for Mamma, with black in store, and for Caro, so fair that black became her, and who could have other new dresses, any time; and for Deborah, who plainly did not care what she wore, as the print dress bore witness. And although Diana had once hoped to—or would have relished an opportunity to—exchange a few careful words on the subject of marriage with Deb, she no longer wished to do so. What marriage meant to Deb was all too plain.

Now Deb said, "All right then. Mamma, if I may, I'll borrow Willy." What she did not want was any fuss about getting the dog-cart home. In a way, yesterday, in insisting upon having the gig, she had defied Tim; and if what she suspected was right, she would be obliged to defy him again and again. But never over small things. Strength must be reserved for real battles.

With a jolt, Mrs Thorley realised that now she was free to come and go.

"No need to borrow Willy, my dear. I'll come myself. An airing will do me good."

Would it? She felt as though the only thing in the world that would do her good at the moment was a stiff whisky and another. To steady her shaking hands and jerking head. But the crisis was past now, and so must the indulgence be, if what her mind planned her body would perform. As it must, if George's inheritance was to be worth anything, if Gad's and Park were to survive, as they must. Life was like a string of beads, some pretty, some ugly, and now and again the string broke and all was confusion. Then you gathered the pretty ones, let the ugly ones roll away, and knotted the string. She had done it before; she must do it again, but she must stay sober.

"Do you think you're fit to drive just yet?" Deborah asked.

"I must start some time. This is going to be a busy autumn for me." The cancellation of the summer shows had meant loss of publicity which must be made

up for at the sales. And the little desk by the window
was piled with papers that needed attention. Amongst
them was a letter from Mr van Haagen, reporting
gladly that the cross between Friesian and Durham
shorthorn had been, so far as one could judge in so
short a time, a great success. Mrs Thorley wondered if
he would come at her invitation, attend a cattle sale or
two and place some fantastic bids for some of her
stock. She could then make it right with him afterwards.
It was worth attempting. Not that she was particularly
eager to see Mr van Haagen again; there was something
uncanny about the man. It was too soon yet to know
about the grandchildren, but almost everything else he
had foretold had come about with such a seeming inevi-
tability that it sometimes made her wonder about pre-
destination, a theory little to her taste.

Had the destination been any other than Foxton,
Geroge would have offered to go, keep Mamma company on the way home, perhaps be allowed to take the
reins for a time. But he never wanted to see Foxton
again; and one never knew what might happen. Their
own horse could have gone lame and that would mean
spending the night . . .

"You and Jenny will have a makeshift lunch, and
we'll have your fish for supper," Mrs Thorley said.

"I'll take mine and have it in the field—my lunch, I
mean."

That should please Mamma; she liked him to show
interest, as she termed it, and George had no objection
to being present where work was going forward; it was
being expected to work, anonymously, like a labourer,
that had irked him. And already a thought, benevolent
if tinged with patronage, was astir in him. Those very
early, very rosy, very sweet and juicy apples were ripe
on the old tree. He'd take a big basketful, enough for
all. That should please them.

Jenny said, "I can't find my bucket, nor my scrubbing brush. I know where I left them and by the look

of this table and this floor they ain't been used since I went away."

George remembered Deb, cleaning up, clanking a pail, throwing things out because Lavinia wouldn't be coming back; would never need her studio any more.

"I think they could be in the attic, Jenny."

"Nip up and fetch 'em, Master George, there's a love. Your legs is younger than mine."

His legs were so young that he could take the first steep flight two at a time; the next, with its two twists, slowed him down a bit. But there, just as he had thought, were the things Deborah had used. Just near a door with a heavy padlock.

George knew the attic floor, he'd been up from time to time to fetch apples and pears and walnuts—but not, of course lately because, however carefully stored, nothing much lasted after Christmas. In Lavinia's studio he had taken no interest; a place where she had mucked about with paints. But the fact that the door should now be padlocked was, well, a bit odd. Not that it mattered to him. He reached down to pick up the two pails, one inside in the other, and something hit him like a thunderbolt. Jenny had just said that his legs were younger . . . But they would age. Year after year would add its burden . . . Until the end . . .

One day I shall be old!

Incredible thought and instantly repudiated. I will not! I will *not* go about creaking and groaning, mumbling and muttering, supported by a stick, two sticks.

But all men must die. *Day follows day and suddenly the dark one calls, and we follow, by that road or this, into the universal silences.* A scrap picked up from the liberal education Mr Spicer offered.

All right! I know. But I intend to live until I die. And live it in my own fashion, in my own place.

George snatched up the pails and clattered down the stairs to tell Jenny that he wanted mustard, not too much, not too little, just enough, on his ham sandwiches.

Mrs Thorley and Deborah drove to Foxton in a silence punctuated by trivialities. The whole affair was over and done with, and the moment of intimacy in the garden had left them both shy. What more could be said?

"I won't come in," Mrs Thorley said as they neared the place. "I still have so much to do."

Harvesting was going on here. In a field close to the road, Tim was doing one of the heaviest jobs, pitching sheaves onto a half-laden wagon. He was at least consistent; never ask a man to do what you were not prepared to do yourself.

Deborah waved, and he waved back; but he did not stop work. It would have pleased all his workmen had he done so, for he set a hard pace.

He could not fairly be said to be angry with Deborah. Half-broken colts—and in a way he regarded her as much—did kick up now and again. Patience and a firm hand were the answer, not anger; but in making him hitch the gig in that sharp sudden way and going off, for no reason that he could see, she had kicked up, after seeming to be so amenable. So she must learn. He was not going to run to welcome her, jump the ditch that divided the field from the yard, unhitch the gig, hitch up the dog-cart, make himself agreeable to Mrs Thorley, offer her tea. Let Deb do it, she was capable . . .

Quite suddenly, as he stood there, a sheaf poised on the fork, a tiny dart pierced Tim's armour of self-confidence, self-righteousness, his certainty that God had made man in His own image and woman as a kind of subsidiary. Deb *was* capable. He had a thought which should have been comforting but was not. If he dropped dead where he stood she'd step in and take charge. Foxton would go on as before. The only real gap he'd leave would be at chapel! A sobering thought for one who had never been anything but sober in all his days.

The man atop the half-loaded wagon rubbed a little salt into the little wound.

"Ah," he said. "Missus is back! She'll see to Bill's thumb."

Getting the scythes ready for the next day's reaping in another field, Bill had nicked his thumb that morning and despite the lavish application of cobwebs, supposedly a sovereign cure, it was still bleeding and Bill was looking a bit whitish round the root of his nose.

Yes, Tim thought, heaving the sheaf on to the load, she's been here two months and she's endeared herself to everybody; old Emma, the men, the chapel people.

Should you not, Timothy Bridges, be glad and proud? Did you not choose well? Yes; and yes; and yes. But she'd stood in his yard and said, Will you harness up, or must I? And he could not forget it. Like the pinch of yeast that could leaven a whole batch of bread, like the teaspoonful of rennet that could turn a whole bowl of milk sour and make it into cheese, the memory of that moment was to rankle in his mind.

"It could be," Caroline said, anxious to be consolatory, "just talk. I believe all men have such fancies. Even Edward! He once told me that as soon as he qualified he thought about going to America where there's only one doctor—in the wild parts—to thousands of people. His father talked him out of it; he said there was plenty of work right here. And look how he's settled down. It may be the same with Everard. Wanderlust. That's the word I wanted."

Caroline could quote the case of Edward. But in fact Freddy had been the same. Always talking about getting away, making a fresh start. Never—give the Devil his due—asking her to go with him but keeping her, between the ecstatic moments, on the knife-edge of apprehension: Will he be there? Will he come? And look how he had settled down! Look!

"I am afraid Everard is more serious in his intention," Diana said. "I don't think wanderlust takes men

to London. Ambition. Everard is very ambitious, and
here he has run into a cul-de-sac. But it is such a
shame, just when I've got the house so nice. And all
that horrid business is over and we could begin to enjoy ourselves. I don't know about you, Caro, but I do
sometimes think life is rather disappointing."

"I'd say, bloody awful. Don't turn that Mamma look
on me, Di. I said bloody awful and bloody awful I
mean."

"I don't see what *you* have to complain about."

"No? Doddering about, befriending this, helping
that, supporting the other. God knows I'm sorry for the
halt, the maimed and the blind. *And* the poor! But I
hate them. Di, I know it sounds terrible, but I do. I always want to cry, and I hate them for making me want
to cry. Honestly, I don't see why misery should be so
contagious. We all have our miseries. Why we should
go about licking other people's wounds . . . ? There
are times when I think I shall go quite mad and say to
some fellow who's lost an arm: Congratulations; next
winter you'll have only *five* chilblains!"

Half a joke, half hysteria; and with neither had Diana any fellow-feeling. She said, "Don't be so silly!"
But something that Caro had said lodged in her mind.
If the worst happened and Everard did get a job in
horrible London and she was torn up by the roots and
wounded, nobody should be asked to give her a lick.
She regretted now that she had said anything to Caroline about her reluctance to move. If it came, the
move, she would pretend to welcome it. She would go
down, no, not down, out, with all flags flying.

George said, "Well, that was nice, wasn't it?"

"Very nice," Mrs Thorley said. But she had hardly
tasted it. Within her an appetite, not for food, had
raged and been with difficulty controlled. This was perhaps the worst moment. There on the chiffonier was
the whisky. And George's presence was no deterrent.
He had seen her drink, had even poured a drink for

her, many times. She had only to reach out her arm, or say: George would you please . . . ?

And why think of it as so evil? It saw you through, didn't it? It served you well.

Yes, a good servant; but a bad master.

How about moderation? Before March, before you were under such stress, you drank a little to help you to sleep. You did not begin to drink to excess until you found yourself in such an impossible situation. Go back to that régime. You *need* a drink, just one good stiff whisky, to steady your head and your hands, especially as you have writing to do. Go on. Just one. No! I know what that would mean: another and another. And within a year you'd be useless, a hopeless alcoholic.

"Have an apple, Mamma," George said, offering the dish. "I gathered them myself. And," his voice grew pious, "I took a great basketful to the field. Everybody enjoyed them."

"I'm sure they did, darling."

What else could he report to show himself in a favourable light? Make himself seem useful and indispensable?

"Oh, and I found Jenny's scrubbing things. They were on the attic landing." With scarcely a pause his mind flitted. "Why is Lavinia's door locked, if she isn't coming back?"

That must be Deb's doing. And why had she bothered? For a second Mrs Thorley wondered if Deb knew more than she had ever mentioned.

"It is because she will never come back, dear," Mrs Thorley improvised. "It had to be cleared out and cleaned up a bit. But while it remains unused it will still be, in a way, Lavinia's room."

And used or unused, so it would remain, while the house stood.

George gave this idea the blessing of his approval.

"I think that is a very nice idea, Mamma. After all we don't need the space. And I expect Lavinia hoped to come back. I know I did, when I was at Foxton. It was a great comfort to me to think that Gad's was here and you were here and everything would be as I left it. Being homesick is a terrible thing." A seed successfully planted? His mind shifted again, and Lavinia, who had never meant anything to him, never seemed real, did for a second take on reality, a homesick girl who would never come home. "Poor Lavinia," he said. "We'll keep that room. And when I am an old man and have a son of my own I shall tell him, and tell him to tell his son—leave that room alone. After all, she didn't have a grave here."

With a jerk of the head which gave the lie to her next words, Mrs Thorley said, "No, she has no memorial."

Historical Romance

*arkling novels of love and conquest against the colorful
ckground of historical England. Here are books you
ll savor word by word, page by spellbinding page.*

TRUMPET FOR A WALLED CITY—Pala	23913-6	$1.75
THE ARDENT SUITOR—Greenlea	23914-4	$1.75
HONEY-POT—Stables	23915-2	$1.75
SOPHIA AND AUGUSTA—Clark	23916-0	$1.75
THE WITCH FROM THE SEA—Carr	22837-1	$1.95
AFTER THE STORM—Williams	23928-4	$1.75
ALTHEA—Robins	23268-9	$1.50
AMETHYST LOVE—Danton	23400-2	$1.50
AN AFFAIR OF THE HEART Smith	23092-9	$1.50
AUNT SOPHIE'S DIAMONDS Smith	23378-2	$1.50
A BANBURY TALE—MacKeever	23174-7	$1.50
CLARISSA—Arnett	22893-2	$1.50
DEVIL'S BRIDE—Edwards	23176-3	$1.50
ESCAPADE—Smith	23232-8	$1.50
A FAMILY AFFAIR—Mellow	22967-X	$1.50
THE FORTUNE SEEKER Greenlea	23301-4	$1.50
THE FINE AND HANDSOME CAPTAIN—Lynch	23269-7	$1.50
FIRE OPALS—Danton	23984-5	$1.75

FREE
Fawcett Books Listing

There is Romance, Mystery, Suspense, and Adventure waiting for you inside the Fawcett Books Order Form. And it's yours to browse through and use to get all the books you've been wanting . . . but possibly couldn't find in your bookstore.

This easy-to-use order form is divided into categories and contains over 1500 titles by your favorite authors.

So don't delay—take advantage of this special opportunity to increase your reading pleasure.

Just send us your name and address and 35¢ (to help defray postage and handling costs).